A NEW LANGUAGE

I do not understand why you Indians do not kiss.

Sun Dancer turned abruptly. There, staring down at her, was the white man. Slowly, he reached out to touch her face. She had the impulse to run, but as he continued to speak she was mesmerized by the sound of his strange language.

"This is a wonderful way to show affection." He brushed his palm across her cheek and slid his hand slowly down the gentle slope of her neck.

Sun Dancer could not understand his words, and his gesture frightened her, making her heart beat quicken. She began to reach for her knife, and as she grasped the handle the white man closed his mouth over hers.

Softly, quietly, Sun Dancer released the knife from her hand . . .

SWEET MEDICINE'S PROPHECY
by Karen A. Bale

#1: SUNDANCER'S PASSION (1778, $3.95)

Stalking Horse was the strongest and most desirable of the tribe, and Sun Dancer surrounded him with her spell-binding radiance. But the innocence of their love gave way to passion—and passion, to betrayal. Would their relationship ever survive the ultimate sin?

#2: LITTLE FLOWER'S DESIRE (1779, $3.95)

Taken captive by savage Crows, Little Flower fell in love with the enemy, handsome brave Young Eagle. Though their hearts spoke what they could not say, they could only dream of what could never be. . . .

#3: WINTER'S LOVE SONG (1780, $3.95)

The dark, willowy Anaeva had always desired just one man: the half-breed Trenton Hawkins. But Trenton belonged to two worlds—and was torn between two women. She had never failed on the fields of war; now she was determined to win on the battleground of love!

#4: SAVAGE FURY (1768, $3.95)

Aeneva's rage knew no bounds when her handsome mate Trent commanded her to tend their tepee as he rode into danger. But under cover of night, she stole away to be with Trent and share whatever perils fate dealt them.

Available wherever paperbacks are sold, or order direct from the Publisher. Send cover price plus 50¢ per copy for mailing and handling to Zebra Books, Dept. 1778, 475 Park Avenue South, New York, N.Y. 10016. DO NOT SEND CASH.

SWEET MEDICINE'S PROPHECY: SUN DANCER'S PASSION

BY KAREN A. BALE

ZEBRA BOOKS

KENSINGTON PUBLISHING CORP.

ZEBRA BOOKS

are published by

KENSINGTON PUBLISHING CORP.
21 East 40th Street
New York, N.Y. 10016

THIRD PRINTING FEBRUARY 1986

Printed in the United States of America

THIS BOOK IS FOR:

Jack Bale,
a man who touched all those who knew him
and for Don—
he knows the reasons why

ACKNOWLEDGMENTS

I have used a great many sources in my research for this book. Probably the most valuable to me was George Bird Grinnell's *The Cheyenne Indians*, originally published in 1923. Mr. Grinnell lived with and knew many plains tribes, the Cheyennes not being the least of these. These two volumes of his work give insight into a truly interesting and honorable people.

I have in no way attempted to write a complete account of the Cheyenne tribe in the late 1700's. The entire tribe, it was estimated, numbered thirty-five hundred and was split into various bands along the Missouri River and in the Black Hills region of South Dakota. I have simply chosen a single band and used them to learn about the tribe's history and traditions, as well as their day-to-day lives and emotions.

Cheyenne history is vague in the early years, particularly pre-1800's. Various sources contradict each other as to dates, places and facts. I have taken the facts from several sources and used them in my fictional account.

The Cheyenne language is an Algonquian based language (as are Arapaho, Blackfoot, Fox, Cree, Ojibwa, Shawnee and others) and is difficult to read and pronounce. It is actually a composite of several dialects and levels of language, and its words are composed of smaller parts. An entire sentence in English can be expressed by a single "verb" in Cheyenne. Similarly, Cheyenne nouns can be made up of several meaning parts. In the few Cheyenne words and phrases which I have included in the story, I have eliminated the extra marks (high stress, whisper mark, glottal stop) to simplify the meaning.

In the course of their conversations, I have also eliminated the use of contractions from the Cheyenne's speech. In every passage or speech where I found an Indian speaking English, he or she did not use contractions but spoke correctly and eloquently. They were not lazy in their speech as many of us are.

When I refer to the "Big River" I am referring to the Missouri. It was an integral part of early Cheyenne history.

I am not sure that a Cheyenne band ever saw the Pawnee Morning Star Ceremony, but I presume it to be possible. For many years, the Pawnees roamed and lived on the headwaters of the Missouri, as well as in their own land to the south. And in the mid-1800's, a young Pawnee chief named Petalesharo rescued a Comanche girl from the sacrificial altar, thus putting an end to the Morning Star Ceremony.

Although I cannot name every book that I used in my research, I would like to name some of my sources and give thanks to their authors and editors.

George Bird Grinnell, *The Cheyenne Indians,*

Their History and Ways of Life, Volumes I & II (Lincoln, Nebraska: University of Nebraska Press, 1972); *English-Cheyenne Student Dictionary*, Language Research Department of the Northern Cheyennes (Lame Deer, Montana: Northern Cheyenne Language and Culture Center, 1976); Oliver La Farge, *A Pictorial History of the American Indian* (New York: Crown Publishers, 1956); John Stands in Timber and Margot Liberty, *Cheyenne Memories* (Lincoln, Nebraska: University of Nebraska Press, 1967); George Bird Grinnell, *By Cheyenne Campfires* (Lincoln, Nebraska: University of Nebraska Press, 1971); John Bierhorst, *In the Trail of the Wind*, American Indian Poems and Ritual Orations (New York: Farrar, Straus, and Giroux, 1971); Elsie Clews Parsons, *American Indian Life* (Lincoln, Nebraska: University of Nebraska Press, 1974); Frank B. Linderman, *Pretty Shield, Medicine Woman of the Crows* (Lincoln, Nebraska: University of Nebraska Press, 1972); Melvin R. Gilmore, *Uses of Plants by the Indians of the Missouri River Region* (Lincoln, Nebraska: University of Nebraska Press, 1977); Helen Addison Howard and Dan L. McGrath, *War Chief Joseph* (Lincoln, Nebraska: University of Nebraska Press, 1941); Donald J. Berthrong, *The Southern Cheyennes* (Norman, Oklahoma: University of Oklahoma Press, 1963); William Brandon, *The Last Americans* (New York: McGraw-Hill Book Co., 1974); William K. Powers, *Indians of the Northern Plains* (New York: Putnam, 1969); Robert Hofsinde, *Indian Sign Language* (New York: Morrow, 1956); George E. Hyde, *Pawnee Indians* (Denver, Colorado: University of Denver Press, 1951);

Owen, Deetz, Fisher, *The North American Indians* (New York: Macmillan, 1967); Reginald & Gladys Laubin, *The Indian Tipi* (Norman, Oklahoma: University of Oklahoma Press, 1957); George E. Hyde, *Indians of the High Plains* (Norman, Oklahoma: University of Oklahoma Press, 1959); Jay Monaghan, *The Book of the American West*, (New York: Bonanza Books, 1958).

Many thanks to my husband and kids, family and friends, who seem to think I am able.

A very special thanks to E. L. Kosanovich for helping to make some order out of a lot of chaos. Thanks Mom.

Karen A. Bale

PROLOGUE

Long before the Cheyennes had ever seen a horse, cow, or a white man, they knew of all three. They had been told of them in an ancient prophecy and warned that their coming spelled the nation's doom. In a far-off time their culture hero, Sweet Medicine, came to earth from the spirit world to guide and teach and advise his children. When his task was done, he called the Cheyennes together to hear his farewell words.

"A time is coming when you will meet other people, and you will fight with them and you will kill each other. Each tribe will want the land of each other tribe and you will be fighting always." He pointed toward the south.

"Far away in that direction is another kind of buffalo, with long hair hanging down its neck and a tail that drags on the ground; an animal with a round hoof, not split like the buffalo's, and with teeth in the upper part of its mouth as well as below. This animal you shall ride upon." Then having told them of the horse he spoke of the cattle.

"In time the buffalo will disappear from the land and when they have gone, the next animal you will

11

have to eat will be spotted." Sweet Medicine warned of many other things but then his voice grew sad.

"Soon you will find among you a people who have hair all over their faces, whose skin is white; and when that time comes you will be controlled by them. The white people will be all over the land, and at last you will disappear."

* * *

The Cheyennes were one of the most highly regarded and respected of all the plains tribes. History picks them up in the Lake Superior region of Minnesota about 1600, when they were a peaceful, agricultural people, living in earthen lodges, tilling fields of corn, beans, and squash, and hunting buffalo and other large animals with crude bows and arrows and sharpened sticks. Among the tallest and handsomest of Indians, they commanded the respect of all tribes because of their generosity and honorable dealings. Their women were noted for their beauty and chastity, and in the men, the love of peace was regarded as a strength rather than a weakness. But in a single day, war came to change the course of their lives and fulfill the first part of Sweet Medicine's prophecy.

A Cheyenne hunting party was closing in on a herd of buffalo when they saw other Indians approaching. Their old men identified them as the Hohe, a northern tribe the whites called the Assiniboins. As was their custom, the Cheyennes made signs of friendship and invited the Hohe to strike the game first. They felt sorry for the newcomers, for they had neither bows nor lances, but only a strange black club which was crooked at one end. Instead of answering their signs, the Hohe made strange medicine over their clubs and pointed them toward the Cheyennes. Smoke and fire came out with a sound like thunder and several Cheyennes cried out and fell to the ground bleeding. The others fled, frightened and bewildered by the strange medicine. They looked back to see the Hohe dancing and waving the bloody scalps of their fallen comrades.

That night they held solemn council; it was the first time they had ever been attacked by enemies. But they agreed that they must learn to fight. It was in Sweet Medicine's prophecy that they would fight other people and that they would kill each other and that they too, would become great warriors.

But at first this was only a gesture, as the Hohe repeatedly attacked them without mercy. The Cheyennes tried to move their villages but the Hohes always hunted them down. They finally came to understand that they would never survive without guns, so they acquired some from a hunting party of Hohes whom they had ambushed and killed. They learned quickly the skills of the gun and they began to kill the enemy for more.

Now, fighting constantly, the Cheyennes moved westward. Their wars with the Teton and Yankton Sioux, the Hidatsa, Mandans and Arikaras ended quickly in a lasting peace. With the latter, the second part of Sweet Medicine's prophecy came true. The Arikaras had horses and the Cheyennes were quick to adopt this new mode of traveling and fighting.

The horse changed their entire pattern of existence. They abandoned earthen lodges and agriculture for the portable skin tipis and the nomad life of the plains hunter. Their tribal organization and customs underwent great change. Individual heros began to emerge and warrior societies came into existence.

In this period, the Cheyennes found their home in the Black Hills. They knew instinctively when they saw it, that it was the promised land in the ancient prophecy. The rich green valleys and streams around the base of the Black Hills became their home, and from there their warpath crisscrossed the Great Plains. They fought the Kiowas, Comanches and Apaches, and enjoyed occasional skirmishes with the distant Blackfeet until a great peace was made in 1840. Their wars with the Utes, Pawnees and Shoshonis lasted half a century, and they fought their most hated enemy, the Crows, for over seventy years.

But despite their ferocity, the intertribal wars followed a code of chivalry that few white men could ever understand. The Cheyennes were noted for their kind treatment of captives, and children were taken into their lodges and raised with all the rights and privileges of a born Cheyenne.

The fighting courage of the Cheyennes was talked about all through the Plains. Men said there was nothing on earth a Cheyenne feared, but this was not true. One thing every Cheyenne feared was the fulfillment of Sweet Medicine's last prophecy—that contact with the bearded white man would bring about the total extermination of the Cheyennes.

CHAPTER I

She was called Sun Dancer because the sun danced across her tiny face as her mother held her up in the first light of dawn. Her father called her his "precious thing," for like all Cheyenne men, He-Walks-the-Mountain doted on his daughter. He was told before Sun Dancer's birth that one day she would hold a special place of honor in the tribe and would be the possessor of great wisdom, and that her name would be passed down for many generations. He-Walks-the-Mountain believed that his daughter was special not only from the words which the medicine man had told him before her birth, but because he could see it in her eyes. She was special.

As a baby, Sun Dancer was bright and quick and was not one to cry easily. She watched everything that went on around her with great intensity and absorbed easily everything which was taught to her. He-Walks-the-Mountain remembered well the first time he set Sun Dancer on a pony. She was only three summers old yet she sat the pony with a straight back and chin held high, no fear showing on her small face. Her father smiled as he watched her automatically command the pony with her legs and pat it gently with her hand; she was a natural rider.

The horse was still a fairly new acquisition for the Cheyennes. It wasn't too many years before Sun Dancer was born that they caught their first horses. He-Walks-the-Mountain and some others were by a lake when they saw two horses, one a dark-colored horse, the other a buckskin, come to drink water at the lake. They remembered Sweet Medicine's vision and they were sure this was the animal he had referred to in his vision. They fixed a snare and when a horse stepped into it, they ran and tied it down. Then they tied a buckskin rope to him and they all hung onto it and that was how they broke him. When he was tame enough to follow on a rope they tried riding on his back. He-Walks-the-Mountain was the first to ride the horse and the first to ride and search for others. It was in this way that they had first acquired the horse.

Still, many of the tribespeople were unable to become accustomed to riding on such a large animal; previously, they had traveled by walking and placing their equipment on the much smaller dog or by using the dog to pull a travois. But in the ensuing years, many men and women had become adept at riding and had shown others in the tribe. It wasn't long before the majority of the tribe saw the advantages to riding.

He-Walks-the-Mountain watched as Sun Dancer rode in the race against one of the boys. She was laughing and she rode well. There was only one boy who beat her—Stalking Horse. Stalking Horse always beat her; he always beat everyone. The boy was only a few years older than Sun Dancer but he was already much larger and stronger. He had a great future as a warrior because he was strong and fearless, and other boys naturally followed him. But Stalking Horse was a loner and wished no other person's company, whether it be boy or girl.

After the race Sun Dancer ran to her father and took his large hand in hers. She kissed it tenderly and looked up at him. "Did you see me, *nehayo?*"

"Yes, and as usual you rode well. Not many can beat you."

"Stalking Horse can."

"Stalking Horse is in a class of his own. I myself have never seen anyone ride so well as he."

"He does everything well. How is it that one person can be so capable, father?"

"I have seen many people in my lifetime who have been so blessed. You are one of these. It is a gift from the Great Spirit."

"I am so blessed?"

"Yes."

"But why? I am no different from the others."

"But you are. It is not important for you to know all the ways now, the important thing is what you do with your gifts. So far, you have done well."

Sun Dancer looked up at her father, a perplexed look on her face. She was not quite twelve summers and had acquired a vast amount of knowledge during that time, but she was entirely confused by what her father had just said.

"I do not understand, father."

"It is just as well. Come." He took her hand and they walked to the edge of the camp and looked out at

17

the hills. "They are majestic, are they not?" Sun Dancer nodded in agreement and looked out at the Black Hills. She was already entranced because she knew that her father was about to tell her a story. He called it his "history." She loved to hear him speak, for he always did so eloquently.

"You were not yet with us and your brothers still young when we crossed Eomitai, the Big River. It was a hard decision to leave our home, the home of our ancestors, but the Hohes drove us away. We had much to learn about fighting then." He smiled to himself as he thought of how little they knew about the warring ways and how quickly they had learned them. "We left everything we knew: the land, the crops, our mode of living. We changed from peaceful, farming people who lived in earth lodges, to warlike people who hunt and live out in the open in hide lodges."

"But you have said yourself it is better this way, father."

"Yes, I have. I feel it is better for our people to know the ways of the white man. We have seen only a few but I know that soon there will be many. It is good that we do not live in ignorance anymore. We now know of the gun, the horse, the trading of furs, and of our friend, the buffalo. We have learned much in a few short years."

"Would I have liked it then, father? Did you?"

"It was my life; I knew no other. It was a peaceful life until the Hohes came. It was then we realized we had to learn to fight."

"Do you miss it?"

His eyes crinkled at the corners as he looked out at

18

the hills, as if contemplating a painful thought. "I miss the peace. Peace is a good thing."

"But peace is seldom possible, is it, father?"

"I suppose not, child. As long as men live together, side by side, there will always be disagreements. Man is an aggressive animal and it does not suit his temperament to live in peace."

"Will we fight the white man someday?"

"I am sure of it."

"You believe Sweet Medicine's prophecy?"

"Yes. We are seeing more and more white men all the time. Soon they will want to live on our land and kill our buffalo. Just as men of their own blood fight among each other, so we will fight with the white man."

"And who will win?"

He-Walks-the-Mountain looked down at his daughter, the ever-inquisitive brown eyes looking up at him. Her thirst for knowledge was a source of great pride to him. He would never lie to her.

"The white man will win because he is greater in number."

"How do you know this if you have never seen him?"

"I have heard many stories from tribes to the east and to the south. It is said the white man is everywhere and that he multiplies quickly. He builds lodges of wood and stone and lives everywhere. He farms and raises strange animals, called cattle. And he moves westward, claiming more and more Indian land as his own."

"What does the white man look like?"

He-Walks-the-Mountain shook his head in confusion. "I do not know. It is said all white men are different. Some have eyes the color of the sky, some the color of the trees, while still others have hair the color of corn or fire."

Sun Dancer stared at her father in bewilderment, her brown eyes large in her small face.

"Eyes the color of the sky?"

"Yes. And it is said that some look like us with dark hair and eyes, but with light skin." He shook his head. "It is all very confusing."

"Yes." She touched one of her long braids and looked at the deep, rich color. "I do not think I would like hair the color of corn. It would always be dirty."

He-Walks-the-Mountain smiled and took his daughter's hand. He enjoyed their talks. He was older now. His sons were all warriors, but Sun Dancer was still young. She was his joy and it was she who kept his heart young and his mind fresh. As they walked back to camp his mind pondered the reality of her youth and his maturity. If he died, he wanted her to be tended well, her mind as well as her body. She still had so much to learn and he wanted her to learn as much as possible. His wife, Woman's Heart, was a good wife and a good mother, but she felt that Sun Dancer should concentrate more on womanly chores and duties, rather than spend so much time with her father educating her mind.

"What is it, father?" Sun Dancer looked up at He-Walks-the-Mountain and saw the troubled expression on his face. "Tell me, please."

"What will you do when I am gone? You have such a fine mind."

"You will not go for a long time. Do not worry."

"You do not know that."

"But I do." She looked up at her father with great sincerity. "I do."

"How do you know this?"

"I just know. I have visions where I see you and I and my husband walking out to our place and looking at the hills."

"And who is your husband?" He-Walks-the-Mountain asked playfully.

Color filled Sun Dancer's cheeks and she became suddenly shy, her voice barely a whisper. "Stalking Horse."

"Are you sure this is not a 'wish-dream' rather than a vision?"

"No," she stated adamantly, "it is a vision. I have had it many times before."

"You have 'sight' then?"

She stopped walking and looked up at him, a troubled expression on her face. "I think I do have sight, father, and it frightens me. I see things which I do not wish to see."

He-Walks-the-Mountain took Sun Dancer's hand and led her to a formation of rocks. They sat down, side by side.

"Now, tell me about these visions." When Sun Dancer hesitated, her father urged her to speak.

"I do not like this, father. I have seen a vision in which there is a fight between our people and the Crows. There is much fighting and I even hear the sounds of the horses as they scream in fear, and the sounds of the war clubs as they land. And then I see Brave Wolf knocked from his horse and trampled by horses, and our riders ride off without him. Do you think it means anything, father?" She looked up and He-Walks-the-Mountain could see tears in her eyes. Brave Wolf was his oldest son, Sun Dancer's oldest brother, and her most loyal friend. A chill went through his body.

"I do not know what it means, my child. I have had many dreams which occur over and over again yet they have never come true. I do not think you should worry yourself over this. Perhaps the vision means something else."

"But what? It can only mean one thing."

"We do not know what it means, we do not even know that it is a true vision."

"But father . . ."

"No, I do not want you to think about it anymore. It is best for you to dwell on joyous things. If it is meant for us to go to the other world, then we will go. But not because of a vision or dream of yours. Do you understand?"

"Yes, father." Sun Dancer replied glumly, not entirely reassured by her father's statement.

As they walked back to their tipi, He-Walks-the-Mountain wondered about Sun Dancer's vision. The medicine man, Horn, had predicted that Sun Dancer would be a visionary. Horn had great "sight" and he could predict things with great veracity. If what he said was true, then Sun Dancer's vision would come true and Brave Wolf would die. The thought weighed heavily on He-Walks-the-Mountain and it was one which he preferred not to believe. For once, he chose to ignore Horn and his predictions, in the hope that his son would not die young.

* * *

Sun Dancer was a good girl and a dutiful daughter, but she didn't always enjoy doing the chores which were bestowed upon her by virtue of her sex. Women's work, she soon found out, was quite tedious; she now fully understood why the men hunted and raced and went to war.

She wandered about slowly, taking her time getting the morning water for her mother. This was also the time when the boys and men came to the stream for their early morning bath, and it was one of the few times she could count on seeing Stalking Horse. She was fascinated by the sight of the men, old and young, who plunged into the stream, even in the dead of winter after breaking the ice. It was said to assure good health and wash away all sickness.

Sun Dancer filled her containers and stood by the side and watched as the men came to the river. She waited impatiently to see Stalking Horse. He was always one of the last to come and he usually came alone. He didn't seem to need the company of others, yet the other boys liked him and wanted to be around him. Her father said this was the sign of a good leader, and he was sure that Stalking Horse would one day be a great one.

Sun Dancer looked around her and smiled as she thought of the life her tribe now lived. She was happy that she didn't know the life her people led before; she felt that life without the horse must have been very confining, and she, like her father, loved to ride for miles and miles roaming the countryside.

She heard someone shout her name and she looked in the direction of the river. It was her friend, Laughing Bird, and he waved and smiled as he called her name. He motioned her to come into the water but she smiled and shook her head. They both knew that any respectable Cheyenne girl wouldn't dare be alone with all those boys, but it was a game they played. She and Laughing Bird had been close friends since they were small, and he always teased her in front of the other boys. Nevertheless, they were good friends and she knew that he held her in high esteem as a person.

Just as she turned away from Laughing Bird and his friends, she saw Stalking Horse dive into the water. She stood and watched him as he swam with long, easy strokes across the deep part of the river. She felt she had loved him since she was a small girl and she had seen him run the long race with the other boys. Her mother said she was too young to know of such feelings, but she knew better.

Stalking Horse stood up and pushing his wet hair back from his face, he looked at Sun Dancer. He had stared at her this way many times before. It was a look which contained neither malice nor kindness, but it was a gesture which Sun Dancer had come to depend on and look forward to. In her mind, it was a special look which he reserved only for her.

As quickly as Stalking Horse looked at Sun Dancer, he looked away and walked away from the stream towards the camp. Sun Dancer sighed deeply and picked up her jugs of water and returned to her family's lodge. Her mother berated her for taking so long with the water but her father smiled indulgently. He knew well her feelings for Stalking Horse but Woman's Heart was very strict in the upbringing of her daughter. She was constantly telling Sun

Dancer that she could never be too good nor too chaste, and she shouldn't wander around the camp alone and be seen with boys. It was important that a Cheyenne girl prove to all in her tribe that she was a good girl and not one to be seen with boys. Sun Dancer knew her mother's words to be true and she believed them, but she also believed that a girl could be on her own and be friends with a boy and still not spoil her reputation. It was a subject over which she continually argued with her mother.

While her mother boiled the meat for their morning meal, Sun Dancer took out the bowls. She used a sharpened stick to pull the meat from the pot and put it into the bowls. She fed her father first, then she and her mother sat down. When they had finished the morning meal, Sun Dancer cleared and washed the bowls, her father met with Brave Wolf and they prepared for the hunt. Before they left, they all stood out to hear the voice of the camp crier. He was an old man who shouted out to the camp the orders of the day, the commands of the chiefs, or some items of personal news. Sun Dancer smiled as she saw her mother edge farther out of the lodge to better hear the news of one of her neighbors. Her mother, for all her respectability and propriety, was one of the best gossips in the camp.

The day was clear and warm and in spite of her protestations to the contrary, Woman's Heart was not totally oblivious to the fact that her daughter was still a little girl. Unlike other mothers who were already training their daughters in lodge-building and the tanning of hides, Woman's Heart let Sun Dancer go her own way most of the time. She knew that while Sun Dancer was just a few months short of being only twelve summers old, in probably three more summers she would be married and expecting her first child, with all the duties and responsibilities of a grown woman. She wanted her daughter to be a child as long as she could be.

"Off with you now," Woman's Heart patted Sun Dancer on the back. "It is a day for swimming and playing with your friends. Anything you have to do can be done another day." She smiled warmly and hugged her daughter to her. "I do not mean to be so harsh all the time. I only want you to be the best person you can be."

"I know that, mother. And I try to be a good daughter but sometimes . . . I think I should have been a boy," she said quite seriously, a confused expression on her face. "I do not like to do woman's work."

Woman's Heart laughed heartily as she rubbed her daughter's cheek. "That does not make you strange, *moksis*. I have been doing it for many years now and I still don't like it. But I must; there is no other way. I cook and look after you, and collect herbs and roots, and build the lodge, while your father hunts and defends us. That is the way of it." Sun Dancer hugged her mother fiercely. She hadn't called her *"moksis"* in a long time. It had been her nickname as a tiny child. It meant "pot belly." Woman's Heart shoved her away gently. "Go along now before I change my mind and put you to work on some hides. And stay away from the boys!"

Sun Dancer smiled and waved back at her mother. She was not supposed to have boys as friends;

Cheyenne custom forbade it. A Cheyenne girl was supposed to be very discreet in her relations with boys; if she was not, she could earn herself a bad reputation. A girl was not even supposed to talk to her older brother once she attained puberty. But Sun Dancer knew she would defy tradition, just as she always had. She played and hunted with Laughing Bird, and she had wonderful talks with her brother. She would never stop being friends with Laughing Bird or Brave Wolf for the sake of traditional beliefs—they were more important to her than these beliefs.

When Sun Dancer walked to the stream, many of the younger children were already swimming and diving into the water, the boys running races along the sandbar. Some of the other boys were modeling images of animals and people out of sand and setting them in the sun to dry. The older boys were practicing with the bow and arrow, others were playing one of the wheel games, or sliding their slender throwing-sticks far along the ground. As usual, Stalking Horse was nowhere to be seen, so Sun Dancer joined the children at the river and swam and dove into the water until she was out of breath. Afterwards, a group of them lay on the warm sand and rested as the sun browned their skin an even darker shade.

When Laughing Bird suggested that they go on a hunt, Sun Dancer expressed her desire to accompany them.

"But you are only a girl," said Elk River, a particularly antagonistic boy.

"I can shoot as well as you," Sun Dancer said

confidently. "Tell them, Laughing Bird."

"It is true. I myself have hunted with her many times. Her hand is very steady and her aim is always true."

"But hunting is man's work," Elk River reiterated boastfully.

"Only if you are a man," Sun Dancer countered confidently.

Laughing Bird looked over at Sun Dancer and smiled. She was stubborn and he had never known her to back down. She would probably face Elk River in a fist fight to prove her point.

"Well, I am going on a hunt and Sun Dancer is coming with me. Anyone else who wants to come with us can come." Laughing Bird motioned to Sun Dancer and she smiled her thanks.

They decided to make it a competition and they split up into four groups of two. The team who came back with the most game by the evening meal was the winner and would get half of what each of the other teams had shot.

After Laughing Bird and Sun Dancer had eaten their midday meals and picked up their bows and arrows, they headed off in the direction of the woods. They were good hunters and each was confident that they would be the winners.

"You are a good friend, Laughing Bird. I seem to cause you problems with your friends much of the time."

"Elk River is not my friend. He does not like girls so he cannot understand how you and I can be friends."

"Do I shame you much then? Is it so unusual for a

boy and girl to be friends?"

"My father says it is good."

"So does my father. He says it does not matter if it is man or woman, boy or girl, a friend is a friend."

"It is true. I know I could count on you to save my life if it were ever endangered. I cannot say the same for Elk River."

"You have already saved my life, Laughing Bird. It seems I owe you mine."

"You were small then and not a very good swimmer. I am glad I was able to pull you out of the river before you drowned. You were foolish to go into the water when you did not know how to swim." They both laughed. "You do not have fear, Sun Dancer, and you must be careful. You cannot go into everything with such carelessness."

"You are right, I know. But it is hard for me to control myself. I want to do so many things. Soon I will be too old to do the things I am doing now. I will have to get married and bear children and then I will be bound by a much stricter code. It displeases me greatly, Laughing Bird."

They stopped walking and Laughing Bird took Sun Dancer by the shoulders. "You are a strange one. You seem too serious for your years, as if you know much more than you are saying."

"I know not what I am saying most of the time. At least that is what my mother says." They both laughed again and continued on into the woods. They displayed immense caution and patience, and they crept stealthily through the bushes and trees. It wasn't long before Sun Dancer shot at a blackbird and as Laughing Bird had bragged to

Elk River, her aim was steady and true. Laughing Bird picked up the bird and stuck its head underneath his waist-belt. Then they moved on. In less than two hours they had shot ten birds between them, Laughing Bird six, Sun Dancer four. Then they decided to travel across the prairie and look for larger game.

Hunting on the prairie was much more tedious and difficult than hunting in the woods. If game was detected, they tried to approach it before they startled it, which was often very difficult. Jackrabbits were likely to hop up right under their feet and then quickly scurry away. If the animal escaped, the children watched it until it stopped and settled down to hide. Then, when they had marked the spot, they very cautiously approached it. If one discovered the rabbit squatting close, he or she indicated to the other the rabbit's position and they tried to shoot it. It was very good practice for hunting larger game.

While the children were engaged in the hunting, they learned other helpful things. They learned to understand the signs of the prairie, the habits of the wild animals, how to observe and become trackers, and how to endure and be patient. While she was hunting and tracking with Laughing Bird, Sun Dancer knew that these were things only a boy-child should be learning, but she also knew somewhere deep inside that all this knowledge and skill could only do her good.

By the end of the day, their catch consisted of ten birds, five jackrabbits, and three small turtles. They caught the turtles by wading slowly through a stream and pushing them until they swam for the bank, then either Sun Dancer or Laughing Bird picked them up with their hands.

"We have done well, little Sun Dancer. I think I shall always keep you as my hunting partner." Laughing Bird smiled and pulled one of Sun Dancer's braids.

"I wish it could be so," she sighed wistfully. "Why do you suppose it is that I am a girl and you are a boy? It could just have easily been the other way."

"I am glad it was not. I am not very good at quilling and having babies.

"Neither am I," Sun Dancer joked. "But I am sure I will learn."

"Do not be sad. It is as it should be. By the time you learn to do all those things you will be ready to accept them as part of your life, and you will no longer want to do these things. Everything will change."

"And do you think we will still be friends?"

"We will always be friends, Sun Dancer." He touched her cheek softly and they walked towards their camp.

It was a curious thing Laughing Bird had done, Sun Dancer thought, as they walked to camp. When he had touched her cheek it was not as a little boy or a friend, it was more like the touch of a lover or a husband. It was something that a young girl like she was not quite ready to deal with. It, like all the other things she would learn to do, would have to wait until later in her life. Right now was her time to be a little girl who played at being a little boy.

CHAPTER II

Sun Dancer smiled as she thought of the way Elk River and the others had grudgingly given up half their catch for the day. They were genuinely surprised to find that she could really hunt, but they knew it was impossible for Laughing Bird to have caught all the game himself.

"You are wandering again." Woman's Heart spoke sternly to her daughter, who was looking off into the distance as she leaned against her root-digger.

"I am sorry, mother, I was just thinking of the look on Elk River's face when he realized that I could hunt. I felt very satisfied."

"You should not feel satisfied about doing a man's job. I have told you often that it will serve you no purpose in the future."

"But father has told me countless times that any knowledge is good."

"But he neglects to tell you that the lack of knowledge is just as bad," she said angrily. "What will you do, Sun Dancer, when a brave takes you to wife and you are unable to cook or quill or tan a hide?

Will you go out and hunt and tell your husband to cook? Or will you bring it to me and ask me to help you? You must accept your role in life, my daughter, whether it is to your liking or not. It is the way of things.''

Sun Dancer frowned and angrily thrust her root-digger into the hard ground, grunting slightly as she did so. She was tired of everyone telling her "it was the way of things.'' Why, she wondered solemnly, couldn't things be changed?

"Put your roots in here," Woman's Heart motioned to her buckskin bag. "Why don't you go for a ride now? You have worked well today. Maybe a ride in the fresh air will take the frown from your face."

Sun Dancer stood up and immediately a smile spread over her young face. "Thank you, mother. Shall I carry the bag back to the lodge for you?"

"No. Go along and pay attention to the sun. I do not want you out alone when the sun starts to go down."

"Yes, mother," Sun Dancer yelled back over her shoulder as she ran back to camp and to her horse. Her father had acquired a beautiful chestnut gelding for her and she was extremely proud of it. It was one he had stolen himself from a Snake warrior.

As soon as Sun Dancer was out of camp and she felt the wind against her cheeks, her mood brightened. She loved being out in the open and riding free. She kicked her horse gently with her moccasin-covered feet and he took off with great, long strides. Sun Dancer lowered her body over the back of the horse and she felt his speed increase. Her braids flew out behind her and she squinted her eyes against the wind; she laughed with the pleasure of it. Hoofbeats sounded behind her and she looked back to see Stalking Horse following her. She smiled and slowed her pace gradually. It was a game they had played often. He would catch up to her while she slowed down, until they were neck and neck. Then by a silent mutual signal, they would race until one of their horses tired or until one of them was far ahead of the other. Usually Stalking Horse wound up the winner, taking himself far out ahead of Sun Dancer. But today, Sun Dancer felt the wind at her back and she urged her horse on with the pressure of her thighs and legs. She felt rather than saw Stalking Horse next to her, his large paint effortlessly keeping pace with her own horse. She looked over and saw the beginning of a smile on his handsome face and it gave her the motivation to ride faster. He had never smiled at her before and she sensed he was now challenging her to a more dangerous game. She was somewhat frightened; she had seen the boys play these racing games but had never participated in them herself. Her father had never permitted her to because of the danger.

She nodded slightly and saw Stalking Horse move out a little ahead of her. Slowly, with infinite care, he swung his right leg over the horse then jumped down to the ground, hitting it with his feet, then jumping back onto the horse's back. He looked over at Sun Dancer and he challenged her with a piercing look.

She swung her leg over the horse, almost slipping over the side as she did so, but she managed to regain control and imitate the same movement as Stalking Horse. When she was back on her horse, she gave Stalking Horse a derisive look, although her heart was pounding rapidly.

Stalking Horse barely acknowledged Sun Dancer's look. He slipped to the left side of his horse and hooked his right leg under his horse's neck. He lowered himself to the ground, picked up a stone, and threw it to Sun Dancer as he righted himself. Sun Dancer frowned slightly as the stone flew past her and she thought of the movement she was about to perform. Often she had seen the older boys perform this and she was always frightened by it. She had seen one boy trampled by his horse when his foot slipped from around its neck. She took a deep breath and stuck her foot underneath her horse's neck. Since she wasn't as tall as Stalking Horse, she had great difficulty getting a hold with her foot, but she refused to be cowed by him. Slowly, she lowered herself down the horse's side until her arm reached down to the ground, but she was too short to touch it. She stretched as far as she could to pick up a rock but her right foot lost its hold around the horse's neck, and she fell to the ground, barely missing her horse's hoofs. She rolled as she hit, and her slight body was bruised and scratched by the rocks and prairie bushes. She immediately tried to stand up but she fell to the ground, her legs weak from fear and excitement. She sat, tears of anger and frustration pouring down her cheeks, as Stalking Horse jumped from his galloping horse to her side.

"Are you well?" he asked as he squatted next to her.

"Leave me," she said angrily and tried to stand up, but she was unable to put any weight on her left foot. She pushed Stalking Horse away as he offered to help and she sat back down on the ground. "Why don't you go away. Does it give you pleasure to see me like this?"

Stalking Horse smiled slightly at the stubborn girl. Her face was covered with dirt and tear-streaks.

"It gives me no pleasure. I was wrong to challenge you. Racing is not for girls."

"I race well. It is just that I am too short."

"That may be so," he said, lifting her against her will to her feet, "but it is not for little girls. Come, we will find your horse." He lifted her up onto his horse and deftly swung up behind her. He wrapped his arms around her as he grabbed the reins. "Does your foot pain you?"

"I do not fear pain," she replied defensively.

"I did not think you did, or you would not have tried so foolish a trick as that one."

She turned halfway around on the horse to face Stalking Horse and she shouted angrily, "I, foolish? But what of you then? You were the one who did it first."

"But I have done it many times before and I do not attempt things unless I am sure I can do them." His voice was confident, not arrogant.

"You challenged me," Sun Dancer's words softened perceptibly.

"Yes, and I was wrong. You are much too young to be doing tricks as the ones I did."

"I almost did them."

"The first you did well," Stalking Horse conceded, bringing a blush to Sun Dancer's cheeks, "but the second one was much too difficult for you. I thought you would give up."

"I never give up," Sun Dancer replied adamantly and held her chin high in the air. "It does not become a Cheyenne to give up."

Stalking Horse smiled into Sun Dancer's hair, breathing in the smell of it. It was fresh and clean like the very air he breathed, and it glistened like black rocks he had once seen sitting at the bottom of a pond. She would someday be a spirited and beautiful woman, he thought, and a difficult one to control.

"There is my horse," Sun Dancer pointed to her horse grazing on some prairie grass. She attempted to jump down from Stalking Horse's horse, but he swiftly jumped down before her and lifted her gently to the ground.

"Can you put weight on the foot?"

"I think so." She stepped slightly on the foot, and with Stalking Horse's help, she limped to her horse. She stared up at her horse's back and then at Stalking Horse. "I will need your help." Stalking Horse nodded and easily lifted her up onto her horse's back and handed her the reins. "Thank you," she said softly and turned her horse toward camp.

Stalking Horse followed closely, his horse easily keeping pace with Sun Dancer's smaller one. He admired her greatly, although he would never tell her that. He had noticed her the first time when she was a very small girl, not yet five summers old. Everyone was swimming in the river and she too, thought she would swim, although she hadn't yet been taught how. He had watched her as she threw herself into the water (which was much deeper than she was tall), and as she vainly tried to keep afloat. He was then ten summers old and a very strong, experienced swimmer. He dove into the water after her but her friend, Laughing Bird, had already pulled her out. When she was sitting on the bank, choking up water from the river, she showed no fear but only a yearning to try the water again. He knew then that she was special.

"This is the first time you have spoken to me," Sun Dancer said suddenly. She pulled her horse up and was now riding evenly with Stalking Horse.

"A brave does not spend his time talking to little girls," Stalking Horse replied arrogantly. He averted his eyes and looked straight ahead of him.

"Ah, but a brave will race with little girls. I find that curious." Sun Dancer smiled as she saw the frown on Stalking Horse's face. "You are silent again, Stalking Horse."

Stalking Horse looked over at Sun Dancer and was annoyed by the amused look on her face. She had a slight dimple by one corner of her mouth and he found himself staring at it. He wondered if she knew what a pleasing sight she was.

"Your mouth is like a running river, Sun Dancer, the flow never seems to cease." His voice was harsh but his eyes were twinkling playfully.

"And yours is like a pond. The water sits and does not go anywhere." She looked at him, dark eyes challenging dark eyes.

"You also have a sharp tongue and someday some man will remove it for you."

"It will not be you," she replied sharply and urged her mount into a full run. It was no race this time; Stalking Horse was upon her in seconds and skillfully lifted her from her horse to sit in front of him. She tried to pull away from him but he held her firmly until they were on the edge of camp, at which point he dumped her unceremoniously onto the ground. She stared up at him, a disbelieving expression on her face.

"The sun will still set tonight and rise tomorrow, even if you do wish it to be so. You are not the center of the universe and things do not come and go at your bidding. You would do well to learn that and accept it." He turned his mount sharply and rode back the way they had come, a small cloud of dust forming at his horse's heels.

Sun Dancer stood up and grasped her horse's reins, slowly walking into camp. Her initial anger had subsided into a somewhat satisfied feeling of accomplishment. Stalking Horse had not only talked to her but had taken her on his horse, in spite of the fact that he had admonished her for her poor behavior. Grudgingly, she admitted that he was right. She expected too much of people and of the world around her. If things were not to her liking she expected them to change, for she did not yet have the capacity to accept them as they were. This she knew; her mother scolded her for it every day. But try as she would, she could never quit asking questions or challenging the way things were. As her mother often told her, "it was the way of things," but she found it almost impossible to accept that explanation.

Cheyenne women were famous among all western tribes for their chastity, and Woman's Heart was relentless in her continual attempts to teach her daughter this. She knew in her heart that Sun Dancer was a good girl and would never compromise herself, but she worried that as she grew older, the boys she now played with would view her differently. She did not relish the thought of making her daughter's protective rope, for she knew that Sun Dancer would reject it as surely as she, Woman's Heart, would make her wear it.

Woman's Heart remembered when her mother had given her hers and had shown her how to put it on. The small rope wound around the waist and knotted in the front, then passed down and backwards between the thighs, each branch winding around each thigh nearly to the knee. It was terribly confining and she remembered not being able to walk comfortably for weeks, the rope always rubbing her thighs. Yet she got used to it, just as Sun Dancer would have to get used to it. Once Sun Dancer passed into womanhood, she would be unable to walk around freely at night or in the day without it. All Cheyenne men, old and young, respected the rope, and anyone violating it would be killed by the male relations of the girl who wore it.

Woman's Heart's greatest worry was Stalking Horse. She knew the young brave; everyone in the camp did. He had distinguished himself in battle at an early age, and it was said that he would be a great war chief someday. He was greatly admired by the young girls and women of the tribe, and many were seeking to gain him as a husband. But he showed little interest in anyone, except Sun Dancer. Many times Woman's Heart had seen the furtive glances Stalking Horse had thrown Sun Dancer; she knew that he already saw the full promise of womanhood in her that others did not. And she worried that he would take advantage of Sun Dancer's feelings for him. He was already a young man. When Sun Dancer made her passage into womanhood, there would be nothing to stop their feelings for each other, however under-stated they now were.

"What are you thinking, wife?" He-Walks-the-Mountain came to stand next to his wife as she looked out on the distant hills. "It is Sun Dancer again?"

Woman's Heart nodded. "I worry for her. She is a girl of great emotion, and she will be a woman of even greater emotion." She turned to look at her husband, the deep lines etched into his brown face from years of laughter, sadness, and living. "Sometimes I look at her and I cannot believe that she is so beautiful. My heart becomes so full." He-Walks-the-Mountain nodded, for he knew only as a parent can know, the extent of joy one can feel for one's own child. "There are other times I feel such anger that I want to take her and beat her until she listens to me. She is determined to pick her own road, I fear."

"Is that so bad?"

She turned to him, the anger apparent on her face. "How can you, a great chief and leader, even say such a thing? You know as well as I, that tradition cannot be broken. Things must go on as they have before us and our father and grandfathers. We cannot change the course of things."

"So it is said," he replied thoughtfully, "and so I have said many times over to Sun Dancer. But is there not room for change? We know from Sweet Medicine's prophecy that a change will eventually

41

come about.''

"But not with our daughter. She is a Cheyenne and I want her to be able to hold her head up high in front of our people.''

"She will.''

"You know this?''

"I know. I was told before her birth.''

"Who told you this?''

"Horn.'' Woman's Heart's expression changed from one of skepticism to one of respect. Horn was the most highly respected seer and medicine man in the camp. His prophecies had always come true. It was said his power came from the *maiyun*, those mysterious powers which controlled the affairs of men and brought good fortune or bad, and his knowledge came from the wolves, as they were the messengers who brought it. When one walked past Horn, one lowered his head in respect.

"He talked to the wolves then, about our daughter?''

"No, he said the wolves came to him with the knowledge. The *maiyun* wanted him to know.'' He watched as the statement had its desired effect on his wife.

"What did he say?''

"He said that Sun Dancer would hold a special place of honor in our tribe and that her name would be passed down for many generations.''

"It is true then,'' Woman's Heart replied softly, her voice trembling noticeably. "Is it the reason that she is so different from the others?''

He-Walks-the-Mountain exhaled slightly, his point made. He wanted his wife to understand that

Sun Dancer was different from the other girls and that her continual search for knowledge did not make her bad.

"I believe so. She is not bad, wife, she only seeks to know all that she can. Perhaps it is for later on in her life. Perhaps it will serve to help our people at some time."

"Yes, it is possible. And does Horn see her married with children, or as one of the old unmarried ones?" There were some old women in the tribe who had never married but who had dedicated their lives to helping others.

"Horn did not say. He said only that we must be patient with her and try to understand that there is a reason for everything she does." The last was a lie, or at least Horn did not say it. But He-Walks-the-Mountain felt it was important to impress upon his wife that she should not stifle that beautiful, living thing which was in Sun Dancer.

"And why did you not tell me this before, husband?" she asked in a bewildered tone. "Were you waiting until she attained the full flower of her womanhood and the time when you knew I would place the most restrictions on her? You must think me a dim-witted old woman then."

He-Walks-the-Mountain touched her cheek, his rough, calloused hands gliding over the lines of his wife's face. He remembered when the skin was young and fresh and unflawed, and his hands had traveled over it with a young man's enthusiasm and energy. He remembered the firm young body before it became worn and used from children and the labors of being a woman, and from time itself. The bodies were well-used but the memory was still vividly clear.

"It is I who am dim-witted, for I did not share this news with you when I should have. I sometimes forget that you are her mother, and the one who carried her and birthed her. In my complete and utter joy of her, I sometimes forget that there is someone with whom I can share my joy and love." He rubbed her cheek gently and wiped the tears that suddenly appeared there.

"I fear we have grown old, husband, and the years have slipped by without our knowledge. We have allowed little time for ourselves." Her voice was sad.

"But we have many years left. We shall grow even older together."

"If it is to be so." Woman's Heart sighed deeply and turned to go back into the lodge. He-Walks-the-Mountain gently took her hand and pulled her away from the lodge.

"There is always time for that," he motioned to the lodge, "but not always time for a walk. Come, let us go and pretend we are a young couple courting for the first time. I will even pick you a flower for your hair."

"Good fortune for me then, that your eyes are so poor you will not be able to see how silly an old woman looks with a flower in her hair."

"My sight has always been poor, wife, but always very clear when I look at you. Come." He took her hand and from the back they looked as any two people in love look, for in the mind, love has no age.

CHAPTER III

Sun Dancer laughed in great amusement as she watched the man before her "sitting" on the ground, his head and shoulders on the ground, his legs high in the air. His name was Long Bow and he was a contrary. A contrary was a person who greatly feared lightning and thunder, most of them old men and women, and they did everything by their actions and words in a backward or reverse manner. They backed into and out of a lodge; said "no" for "yes"; if asked to ride, they walked; if asked to bathe in the river, they bathed in the dirt. Long Bow always made Sun Dancer laugh, performing his antics for her, but when she tried to speak to him he walked away. Contraries might perform and entertain others, but they didn't speak to them. They were always alone and no one was to associate with them, unless it was another contrary. Although Sun Dancer had tried often to talk to Long Bow, his only reply was in performing for her and making her laugh.

It had been many weeks since Sun Dancer had last seen Stalking Horse. He had been on a raid with some others to steal horses from the Snakes. Sometimes they rode for weeks before they spotted a small encampment of them. They usually raided at night when the Snakes were asleep and their horses grazed outside the camp. It was easy for an experienced Cheyenne horse-stealer to sneak up and steal many of their enemy's horses. Stealing horses was vital to the existence of the Cheyenne, but it was also vital to his manhood to prove that he was an able and skillful horse stealer. Stalking Horse was one of the most able, and indeed, that was how he had acquired his permanent name.

Stalking Horse was barely thirteen summers old when he accompanied a war-party which was setting out to steal some horses from the Snakes. They had ridden three days and nights when they spotted a small encampment of them and they waited until the cover of darkness to make their way into the camp. While they waited, some talked of the best way to retrieve the horses without alerting the Snakes; Stalking Horse spoke up and said he thought he could do it. Some of the older warriors laughed at the arrogance of the young boy, but others who had seen Stalking Horse during his training decided to give him a chance. So it was that when the moon was very high that night and the Snakes asleep in their lodges, Stalking Horse made his way into their camp. Daringly, he walked through the center of camp, throwing bits of meat to the snarling dogs to quiet them while he made his way to the remuda of horses. Softly, he talked to the horses, shushing them while he placed a rope through their halters and around the necks of the unhaltered ones. He led them around the camp and out to his astonished companions. Thus, the boy who had been called Lone One, was renamed Stalking Horse.

Sun Dancer sighed deeply as she thought of the day she and Stalking Horse had ridden together. She wondered if she were much in his disfavor. She still couldn't believe that they had talked and had even bandied words about as if they had been old friends, or at least, old acquaintances. But she knew in her heart what a game it had been between them, and that Stalking Horse was just teasing her. He was, after all, already a man, almost seventeen summers old, and she was still just a little girl. It wouldn't be long before he took a wife or two wives, and became a father. When she reached marrying age, Stalking Horse would have been married a long time and completely forgotten about her, if indeed, he'd ever thought about her.

She wandered through the camp until she encountered her oldest brother, Brave Wolf, who had been married many summers and who already had three sons. His face lit up when he saw her.

"How is it, little one? Does the sun smile upon you today?" He was sitting in front of his lodge, working on a leather halter for his horse. A slight frown settled on his strong features. "I can see that it does not."

Sun Dancer sat down next to her brother, automatically taking the halter from him and beginning to work it. It was something he had taught her to do many years ago and she always loved helping him. "It is always the same, Brave Wolf, I feel I do not belong."

"Why is that, *nekaim*, my sister?"

"I am different."

"You are different from me and our brothers and father, but you are the same as our mother and my wife."

"No, I am not."

"What sets you apart then?"

"I like to ride as fast as my horse will take me, I like to shoot with my bow and arrows, and I enjoy footraces and games. I think I am a boy in a girl's body," she said glumly.

Brave Wolf laughed loudly and clasped Sun Dancer around the shoulders. "I will share something with you, little one, but it must be something that is only between us." Sun Dancer nodded in anticipation.

"When I was your age, perhaps a little older, I went on a hunt with some of my friends. We had started out with small game but we sighted some mountain lion tracks and decided to track it. We followed the tracks deep into the woods where the trees and brush were thick and it was dark. I felt unsure in there; it was not like the prairie where you could see anything which approached. While we were stalking the animal, we became separated and I was all alone. There were sounds in the woods which I had never heard before and I was frightened; I have never been so frightened since." Brave Wolf paused for a moment, smiling at the look of fear and awe on Sun Dancer's face.

"What of the lion, brother, did you find him?"

"He found me. As I was trying to find my way out of the woods and back to my friends, I heard a rustling sound in the brush and I turned around. Standing there was a large lion, not quite fully grown but large enough to scare me. I was unable to move; I just stared into its golden eyes. I was unable even to lift my bow. It would have been simple for the animal to kill me but after a few moments he left. I stood there for a long time."

"Why do you suppose he did not kill you?"

"Possibly he was as frightened as I, I do not know. I only know at that moment when I saw his golden eyes, I wanted to cry and I wanted to be safe inside our lodge with our father and mother. It did not matter that I was a boy and trained to feel courage in spite of the danger, I felt fear and I was doubtful from that time on that I would ever become a warrior."

"But you did. How did you overcome your fear?"

"Father told me that we all feel fear of some kind and there is no shame in that. But he also said that we must not give in to that fear and let it cow us. I overcame my fear by forcing myself to face situations like that. It was not easy; there are times when I am still fearful."

"What of this feeling I have, Brave Wolf? Is it not strange that I do not wish to be like the other girls? I fear I will never be like them."

"Perhaps it is better if you are not."

"What do you mean? Shall I be an outcast similar to a contrary? I do not think I could bear that."

"Do not fear being different, little one, we are all different in some ways. Look at Stalking Horse. He is very different from all the other boys, yet he is well-liked and respected."

"Yes," Sun Dancer agreed, her face diffused in red. "But I am not Stalking Horse and I am not a boy."

"No matter. There will be a man who will want

you the way you are and not try to change you. Someone like Stalking Horse, perhaps." Sun Dancer looked over at her brother and smiled; she knew that he knew her feelings for Stalking Horse, yet he did not tease her about them. She laid her head against his shoulder.

"Whatever would I have done without you, Brave Wolf? There is no finer brother."

"Well, you are lucky then sister, for not all girls have such fine brothers as I," he said pointing to his chest. "Remember that when I assign you some task to do."

"The mountain blows only smoke, Brave Wolf; you are too soft. I should marry someone like you."

"I should not like to marry someone like you. You are too wild for me. Better a man who would beat you occasionally."

"A man who would beat me would receive a like beating."

"Of that I have no doubt."

"They are back," Spotted Calf's voice breathlessly interrupted Sun Dancer and Brave Wolf. Spotted Calf was Brave Wolf's wife and she had just come from the other side of the camp. "The war-party is back and they have brought many horses. Stalking Horse and Lame Deer were both wounded."

"What of Stalking Horse? Is he all right?" Sun Dancer jumped to her feet.

"I do not know. He and Lame Deer were taken to be tended by Horn."

"I must go. Thank you, brother. As always, you have eased my mind." She ran off in the other direction without looking back.

"What ails Sun Dancer?" Spotted Calf asked curiously. She, like her mother-in-law, was a busy gossip.

"Nothing ails Sun Dancer. She will be passing into womanhood soon and it is a troubling time for her."

"Then she should talk to her mother, not to you."

"She is my sister, Spotted Calf, and if I wish to help her when she needs my help, then it is no concern of yours. You would do well to close your mouth and open you heart; there is much you can learn that way." The conversation was finished and Brave Wolf went back to working on his halter, while Spotted Calf, justifiably admonished, went into the lodge, uncharacteristically quiet.

Sun Dancer stood outside Horn's lodge for many hours until he appeared. Unlike others in the tribe, Sun Dancer had no fear of the medicine man, for he had always been kind and friendly to her.

"Is Stalking Horse well, Horn?"

Horn smiled at the worried expression on the young girl's face, for he had known she would be here inquiring as to the health of Stalking Horse. He was always pleased when one of his visions came true.

"He is well. He will stay in my lodge tonight."

"No," Sun Dancer stated with alarm. Everyone knew that if a person stayed the night in Horn's lodge, it was serious. "You said he was well."

"He is well for a strong, young man, but it is best he rests here for the night rather than be moved. He will be sitting up by tomorrow."

"It is true then," Sun Dancer relaxed noticeably.

"May I see him? I would not disturb him. I would just like to see for myself."

"Ah, you don't trust me and my medicine?"

"Oh, no, Horn, I mean no disrespect. Forgive me. I only wish to see with my own eyes."

"You may go in then."

Horn watched as the young girl bent down and went into his lodge; he smiled again as he thought of her and Stalking Horse. He knew they would marry someday and it would be a strong union. But until that time came there would be strong words between the two.

Sun Dancer moved slowly across Horn's lodge, gingerly stepping over bowls and parfleches of different concoctions and brews. Stalking Horse was lying on a robe near the fire, his eyes closed, his breathing even. Sun Dancer knelt next to him, waiting until Stalking Horse opened his eyes.

"Are you in pain?" Sun Dancer asked gently.

"I do not fear pain."

"That is not what I asked you."

"That is what you replied when I asked if your foot pained you."

"But that was nothing."

"This is nothing."

"You are stubborn, Stalking Horse. I find it easy to lose my patience around you."

"It is the same with me. So we are in agreement about something." Sun Dancer smiled and picking up the cloth in the bowl next to him, she wiped Stalking Horse's face. "Do you thirst?" When he nodded, she placed one hand behind his head, lifting it while he drank from a bowl.

"Do you plan to be Horn's assistant then? I find I do prefer your face to his."

Sun Dancer blushed slightly. "I wanted to see for myself that you are well." She motioned to the poultice on Stalking Horse's shoulder. "How did it happen?"

"We were attacked by some Sioux; I was lanced by one of them. It felt as though it went through my shoulder. Horn said it will not hinder any movement of my arm. I will remember next time to always keep the enemy in my sight."

Sun Dancer sat back on her heels and watched as the flames of the fire played over the bronze of Stalking Horse's skin. She felt a strange, unfamiliar feeling in her stomach, as though she would faint. She did not understand or perceive that it had anything to do with Stalking Horse.

"Are you ever frightened when you fight?"

"I do not think about it. If I did, I am not sure what I would do," he replied honestly. "And you, what do you fear, Sun Dancer?"

"Everything," she said in a shocked tone, surprised by her own honesty. "I fear I would make a poor warrior."

"You do yourself a disservice. You have a courageous heart."

Sun Dancer looked up and met Stalking Horse's eyes; she was moved by his statement and her eyes betrayed her feelings. "Thank you," she said simply. She felt suddenly shy and unsure of herself. She rose. "I must return to our lodge. My mother has many things for me to do. She says I am lazy and I find excuses to run away."

"Do you?"

"Yes," she laughed. "There are always more pleasing things to do than the tasks which my mother has set for me. Perhaps I should have been an eagle and then I would be free to do as I please."

"Perhaps you were once."

"I think not. My stomach turns sour when I climb too high. I have not yet seen an eagle who was afraid of heights." Stalking Horse laughed and Sun Dancer wrinkled her small nose in irritation. "Are you making fun of me?"

"No, I am only laughing because you make me do so. You have a fine wit."

"My father says I have a fine mind," Sun Dancer said honestly, without any trace of conceit.

"I believe your father is right. And it will be an even finer mind when you learn to use it in the right manner." At the antagonistic look on her face he added quickly, "I mean it to be a compliment, Sun Dancer. You are too quick to take the wrong meaning in things."

Sun Dancer thought for a moment and then nodded. "You are right, I must learn to have patience. I have much to learn."

"We all have much to learn." He moved on the robes and winced slightly. Sun Dancer quickly moved to his side.

"You are in pain." She dipped the cloth in the cool water and ran it over his forehead. Stalking Horse took her small hand in his and held it gently.

"It does not hurt so much. Every minute that you fuss over me I feel like less of a man. Please, I know your intentions are well meant, but I am fine. I am young and strong and I will probably be wounded many times in battle. Do not worry yourself." His voice was gentle and for the first time, Sun Dancer did not take exception to what he said. She knew how strongly Cheyenne men felt about their manhood, and again she rose to leave.

"I am pleased that you are well, Stalking Horse. Perhaps we will talk more when you are better."

"Perhaps," Stalking Horse said noncommittally, and watched her as she left the lodge. It was not wise to foster hope of love in one so young, he thought ruefully. Nor was it wise for him to dream of the day when she would be a woman and of marriageable age. Life was too fickle and filled with too much uncertainty. Better to remain true to one's self.

Stalking Horse pulled the string on the bow back as far as he could but the pain in his shoulder was still excruciating. Horn told him it would take some time for him to work out the stiffness and soreness but it seemed to be taking much too long. He took another arrow from his quiver and placed it in the bow. He pulled the string back as he always had, with his thumb and first two fingers, but the pain was now too much and he quickly pulled on the string with his other fingers. Smoothly, he pulled back the string and aimed at his target on the tree trunk. When he let go of the string, his arrow flew straight to its destination. He smiled. The pain was great but he was still able to hit the target.

He let his arms drop for a moment and began rotating his sore arm and shoulder. The muscles were tight and they needed to be stretched and strengthened again. He then picked up the exercising instrument which Horn had made for him. It was a large rock, one which a man would have trouble lifting with one hand, with a strap of rawhide secured around it so one could swing it. Horn wanted Stalking Horse to start swinging the rock around in the air, forward and backward, until he could do it quickly and without pain. The first circular movement caused a great deal of pain, but Stalking Horse persisted until he had done many rotations each way. The shoulder felt no better and now suffered a throbbing pain, but he knew that if he followed Horn's advice he would be normal again. After he had performed the exercise a few more times, he picked up his weapons and equipment and headed back toward camp.

Walking back from the woods along the stream, he happened to see Sun Dancer sitting with Laughing Bird. They were sitting on the edge of the bank, their bare feet dangling in the water. Their heads were close together and they were laughing about some matter. He stopped and stared at them, the sight of the two together angering him. It had always been that way—for some reason he had always resented their closeness. He resented the fact that any boy outside of her family could know Sun Dancer so well. He watched as they jumped into the water and Laughing Bird dove down and playfully tugged at Sun Dancer's legs, while she splashed water in his face and swam away in crisp, even strokes. It angered him even more that Laughing Bird had been the one who had saved Sun Dancer when she was a child. He started back to the camp, not wanting to see more of the child's play, when he heard Laughing Bird call out to him.

"How is your arm, Stalking Horse? I see you have been practicing with your bow." Stalking Horse turned back to see the two standing up in the water, Sun Dancer looking at him in expectation. He walked to the bank.

"The arm is well, Laughing Bird. It will soon be stronger than ever."

"That is good to hear. We could not afford to lose so valuable a warrior as you."

Stalking Horse looked at him, a slight smile of thanks appearing on his face. Laughing Bird was one of the few boys whom he genuinely liked and respected. He was a good athlete and already had proved himself to be an adept horse stealer. He hadn't yet proved himself in battle, but that was only a matter of time. He was friendly and outgoing and he had a sense of fairness about him that most people didn't have. Stalking Horse supposed the only reason he felt any resentment at all toward Laughing Bird was because of his relationship with Sun Dancer.

"It is a fine day for a swim." He then looked at Sun Dancer. "I remember a time when you could not swim so well."

"But thanks to Laughing Bird I am here and I am a good swimmer."

"Yes," Stalking Horse answered shortly. "Are you being lazy from your chores again, Sun Dancer?" he asked sharply.

"I think your wound still causes you pain, Stalking Horse, for your mood is not at all pleasing. I would rather carry on a conversation with the snapping turtles, for they at least give warning before

57

they bite." She abruptly dove into the water and swam away from the young men.

"Do not mind Sun Dancer, she has much too sharp a tongue," Laughing Bird stated in defense of the girl.

"I know about her tongue," Stalking Horse said angrily, "and one day I should like to cure her of it." He picked up his things. "A good day to you, Laughing Bird. Let us ride sometime." He strode back to the camp in anger, wondering all the while, how a little nothing of a girl could try his patience so.

The camp was quiet and most of the older people were asleep. Sun Dancer's parents had gone to sleep but she herself was unable to lie still. She arose and decided to take a walk. She heard a flute being played, a love song for some young Cheyenne maiden. In the distant hills, she heard the shrill cry of a pack of coyotes as they struggled over some recent kill. There were very few people about now, and this was one of Sun Dancer's favorite times to walk. The fires had burned down and the camp had grown silent except for the usual nocturnal sounds. She walked through camp to the stream to sit on the bank and look at the light of the moon reflected on the water. She gazed up at the moon and wondered how so much light could come from such a small object. This was her best time to think; she savored the stillness and the silence of the night to enjoy her own thoughts.

She knew that soon her "little girl" days would be over and she would have to accept her rightful place as a woman. The thought scared and excited her at the same time. There were some things about being a woman which did not disturb her; one was the possibility of marriage to Stalking Horse. She knew in her heart it was a silly idea, one unsuited to one so practical, but she could not imagine marriage to anyone but Stalking Horse. She wondered if her vision were true and if she would marry him, or if, as her father had suggested, it was just a "wish dream." If she did not marry Stalking Horse, the only other man she would even consider would be Laughing Bird, and even then, she couldn't imagine sharing the intimacies of marriage with her best friend.

She was not even sure what the intimacies of marriage were. She had heard her mother and father since she was a child, but it did not sound so bad. They made noises and she had looked and seen her father on top of her mother, but as to the truth of the situation, she knew very little. She knew only that one had to care for a person very deeply to share a robe. She sighed deeply. Perhaps she would never know if her time didn't come. She knew three girls her age who had already come into their time and were already spoken for in marriage. She was beginning to feel odd.

"What keeps you up at this hour? Are your dreams not pleasant?" Stalking Horse's voice broke the stillness of the night. Sun Dancer, startled, turned to find him standing behind her.

"Do you always sneak up on people so as to frighten the wits out of them?"

"I doubt the wits could ever be frightened out of you, Sun Dancer." He sat down next to her before she could reply. "Truly, what brings you out here alone this night?"

"I often come out here at night. It is a good time."

"For what? For thinking of things which might not be?"

"Or for things that might," Sun Dancer replied softly. "Did you follow me here, Stalking Horse?"

"Yes. I saw you wandering through camp alone and I wondered where you might be going. It is not safe to wander out of the camp at night."

"You are worried for my safety now?" she asked in a bemused tone.

"I would worry for your parents if something should happen to you."

"I have never known you to be overly worried about me before. Do I present a helpless picture?"

"No. In all truth, I do not know why I followed you here. Perhaps it was just to talk."

"Why did you not tell me that to begin with. I am not always so quick to be sharp. What do you wish to talk about?"

Stalking Horse shook his head. "I do not know. Perhaps it is to say that I should not talk to you anymore."

"Why is that?" she asked directly, her eyes not giving away to the alarm she felt.

"I do not think it becomes a warrior to be seen talking to a little girl."

"I am not so little and you are only five summers older than I. You are barely out of boyhood yourself."

"I am no longer a boy now that I have been on a raid. It does not become my stature as a warrior to be seen talking to you."

"Then why do you continue to talk? Why do you not leave?" She looked away and stared at the water. Tears stung her eyes but she refused to let Stalking Horse see them.

"I should be talking to girls of marriageable age."

"Then be off," she shouted angrily. "I do not wish to keep you from your young maidens. I am sure there are many who would be pleased to become your wife. Or do you plan to have more than one?"

"I do not know. Perhaps I will have five, if it suits me."

"Why not ten?" Sun Dancer replied sarcastically.

"Jealousy does not become you, Sun Dancer."

"I feel no jealousy, Stalking Horse, only relief that I am not of marriageable age and do not have to be selected by you."

Stalking Horse stood up. "You do not have to worry; you would not even enter into my choice for a wife. The woman I would choose would know her place and would do anything to please her husband. She would not be a sharp-tongued, short-tempered she-wolf. A good life to you, Sun Dancer, for we need not speak again."

Sun Dancer didn't watch him as he stalked away, her eyes were clouded by the tears which filled them. Her vision had indeed been a "wish dream," as her father had expected, because now there was no possibility of Stalking Horse ever becoming her husband. She, in her infinite stupidity, had just laid to rest all hopes of that.

CHAPTER IV

Sun Dancer looked up from her task to wipe the sweat from her brow. She was scraping the flesh from a buffalo hide. It was stretched out and pinned down to the ground, and she was scraping all the blood, fat, and bits of flesh that still clung to it. It was important that the hide be freed of everything that might hinder its drying evenly.

She stood up and stretched her back, which was sore and cramped from staying in the same position for so long. She looked beyond the camp to the riders and the buffalos which they were killing. The large herd had started to move and the riders killed as many as possible before they did so. The prairie was littered with corpses of the large animals, and already the scavengers were making a feast of some of them.

If the buffalos were plentiful, men were not permitted to chase the buffalo alone. There was no individual hunting. If one man hunted, all men joined in the chase. Anyone who was discovered going out alone was severely whipped by the soldiers of the tribe. It was a strictly enforced rule because the tribe depended on the buffalo for most of its food. It was necessary that the hunting be organized so that large quantities of food would be killed at one time, and that the animals would not be frightened or disturbed so as to be driven beyond the reach of the people.

The chiefs decided when the buffalos were to be surrounded and they gave their orders to the soldiers. From that time on, the soldiers had charge of the hunt. The word was spread throughout the tribe when the hunt was to begin and then all would join in.

The favorite method of killing the buffalo was with the lance. A rider rode up on the right side of the animal and holding the lance across his body, right hand held higher, he thrust the lance downward and forward. When the buffalo felt the lance he usually ran faster, and sometimes he turned to charge. But it wasn't long before the crippled animal broke down and stopped, and the kill was made.

Some men felt that the bow and arrow was the most effective method of killing the buffalo—it could kill from up to three and four hundred yards. If the arrowhead entered at the right point, an animal could be killed with one arrow.

Once the buffalos were killed, the women and children ran from the camp to assist in butchering the meat. When the animal was skinned and butchered, every man, woman, and child carried a pack back to camp. They left nothing behind. Even the bones and entrails were taken as they felt nothing should be wasted. The tongue and nose were considered delicacies, while the liver sprinkled with gall was a favorite. The small intestine filled with chopped meat was roasted or boiled; the lungs of the animal were cut open, dried, and roasted on coals; the marrow bones were split and the contents eaten. The blood was cooked in the rennet of the buffalo over hot ashes until the blood turned to the consistency of jelly, and was then eaten. The hide of the buffalo-bull was eaten by cooking it in a small depression in the ground and covering it with layers of leaves, over which several inches of clay were spread, pounded, and smoothed off. Over the clay was built a fire which burned for three or four hours, and when the fire was swept aside and the clay and leaves removed, the hide was taken out. The hair slipped easily from the hide, which was now quite tender and palatable.

The women saved the scrapings from the hide which they later boiled and made into food. They made pemmican by roasting the dried meat and pounding it with a stone maul on a stone. The flesh of the buffalo, including the back fat, was cut into strips and dried in the sun or on lines stretched in the lodge.

Sun Dancer had cleaned many hides this morning, and her mother said that after she finished this one, she could go watch the rest of the hunters. Again she stooped down and applied the mixture of brains, liver, soapweed, and grease to both sides of the hide, rubbing it in thoroughly. She then folded the hide up and put it aside with the others she had done. They would sit overnight while the mixture soaked through the skins. The next day the women would unfold them and lay them out in the sun to dry and soften. But that was tomorrow; she had other plans for today. She ran to the stream to wash the blood and bits of flesh from her hands and hurried to the edge of camp.

The hunters were almost done. They had killed a great many buffalo and the village would have plenty of meat and robes for the winter. Sun Dancer spotted Stalking Horse on the ground, taking the hide from a huge bull. It had been a long time now since she'd spoken to him, since the spring, and already it was the fall and she was twelve summers old. They'd met often but he always avoided her eyes and continued on. Once, while she was out on the prairie butchering an animal, he rode past and stopped on his horse. He looked as though he might speak to her but he did not. He only sat on his horse for a few seconds looking down at her and then rode off in the direction of more buffalo.

Sun Dancer had changed a great deal since that night when she had argued with Stalking Horse. She had thought on what he had said to her, and she knew that he was partly right. She was too sharp-tongued and she did not accept her responsibilities as a girl. Since that time, however, she did all that her mother told her without complaint, and she found that it was not all so bad. When she finished doing the things which her mother had assigned her for the day, she was still able to do the things she loved most: ride, shoot, swim, and walk. While always stern about her daughter's duties, Woman's Heart never prevented Sun Dancer from doing the things which she most enjoyed doing; she knew that would only make her daughter more rebellious.

Sun Dancer walked farther onto the prairie and

decided to skin another animal. She knew it would please her mother, and she found she liked doing things which would please her. Most of the herd was now grazing farther away from camp, and Sun Dancer had no fear of the animals. She knew that when they charged, it was only from fear or the pain which they suffered from a wound. She reached a large cow and took out her knife and began the laborious task of skinning the animal. She had been taught by her father, who, like most Cheyenne men, was an expert at removing the hide from an animal in one piece. Sun Dancer was engrossed in her work when she heard a noise from somewhere beyond. She looked up to see a large bull, blood pouring from a wound in his side, looking at her and pawing the ground. Sun Dancer did not move; she stared at the animal with eyes transfixed. She had never seen one so close before. The closest she had ever been to a live buffalo was on horseback with her father, and they had been well behind the animal. She had never confronted one this close before, and certainly not alone and on foot.

She stared up at the large animal, who was snorting and pawing at the ground angrily, clods of dirt flying from beneath his feet. Her heart beat frantically but she remained calm, her body not betraying any signs of fear. She knew that if she remained still, the animal probably would not attack her. She clenched the knife in her hand even tighter, just in case the huge bull decided to come at her. Her chances were slim if the animal decided to attack, but she had also heard stories of great men who had survived an attack by a wounded buffalo.

The buffalo bellowed loudly, throwing up bits of dirt which hit Sun Dancer. He stopped suddenly, as if unsure of what he was confronting, then charged forward. Sun Dancer lay down next to the body of the cow, pressing her smaller body next to the larger one. She felt the impact when the bull's horns crashed into the dead body of the cow, and again and again as he punctured it with his sharp horns. Sun Dancer knew the bull would gore the dead cow until she was forced to flee; her only option was to run for camp when the bull was distracted. She found her chance when the bull ran off again to renew his charge. Sun Dancer leaped from behind the carcass and quickly ran for the camp. She looked behind her and saw the large bull following, his speed somewhat diminished by his loss of blood. She rapidly swerved to the side and headed for another carcass, diving beside it just before the bull rammed its horns into it. The bull repeatedly rammed the dead animal with its horns until he grew tired and looked for more movement. He waited in silence, shaking his large head, then he circled around the dead animal. Sun Dancer lay very still. When she saw the bull headed toward her again, she jumped up and ran for the camp. She waved frantically when she saw a rider in the distance. She changed direction slightly and headed for the rider, carelessly stepping in a prairie-dog hole and falling down. She turned over and quickly pulled herself to her feet just in time to see the bull lumbering down on her. She was tired but she continued to run in a zig-zag fashion, knowing she couldn't continue for much longer.

It was then she saw Stalking Horse, the rider she

had seen in the distance, bearing down on her and the buffalo. He was yelling and waving his lance in front of the bull and the dazed animal followed the distraction. It ran after Stalking Horse for some distance until tiring, then fell to its front forelegs. Stalking Horse thrust his lance into the animal's side, then turned his horse and rode back to Sun Dancer, who had fallen to her knees, her knife still grasped tightly in her hand. He jumped from his horse and knelt by her.

"Are you well?"

When the girl would not reply, he lifted her face up; there were tears in her eyes. "Tell me, Sun Dancer, are you well?"

She looked at him then, the dark eyes betraying a kind of sadness. "I am well, Stalking Horse."

"What is wrong then?"

"I feel great shame."

"Why do you feel shame? I do not understand."

"It seems that again I have been foolish and put myself in a dangerous position without thinking. And to my further shame, you are the person who has saved my life. Perhaps it would have been better if the bull had killed me."

"That does not sound like you, Sun Dancer. The experience has caused you much fear."

"Yes. Fear and shame. They are bad feelings even alone, but together almost unbearable."

"Why do you react like this? It is over now and you are well. Does it bother you so that I helped you?"

Sun Dancer was silent for a long time, her head hung low. When she answered, it was with a soft, trembling voice.

"Yes, it bothers me, and it shames me. You said things to me once before, and I know that you do not respect me. A man cannot respect a girl like me. Now you have seen me put myself in a shameful position so that my life depended on yours. I cannot bear it." She stood up, putting the knife back into its sheath. "I thank you for saving my life, Stalking Horse; I will never forget it. I will be forever in your debt. But I think it best that we continue on the road we have traveled these last months and let the silence between us continue. I am sure that being seen with a girl like me can only bring you dishonor." She started to walk away then stopped, without turning back to look at him. "Please come to me if you need my help for anything. I only hope that someday I can repay the debt I now owe you."

Stalking Horse watched the girl walk away, her once proud gait reduced to a slow, slump-shouldered walk. Had he done this to her? Had he shamed her so that she would rather have been killed by the buffalo than be saved by him? He walked back to his horse and mounted it, turning to ride back out to the other hunters. Were all girls as complicated as Sun Dancer, or was she as he had suspected for sometime, someone different? Perhaps it was time to go to Horn for some answers.

Woman's Heart watched her daughter as she glumly went about her work. She was now working better than she ever had, but her mood was very solemn. Her mood had been the same for weeks and she had lost the vitality and enthusiasm which was so characteristic of her.

"How is this mother?" Sun Dancer held up the softened hide for Woman's Heart to see. She had been pulling the hide back and forth across a rope which was tied above her to a post, and then ran diagonally down to a peg in the ground. The work was long and tedious, but there was never a complaint from Sun Dancer. She continued on, without break, until the hide was softened to her mother's liking. Woman's Heart took the hide from Sun Dancer and ran her fingers along the smooth texture.

"It is good, daughter. You have done well." She handed it back to the girl. "Perhaps we can make you a new dress from it," she said enthusiastically, hoping to entice the girl from her mood.

"Do not waste the hide on me, mother, I do not need a new dress. Use it for something more important."

"What is more important than you, *natona*, my daughter?" Woman's Heart walked to her daughter and placed her hands on either side of her face. "What is it? What ails you?"

"I cannot say, mother." She pulled away from Woman's Heart and knelt down to start a new hide.

"Come here, Sun Dancer." Woman's Heart's voice was stern. Sun Dancer complied immediately, knowing well her mother's tone of voice. "If you cannot talk to me about what ails you, I wish you to talk to your father or brother. I do not like this change in you and I want you to talk to someone who can help you."

"No one can help me, mother," Sun Dancer replied resignedly. "I have brought myself to this point."

"Then you must take yourself past it. You are a strong girl and you can do anything. You will talk to your father or brother; I will hear no more about it."

Sun Dancer sat quietly next to her father as they watched the sun begin to set on the vast prairie. It was a favorite time of day for Sun Dancer, for in those last few minutes before sundown, the landscape continually changed because of the light and shadows. Father and daughter sat quietly until He-Walks-the-Mountain broke the silence.

"What is it that ails you, daughter? Your mother worries for you."

"She need not worry."

"Parents always worry when something is wrong with their children."

"Do I look ill of health?" Her father shook his head. "Then I am well."

"I have been a chief for a long time and have seen many things through these eyes. One thing I have learned is never to believe what I see. Things may not be what they seem. And with you I know that to be true." Sun Dancer voiced no reply and He-Walks-the-Mountain continued, undaunted by her silence. "Perhaps we should take you to Horn. He knows ways of finding out what is wrong with a person." At the startled look on Sun Dancer's face, He-Walks-the-Mountain knew he had gotten through to her. Although Horn was revered and greatly respected, he was known to use strange methods of finding out why people were ailing. Sun Dancer, still a little girl, was frightened of the stories she had heard about Horn.

"I do not wish to see Horn; he will make me confront the spirits."

"We must get at the truth somehow."

"No. Horn frightens me."

"Horn has always treated you kindly."

"Yes, but I have never been to him for a problem. Perhaps then he would make me face demons and spirits."

"You know those are only stories to make Horn appear evil, do you not, daughter?"

Sun Dancer nodded. "You were trying to frighten me then? Why?"

"Because I wish you to talk with me. I have lived much longer than you and I possess more knowledge of the world. Perhaps I can help."

"Something is wrong with me; I do not think I can be helped."

"Tell me what, Sun Dancer. I cannot help if you do not confide in me."

Sun Dancer lowered her head and thought for a moment. "I do not seem to be able to do anything right. Brave Wolf told me there is nothing wrong in being different, but I feel I am too different. I do not seem to be content in anything I do."

"You are still a girl; things will be different when you are a woman."

"Are you sure, father? Will I really change that much?"

"Your body will tell your mind when it is time."

"It is hard for me to believe. Already there are girls who plan for their weddings: they make robes and quill on them everyday, they make dresses and moccasins for their wedding day, they make shirts for their husbands. I have no interest in any of this. My mind is still occupied with thoughts of swimming and riding and taking long walks. I do not seem to be able to control my wild ways, father. I would not know how to make a good wife."

"I, myself, feel you are too young to be thinking of marriage. Some of the other girls are ready for it, that does not mean you are. Has your mother told you that we did not marry until she was almost seventeen summers old?"

Sun Dancer looked at her father in surprise, her mouth open in a gasp. Most girls married quite young, at the age of fourteen or fifteen; seventeen was fairly old for a bride.

"But why? Mother is beautiful and surely she had many suitors."

"She simply did not wish to marry so young. It was her own choice."

"I do not understand. That does not sound like mother."

"I do not think you know your mother very well, Sun Dancer. She is stern with you because she loves you. When she tells you to watch your conduct around the young men it is only because she cares. She wants you to have a good reputation when you marry, so you may marry the man of your choice. She does not want you to be forced into a marriage because of your poor conduct."

"I did not know."

"There is much you do not know about her. In some ways, she was as wild as you. In the old days we did not have horses, but we hunted on foot. Your mother was swift and her eye as sharp as an eagle's.

She made many young braves look foolish."

"Mother liked to hunt, too?" Sun Dancer asked with a smile. It comforted her to know that her mother had done some of the same things she now did. "And did she swim well also?"

"When we were children, she was never out of the water. She was as fast in the water as she was on land. I had to chase her everywhere."

"You chased her?"

"Until she realized I would make a good husband for her. Then she stopped running."

"Was she happy then, after she changed?"

"Yes, I think so. She was ready to be my wife and raise our children. I do not think she felt any less free."

"I do not think I will ever be married."

"Why? There are many young men who would be willing to wait until you are ready. Of that, I am sure."

"But I do not want just anyone."

"This mood of yours, has it to do with Stalking Horse?"

"Yes. He told me I would never be his choice for a wife."

"He told you that out of the blue? There was no reason for this?"

"There was a reason. I told him I am glad I am not of marriageable age so that he cannot choose me."

"And this is what put you in your mood?"

Sun Dancer shook her head in agitation. "No, father. It is much worse than that. He told me that in the spring; we had not spoken since, until a few weeks ago. I decided to talk out on the prairie and skin another buffalo. I wanted to bring the hide back and scrape it for mother as a surprise. While I was out there, a wounded bull attacked me. I lay down beside a dead one and he didn't see me, but he knew I was there by my smell. I decided to run for camp and when I did the bull came after me. It was then I saw a rider and signaled for him to come. It was Stalking Horse. He distracted the bull and killed him, then he came back to see if I was all right."

"Why did you not tell me this before?" He-Walks-the-Mountain asked in alarm.

"It was not important. It was over and I was well and unhurt."

"I must take a gift to Stalking Horse and give him my thanks. I will give him the shield I have been working on."

"No," Sun Dancer cried vehemently. "Not your shield. You have been working on it for so long. It is special to you."

"Yes, which makes it an even better gift. Do you not know, daughter, that I would give all my shields, robes, weapons, and horses for your life? They are trifles in comparison to your worth to me. I am pleased that I have such a good gift to offer Stalking Horse."

"I am ashamed."

"Why?"

"Because I was foolish. Now, not only do I owe my life to Stalking Horse, I have put you in the position where you must give up something on my behalf. I am truly sorry, father, I do not seem to be able to behave as the daughter of a great chief should."

"You make too much of this, daughter. We should rejoice that Stalking Horse was there to help you."

"I wish he had not been. I belittled myself in

his eyes."

"Ah. This has to do with pride then?"

"Yes. You have told me many times that one must have pride in one's self."

"But I have also told you that humility is just as important as pride. Too much of either one is not a good thing. That is why they balance each other out so well."

"But am I not humble now?"

"No, you are ashamed; that is different. Your pride has been damaged by something Stalking Horse told you in anger, much the same way you probably hurt him by saying the things which provoked his outburst. Is that not right?"

Sun Dancer hesitated a moment, then nodded. "Yes, father, you are right. It was I who started the argument. As usual, my tongue was quicker than my mind."

"And you hold a grudge against Stalking Horse because he played your same game? You are smarter than that, daughter. Why did you not see that his words were spoken in anger?"

"I knew that, father, but the words still stung. I believe what he said was true."

"It probably was true at the time. But did he not show concern for you when he saved your life?"

"Yes."

"And did you thank him rightfully?"

"I thanked him, but I was not kind. My shame did not permit me to show my true thanks. You would not be proud of me, father."

"I am always proud of you, daughter, but it is time you began to think on the mistakes you have made and to learn from them. I propose that you, too, make a gift for Stalking Horse and take it to him when I take my gift to him. If you ever want him to think well of you, show him you have a kind and forgiving heart. Show him you are worthy of being a chief's daughter."

"It will be difficult," she sighed. "He provokes my anger easily."

"Then how much more meaningful to you, if you can show a little humility and admit that you were wrong. You will become better for it."

"You are right, I know, but . . . Yes, I will do it. If only to prove to you that I can."

"Do not prove it to me, daughter, prove it to yourself. Learn that you can sacrifice a little of your pride sometimes and be a better person for it."

Sun Dancer looked at her father and then threw her arms around him in a loving embrace. "How did you become so wise, father? I fear I will never learn the things you have."

"You will learn them and much more," he said thoughtfully, thinking of Horn's prophecy. "Just remember to keep your mind open at all times. If you close your mind, then you will only remain as you are."

"I will learn, father, and someday I will make you proud of me. I will make myself worthy of being your daughter."

In his silent thoughts, He-Walks-the-Mountain realized that Sun Dancer would have to do no more than hug him and love him, as she was now doing, to make herself worthy of being his daughter. Although he could never tell her this, her love was more than enough.

CHAPTER V

Sun Dancer sat by the fire, a robe around her shoulders, trying to warm her stiff fingers. She had been working on a shirt for Stalking Horse for almost two moons, and her fingers showed the signs of her labors. Many nights when the wind blew coldly through the lodge and the snow was too deep to walk in outside, Sun Dancer worked on the quilling of the shirt late into the night. She was an inexperienced quiller, but her mother showed her certain stitches and beadwork which could be used to accent the shirt. She made concentric circles and a many-pointed star which represented the sun. Her favorite design, which she thought of herself, was on the back of the shirt and in the shape of a prancing horse, hoofs high off the ground. In her mind, it represented Stalking Horse. Her mother, who was a highly respected quiller and a member of the women's Quilling Society, was greatly impressed by her daughter's work. Sun Dancer had never before shown an interest in quilling and Woman's Heart had not known that her daughter possessed such talent.

Sun Dancer rubbed her fingers together and then

blew on them, trying to get the circulation going in them again. The tips were sore and bleeding slightly from the blisters. In time, the blisters would turn to callouses. She picked up the shirt and turned it toward the light; it was indeed a pleasing sight. She surprised even herself with the work she had done. She could see the shirt on Stalking Horse's large frame. He would look handsome in it, of that she was sure. Her only worry now was whether or not he would accept it from her. He could refuse the gift and she would be forever shamed. But she did not wish to think of that. She hoped that he would forgive her and take her gift offering and be her friend. For other than Laughing Bird, she could think of no one else whose friendship would mean so much to her.

Winter had come early this year and the band had to make haste to find their winter encampment after they finished their hunting of the buffalo. Stalking Horse sat opposite Horn in the elder's lodge. Both sat with their legs crossed, heavy robes around their shoulders. After the smoking of the pipe, they talked of general things: of people in the camp, the long winter ahead, the supply of food, things which affected them everyday. After a while, Horn spoke.

"What is it you wish to speak to me about, Stalking Horse?"

"It is a person I wish to speak to you of, Horn. It is Sun Dancer." Although Stalking Horse might have felt some embarrassment talking to another man about a young girl, he felt none where Horn was concerned. Horn was too learned in too many ways to scoff at another man so easily.

"What is it you wish to know?"

"I feel there is something about her, I do not think I can explain it. She seems too old sometimes and she says things which only a woman should know. She provokes me to anger faster than anyone I ever knew. I wonder if you know, Horn, is she 'special'?"

"How do you mean 'special'?" Although Horn knew exactly what Stalking Horse meant.

"She feels too deeply," he said simply.

Horn nodded in agreement and in admiration of the youth; Stalking Horse, too, felt deeply, although he didn't yet realize it.

"You are right, my son, Sun Dancer is 'special.' Before she was born, I had a vision brought to me by the wolves from the *maiyun*."

"The *maiyun*?" Even Stalking Horse was impressed.

"Yes. They told me that one day Sun Dancer would hold an important position in the tribe, and that she would serve her people well. I believe she has visions, too."

"How do you know this?"

"We have talked and she has told me things which make me believe that she is also a possessor of certain gifts. What is it that troubles you about her?"

Stalking Horse shook his head in puzzlement. "I wonder why I take such interest in a mere girl. I do not understand it."

"Perhaps it is because you know the child will be a woman in a few years. You know deeply inside of you that she will be quite different from all the others— quite special. You feel some attachment to her then?"

"Yes, I believe I do. We do not talk often, but I

think of her and I look for her in the camp. Right now she will not speak to me."

"Why is that?"

"It started back in the spring. We fought and we both said things which should have been forgotten. I did not mean what I said; I only spoke out of anger. We did not speak until the hunt, when I saw her endangered by a wounded bull. I distracted the bull and killed him. When I went to Sun Dancer she was so shamed by what I had done, she would not even look at me. She said she would rather have been killed by the thing than be saved by me. She seemed to hate me."

"I think just the opposite. You said it before, she feels too deeply. She was probably hurt by the words you both said; and when you saved her life, she felt even more hurt, more ashamed. I do not think she wanted you to see her as a helpless thing."

"But that is how I first saw her, when she almost drowned in the river, and I know Sun Dancer to be anything but helpless. She has the skill and the pride of some braves."

"Yes, I believe that to be true. But she is still a young girl with all the feelings and sensitivities of one."

"I do forget that at times. It is difficult for me to see through my anger."

"For Sun Dancer also."

"You care for her, Horn. You speak very kindly of her."

Horn smiled, the gesture looking incongruous with his dark, craggy face and long, white hair. "Yes, I care for Sun Dancer. It is I who named her. He-

Walks-the-Mountain brought me to his lodge and we both saw the sun coming through the top of the lodge, shining on her face. I knew it to be a sign. She was a calm, peaceful baby, willing to wait until she was older to find out all the things she wished to know. The first time she saw me, she smiled. I believe she won my heart at that time."

"I believe she has won everyone's heart. I do not think there will be anything less than half the warriors in this camp who will court her when she comes of age."

"Will you be one of them?"

"I do not know. I only know I wish her to be my friend. And you have helped me with that. For this I thank you." Stalking Horse stood up, leaving Horn the robe which was on his back. "I wish you to have this robe, Horn, it is very thick and warm, and it looks to be a cold winter."

"Thank you, Stalking Horse. It is a fine robe." Horn knew that the boy probably did not have another robe so fine as the one he now gave away, but it would be an insult to refuse his gift. As Stalking Horse started for the door of the lodge, Horn's voice stopped him. "Stalking Horse." The boy stopped to look at the old man once more. "Sun Dancer will go through many changes before she attains her womanhood, not all of them favorable to others. But when she attains the full flower of her womanhood, it will be something to behold. The man who shares this with her will only be the better for it." Horn watched the broad-shouldered youth stoop down and go through the door of the lodge. He reached for his pipe and relit it, puffing on it a few times, while lying

82

against his backrest. He had lived a long time and few things gave him joy anymore: the birth of a new child, the recovery of a wounded or sick person, the marriage of a young couple. But he knew that there would be few greater joys in his lifetime than the one he would feel when he blessed the union of Sun Dancer and Stalking Horse. For from their union would come a strength that others in the tribe would draw on, and eventually, be guided by.

The day which Sun Dancer and He-Walks-the-Mountain picked to go to Stalking Horse's lodge was a good day; there had been no snow for two days and the air was cool but not freezing. Patches of blue had shown through in the sky, and He-Walks-the-Mountain said that was a good sign.

Sun Dancer had finished the shirt and with her mother's approval, had folded it up and wrapped it in a large piece of rawhide. Sun Dancer felt pleased when her mother complimented her on the shirt, as her mother was an experienced and seasoned quiller. She had even said that it was time for her to join the Quilling Society. Sun Dancer was honored.

He-Walks-the-Mountain and Sun Dancer walked to Stalking Horse's lodge after the morning meal. There had been a large hunt the day before, so the men were not venturing out of camp. Stalking Horse's lodge was not large, although he owned many horses. When a man owned as many horses as Stalking Horse, he usually had a large lodge. Many horses could carry all the lodge poles which were needed for a larger lodge, and a man with a family needed a larger place in which to live. Stalking Horse had no family. His parents were killed by the Hohes when he was young, and he lived with his mother's family until he went on his first raid. He then moved into a lodge of his own. As they approached Stalking Horse's lodge, He-Walks-the-Mountain cried out to Stalking Horse for permission to enter. One did not enter another's lodge without permission; it was regarded as bad manners and was a discourtesy to the owner. At Stalking Horse's bidding, He-Walks-the-Mountain and Sun Dancer entered the lodge.

When they entered the lodge, they turned to the right and waited until Stalking Horse bid them to come to the back of the lodge. He was sitting against his backrest, working on a shield. The place of honor was at the left of and next to the owner and although He-Walks-the-Mountain was a chief, Stalking Horse requested that Sun Dancer sit there. She was distinctly honored and knelt with her legs to one side.

The owner and his family, if he had one, lived to the left side of the door, though their sleeping place might be at the back. It was not good etiquette to go to that part of the lodge occupied by the owner or his family, nor to pass between the fire and the owner of the lodge, nor to pass between anyone sitting in the lodge and the fire. A well-mannered person passed behind the sitters in the lodge.

Before He-Walks-the-Mountain or Sun Dancer spoke, Stalking Horse took out his pipe. He began by pointing the pipestem to the sky, to the ground, and to the four directions, in order, and then said: "Spirit Above, smoke. Earth, smoke. Four cardinal points, smoke." Then he made his prayer for help. The smokes to the four cardinal points were offered to the spirits who dwelled in the lodge.

Stalking Horse then passed the pipe to He-Walks-the-Mountain, from right to left, and then back to Stalking Horse, until the pipe was smoked out. If there had been a large circle of men, the owner would start and pass it from his right to his left, with the sun, and when the man sitting next to the door had smoked, he was not allowed to pass it across the doorway; instead, it was handed back all around the circle, no one smoking, to the man on the opposite side of the door. He smoked, and then the man to his left, and so it went until it went back to the owner or until it went out.

Normally, young men did not smoke, nor would men smoke in the presence of a woman, but in deference to He-Walks-the-Mountain's position in the tribe, Stalking Horse smoked with him, in front of his daughter. It was not advised that young men smoke because it would make them short-winded and unable to run long and fast.

"Why do you and your daughter honor me so on this day, He-Walks-the-Mountain?" Stalking Horse was the first to speak in his own lodge.

"I have come to give my thanks to you, Stalking Horse, for a deed well-done."

"And what is this deed I have done?"

"You have saved my daughter's life; I know of no deed greater than that to me," He-Walks-the-Mountain stated solemnly.

Stalking Horse was genuinely surprised; he didn't think that Sun Dancer would tell anyone about what had happened.

"It was easily done and one which any man would

have done had he been there."

"But you were the one who did it and I came here on this day to honor you with a gift." He lifted up the shield and handed it to Stalking Horse. The younger man's eyes shone in disbelief—the shield was magnificent. It was painted red and on either side were attached eagle's and owl's feathers, together with two pairs of bear claws. The eagle's feathers would give the user the swiftness and courage of the bird; the owl's feathers would give him the bird's power to see in the dark and the ability to move silently and unnoticed in the night; the bear claws represented the strength and courage of the bear and would make the user of the shield hard to kill.

Stalking Horse was speechless. The shield he was now working on was his first, to be used at a time later on when he felt ready to carry a shield. Shields were usually carried by men of years and discretion, who had distinguished themselves in battle. To have someone as respected as He-Walks-the-Mountain give him a shield, a shield which had been made by his own hands instead of by those of a shield-maker, was an honor difficult to equal. The protection afforded by the shield was in part physical and in part spiritual; therefore, the ceremony connected with it was very important.

"I am deeply honored, my chief. I am without words."

"You do not need to say words, Stalking Horse. You deserve to wear this shield by the deed you performed."

"Then you must tell me what to do with it now; I would not break your tradition." He-Walks-the-

Mountain nodded in agreement. A young man who carried a shield and failed to perform the ceremonies appropriate to it was sure to be wounded in battle.

He-Walks-the-Mountain explained the powers imbued by each bird's feather and those of the bear claws, and stated that although he had once owned the shield, no one, not even he, was permitted to handle it without Stalking Horse's permission now. The shield was to rest on a tripod-like stand behind the lodge, where it would remain until Stalking Horse was ready to go to war. If it fell to the ground, Stalking Horse was not permitted to pick it up at once. He must cover it with a skin or a blanket and allow it to lie on the ground for a time. When he finally picked it up, he would sprinkle some of the medicine from the bundle tied to the shield on a coal and pass the shield through smoke. After this, the shield could be hung on the tripod as before. When He-Walks-the-Mountain finished telling Stalking Horse about the ceremonies concerning the shield, he turned to his daughter, who then knew it was her turn to speak.

"I, too, bring a gift to honor your bravery, Stalking Horse." She placed the bundle in front of him and waited as he opened it. He lifted the shirt up in front of the fire and examined the intricate quilling and ornamentation which Sun Dancer had painstakingly worked on for so long. "I hope that I did not offend you with my behavior. I am truly gratified that you were there to save me from dying a horrible death at the horns of the buffalo. I will always be indebted to you."

Stalking Horse looked from the shirt to Sun

Dancer and he was quick to notice the unwavering look in her eyes. Her words were not forced; she meant what she said.

"Thank you, Sun Dancer, but as I told your father, anyone would have done as I did. You did not need to honor me so by bringing such an elegant gift."

"You like the shirt then?" Sun Dancer asked in expectation.

"It is a fine shirt," Stalking Horse remarked honestly, as again his eyes went over the intricate details.

"You did not look at the back."

Stalking Horse turned the shirt over and saw the distinct outline of the horse; he was amazed that one so young could do such fine work.

"Ah," he said admiringly, running his fingers over the stitches, "it is wonderful. You have great skill."

Sun Dancer smiled and looked over at her father. "Thank you. I will more fully repay the debt I owe you someday."

"Let us not talk of it anymore." Stalking Horse stood up and walked to the door of his lodge. "Let me walk you back through camp; it is good to have a clear day for a change."

The three started off through camp, Sun Dancer inwardly excited at the presence of Stalking Horse. It was good to have him as a friend again. As they walked through the snow, one of the elders of the tribe waved at He-Walks-the-Mountain and bade him come to his lodge and smoke.

"You two walk for awhile. I believe the snow will come again this night and it will be many days before we can venture outside." He-Walks-the-Mountain waved them off and the two younger people continued on through camp and down to the frozen stream. Few people were out because the air was still cold. Sun Dancer could see her breath, and her nose and cheeks felt prickly from the cold air. She pulled her robe tighter around her shoulders and neck.

"Are you warm?"

"Yes, it is good to be outside. I do not think I could have stayed inside much longer. I grow impatient in winter."

"As do we all. The shirt is truly fine, Sun Dancer. You surprise me."

"Why?"

"Because I thought you were so shamed by what had happened. I did not think you would tell anyone of it."

"I was shamed but my father helped me to see things clearly, as he always does. I was foolish for feeling so, and truly, I am glad it was you who saved me."

Stalking Horse looked at the girl in surprise and then grinned. "And why are you glad it was I and no other?"

"Because you are so good with a lance, of course," Sun Dancer said laughingly, a slight blush spreading over her cheeks.

"You do not speak the whole truth, Sun Dancer, but I will not press you further. I am satisfied for now that we are friends again."

"Truly?"

"Truly." He took her arm as they walked along the slippery bank. "I think I will save the shirt for my wedding."

"What?"

"I will save the shirt you made me for my wedding. It is a very special shirt."

"Indeed," Sun Dancer replied sullenly. "Perhaps I should make your bride's dress also?"

"I think that a fine idea. You have a talent with the quill."

"I may be young but I am not slow. If this stream were not frozen, I would take great pleasure in pushing you into it."

"And why would you do that?"

"Because you are baiting me. You wish for me to lose my temper and become churlish and sharptongued. But I will not; I will not play at your game."

"I was not playing a game. I was honest when I say you have talent with the quill."

Sun Dancer stopped and turned to look at Stalking Horse. "I thank you for that, but would you really ask me to make the wedding dress of your bride?"

Stalking Horse put his hands on Sun Dancer's shoulders and met her eyes directly. "It would depend on who the bride is."

Sun Dancer's heart beat so rapidly that she felt uncomfortable. She wasn't sure what he meant by his words but she felt that it was something serious. She was frightened suddenly—frightened to feel so strongly and then have her feelings trampled on as he had done before. She turned abruptly away, as if his words held no meaning for her.

"Well, I am sure when the time comes, your bride's family will make the dress for her." She was cold suddenly, thinking of Stalking Horse taking a bride. It wouldn't be long now because he was distinguishing himself in battle and would need a wife to do all the things he now did so he could save himself for the hunting and fighting. She pulled her robe and held it tightly around her. She looked up at the sky. "I do not like winter overly much. Sometimes when all I can see are the gray clouds and the white snow, I am frightened I will never see the sun again. I feel trapped and sometimes I can hardly catch my breath, I am so fearful." She hadn't meant to tell Stalking Horse of her fears; she had never told anyone how she felt about the winter. Stalking Horse came to stand next to her on the bank.

"It is probably because you are kin to the sun; you feel it more strongly than most. But the cold and snow will always come and when that time is over, the sun will shine again. It is the way of things; do not be frightened of what is inevitable."

Sun Dancer nodded her head slightly and looked over at Stalking Horse. His words made sense and his voice was calm and knowing. She could see spending the rest of her days with him and always feeling safe and assured.

"You are right; I am just being foolish. When the summer sun blazes down on me and I am so hot I find it difficult to breathe, I will wish for the snow again. I am a very contrary person, Stalking Horse."

"So are we all, Sun Dancer." He took her arm and they walked back along the bank toward the village. "Come, it is cold and your family will worry."

"Do you ever feel lonely?" Sun Dancer asked suddenly. The words had come before she could stop them.

"There are times when I wish I still had my parents

91

and my brothers, but they are gone and I have made a life for myself now. But I still have my aunts and uncles."

"But do you not long for something close, something deeper? I sometimes feel that Brave Wolf and my father are a part of me and I do not know what I would do without them."

"And what of Laughing Bird? Is he a part of you also?"

"Laughing Bird?" Sun Dancer thought of him and she smiled. He had helped her and loved her as much as her father and brother had. "Yes, he is also a part of me. I am very fortunate."

"Indeed you are. But will there ever be room for a husband in your life, Sun Dancer? Will there ever come a time when you can sever the bonds you have with these other people in your life to make room for your husband?"

Sun Dancer looked at Stalking Horse, again not understanding why he was saying such strange words. She wanted to talk further with him but they had come to the village, and after bidding her a curt good-bye, he left her.

Perhaps when I become a woman, she thought, things will be easier. Or perhaps, as she suspected, she would have deeper and more complex feelings. Everything was confusing except her feelings for Stalking Horse—those, she knew, would never change.

CHAPTER VI

Sun Dancer breathed deeply of the fresh, warm air, feeling the cool breeze against her skin, reveling in the blue sky above her. It had been a long winter and very hard toward the end. The village had run out of dried meat and had subsisted almost totally on pemmican and dried roots. Occasionally, a hunter was able to catch a rabbit or a deer, but the snows were so deep that it hampered the hunting. When at last the snows began to melt, they made their way back down to the prairie below the mountains. Her father had wanted to go farther south this year, where he had heard some of their other brothers had gone. But her mother had wanted to return to the place which she knew best. Her father said that the following spring they should go south to see the land.

Although the Cheyenne tribe was large, many separate camps existed throughout the large area between the Missouri River and the Black Hills. The movement of a camp or village followed its own leader's ideas as to where they should go, and what was best for that individual village. The entire

Cheyenne tribe could converge on a certain place to meet and discuss matters of importance, but for the most part, it remained separate bands which lived in areas to which they were most adapted.

The days were long and arduous, riding horseback nonstop in the sun, but Sun Dancer never complained. She loved the sky and the warm air, and she loved being alive so she was able to enjoy it all. Occasionally, when she wasn't pulling a travois, she would urge her mount into a gallop. They would ride far ahead of the others, feeling the freedom that only a rider and her horse can experience.

She had seen little of Stalking Horse since the day she had given him the shirt. She had thought a great deal about it and decided that Stalking Horse didn't hate her, but he did not ever want to be more than friends. She knew that if she were ever in trouble or needed his help, he would be there. But in their day to day routine, he seemed to ignore her and go on about his own life.

Sun Dancer knew that before too long Stalking Horse would be taking a wife, and she looked for any signs that he was interested in one. She had heard rumors, that when he and some of the others had ridden to their friends, the Arapahos, after the snows had first cleared, Stalking Horse had taken one of the Arapaho girls into his tipi. She snorted smugly; everyone knew that Arapaho women were notoriously free with themselves, not like the Cheyenne women, who were discreet and chaste. Still, the thought plagued her—what if a woman loved a man and he did not want to marry her—would it then be right to give herself to him out of love? She shook her head; she did not know. It was all the more confusing because of things her friends had told her. One of her married friends, Fawn, had told her that she did not like to do what her husband wished her to do, but it was her duty as his wife. They had been married less than one summer, and Fawn was with child. She had told Sun Dancer that her husband was very large and he hurt her when they came together, but still Sun Dancer did not understand. When Fawn told her this, she nodded her head as if she knew, for she did not want to seem a child in her friend's eyes. What happened between a man and a woman when they married was still a mystery to her.

This night they were to camp with some of their Arapaho allies, the same ones whom Stalking Horse and the others had gone to after the snows had melted. They had traded for some food and had been told to stay for awhile on their trip back north. Sun Dancer always liked it when they visited the Arapahos because they were gracious and friendly hosts, and it was always an occasion for game-playing, horse-racing, feasting, dancing and singing, storytelling, and general revelry.

When they arrived at the Arapaho encampment, they quickly set up their lodges. The women made fires for the evening meal and the men put the horses out to graze, while the children played. Arapaho and Cheyenne women shared their food and combined it to make larger communal meals. The chiefs and elders sat in front of their lodges and smoked, telling one another about the long winter, while the younger men went to the sweat lodges to purify themselves and exchange stories of the raids and hunts they had been on since they had last been together.

Woman's Heart, who was busy exchanging gossip with some of her Arapaho friends, did not notice when Sun Dancer left and made her way through the large camp. People were laughing and the gaiety spread throughout the camp. Tomorrow there would be games of skill and courage, and much gambling on the outcome. The men showed each other the valuable pieces with which they were going to bet and boasted of their ability to gamble. Some of the younger men were showing each other their newest horses, ones which they had claimed in raids on the Snakes or the Utes or the Kiowas. Sun Dancer was fascinated by it all; when they were all together, it was as if life were always good and peaceful.

Sun Dancer passed by the lodge of an important chief, Spotted Elk, and saw her father and Brave Wolf and others. She waved as she walked by but she did not stop; it would not be proper for her to sit in while respected chiefs and warriors were talking. She saw a group of girls and recognized some friends whom she had met the year before, and some of her Cheyenne girl friends. They welcomed her enthusiastically, and they all walked about the camp laughing and giggling, pointing to the handsome young men, or to those who had distinguished themselves in battle. As usual, the topic of conversation ran to the physical aspects of the young men, and how proficient they might be at other things besides battle. This topic always embarrassed Sun Dancer, for she knew so little about it; she did not want to look silly in front of the other girls by admitting her innocence in the matter. She had played with boys for so long she did not think of them as different from herself. She had never thought of Laughing Bird as someone of the opposite sex with whom she might someday co-join, and she was now acutely embarrassed when her Cheyenne friends told the others how she played with boys but knew so little about them.

"Sun Dancer wishes that she were a boy," Fawn said playfully, while the others burst into fits of laughter. "Only I am afraid if she were, she would not know what to do with it." Sun Dancer, who was seldom at a loss for words, was too hurt to think of a reply. Instead, she looked at them all and turned away, her head held high and shoulders squared, in spite of her humiliation.

She left the group of girls, their laughter echoing in her ears, and walked back through the camp. It was then she saw Stalking Horse, who, talking with a lovely girl by one of the lodges, looked up and saw her as she walked past. Their eyes met and in spite of her efforts not to show any emotion, Sun Dancer began to cry as she drew even with him. Determined not to let him see her so weak, she ran past him and out of the camp to a wooded area where she could be alone. She put her hands on the trunk of a tall cottonwood and laid her head against it for support. Perhaps, as her father had told her, this was one of the difficult times she was going to have to endure before becoming a woman. Normally, she would have had a witty reply or simply have knocked Fawn on the ears, but this night it had been too much for her. Ridicule was more than she could stand, especially when what they said was the truth. She heard footsteps behind her and she moved farther into the woods. She wanted only to be alone and for no one to see her crying so shamefully.

"It is not good for you to be out here alone." Stalking Horse walked up behind her. She turned to face him, her hands quickly going to her face to wipe away the tears. "Come, we will go back."

"No," Sun Dancer said angrily and walked away from him. "Why did you come here? I want to be alone." He had a peculiar habit of following her which unsettled her.

"I thought you were in need of my help."

"I do not need your help."

"I think to the contrary," Stalking Horse said firmly, putting his hand on Sun Dancer's thin arm and pulling her out of the woods. "Now, why are you troubled?"

"It is no concern of yours." She pulled her arm away and turned her back to him. "Go back to your Arapaho woman."

"Ah, so that is it. You did not like seeing me with her?" His voice was taunting her.

"I do not care whom you are with. You think too highly of yourself, Stalking Horse, to think that everything you do affects me."

Stalking Horse turned Sun Dancer around so that she faced him. He placed a single finger on the still quivering lips and said gently, "But I know that it does." The finger traced the lines of her mouth and then ran softly over her face. "You will be a lovely woman, Sun Dancer."

She looked up into his eyes, not able to see them fully because of the dark night, but she knew the look in them was gentle. She could fight him no more. She moved closer and laid her head on his chest and shut her eyes. She felt his arms encircle her and she sighed contentedly. Again, she had the feeling that being with him was natural; the feeling of well-being and security which she felt in his arms was beyond anything she had ever before felt.

"I know I am young and have much to learn, but my emotions are deeply felt. You asked me once if I could break the bonds which tie me to the other people in my life and form another bond with my husband. I know now that I could do that." She did not say that he would have to be the husband.

"Yes, I believe you could." Stalking Horse's arms pulled tighter around her. "But you have much growing up to do before that time. It is something we can talk of later." He loosened his arms and took her hand. "Let us go back to camp; your reputation will be ruined if anyone knows you have been with me for so long."

"I hope so," Sun Dancer replied glumly.

"Why would you say such a thing, Sun Dancer? You surprise me."

"All my friends laugh at me and say that I do not know . . . that I do not know certain things. They say I would not know how to . . . I cannot say it."

"I know what you are speaking of. Let us walk by your friends together, and then they will think differently. Without a word from you, they will think only the worst. But you and I will know the truth."

Stalking Horse took Sun Dancer's hand firmly in his and they walked through camp, as if they had been lovers for a long time. The look on Sun Dancer's face was glorious, and Stalking Horse found pleasure in knowing he helped put it there. In his mind, he could imagine a time not long from now when he and Sun Dancer, the young woman, would walk through camp and people would stop to stare at them. She would be so beautiful that every man in camp would desire her, but she would be only his.

"They are there," Sun Dancer pointed out the small group of girls who sat by one of the fires. "I would like to push Fawn's face in the mud. She thinks because she is married that she knows everything. I am not totally dim-witted."

"Do not worry so about her; she only tries to make you feel inferior now, because she knows that one day you will be far superior to her."

"But how can she know that?"

"She knows, just as many people in the tribe know it." He leaned his head closer to hers. "They are looking this way. Perhaps you should laugh and make them think we are lovers."

Sun Dancer looked up at him, a blush spreading over her small face. Then she did laugh, for she realized how silly it was: he could not be her lover for she had not yet attained her womanhood. But the girls were such gossips that they would fail to remember this. Her laughter rang out as she and Stalking Horse walked by the group of girls, all of whom were shocked into an uncommon silence.

The day dawned early and the sun was already warm by the time everyone had eaten his morning meal. Many of the men and boys had gone off to hunt, so there would be fresh meat for the feasting on this night. The women collected roots and herbs and searched for berries in the woods. Young children splashed playfully in the water of the river, older ones watching so they were in no danger. Many took their turn at catching turtles, wading along in the water and feeling them with their feet, then grasping them with their hands when they tried to swim away. Still others used spears or small nets to catch fish.

The boys of the Cheyenne camp and the boys of the Arapaho camp had already entered into competition. Some shot their arrows at certain marks, others threw sticks, wrestled, or played the kicking game. Another group of boys played the coyote game. A group of boys lined up, tallest to the smallest, in front of a leader. In front of him stood the coyote, who made leaps at the boys behind the protector. If he touched a boy, that boy was out of the game. They played another game called running through the line. A group of children formed a circle and held hands, locking fingers with each other. Another child stood in the middle of the circle and tried to break through. If he succeeded, the others pursued him and slapped him playfully with their hands. Some of the boys engaged in mock battles, attacking each other on foot or on their ponies.

The kicking matches were played by the older boys and some of the men. The men kicked each other with one or both moccasined feet, kicking from the ground or jumping up in the air and lashing out sideways with both feet. This was a favorite game between the two tribes, and often the sound, *"Coho! Coho!"* could be heard as one tribe challenged the other. The contestants might number several hundred. The Cheyennes were great wrestlers and practiced it from the age of seven or eight years to middle life. They didn't use their feet or legs in tripping, but tried to swing the opponent off his feet or bend him back by sheer strength.

As Sun Dancer walked around the camp, looking at the different games and amusements, her friend, Bird Song, ran up to her.

"Come, Sun Dancer, we need you for the ball game. The Arapaho girls have challenged us and you are such a strong player."

"Yes, I would like to play, but I will not be at my best. I have not played since the fall."

"So, none of us has. It will be good competition. I hear one of their girls can bounce the ball two hundred times!"

"Two hundred times! I am not sure I can even do one hundred fifty. Let us hurry."

The game was played with a ball stuffed with antelope hair and covered with deerskin. Three hundred slender sticks were prepared as counters and were placed in the center of a circle where two girls cared for them. This day there were twenty girls on each team and they stood alternately around the circle in a close ring. The one who would begin the game would take the ball and balance it on her instep, kick it up a little ways and then catch it on her instep, kick it again, and continue on this way as long as she could. As the girl kicked, she would count aloud, while the opposite side watched her kicks and listened to her counts. A girl was permitted to support herself by her left hand by holding a stick or placing it under her armpit as she kicked. When the kicker finished her turn, she stepped up to the counters and took as many sticks as she had made kicks and put them to one side. Each one who kicked thereafter would put the sticks she had gained with those of her side. When the counters in the center were used up, the girls would take from each other's piles, until one side or the other had won all the sticks. On the outcome of this game, the girls wagered their beads, necklaces, bracelets, or anything which was of worth to them.

The Cheyennes went first, as they were the guest team, and Fawn was the first player. She was good at the ball game, and the only one who could beat her was Sun Dancer. Fawn grabbed her stick, held onto it with her left hand, then kicked the ball up and proceeded to catch it on her instep. She counted loudly each time she caught the ball to make sure she didn't miscount. Fawn made it to ninety before she missed. Then one of the Arapahos picked up the ball. They were starting their best girl first, the girl Sun Dancer had seen Stalking Horse with. Their team hoped she could pick up the rest of the sticks.

The girl stepped into the circle and with a smug look toward Sun Dancer and the others, kicked the ball up with her foot, deftly and quickly catching it with her instep. She did not use a stick but her kicks and catches were just as good. As she counted higher in number, her kicks were as good as they had been at the beginning. She made it to one hundred before she missed, a very good number in competition. Sun Dancer was next. She had kicked the ball well over a hundred times during play, but competition was something else.

She walked to the circle and as the Arapaho girl had done, declined the stick. She kicked the ball up slightly and caught it with her instep and the count had begun. Sun Dancer concentrated only on the ball as it went into the air and came back down on the top of her foot. When the count had reached seventy-five, she almost dropped the ball when she swayed slightly, but she managed to balance it and kick it back up into the air. Her left leg grew tired and weak and she could feel herself begin to sway, but she continued to concentrate on the ball. She counted but didn't realize that she had surpassed the Arapaho's mark when she dropped the ball. She had counted to one hundred ten, and with the ninety points of Fawn's, they had two hundred points. They won the competition.

"You were wonderful, Sun Dancer." Fawn ran to congratulate her. "You are still better than I at the game."

"Thank you, Fawn. I believe I was lucky today. My legs were very weak."

"But you were strong enough to hold out." Fawn brought over the basket in which the wagers were placed, bringing out a beautiful black stone. "It was the Arapaho's and now it is yours. It looks like it may be a lucky stone."

Sun Dancer took it in her hand and rolled it around. The stone was incredibly smooth and shiny and reflected different colors as the sun shone on it. Someone else walked to her and she saw it was the Arapaho girl.

"My name is Broken Leaf. You are very good at the

ball game. Perhaps we could play it again some-time."

"Yes, I would like that. My name is Sun Dancer." She looked down at the stone in her hand. "The stone is wonderful."

Broken Leaf looked at the stone with deep regret etched on her young face. "Yes, my grandfather gave it to me before he died. He said it came from our hills when he and his people first arrived here. He said it would bring me luck."

Sun Dancer put the stone in Broken Leaf's hand. "I cannot take your stone. A stone that is lucky for one person may not be lucky for another. It is yours."

"Thank you," Broken Leaf replied happily. "You must come with me to our lodge so I may give you something in return."

"There is no need."

"But there is. I should not have been so foolish as to wager my stone; I was sure I would win. But you are a winner and you deserve a prize." She took Sun Dancer by the arm and pulled her along. "Come."

The two girls walked through the camp and Broken Leaf took Sun Dancer to her parents' lodge. Her parents were very honored when they discovered she was the daughter of Chief He-Walks-the-Mountain and further when they found out about Sun Dancer's generosity. They bade her stay and eat their midday meal with them. Sun Dancer complied with pleasure. After the meal, Broken Leaf suggested they go for a swim and Sun Dancer agreed. While they were walking to the stream, Broken Leaf handed Sun Dancer a small leather pouch.

"These are for you."

Sun Dancer opened the pouch. It contained different colored beads.

"They are truly wonderful; I have never seen such colors. They are almost transparent." She held them up to the sun and could see through them clearly.

"My brother traded with a white man for them. They are called 'glass.'"

"Glass? I have never heard the word."

"Yes. And the white man told my brother that many white people have lodges built of wood and have this glass in the house so they can see out."

"It must be wonderful with such colors. Where did your brother see the white man? I did not think any ventured this far north."

"He was a trapper and came here for beaver. Many trade with the Arikaras and Mandans, and it is said they have wooden lodges in the north from which they trade. My brother said he was kind and gave him food. My brother was not at all frightened."

"I do not wish to meet up with any white man for I know all that is in his mind is to destroy us."

"That is a prophecy, Sun Dancer, and probably one that the old men of the tribe made up to scare the younger ones."

"You do not believe in the culture heroes?" Sun Dancer asked, an incredulous look on her face.

"I do not know for sure. Some things are true, I believe, and others are superstition. It is better to believe in what is real."

"But what of the old beliefs and traditions? Surely, you would not throw all of them away."

"No, but I would change some of them. At least in

our tribe a woman can be with a man if she wants to, and not be ostracized because of it. I could never live in your tribe."

"Our tribe is good. Our rules are for our protection."

"Perhaps, but would you not like to do as you please and not answer to anyone?" Broken Leaf saw the look in Sun Dancer's eyes and continued. "I saw the way you looked at the warrior Stalking Horse as you walked with him through the camp. Would you not like to give yourself to him and not be punished for it?"

Sun Dancer met the other girl's eyes and admitted to herself that she would like to do as Broken Leaf suggested. But she was Cheyenne and she would not bring disgrace on her family or her people. "Perhaps I would like to, but I would not do it. I would not dishonor my family so. I love them very much."

"I love my family also but they have nothing to do with my desires as a woman. Do you not see that?"

Sun Dancer shook her head in confusion. "I suppose I do not. Perhaps I am too young or too slow to understand."

"Or perhaps you take your responsibilities too heavily. I think, Sun Dancer, that you are an honorable person. Be not ashamed of that." Sun Dancer smiled and Broken Leaf pulled her along. "Come, I will race you to the stream."

As they ran, Sun Dancer thought of her new friend; she admired Broken Leaf in many ways. She was the type of woman who would probably do as she pleased. Broken Leaf would follow her own beliefs, while she, herself, would always accede to the wishes of others. How she wished she had the strength of will which Broken Leaf possessed.

"You are swift on your feet; do you do all things well?" Broken Leaf asked as they reached the water.

"I try to do all things the best that I can but I fail at many."

"What do you fail at?"

"I seem to fail at the most important thing."

"And what is that?"

"At being a girl. I do not seem to behave as I should."

"And why should you? Ah, but I forget, you must conform to tradition. But you can respect the old ways and still behave as you want."

"No, I cannot. I am the daughter of a chief and I am expected to act in a proper, well-mannered way. If I did not, I would bring disgrace on my family. As it is, my father lets me do as I wish most of the time. And my mother, she says I will not be a child forever and so I must enjoy myself now."

"Your parents sound good. Perhaps now I understand why you do not wish to disgrace them."

"Yes, I am most fortunate." They sat down to take off their moccasins and Sun Dancer had a sudden urge to tell Broken Leaf her true thoughts.

"I like you, Broken Leaf. I think I would be like you if my responsibilities were not so great. I admire your honesty and forthrightness."

"Thank you. Not many girls have said they like me. Most usually feel I am too wild and free in my ways." She shrugged her shoulders. "Perhaps I am."

"But you are true to yourself."

"Yes, I am that." Broken Leaf dangled her feet in

the water, splashing slightly from time to time. "Are you in love with Stalking Horse?"

Sun Dancer looked at Broken Leaf and she knew she could not lie. "I have been in love with him since I was a child, and he was already showing great skill in all manner of things. How is it that a person can fall in love at so young an age? Is it some kind of torture perhaps, that I will love him all my life but never have him?"

"I think not, for I noticed the way he looked at you that night. His eyes were filled with desire."

"Desire? For me? I do not think so, Broken Leaf. I am only a child, as he himself has so often told me."

"Is it possible that he tells you this so you do not get interested in any others? I think it is already in his head to have you when you become a woman; he does not wish to fight any others for you."

"You think that?" Sun Dancer's eyes shone brightly; Broken Leaf had just voiced the things she herself had so often thought. "But why? He is so handsome and it will be some time before I attain my womanhood. Why would he want to wait for me?"

"Because you are worth waiting for. But do not fool yourself into believing that Stalking Horse has no desires of his own. I, myself, can assure you that he does."

Sun Dancer felt her cheeks burn but she looked her friend straight in the eyes. "You were with him then?"

"Yes, and he is truly a man. You will be happy that he is the one." Sun Dancer didn't answer and looked away; Broken Leaf turned Sun Dancer's face toward her. "Do not be angry with me, Sun Dancer. We only fulfilled our mutual desires. With you, it goes much deeper. I think he has already decided you will be his wife."

Sun Dancer looked at Broken Leaf and then put her arms around her and hugged her close. "I am not angry with you, Broken Leaf. How can I be angry with one who shines so true?" She sighed deeply. "I only wish that I could be the one who fulfills Stalking Horse's desires."

"You will be, *navese*, my friend. Have patience. Stalking Horse is willing to wait, and so must you. Now, let us swim and then lie in the sun and pretend pretty thoughts." For your time for pretending will soon be over, Broken Leaf thought to herself, and you will soon be a woman.

CHAPTER VII

Sun Dancer screamed wildly and clapped her hands; her voice carried above those of the crowd. Stalking Horse had just scored another goal for his team, and they were now far ahead of the Arapahos. They had been playing on foot for a good many hours and had decided to switch to horseback. The object of the game was to hit a flattened ball between two mounds of earth, the goal. Most of the players stood near the goals, but the fastest runners stood off at either side. Two leaders stood in the middle of the field and at the same time, each tried to strike the ball with his stick and to knock it toward the fastest runner on his own side. When one of the players got the ball, he might run along the prairie for a long time to try to outrun his opponents before he came back to the playing field to try to score a goal. Stalking Horse, Laughing Bird, Brave Wolf, and some of the others did well on foot but when mounted, the Cheyennes completely dominated the game.

Sun Dancer walked to Stalking Horse when the game was over to offer her congratulations. "You did well, Stalking Horse. I felt sorry for our Arapaho brothers."

"I did not," Stalking Horse smiled, as he led his horse to his lodge. "I always enjoy beating them. Some of them are too boastful and I enjoy showing them that they are wrong in their boasting."

"Yes, I could see that. And what did you wager?"

"It is what I won which is more important." He lifted his arm. On it hung a braided leather bridle. "Do you like it?"

"Yes, it is lovely. There is much workmanship there." She looked at his horse. "What will you do with yours?"

"I believe I will give it away. I have no use for two of them." He removed the bridle from his horse and placed the new one on him. "What do you think?"

"It looks handsome."

"Yes. But whom should I give this to?" He held up his old one.

"I do not know. To a friend, perhaps."

"Yes." He handed it to Sun Dancer. "I would like you to have it."

Sun Dancer held it in her hands. "For me? I cannot accept this, Stalking Horse. It is very fine and I am sure you worked long on it."

"Yes. That is why I want to give it to someone who will take care of it. I know you will do that."

"It is wonderful, thank you."

"You are welcome. Would you like to walk with me?"

"Yes."

"We can go by the woods and perhaps catch some game while we are there."

After Stalking Horse had taken his horse to his lodge, he and Sun Dancer left for the woods. As they walked, Sun Dancer stooped to pick wild berries and put them in the parfleche she carried around her shoulder. They walked in silence, enjoying the warm day and the beauty around them.

"You have met Broken Leaf?" Stalking Horse asked suddenly, and Sun Dancer turned to look at him.

"Yes, we are friends."

"What did you speak of?"

"We spoke of everything. Broken Leaf does not keep things inside; she says whatever is on her mind."

"Yes, I know." Stalking Horse started to speak further but stopped. He looked as though he wanted to ask Sun Dancer something, but he didn't know how.

"We spoke of you, Stalking Horse. Is that what you wanted to know?"

Stalking Horse looked at her and nodded. "I am brave in many ways and cowardly in some."

"Broken Leaf said only good things of you." Sun Dancer smiled warmly.

"That is all?"

Sun Dancer turned away and bent down to pick more berries. "She told me you two were together." Her voice was low, barely audible.

Stalking Horse pulled her up until she looked into his eyes. "And what did you think when she told you that?"

"I thought, 'I wish I had been the one.'"

Stalking Horse looked at her, his eyes soft, his

113

voice gentle. "It is not in you to lie, is it, Sun Dancer? You must always be true to yourself no matter what."

"Not always. I am mostly governed by outside forces. Broken Leaf says I should be more true to myself, but I fear I cannot. My responsibilities are too great."

"And that is what makes you so good."

"Thank you, Stalking Horse, that is a kind thing to say. Do you think me foolish for what I said before?"

"No more foolish than I for asking." He took her hand. "Come, let us walk more. This talk grows much too serious."

There was great feasting that night in the Arapaho camp. The men of both camps had gone hunting and there was fresh meat for all. The women roasted the meat on spits over the fire, while corn and squash cooked in pits below the ground. The smell wafted throughout the camp. Entire families joined together and prepared their meals, while others played songs on flutes and beat rhythms on the drums. Sun Dancer, Woman's Heart, and Spotted Calf, together with their invited guest, Broken Leaf, served the men of their family and their guests first, and then they sat down to theirs. When the meal was over and Sun Dancer and Broken Leaf had cleared away the bowls for Woman's Heart, the girls walked through the camp. Men were smoking pipes and wagering on games of chance while others were telling stories that had been handed down to them for generations. These stories were sacred and some belonged to certain families. The stories which were passed on from parents to children were taught exactly as they had been learned, so that they would be passed on intact. A child had to listen and repeat the story several times over until he could repeat it from memory, the same way it had been told to him. Sun Dancer stopped Broken Leaf as they passed the lodge of an old story-teller.

"Let us listen, Broken Leaf. I could listen to stories forever." Broken Leaf nodded and they sat down to listen. The old man was practiced and knew well his art. He used his hands and his voice, and he had the entire audience entranced. When he was through with his story, Sun Dancer asked, "Would you please tell the story of the creation, Old Man?"

The old man nodded and spoke solemnly.

"The story speaks of a person floating on the water which then covered the whole earth. Surrounding him were ducks, swans, geese, and other water fowl. These birds had already been created and of their origin nothing had been said. This person called some of the birds and directed them to locate some earth. The birds dove into the water trying to reach the bottom and find earth. None was successful until a small blue duck came to the surface with a little mud in its bill. This duck swam to the man, who took the mud from it and worked the wet earth between his fingers until it was dry. Then he put little piles of the earth on the water near him which became land that spread out and grew until all was solid land, as far as the eye could see. Thus the earth was created."

The old man continued.

"After the earth was created, a man and woman were created and put upon the land. When the Creator, *Heammawihio*, made the man, he formed him from a rib taken from his own right side; the woman was created from a rib taken from the left side of the man. These two persons were made at the same place but were then separated, the woman being placed in the north, the man in the south. The Creator said that where he had placed the woman it would be cold, and where he had placed the man it would be warm. He said that the animals and birds who were from the north would be different from those in the south, but in summer, the birds from the south would fly north. The woman controls *Hoimaha*, Winter Man, the power that brings snow and cold, and also sickness and death. The man in the south controls the thunder. Twice a year there is a struggle between the *Hoimaha* and the Thunder Man, the changing of the seasons. At the end of summer, *Hoimaha* comes down from the north and drives the Thunder back to the south; but toward spring, when the days begin to grow longer, the Thunder returns from the south and forces the Winter Man back to his place. When the Thunder comes up from the south, he brings with him the rain and the warm weather, and the grass grows and the earth becomes green.''

Sun Dancer looked over at Broken Leaf and smiled. "It is a wonderful story, do you not think so?"

"Yes, I like it very much." They got up and continued walking through the camp. "My mother used to tell me many stories as a child."

"Mine too. I would sit for hours and plead with her to continue but she would wave me away. Then I would go to my father and when he would tire of me, I would go to my brother. After that, I would go to anyone who would be willing to talk to me." Broken Leaf laughed and Sun Dancer continued. "I remember once when I was still very small, I could not sleep and I went over to my father and tapped him on the shoulder. He woke up and inquired as to whether I was ill. I told him I could not sleep and wished to hear more stories. He told me if I did not go back to sleep he would make me sleep outside with the horses."

"You were persistent as a child. Or is stubborn the word?"

"Both, I think. Look, they are playing 'hands.'" The girls rushed to the group of men and watched in delight; this was a favorite game for spectators, as well as players.

The girls watched as one of the old men took two bones, one marked, the other unmarked, and held one in each hand. The wagers had been placed—many horses, robes and weapons—and the old man began. The drum began beating and the old man moved his hands around his head, down to the ground, around in circles, behind his back, all movements designed to confuse his opponents. Then he thrust his still closed hands out in front of him for his opponent to pick the marked bone.

"It is the left hand," Broken Leaf muttered to Sun Dancer.

"Yes, I agree."

After a few moments of serious decision-making, the old man's opponent pointed to his left hand. The old man smiled and opened his left hand—it contained the unmarked bone.

"But I cannot believe it!" Sun Dancer exclaimed

with the others. "I was sure it was in his left hand."

"So did we all. That is why Old Beaver Tail is so rich—he grows wealthy on this game and wins heavy wagers. I have not yet seen him lose."

After a while, Broken Leaf left Sun Dancer to walk with a young Arapaho boy, and Sun Dancer continued on by herself.

"Ho, Sun Dancer," she heard a voice and turned to see Laughing Bird approaching.

"It is good to see you, Laughing Bird. I have not seen you for days."

"Yes, I have been busy. This is great fun."

"Yes, I always enjoy visiting our brothers. They are generous hosts."

Laughing Bird nodded then grew serious. "I have seen you with Stalking Horse."

"What do you mean?"

"I saw you walk through camp with him the other night and again today. It is not good for your reputation to be seen with him."

"Why is that?"

"Because you are so young and he is more experienced than you. People will talk."

"People already talk about me. I do not feel the less because of it."

"I know that, I mean your reputation is at stake here. If men think you have been free with yourself before you marry, your prospects will be few."

Sun Dancer laughed and took Laughing Bird's arm. "You sound like my mother, Laughing Bird. You know that I would never do anything to bring dishonor to my family. I may dream of the things I would like to do, but I do not do them all. It is not possible anyway. Some of the things I would like to do only men do."

"That has not stopped you before. You do many things which men do."

"Yes, but I am still a child and people do not frown on me so. When I am a woman I will not be permitted to do the things I wish."

"It is true; this I can understand. In a short while, your responsibilities will be even greater. But what of Stalking Horse?"

"What of him?"

"You always question me when I question you. Tell me directly, Sun Dancer. What do you think of Stalking Horse?"

"I think he is brave and good and handsome, and he will not dishonor me."

"You are sure?"

"Yes. He knows I am still a child. He is, after all, a man grown, who has distinguished himself in battle. He only befriends me as you have. I am not of marriageable age; you know that."

"Yes, I know that. But I think Stalking Horse seeks to stake his claim now for the future."

"I have heard that before. I do not believe it."

"I do. Stalking Horse knows what kind of woman you will be."

"How is it that everyone else knows what kind of woman I will be, when I do not even know myself? Do you all have Horn's powers and his ability to see into the future?"

"It is not necessary to have Horn's power to see into the future. In the natural course of things, you will turn into a beautiful, desirable woman. You do not see it because you do not see yourself as others do."

"Perhaps not, but I am not ready to be a woman yet. I have enough trouble being a child." She walked ahead. "Walk with me to my parents' lodge. I am tired and wish to retire for the night. I have had too much talk today."

The Cheyennes stayed with their brothers, the Arapahos, for more than a week, then they continued on to their spring and summer home on the prairie. When most people complained of the daily travel, Sun Dancer relished the fresh air and open spaces and the fact that she did not have to answer to anyone until the end of the day. She already missed Broken Leaf and wished she could form such a tight bond with someone of her own tribe. But she knew that the reason she and Broken Leaf got on so well together was that they were both different and their beliefs did not necessarily conform with those of other people. She thought of the many conversations she had had with Broken Leaf; she respected and admired the girl for her truthfulness and honesty. She had never formed such a tight bond with a girl before and she felt pleased that it was possible for her to do so. There were things she had discussed with Broken Leaf that she could not discuss with any other person. She would miss her greatly.

Sun Dancer felt happy this day because they were almost to their camping spot and she wouldn't have to suffer through any more snow until another summer passed. She really did feel akin to the sun, as her father said she was, and she felt she grew and blossomed during the spring and summer. She was sure she would attain her womanhood during those seasons.

They reached their home only one week after leaving the Arapahos. They camped in a small valley below the hills which afforded them shade, water, and grass for the horses. Horn had said it would be a particularly hot summer, and they should seek any relief they could from the sun. The weather was still cool, although the sun was shining, but in summer and early fall it would be extremely hot.

As soon as the chiefs had decided on a camp location, the separate families dismounted and went about their various routines. The men saw to the horses, while the women and girls erected the lodges, started fires, and got fresh water. Sun Dancer helped her mother erect the lodge first of all, while neighbors and friends pitched in.

Theirs was a sixteen skin lodge which required twenty poles. It was large and required plenty of space. Woman's Heart chose a site northeast of a clump of trees so the lodge would be in shade from late morning until late afternoon, while sun would shine in it in the morning. The site was also high enough to be above water in case of a prolonged rain or a flash flood. Water, grass, and firewood were all near. Women chose their lodge sites carefully.

The women preferred hides of old buffalo cows for lodge making. These hides were easiest to tan because the old cows were thin in flesh and their hides thicker. This made them easier to work. The lodge poles were cut in the season when the sap was in the tree and the poles were easy to peel.

After tying the three longest poles on the ground, the tripod was erected. Woman's Heart, Sun Dancer, and the other women set the remaining poles against the tripod in a circular position laying them inward so their tips met in the middle. Woman's Heart tied one end of the covering to the lifting pole and she and Sun Dancer lifted the entire bundle and placed the butt of the pole into the ground. With the support of the other women, Woman's Heart and Sun Dancer unrolled the covering to fit tightly around the frame and secured it on either side of the lodge opening. Sun Dancer went inside and pushed the poles against the hide to make sure the hide fit snugly over the frame. The women brought in heavy rocks to anchor the lodge in case of strong winds so that a ring of rocks was left on the ground when the family broke camp.

All the women went inside and tied a buffalo cow skin lining to the inside poles which reached to a height of five or six feet above the ground. It protected the person lying under it from any water which might leak through the lodge skins, and from any wind that might blow under the covering. The windward side, that opposite the door, the women had made shorter and more inclined so that it might offer greater resistance in the case of a heavy wind.

Once the lodge was erected, the women began to dig a fireplace. They dug a rectangular shape in the earth about six inches deep, longer from east to west. They cleared away all the grass, sagebrush, and roots on the ground and left a border of earth about four feet wide around the walls of the lodge.

They removed the dirt with knives, spoons, or their hands, piling it on a blanket to take outside. They sprinkled the floor with water, walked over it, then patted it. When it was partially dried, Sun Dancer swept it and threw the dust into the fireplace. The earth was dug so that the border around was a few inches higher than the general surface of the lodge floor. On this little "bench," Woman's Heart spread rye grass and then laid their beds.

The mattresses were seven or eight feet long and about four feet wide, formed of willow rods strung on lines of sinew. They were very flexible and could be easily rolled up and packed on a horse. They were used to raise the bed above the soil and to smooth out the uneven ground. Over the mattress the women spread a mat woven of bulrushes. They placed the mattresses about four feet apart and between the head and foot of two mattresses, a tripod was raised. It was made of slender, painted poles and was tied together near the top with strings passing through holes which had been burned through the ends. These were spread, and from two of the three poles where they were tied together, two backrests were hung, one for each bed. These were supported by the tripods, and the empty spaces between the backrests formed convenient cupboards for storing articles. The backrests were made from slender willow shoots strung on sinew. The shoots were much smaller than the rods used in the mattresses and the backrests were usually not less than eight feet in length. When prepared for transportation, the backrests and mattresses were rolled up into compact bundles and lashed with strings so they could carry well on a horse.

In the vacant spaces between the backrests and in

the narrow spaces between the edges of the beds and the lodge lining, Woman's Heart and Sun Dancer stored practically all the lodge furniture and the extra food that they had laid up for use in case of scarcity. The food, for the greater part, was in the form of dried meat, pounded meat, dried corn, dried roots and fruit, and was stored away in parfleches.

The parfleche was the Cheyenne trunk. It was made from heavy buffalo rawhide from which the hair had been removed. It was cut so as to be from two to three and a half feet long and a foot to eighteen inches wide when folded. The oblong piece of rawhide was folded over at both ends, at right angles to the first fold, so that these ends almost met. Leather strings laced together the two ends and the shape of the case was convenient for packing on a horse's back. Often they were ornamented by painting and Woman's Heart took great effort to see that they were kept clean and freshly painted. Other containers which the women used were "possible sacks," tanned deerskin sacks which held anything a woman might carry, such as: small ornaments, medicine, sewing articles, counters for a game, baskets, and ornamented plum-stones used in the seed game. They were used to keep together anything that might get lost in a parfleche. After everything was set up in the lodge, Sun Dancer went along the banks of the stream to look for driftwood for the fire, while her mother brought fresh water in earthenware pots.

The evening meal was very simple that night, as everyone was tired from the long journey. Most families ate dried meat and berries, and soon after eating, went to bed. Although she was tired and her body was sore from the long days of riding, Sun Dancer went for a walk. She was always somewhat restless when they moved camp, and it took her a few days to orient herself. This camp was not far from the other of the spring before, but it was a little different and she needed time to feel at home. She took a deep breath and smiled as the fresh, cool air filled her lungs. She pulled her robe tighter around her shoulders. Although it was spring, they were still close to the mountains and the air was still cool. It wouldn't be really hot until summer, when the snows had melted and the sun moved up farther in the sky.

Not far into the summer, Sun Dancer would be thirteen summers old, a time when many young girls attained their womanhood. She was anxious yet frightened. She wanted to know what it was like to be a woman, but she didn't want to leave this wonderful childhood behind forever. It had provided her with such joy and freedom—she was frightened she would have neither again.

She walked through the quiet camp until she came to Stalking Horse's lodge, which was erected on the edge of camp. She stood and looked at it and wondered if she would ever share it with him one day. She decided she would not. It would be too long a time before she attained her womanhood, and Stalking Horse would not wait forever, even if he really did care for her. And the vision she had had of being married to him? Maybe her father had been right, maybe it had been a wish-dream on her part. She turned away from the lodge and strode back across camp to her parents' lodge. It was time she became realistic and not live in such a dream world. Stalking Horse was a fine, young warrior who would soon be ready to take a wife. And she was just a girl who was biding her time until she would become a woman who would be taken to wife by a man for whom she would cook, have children, and never love. Because dream or not, she would always love Stalking Horse, and no one would ever take his place in her mind, or in her heart.

CHAPTER VIII

Stalking Horse and Laughing Bird looked down at the camp on the prairie below them and nodded silently to each other. They made their way by foot, back to the rest of the war party and reported what they had seen. It was a Kiowa encampment and there looked to be hundreds of horses. Brave Wolf conferred with He-Walks-the-Mountain and they decided to wait until dark when everyone was asleep, then steal into the Kiowa camp. Their horses would be left at a site near the hills where they now were and they would go in by foot. They would leave everything but their ropes and a few arms, steal the Kiowa horses, then pick up their own horses to begin the journey home.

Patiently, they waited well into the night. When the Kiowa camp showed no signs of life, the Cheyennes left their horses and equipment with the young boys who accompanied the warriors. The main party moved silently across the prairie to the Kiowa encampment. They separated into pairs and entered the enemy camp. It was the work of the older and more experienced men to cut loose the more valuable horses which were tied in front of the lodges and to lead them out; since both Stalking Horse and Laughing Bird had distinguished themselves in battle and in horsestealing, they were allowed to accompany the older men of the tribe. While this was being done, the younger men and boys gathered up the loose horses grazing on the prairie nearby and drove them to the meeting place. Stalking Horse looked over at Laughing Bird as they neared the camp, his stomach tightening slightly. Laughing Bird acknowledged the look and smiled. Although both had been on numerous raids, their experiences still did not equal those of the older men, who were able to slip in and out of an enemy camp unnoticed. Stalking Horse and Laughing Bird were realistic enough to worry that they might make some sound or movement which might arouse the entire Kiowa camp, thereby putting their own men in danger. Following Brave Wolf and several of the older men, they carefully made their way into the enemy camp.

The horses which were tied in front of the lodges were the most valuable. They were the war-horses and the buffalo horses, animals which had been trained specifically for war and in the killing of buffalo. These horses were so well-trained they would not flinch at the sight of an attacking buffalo or an onslaught of twenty riders.

The Cheyennes moved silently about the camp. Each man went to a lodge, cut loose a horse or horses, and led them outside the camp. Stalking Horse and Laughing Bird moved quickly, each returning several times to take as many horses as possible. The camp dogs growled and some of the horses whickered softly. Stalking Horse sensed the tension in the animals and he quickly led his horse from the camp. A loud whinny from one of the horses stopped him and he turned around. He-Walks-the-Mountain had picked a horse who was shy of everyone but its master. He dropped the rope which held the horse and started for the periphery of the camp. The horse's owner came from his lodge and yelled, his voice bringing people from their lodges. The owner of the horse unsheathed his knife and threw it at He-Walks-the-Mountain but Stalking Horse yelled at the older man to move and quickly threw his knife at the Kiowa. His knife hit the man in the stomach and he fell to his knees, while the Kiowa's knife missed its mark. Stalking Horse and He-Walks-the-Mountain quickly fled the enemy camp and ran across the dark prairie to their horses. Stalking Horse glanced back as they rode away, keeping their newly stolen horses closely guarded. Some of the Kiowas had already mounted to follow, while others stood waving their arms in anger. They had done well; many horses had been taken and no Cheyenne lives lost. But Stalking Horse felt no joy— it was the first time he had ever taken another man's life.

The Cheyennes rode hard all night. When day came, each man would identify the horses which he had taken, but now they were all thrown together in one herd. They were driven hard, with most of the men following them and one or two riding on either side to direct the herd. Since the warriors were able to change mounts at any time, they kept the horses galloping for some distance without stopping. Constantly, they checked the prairie behind them—were the tenacious Kiowas still following? Toward the end of the first afternoon, Brave Wolf ordered two of the younger men to watch the back trail and see if Kiowas were still pursuing them. They slowed their pace as the horses tired, but always looked to their backriders to see if there was any sign of the enemy.

"It was good, eh, Stalking Horse?" Laughing Bird rode beside Stalking Horse. "It is the best raid I have ever been on."

"I, too," Stalking Horse agreed.

"You counted a great coup and saved He-Walks-the-Mountain's life. I think you will be honored when we get back to camp."

"I do not wish to be honored. If you had been there, you would have saved his life."

"Yes, but you were the one and you saved the life of a great chief. He will feel he owes you a debt."

Stalking Horse nodded glumly, reflecting on the fact that chance again had put him in a certain place at a certain time. He wondered why he had been the one to save Sun Dancer's life, and now her father's. It made him feel strange, as if it had all been prearranged in time. He would have to ask Horn about it.

"How many horses have you, Stalking Horse? I count nearly thirty."

"Yes, that is right."

"I have twenty-seven. We are wealthy young men almost. A few more raids like this, and we may choose any bride in the tribe. Who will you choose?"

Stalking Horse didn't look at Laughing Bird; he was irritated by the question. "I have not thought on it. I do not wish to marry yet."

"Well, I have thought on it. I will choose Sun Dancer, and I believe she will accept."

"You two are great and good friends," Stalking Horse said mildly, as if uninterested by the news of Laughing Bird's choice of brides. "You would have a friendly marriage."

Laughing Bird looked over at Stalking Horse, irritated by his choice of the word "friendly." "Yes, I think it would be a good match. We have known each other since we were mere children. Sun Dancer is growing into a beautiful woman, do you not agree?"

Stalking Horse shrugged his shoulders indifferently. "I suppose. I have not really noticed. Children hold no fascination for me."

Laughing Bird grew angry at Stalking Horse's remark. "That is why you walked with her, holding hands, throughout the entire Arapaho camp? It looked to me as if you two were lovers. Had I not known Sun Dancer so well, I would have believed it."

Stalking Horse looked over at Laughing Bird now, his black eyes ablaze with fury. "I did not realize my life was of such concern to you, Laughing Bird. Perhaps you would like to know what I do with every minute of my day?"

"It is not your life that concerns me, it is Sun Dancer's. I do not wish for her to be publicly humiliated. She is from a good and influential family and has prospects for a fine marriage."

"With you?"

"With whomever she chooses. If she remains chaste."

"That is her decision. I have nothing to do with her chastity."

"You have everything to do with it. Do not play with her or her emotions. She is yet too fragile and only a girl unsure of her feelings. Wait until she is a woman and more sure of herself before you tantalize her with your manhood. If she chooses you then, you will have all the more because she has made a free choice. I ask you this because you are an honorable man."

Stalking Horse met Laughing Bird's eyes and in spite of his anger, he admired Laughing Bird and the loyalty he showed Sun Dancer. He wished he could be as true.

"Sun Dancer has nothing to fear from me. There are others in whom I am interested. I cannot wait forever until a girl turns into a woman."

Laughing Bird watched Stalking Horse as he rode forward, wondering at his words. He believed Stalking Horse would not dishonor Sun Dancer but he did not believe that he was interested in anyone else. He would wager every horse he'd just captured, that Stalking Horse was just biding his time until Sun Dancer was a woman. And then he would make his true feelings known.

The Cheyenne war party stopped a distance from their village to prepare for their entry. This was done if the party had returned successfully—taken horses, killed an enemy, or counted coup. Brave Wolf sent a scout to the village to give advance warning of their return, while they themselves stopped to prepare for their entry into the village. They wore the same clothes they had worn during their raid but they painted their faces with burnt willow branches, each with his own design. When the scout returned to say the village knew of their arrival, the party set out, riding side by side in two lines. At the head of one line was Brave Wolf and at the head of the other was Stalking Horse. Stalking Horse had performed a noteworthy deed and had saved He-Walks-the-Mountain's life, so he would be honored for his bravery.

The entire camp came out to greet the returning warriors when they were just outside the village. The women sang songs of victory in which the names of the warriors were mentioned, and many of the camp followed Stalking Horse to his lodge to dance in his honor. Each member of the party went directly to his own lodge, where he turned out the horses he caught. Everyone was joyous that none of their warriors had been killed or wounded, and that so many horses had been captured. Almost all of the warriors who had stolen horses gave some of them to the poorer people of the village, and this was also a great thing to celebrate.

When He-Walks-the-Mountain returned to his lodge, followed by Woman's Heart and Sun Dancer, he wore a bleak expression on his face.

"What is it, my husband? You should be joyous this day when you have brought us so many valuable horses."

"Yes, I am joyous. But I am in debt to someone and do not know how to repay him."

"To whom, father?"

"To Stalking Horse. He saved my life. He killed a Kiowa warrior who was going to kill me. It seems again I owe this young man much."

"What do you mean again?" Woman's Heart asked in puzzlement.

"During the hunt he saved Sun Dancer's life. She was trying to bring back another skin to clean for you but was attacked by a wounded bull. Stalking Horse drew the animal away and killed him."

"No one told me of this." She turned to Sun Dancer. "Why was I not told?"

"Because I was too ashamed at the time, mother."

"Ashamed, why?" Then she stopped, for she realized how Sun Dancer felt about Stalking Horse. "Yes, I think I understand now. And the shirt that you worked so hard on, it was for Stalking Horse?" Sun Dancer nodded and Woman's Heart turned to her husband. "And the shield that you had worked on for so long?"

"I gave it to Stalking Horse as a gift. I felt it was nothing compared with Sun Dancer's life."

"Yes, I agree." Woman's Heart walked around quietly and then turned to her family. "Do you not find it strange that this young man seems to be tied to us in some way? It is as if . . ."

"As if what, mother?"

"As if it was meant to be." She thought for a moment then quickly changed the subject. "Well, I must hurry to prepare some food to take to Stalking Horse. Sun Dancer, you will help me. You will rest before joining the others, my husband?"

"Yes, I am growing old, wife. These raids tire me

out much more than they used to. I am glad Brave Wolf is a war chief and I only have to go occasionally. Wake me when the feasting begins."

The celebration in honor of Stalking Horse's bravery was to be a great one. In the Cheyenne world the greatest act of bravery was to count coup on the enemy or to touch him while he was still alive. Often, many warriors went into battle without arms so that they could count coup on the enemy and ride back among their own ranks. The Cheyennes counted coup on the enemy three times; that is, three men touched the body and received credit according to the order in which it was done. Since Stalking Horse had been the only one near when He-Walks-the-Mountain was in trouble, he was the only one to count coup on the enemy.

Soon everyone from the village had brought firewood to the center of camp. After it was lit, the old men and women of the village danced and sang war songs and songs of victory to their warriors. The esteemed warriors sat around the fire and feasted on the food that was brought to them. Fresh game was killed and the meat was roasted over large spits. The warriors sat and talked of their great deeds; they talked proudly of their warrior, Stalking Horse, who had counted coup on the enemy and saved their chief's life. Stalking Horse felt slightly disconcerted being the subject of everyone's praise, but he did enjoy the privileges that went with it. He was served the finest food and was waited on hand and foot by Sun Dancer, whom he knew had been ordered to do so by her father. He knew that it galled her to be his servant but it was her duty to do as her father bade. She kneeled quietly beside Stalking Horse and when he wanted a drink or something more to eat, Sun Dancer quickly jumped to her feet and heeded his every wish. He smiled devilishly; he could see the frown deepen on her forehead every time he ordered her to do something.

Hours had gone by since the feasting and dancing had begun, but it would go on late into the night and early morning. Stalking Horse was satiated and exhausted. He stood up to stretch and asked He-Walks-the-Mountain if Sun Dancer could accompany him on a walk.

The two walked in silence for a while and Stalking Horse was not quite sure how to address Sun Dancer. He had thought a great deal of what Laughing Bird had said, and he knew that Laughing Bird was right. He knew that Sun Dancer had deep feelings for him and he had no right to toy with those feelings. He did not wish to hurt her. And in truth, he did not know if he could keep from hurting her or dishonoring her once she became a woman.

"You enjoyed that, didn't you?" Sun Dancer broke the silence.

"Enjoyed what?"

"You enjoyed ordering me around as if I were your slave. You play the master very well."

"I just enjoyed seeing you silent, for once."

Sun Dancer glared at him and continued on ahead of him.

"Why did you ask me to walk with you?"

"Because I want to say something to you." He stopped and lightly grabbed Sun Dancer's shoulders. "I do not ever wish to hurt you, Sun Dancer, in spite of what you may think. I admire you greatly and think that one day you will become a fine woman."

"And where does all this glowing talk lead, Stalking Horse?"

"I hope you do not feel too deeply for me because I cannot return those feelings to you. Do you understand what I am saying to you?"

"Yes, Stalking Horse, I understand. I am not that much of a child. You are telling me not to love you because you can never love me back. You will always think of me as a child because that is what I am now. But it will be different someday. When I am grown and many young warriors come courting me, you will quickly change your mind about me. You will see what you have missed and then it will be too late." She turned away from him, not wanting him to see the fire in her cheeks and the wetness in her eyes. "Let us return to camp now. They will want to sing more songs to your bravery and courage."

"Sun Dancer . . ." Stalking Horse reached out to touch her but she was already gone. He knew that what she said was true, he would someday wish he'd never said these words to her. But they had to be said now to keep her safe from him and his own desires, even if one day he would tell her to forget everything he'd said to her this night.

He-Walks-the-Mountain had decided to give to Stalking Horse all of the horses he'd captured the night of the raid. He'd thought on it a long time and could think of nothing else that would repay Stalking Horse for his brave deed. Some men gave away one horse in payment to another man; perhaps if he gave Stalking Horse twenty horses he would consider that just payment for his deed.

The day after the feasting, He-Walks-the-Mountain took his string of horses through camp to Stalking Horse's lodge.

"A-hey, Stalking Horse," He-Walks-the-Mountain cried for the younger man to come out.

Stalking Horse immediately appeared at the door of his lodge and looked out. "Yes, He-Walks-the-Mountain, what is it?"

He-Walks-the-Mountain gestured to the horses. "These horses, they are yours. I give them to you as a gift."

Stalking Horse looked at the horses, nodded slightly, then frowned. "I cannot accept these, my chief."

He-Walks-the-Mountain showed genuine concern. He had thought the gift great enough. "The horses, they are not enough? I can give you more if that is what you desire."

"Leave the horses, my chief, and enter my lodge. There is something I wish to talk with you about."

He-Walks-the-Mountain nodded his assent and bade one of the younger boys of the camp to watch the horses until he came out. He entered Stalking Horse's lodge and after they had smoked the pipe, Stalking Horse began. "Your gift of the horses you have just captured is a generous one, He-Walks-the-Mountain."

"Then why do you not accept them?"

"I have thought on this matter a long time. Being the honorable man that you are, I knew you would come here with an offer of a generous gift. But I thought to myself, 'What do I need? I have everything

I want.' Then I realized there is something I do not have."

"And what is that?"

Stalking Horse was quiet for some moments before answering. "A wife. I do not have a wife."

"A wife? I do not understand." But suddenly he did and he looked at the younger man, a shocked expression on his face. "You cannot mean Sun Dancer. But she is only a child." He maintained a semblance of self-control, but his mind was racing at the thought of having to give his only daughter away in payment for his own life. It was a dread thought. "She is only a child, Stalking Horse," He-Walks-the-Mountain reiterated firmly.

"I know this, my chief. You move too quickly. You do not yet know what I want to say."

"I am sorry. I do not mean to interrupt you in your own lodge. Please, speak your mind."

"It is my thought that in a summer or two, Sun Dancer will attain her womanhood and will be courted by many young men. Indeed, she will probably be courted by every young man in the tribe."

"Yes," He-Walks-the-Mountain nodded his head, "I also foresee this as happening."

"I would wish it that you and your wife do not press her to accept any of the proposals of marriage. I want you to give her the time to decide by herself with whom she wishes to be wed. This is my wish."

"And do you intend to be one of these young men?"

"I want her to enjoy all the attention she will receive from her suitors. It happens to a woman only once, and I think she should not be hampered by my proposal."

"So you think she will accept your proposal?" He-Walks-the-Mountain smiled inwardly as he asked the question. He knew the answer to the question without even having to ask it. Still, he enjoyed Stalking Horse's discomfiture.

"I think it is likely," Stalking Horse replied, somewhat less sure of himself.

"But what if Sun Dancer herself asks me to accept one of the proposals for her? Perhaps she will choose one of the young men. Do you concede that it is possible?"

"Yes, it is possible. If that is the case, then you should accept for her. She will know her own mind."

"So, you ask that my wife and I let Sun Dancer have her suitors and play at this game of courtship for awhile, but we are not to let her marry. Is that correct?"

"If she wishes to marry someone else, let it be her choice."

"And when will you present your proposal to her?"

"When the time is right."

"I see. Do you intend to dangle her on a string as one would a puppet? I would advise you not to do that, Stalking Horse, for in the end you will lose her. Do not play at the game too long or she will tire of it and think you are not interested."

"I know this."

"Why do you ask this of me, Stalking Horse? Surely, you must know that Sun Dancer has strong feelings for you. You would have only to court her and she would not need to be courted by others."

"It is because of her feelings for me that I will back away from her for a time. Even though she is yet a child, I see her as a woman and I find myself wanting her as one. I feel it is better for both of us if we are not around each other much."

"You have told her this?"

"Yes. Not in the same words, but I have told her we should not be together. I do not wish to hurt her or ruin her reputation."

He-Walks-the-Mountain smiled knowingly. "I am sure her reaction was one of anger." Stalking Horse nodded. "I think I see now. Because she will not speak to you anymore, you want to make sure she does not do something foolish to spite you? Yes, I know my daughter, and that is something she would do." He narrowed his eyes and looked at Stalking Horse. "You are an honorable man, Stalking Horse. I can think of no finer son-in-law than you."

Stalking Horse stared at He-Walks-the-Mountain, a look of embarrassment spreading across his face. The man had already accepted him as his son-in-law.

"Thank you, my chief, you honor me greatly."

He-Walks-the-Mountain stood up and walked to the door of the lodge. "And I would advise you to keep the horses, Stalking Horse. You will need them and many more to pay for my daughter."

CHAPTER IX

The day started out as any other. The air was clear and the sun was high in the sky, causing what breeze there was to blow languidly through the camp. The majority of the village was resting, the men telling stories and gambling, the women quilling or working on some piece of clothing, and the children playing in the stream and running along the banks. Sun Dancer had been walking along the bank of the stream trying to find a quiet place to sit when she felt a terrible pain in her stomach. At first she was frightened and then she wondered. Her mother had told her that many women suffered pain when they made their passage into womanhood. Was it possible this was what she was experiencing? She couldn't believe it. Already fifteen summers had gone by and nothing had happened. Some of her girlfriends looked at her and laughed and said that because she wished to be a boy, she would turn into one. She was beginning to believe them.

Hurriedly, she ran back to camp and to her family's lodge. Her mother was sitting out in front with some women chatting and sewing.

"Mother, can you come with me, please?" Sun Dancer reached down for her mother's hand. "Hurry, mother."

Woman's Heart looked up at her daughter, an anxious expression appearing on her face. "What is it daughter? Are you ailing?"

"No, mother, just come with me."

Woman's Heart followed Sun Dancer into the lodge and while Sun Dancer removed her leggings and lifted up her dress, her mother began to understand. "It has happened then?" She looked at Sun Dancer thankfully, then grabbed the medicine bag which hung around her neck. She had asked Horn to make it the previous summer when nothing had happened to Sun Dancer. She smiled as she dropped the bag back onto her chest. She must remember to make a gift to Horn.

"It is true, mother. I cannot believe it. I am finally a woman." She smiled brightly and Woman's Heart hugged her tightly. She had known by her own intuition that it would happen soon; the signs were too obvious. Sun Dancer had grown taller and where before she had been straight, there were now curves and a slight swelling of her breasts. Her face had matured and was now pretty rather than cute. They had to make new clothes for her because nothing fit the way it once had; Woman's Heart knew it was going to happen, yet she also felt that Horn's medicine hadn't hurt. Perhaps it had helped it along a little faster.

"Well, then, we must make the announcement." Happily, Woman's Heart walked to the door of the lodge. It was a good day for celebration. She told

Spotted Calf to find He-Walks-the-Mountain and bring him back to the lodge immediately. Shortly, He-Walks-the-Mountain entered the lodge and gladly received the news of his daughter's passage.

"At last," he said proudly, taking both of Sun Dancer's hands in his. "Are you not glad, daughter?"

"Yes, father, I am. But I am also frightened. I do not know if I am ready for womanhood."

"You will have time to adjust. It will come upon you gradually so that it will be a natural thing. We do not expect you to change from child to woman in one day."

Sun Dancer smiled brightly and hugged her father. "Thank you, father. Truly, I am happy this day."

"Then I must make the announcement. The people are lazy this day and need an excuse for a celebration." He-Walks-the-Mountain walked outside the lodge to publicly proclaim that his daughter was now a woman. It was a custom which all wealthy families participated in, and part of the custom was to give away a horse. He-Walks-the-Mountain gave away twenty.

Sun Dancer unbraided her long hair and was led to a secluded part of the river by the women of the village. After she had bathed, her entire body was painted red and a robe was placed around her naked body. Sun Dancer wasn't frightened by the ceremony because she had heard about it countless times from her mother and her friends. She was then led back to the lodge fire where a coal was drawn from it and placed in front of her. Sweet grass, white sage, and juniper needles were sprinkled on the coal, and Sun Dancer bent forward over the coal and held her robe over it, so that the smoke passed over her entire body. Then she and her mother left their lodge and went to a small one nearby, where she would remain for four days. It had finally begun.

It was custom for a girl's grandmother to accompany her to the ceremonial lodge, but as Sun Dancer had none, Woman's Heart took over the position. Sun Dancer knew from the many talks she had had with her mother, that there were many tabus connected with the cycle. She wasn't supposed to ride a stallion, only a mare; young men were not permitted to eat or drink from a pot which was used by her; she was not permitted to touch a shield or any other weapon during this time, nor to touch any sacred object; if she were married, she was not permitted to sleep in her own lodge, or her husband would have bad medicine and would most likely be wounded in the next battle; she was not permitted to enter a lodge where a medicine bundle hung. The owner of a shield had to use special care to avoid a woman who was bleeding. He couldn't go into a lodge where one was or one had been, unless a ceremony of purification had been performed. If the woman accidentally went into the lodge of a neighbor, a shield owner couldn't enter until sweet grass and juniper leaves were burned in the lodge, the pins were removed and the covering thrown back. Once it was purified, the pins could be put back in and the lodge covering thrown forward again.

The first night in the bleeding hut was somewhat confining for Sun Dancer, but she was too excited to think about it. She heard the sounds of celebration from outside and wished to join in. It didn't seem right that she was the cause of the celebration and yet she couldn't be a part of it. Midway through the second day in the lodge she was growing increasingly short of temper.

"You are of ill humor today, Sun Dancer. It must be the changes you are going through."

"It is not that, mother, it is that I am so bored. I do not want to stay in here for two more days. I will go mad."

"Then you will go mad. But you must stay in here for most of the time, especially since this is your first time. People will say you are not grateful if they see you walking around."

"It is a silly custom. We are punished for what our body does naturally. And men are silly creatures. Do they not understand that if we did not do this, we could not give them children?"

Woman's Heart smiled indulgently. She especially enjoyed her daughter's use of the word, "we." "Of course they understand that, but they are still frightened of it. They believe it is strong medicine and will place them in danger should they have to fight."

"And what do you believe, mother?"

"I? I believe that it is only as it seems, something natural that happens to a woman so that she may have children. I do not think it has anything to do with medicine or spirits."

Sun Dancer laughed. "You surprise me, mother. You are not so steeped in your tradition as I thought. I know women my age who do not think as you do."

"I was young once, also. I have never liked being treated as an outcast during this time. Perhaps by the time you have a granddaughter, things will have changed."

"I hope that is so. And what does father think?"

Woman's Heart smiled, a knowing look on her face as she shrugged her shoulders. "Your father is a great chief and has fought many battles. We have spent many summers together, almost thirty, and he has lived long enough to see that I have nothing to do with whether or not he is wounded in battle. But we keep this to ourselves; his people would not respect him if they knew he did not fear his wife during her time."

"Mother . . ."

"What is it, daughter?"

"I do not think I need the rope."

"You do not need the rope? What are you saying? All women wear the rope."

"It is ugly and uncomfortable."

"You have not worn it yet, but you know it is uncomfortable?"

"I have seen it. My friends have shown me their legs. It gives them a rash."

"You will get used to it."

"I will not wear it."

"You will wear it or you will not leave the lodge."

Sun Dancer looked at her mother, her expression reflecting the disgust she felt at such a tradition. "You do not trust me."

"It is the young men of this camp whom I do not trust."

"But mother, I have been playing with boys since I was but three summers old."

"That is what disturbs me. You must wear the

rope, Sun Dancer. It is for your own protection."

"But mother . . ."

"Sun Dancer!"

The girl met her mother's stern expression and knew that Woman's Heart would not give in on this. "Then I will not wear it after I am married."

"That is up to your husband."

Sun Dancer looked at her mother despairingly; this was one argument she would not win.

Many thoughts ran through Sun Dancer's mind before she again spoke to her mother. "I do not think I wish to have children right away, mother. Are there ways to keep from having them?"

"There are ways and I will speak to you of these when you are married. I myself had great luck with one way. None of you was unexpected."

"I am glad. I do not wish to be a mother yet. I have only just become a woman."

"Yes, it is good to wait and learn the ways of your husband first."

Sun Dancer nodded her assent and looked into the fire. Her husband. Soon many young men would come courting her and she would have to make a decision as to which one she would choose. She knew that Stalking Horse would not be among them; she had barely spoken to him in over two summers. They had avoided each other, although there were times when it was not possible to stay out of each other's way during the course of the day. She had watched to see if he would take a bride but he did not; he did not even court anyone in particular. Many times in her fantasies and dreams, she thought that he did not court anyone because he was waiting for her, but in reality, she knew this was not true. Stalking Horse had always been somewhat of a loner and perhaps he would never marry.

"What are you thinking of, daughter?"

"Marriage. Is it a good thing, mother?"

"It is good."

"Even when you do not care for the person you are wed to?"

"I do not know that for I have always cared deeply for your father. I cannot say what it would be like if I had lived with a man I did not care for."

"But you would have, if your parents had told you to."

"I would have."

"But you would not make me marry someone I did not care for, would you? I would rather die than live with a person I did not like or respect."

"Do not excite yourself, daughter, there is plenty of time for you to decide. I do not think your father and I will have to push you into marriage." As she looked at her daughter, she thought of her husband's words and Stalking Horse's request. And she was glad. She had always known Sun Dancer's feelings for Stalking Horse ran deeply, and she was glad to find out that his ran as deeply for her.

The weeks that followed Sun Dancer's passage into womanhood were hectic and exciting. No sooner had He-Walks-the-Mountain made the announcement to the village and Sun Dancer had left the hut, than young men began to court her. A day didn't pass that there weren't at least three young men waiting outside her parents' lodge. When she came back from a walk or doing some errand for her mother, she would find young men waiting for her. Some young men followed her as she walked and plucked at her robe to attract her attention, but she only smiled and continued on. Even a smile from Sun Dancer was encouragement to some, for she found she couldn't coldly turn away from them.

Young men would send friends or an old relation such as an uncle or grandfather to ask Sun Dancer for her hand in marriage, but she refused them all.

Many young women of Sun Dancer's age wore wristlets. It was the custom for a young man to remove the girl's wristlet and take it home. If the girl were willing for him to keep it and show him that she returned his affection, she would say nothing. But if she did not want him to keep it, she would tell her mother and she would send one of the family to get the wristlet. Sun Dancer lost her wristlet many times. Young men hoping that she would assent to marriage would take her wristlet without her permission, and would soon find out that she was not willing when they had to give it up.

Sometimes while she lay awake on her robes at night, Sun Dancer could hear the sounds of flutes being played outside the lodge. Some flutes were believed to have certain powers because the young men took them to the medicine men to have them exercise their power over the instruments. Sun Dancer enjoyed the sweet, lyrical sound of the instrument but she wasn't compelled by any force to come out of the lodge and go to any young man. Some young men went to the medicine man for help in other ways. They might take a filled pipe and again the medicine man might exercise his powers over the pipe. Or a medicine man might give a young man spruce gum to give to the young woman so that when she chewed it, all of her thoughts would be of the young man. Some young men sent gifts to Sun Dancer's father: buffalo hides, horses, bows, arrows, quivers, moccasins. But the gifts were always returned within twenty-four hours and no acceptance of marriage was granted.

Weeks went by and Sun Dancer began to grow tired of all the attention given her by the young men of the tribe. It made her proud to think so many young men thought her worthy of being their wife, but not one of them even came close to her idea of a husband.

There was only one man whom she thought of as her husband, and not once had Stalking Horse ventured to make his intentions known. Indeed, for most of the time he had been off making war against the Kiowas and the Gataka Apaches, and had no idea that she was being courted by so many young men. If her parents were growing restless of her constant rejection of suitors, they made no mention of it to her. But she was sure that if she did not decide in a fair amount of time, she would be forced into marriage with someone she did not care for.

She was surprised too, that Laughing Bird had not courted her. She had expected that he would bring many horses and ask for her hand, but he had not. She had already decided that if Laughing Bird did ask for her hand in marriage, she would accept. She could think of no man other than Stalking Horse with whom she could be happy and content. But it was as if the two men she cared for and admired the most had rejected her without even a chance. She could not understand it.

During the weeks of her courtship, Stalking Horse and Laughing Bird had been with a war party in the Kiowa and Gataka Apache country. They were out for horses and to settle some earlier wrongs which the Kiowas had perpetrated against them. Daily, Sun Dancer would go to the village crier to ask if he had heard anything about the war party, but every day his answer was the same: no, he had not heard. She began to worry that something had happened and that both Stalking Horse and Laughing Bird had been killed, but stubbornly she pushed the thought from her mind.

One of the young men of the tribe was carrying water back from the stream for Sun Dancer when they heard the crier announce that the war party was on its way. They had sent a scout to report that they would be back by the evening. They had lost five men in the battle with their enemies but had counted many coup. Sun Dancer walked about the camp impatiently until word came that the war party was on its way in. She ran to the entrance of the camp and waited until she saw the riders coming. Slowly and solemnly, the party rode into camp, the dead hanging over their horses. Toward the end of the column were Stalking Horse and Laughing Bird, both unhurt. Sun Dancer breathed a sigh of relief and moved back as the men passed. There were many horses behind them and they were let out on the open prairie to graze. Cries and moans from relatives of the dead men started throughout the camp and Sun

Dancer walked back to her parents' lodge. She hated when someone was killed; the relatives always grieved so terribly. She thought of her dream and of Brave Wolf's death, and she suddenly grew very, very cold. She felt his death throughout her body and she was sure then, that it would happen as she had dreamed. She ran to her brother's lodge. He hadn't been with this raiding party because he had just returned from another raid. Sun Dancer asked for permission to enter when she reached the lodge.

"Are you well, Brave Wolf?" Sun Dancer asked as she sat opposite him in the lodge.

"I am well, sister. And you? How many suitors have you today?" He smiled broadly and Sun Dancer looked at his large shoulders and the muscles which rippled through them, and she admired his strength. Surely, one so brave and strong and good as Brave Wolf would not die.

"I do not know, Brave Wolf. I already grow tired of this courting game."

"You wish to be married then?"

"No, I wish to find the one I will be with for the remainder of my life and dispense with these games."

"So you tire of the courting already? It does not seem possible that a girl could ever grow tired of the attention given her by starry-eyed young men."

"But I do."

"You have already picked then?"

"Yes, but it seems he has not picked me."

"Stalking Horse?"

"Yes. I fear he still sees me as a young child. He will not permit himself to see that I am now

153

a woman."

"Perhaps he sees but he is not ready. Give him time."

"I have given him all the time I can; I fear I shall have to choose soon."

"Choose only when you are ready, *nekaim*. You must take the time to decide; you will live with the man the rest of your life."

"Were you born wise, brother?"

Brave Wolf laughed. "If I do possess any wisdom at all, little one, it is by virtue of my years and experience. Wisdom comes from learning and that is something we must all do."

The Cheyennes were not the only Plains Indians who were capable of stealing horses. Most Plains Indians were adept at horse stealing and the Kiowas were no exception. It had taken the Kiowa war party almost two weeks to track down the Cheyenne camp. Although it had taken them far from their own land, this time they had followed. It was now a matter of pride. The Cheyennes had raided their camps too many times and had stolen too many of their best horses. It was time to retaliate.

The Kiowas camped several miles down the river from the Cheyenne camp, trying to avoid any riders who might be coming or going. They waited through the first night when the Cheyenne war party returned because their camp was too well-lit and the people celebrated late into the night. The Kiowas decided to raid on the second night because they knew the people would be tired and in need of rest from their dancing and celebrating of the night before. They waited until the camp was quiet and most of the campfires had died down.

The Kiowa warriors entered the camp silently, much the same way the Cheyennes had entered their own camp, placating the hungry dogs with scraps of food. They chose the best war and buffalo horses, cut them free, and led them outside of camp. It was during this time that Sun Dancer was returning from her nightly walk from the stream. The night was warm and her thoughts were elsewhere as she walked into the middle of the camp and saw figures stealthily moving around. It was but a few seconds later that she realized they were enemies, and she began to scream. She barely emitted a small, stifled sound, when a hand was thrown over her mouth, and she felt herself being dragged from camp. She heard her people come from their lodges and yell to one another, but by that time the Kiowas had succeeded in taking some of their best horses and the daughter of one of their chiefs.

Sun Dancer fought her captor but before she could put up much of a struggle, she was struck across the head. It was sometime later when she woke up to the pounding of the horse and the sound of its heavy breathing. She lifted her head but saw only the ground. She had been tied across the horse and the upper part of her body slammed against the horse's side in time with its steps. She felt sick with fright. She had never been without her family to protect her and now she was completely alone in the hands of an enemy. She shut her eyes and concentrated on being strong; that was what her father would have expected of her and she did not want to shame him by acting like a frightened child.

She knew it would be a long time before the Kiowas would let up in their flight. They wanted to put as much distance as possible between them and the Cheyennes. Sun Dancer didn't dwell on visions of rescue by her tribe; she concentrated on how she could escape at the first possible chance. She was sure her captors would be cruel and she was unsure if she could survive the kind of torture they had in mind for her. She suspected she would be used as an instrument of revenge. She knew only that she had to depend on herself for survival. That was one of the first lessons her father had taught her. He had often said that if she were ever captured by the enemy she must show courage, no matter how great the pain. He also said that it might not be possible for him to find her, so she must depend on her own skills and knowledge to survive and, eventually, to escape. And if escape were impossible, then she must make her own judgment as to whether or not she could make a life with her captors. Hers was the final decision.

He-Walks-the-Mountain was one of the first men out of the lodges, and he watched helplessly as he saw his daughter being dragged away. He yelled loudly and soon the entire camp was awake and ready to ride after Sun Dancer. Woman's Heart begged her husband to find their daughter; she was in an emotional state. Brave Wolf quickly found another horse and was ready to ride, as were Stalking Horse, Laughing Bird and other loyal warriors. Suddenly, the stolen horses were not as important as Sun Dancer's life.

The Cheyennes had a slight advantage; they had raided many Kiowa encampments and knew of their various locations. They were determined to try them all until they found where Sun Dancer had been taken. As they rode out of camp, each man had the same thought—Sun Dancer could be violated, tortured, or killed before they could find her. It was a thought that made each of them ride faster and more furiously.

Sun Dancer watched the people of the Kiowa camp move about her as if she did not exist. She grimaced as she tried to move her wrists about in the tight, constricting ropes. She stood toward the center of the camp, her arms and legs lashed to a tall pole. She was bound so tightly she could barely wiggle her hands, and she was placed where everyone could see her. So far no one had touched her. When they arrived at the camp, she was immediately tied to the pole. After a few curious looks by the women and children of the camp, she was completely ignored. She didn't know how long she had been standing there, but it was long enough for her arms and legs to feel numb and her mind to picture all the tortures that the Kiowas could inflict on her. There was no possible way for her to escape; she could do nothing but endure whatever they had in mind for her.

The next day was in itself a torment for Sun Dancer. She was exposed to the hot sun without any respite; she could feel the skin on her face and arms begin to blister. Her tongue seemed to swell, especially when she saw someone drinking water. The night was cool and she felt herself shiver against the pole. At times she grew so weary that her limbs gave out and she sank down against the pole, constricting the ropes even further. The pain was such as she had never known. She realized that the Kiowas were already torturing her by making her go without water and food and exposing her to the elements. It was cruel but very effective; she could already feel herself succumbing to the thirst and pain.

She tried to think of other things, of times well-spent with her family and friends, but her mind always came back to her present situation and the reality of it. One time she opened her eyes to see some children drinking water out of a bowl. They watched her slyly as they slowly trickled the rest of the water on the ground before her. She shut her eyes to still the sting of tears; she wasn't sure she could survive with the kind of dignity that would make her parents proud.

When Sun Dancer didn't think the torture could be any worse, she opened her eyes to see women and children carrying sticks and placing them all around her in a circle. They were laughing gaily, as if it were great sport to burn a person. She couldn't believe that this was going to happen to her, and she cried out at the women in anger; they looked at her disdainfully. As far as they were concerned, she was less than a dog and deserved far less attention.

That night there was a feast and Sun Dancer knew by the stares and hands which pointed in her direction that it was in her honor. She also knew that as soon as the feast ended, she would be burned to death. The thought made her ill and her legs weakened against the ropes supporting her body. Death by burning was something she had never considered; indeed, she had never considered her own death. Why, she had not even been with a man, been married, nor had a child, and now she confronted her own death. It was too much for her to contemplate; she shut her eyes and tried to blot out the sounds of the merry-makers who were about to murder her.

The Cheyennes found the Kiowa camp—it was easy to trace their own horses. Stalking Horse and Laughing Bird scouted the camp and found that there were two guards around the horses who were anticipating a retaliation by the Cheyennes. They had seen Sun Dancer in the middle of the camp. She was tied to a pole surrounded by brush and wood. They looked at each other in dismayed silence and returned to the others to tell of their news. No time could be lost entering the camp; this could be the night the Kiowas killed Sun Dancer.

The Cheyennes could not wait until the entire camp was asleep to sneak in. It looked as if the Kiowas planned to celebrate far into the night. The camp was well-lit and most of the tribe was centered around a large campfire in the middle. Stalking Horse suggested that they eliminate the guards surrounding the horses and he, Laughing Bird, and Brave Wolf create a distraction with the horses. While this was going on, one of them would sneak in behind Sun Dancer, cut her loose, and carry her out. The rest of the Cheyennes would be waiting outside the camp for the Kiowas to check their newly stolen horses.

They waited until late when some of the Kiowas returned to their lodges for sleep. Then Stalking Horse, Brave Wolf, and Laughing Bird made their way to the horses. They moved quietly in the night, their feet making no sound on the ground. It was easy for them to kill the two guards for their anger made them deadly. When the guards were dead, Laughing Bird went out onto the prairie and signaled the rest of his people to come. The Cheyennes rode to a distance outside the camp and dismounted. The younger men cared for the Cheyenne horses while the older and more experienced warriors made their way to the Kiowa horses. There was no room for error this night for they were greatly outnumbered. Suddenly, a large flame shot into the air and lit the sky. He-Walks-the-Mountain stopped and turned. He knew that the fire had been set around his daughter. He ran to Brave Wolf.

"It must be now; the fire has been set!" They all looked toward the flames. The horses trampled the ground excitedly as the Cheyenne war cries trembled in the air. The Kiowas heard the war cries and some of them ran from the camp to confront their enemies. When they reached the area beyond their camp, the small war party of Cheyennes was awaiting them. They killed the Kiowas without mercy. Stalking Horse, Brave Wolf, and Laughing Bird made their way around the camp to where the fire burned so brightly. They entered behind Sun Dancer.

Stalking Horse quickly cut the ropes which bound Sun Dancer, while Brave Wolf and Laughing Bird fought off some of the defending Kiowas. Sun Dancer was vaguely aware of being lifted into the air; the intense heat of the fire was suddenly gone and her legs were free of the terrible heat. She opened her eyes as Stalking Horse carried her from the camp. She looked over his shoulder and saw Brave Wolf fighting two Kiowa warriors. As she watched, one of the warriors smashed Brave Wolf over the head. She shut her eyes then, for she was sure her vision had come true and Brave Wolf was dead.

The Cheyennes waited for Brave Wolf, Stalking Horse, and Laughing Bird to leave the Kiowa camp, then they herded the Kiowa horses back to their own tethered horses. There, they mounted their own horses and rode homeward. Stalking Horse held Sun Dancer in front of him as he rode. He looked around him, unable to see Brave Wolf, and he wondered if the war chief had been killed.

As any other time when the Cheyennes had stolen horses, they kept a rapid pace to put distance between them and their enemies. The Cheyennes knew that the Kiowas couldn't follow them for long, for they had stolen most of their own horses back, as well as many of the Kiowas'. The Kiowas had little chance of catching the Cheyennes now for they had no alternative mounts. The Cheyenne backriders assured their men that they were safe; there were no Kiowas following them. They slowed their pace slightly. They kept the horses at a canter, because they knew they were safe only in their own encampment with guards keeping constant vigil. And there would be Horn to care for Sun Dancer.

Sun Dancer moaned slightly as she moved her burned legs against the horse. Stalking Horse placed his arms tightly around her. He wanted to protect

161

her; he wanted no one, not even her father or brother, to take her from him.

After awhile, He-Walks-the-Mountain rode up next to Stalking Horse. "Does she suffer much?" The pain was obvious in He-Walks-the-Mountain's voice.

"I believe she does," Stalking Horse replied. "Her legs are badly burned from the fire, as are her face and arms from the sun. I think we should send someone ahead to tell Horn to prepare."

"Yes, I will do that. Brave Wolf is also wounded."

"Is he bad?"

"He was hit in the head but he is riding. I think he will be fine." He-Walks-the-Mountain rode off to assign the task of riding ahead to some eager young brave and he returned to the head of the party. It would not do to have his men think him weak, but his mind still dwelled on Sun Dancer. It was too much to have his only daughter and his favorite son wounded in the same day. He would rather have given himself to the spirits than see either of his children hurt. His outward countenance betrayed no emotion, but on the inside, He-Walks-the-Mountain felt as if a part of him had died this night.

CHAPTER X

Horn changed the poultices on Sun Dancer's legs and arms and applied a fresh one to her face. Her face and arms wouldn't scar, he was sure, but her legs were deeply burned. There would be scars on her legs for the rest of her life to remind her of what she had been through with the Kiowas. When she had first been brought to him, he had given her small sips of water, although she had begged for more. He knew that a large amount of water in her stomach would only make her ill and sap her remaining strength. When she was able to keep more water in her stomach, he made her sip broth into which he had boiled special types of plants and herbs to soothe her and to make her sleep without pain. He had been prepared for this, even before the scout had ridden into camp to tell him of Sun Dancer's wounds. It was another part of the vision he had seen; he knew she would be hurt but that she would survive. It was up to him to see that she could be made as healthy as possible again.

When Sun Dancer was able to sit up against the backrest, Horn gave her small pieces of meat. He made her chew them until they practically went down her throat of their own accord. Various times during the day he changed the poultices on her arms and legs and applied a healing salve to her face. Sun Dancer had not spoken since she was brought to him and he decided it was time for her to speak of her ordeal.

"How great is your pain, Sun Dancer?"

Sun Dancer shrugged, not looking up at Horn. "It is not so great that I will not live, Horn."

"That is not what I asked you, child. I want to know if my medicine works and keeps you from pain. I cannot know how it works unless you tell me."

Sun Dancer looked up. "The pain is great at times, but at others, I do not feel it." She put aside the bowl from which she was eating and asked in a low voice, "Will I be very ugly, Horn?"

"Is this what concerns you most, child?"

"No, I am most grateful that I am alive."

"Then why do you ask such a foolish question?"

"I ask it because I am not yet married. If I am ugly and scarred no man will choose me for his wife. I will never know what it is like to marry and have children." She looked down at her bandaged legs. "I have seen my legs when you have changed the dressings; they are so ugly I can barely stand to look at them. How do you think a man will feel?"

Horn moved the bowl and sat down next to Sun Dancer. He picked up one of her hands. "Move your fingers." She did as she was told. "Now, run your hand over mine. Now, run it over the robe, and the mat. Can you feel them, their texture?" Sun Dancer nodded. "And your arm, move it around in a circle, then reach up and touch your nose." Sun Dancer smiled slightly but did as she was told. "It is a wonderous thing, is it not, that you are able to do such things with your body? Think how the eagle must feel, or the owl, or a fish, who can't even walk on the earth and is unable to touch and feel things as only we can do. Do you feel the textures any less because your skin is burned and scarred?" Sun Dancer shook her head and looked at Horn in wonder. "And when your legs heal, they will still carry you wherever you wish to go. You can walk and run on the land, you can swim in the water, and you can ride a horse. You can still do all these things. Think of the man or woman who is crippled, who can do none of these things. Do you think that they would not trade your scarred skin for their flawless skin so that they might run and swim? You think too much of your bad fortune, Sun Dancer, and little of your good."

"It is true, Horn, I am fortunate. But I am a woman and I want to marry. Will I be forever alone to walk and run and swim?"

"If that is the way of things, then you cannot change them. But if you find a man who accepts you as you are then your life will be even better."

"And if there is no such man?"

"Then you will live alone. But at least you will have more than the people who cannot move. Learn to think of the good things in this life, Sun Dancer."

Sun Dancer reflected for a moment on what Horn had just told her. "I know you are right and I would rather die than not be able to do those things of which you speak, but still I think of the other. Perhaps this makes me a small person, Horn, but I cannot stop the things I feel."

"You are a good person, child, and you feel what any other person would feel. But you are also strong and you can rise above this thing. You can hold your head up high as you walk."

"I do not feel strong. I wanted to cry when I was so thirsty my tongue swelled in my mouth and my legs blistered from the fire. I wanted to scream out in pain."

"But you did not."

"No."

"Why did you not scream?"

"Because I wanted to make my family proud of me, and I wanted to show the Kiowas that even Cheyenne women have brave hearts."

"I believe you showed them this, child. It took great courage for you to do what you did. Why then, can you not accept what has happened to your body and go on about your life? Was there not a time during your torture that you wished you could be anywhere from there, to do the things you have always done?" Sun Dancer nodded. "Well, you are free, and when the burns heal you will be able to do all those things again. You are alive and destined for great things. You must learn to live up to your greatness, Sun Dancer."

Sun Dancer looked at Horn. She didn't entirely understand what he'd just told her, but then she never fully understood everything he said. She smiled at him. "I have never understood why people fear you, Horn, you are as gentle as a fawn but with the understanding and wisdom of the *maiyun*. You are a good teacher."

"To teach is my job, as well as to cure. Have I cured you?"

"I believe so. When I am healed, I will walk from here with my head held high, proud that I am still alive and able to walk. If a man does not choose me, then I will live alone, but with honor."

"That is good, child. But do not spread the news that I am gentle like a fawn; people will not fear me if they know the truth."

"It would not matter, Horn, because everyone knows the truth about you already."

Sun Dancer looked down at the scars on her legs and shrugged her shoulders; they were no longer pleasing to the eye but she could still swim as well as anyone. She dove into the cool water and laughed gleefully. Horn had been right, of course; once she had healed and was able to walk and ride and swim, the scars no longer seemed important. The most important thing was that her brother was alive; he'd only been wounded. He visited her often when he came for Horn to check his wound. He told her how Stalking Horse devised the plan to rescue her and how he had held her while they rode back to their own people. Sun Dancer felt herself blush when Brave Wolf recounted the story, but it gave her a deep satisfaction to know that Stalking Horse cared so much. She had not seen him, however, since they'd all returned to camp. He hadn't come to see her nor had he inquired after her health. Perhaps he had thought of her legs and knew he could not live with a scarred woman.

She dove to the bottom of the stream and swam along its length for awhile, feeling the rocky bottom and seeing the turtles as they scurried away. When she came up for breath she slapped the water with her hands and turned onto her back, floating aimlessly on the water. Horn had been right about other things as well: she now looked at life differently and the things she had taken for granted before. She touched things and felt them and smelled them, she enjoyed every sense to its fullest. When she rode her horse she felt at one with him and she reveled in the feel of his coat against her thighs and the wind against her face. When she drank water, she savored its fresh taste as it moved gently down her throat. Since she had been so close to death, life had more meaning for her now. Everything had been elevated in importance.

Her parents hadn't forced her to marry and she was surprised to find that the young men still courted her. Many young men courted her simply because it was a great honor to have a wife with such courage, and many sought to gain her hand because it would elevate their position in the tribe. But Sun Dancer cared little for marriage now; she knew she could never marry anyone but Stalking Horse. She had already decided that she would become an unmarried one and the holder of great wisdom and knowledge. She would have Horn teach her, and eventually the younger people of the tribe would come to her. They would say how brave she had been as a young woman and they would hold her in awe. It would not be so bad; she would not have children of her own, but she would have all the children of the tribe.

"Be careful or you will float away," Stalking Horse

said as he walked up to the edge of the stream. Sun Dancer stood up, surprised by his sudden presence.

"I did not know you were there; my mind was far away." She walked to the edge of the stream and Stalking Horse pulled her up. She sat down, shaking her long braids.

"What were you thinking on so seriously?"

"Truly?"

"Yes."

"I was thinking on my future. I have finally decided what it will be."

"And what will it be?"

"I will be like Horn, only a great, wise woman. Horn will teach me everything so that I will take over his position in the tribe when he dies."

"What does Horn say of this?"

"Horn does not know it yet. But I will tell him when I am ready."

"What if Horn is not ready?"

"He must be; I cannot do it without him!" She pulled her dress down farther over her legs when she saw Stalking Horse staring at them.

"Your legs are healing well."

"They are ugly."

"What do you expect them to be? They were nearly burned off, woman!" Stalking Horse retorted angrily. Sun Dancer looked at him in shock; he had called her "woman." "You are fortunate you are even able to walk."

"I have been told that."

"Then why do you not believe it?"

"I believe it. Do you think my legs are ugly, Stalking Horse?"

"I do not think either way, Sun Dancer. It is not your legs I am interested in."

"What is it about me that interests you then?"

"Many things." He paused. "Your courage, for one. You have the heart of a warrior."

She was greatly moved. "Thank you, Stalking Horse, that is a truly wonderful thing to say." Her stomach jumped with excitement. When she was near him, she felt special.

"Where are you now, Sun Dancer? You go away too often."

She looked up and smiled, a smile which melted Stalking Horse's heart. "I am here with you; no other place matters." She'd said what was in her heart and for the first time, she was not embarrassed by it. Stalking Horse took her hand.

"It pleases me." He pulled her to her feet. "Let us walk back to camp."

"But I like it here; let us stay." She implored with her eyes.

"No, let us go back to camp. Your parents will worry."

"My parents do not worry about me." But at the look on Stalking Horse's face, she relented. "As you wish."

He held her hand as they walked back into camp, the eyes of many of the villagers on them. Sun Dancer had never felt quite so bold and was surprised that Stalking Horse would hold her hand in public. She relished his touch for soon she knew she would be all alone and an old maid of the tribe. As they neared her parents' lodge, there was a commotion and many people standing about gesturing and talking.

"What is it? Has something happened to my family?" Sun Dancer pulled away from Stalking Horse and ran through the people. She stopped short when she saw the string of horses in front of her parents' lodge. Her father's war shield, a sack of beads, a war lance, and fresh meat were piled in front of the lodge. The gifts were so magnificent that many of the neighbors came to look at them. Some warrior was willing to pay a grand price for her, it seemed.

"Mother, father, what is all of this? There are many fine things here. And here is your war shield, father." She walked over and picked it up and realized then that the shield was Stalking Horse's. He was returning it to her father. He was also asking for her hand in marriage. She shut her eyes for a short moment, afraid to believe the truth. Her eyes begged to cry. Her mother walked to her.

"Did you see these fine beads, Sun Dancer? We could adorn many shirts and dresses with these. And the horses. Do you realize there are over one hundred horses here?"

Sun Dancer turned to look at the horses which were strung out far beyond the lodge. She walked to her father and handed him the shield.

"He is a sly man, father. He knew you would not take the shield otherwise."

"Yes, and he is a very determined young man. He also includes a war lance for Brave Wolf. And these horses we just took from the Kiowas. There can be no greater honor, Sun Dancer." Sun Dancer looked behind the crowd of people for Stalking Horse but she knew he would not be there. He had presented his presents to Sun Dancer's family, and now it was up to her to decide if she would accept his proposal. If his gifts were returned within twenty-four hours, he would know the answer was no.

She felt an arm go around her shoulders and she looked up to see Brave Wolf. She hugged him tightly, happy that he was alive and able to enjoy this moment with her.

"You are well-honored, *nekaim*. You would be foolish to turn this one away."

"I would never be that foolish, brother. Here, this is for you." She brought him the war lance. "It looks to be very fine."

"Yes," Brave Wolf agreed as he ran his hand along the wooden shaft to the stone point which was sharp and hard. Feathers from different birds of prey hung from the shaft. "It is fine work. Stalking Horse has given me his own lance. Your price is high, little sister."

"I am worth it, am I not?" Sun Dancer smiled with delight, quite happy at the prospect that she would not become an old maid.

"I need not ask whether you will accept the proposal?" He-Walks-the-Mountain walked up next to his son and daughter.

"I told her she would be foolish to turn this one away, father. I am quite pleased with my gift and do not wish to give it up."

"Yes, your mother already has plans for the beads. You would ruin everyone's plans if you said no, Sun Dancer."

"You both know I have no desire to refuse. This has been my wish since I was a child."

"Do not be too quick to reply, child, or he will

think you too anxious. Make him wait for awhile. Let him think you are not yet sure."

"But he knows that I am, father. It would be silly to wait."

"Still, that is what we will do. When the final hour is up, Brave Wolf will go to him and say you have accepted."

Brave Wolf nodded his agreement.

"Yes, that is the way it will be done. You will stay close to the lodge, little one, for people will seek you out and want to know your answer. No one will know your answer before Stalking Horse."

The ensuing twenty-four hours were busy ones for Sun Dancer. Much to her surprise, she found that her mother had already made a wedding dress for her. To finish it off, Woman's Heart wanted to add some of the beads which Stalking Horse had given her. She wanted Sun Dancer to try the dress on so she would know where the beads should be put. When Sun Dancer queried her mother as to how she knew she would be married, Woman's Heart replied that all mothers want their daughters to marry, and she was only being prepared if the event ever came about.

The dress was similar to the ones she wore for everyday living, but this one was more decorative. The deerskin had been tanned to a special softness, and the fringes below the arms hung far down the sides, as did those on the hem of the dress. The seams were tied with thin strips of sinew on which beads had been strung. On the left side of the dress over her heart, Woman's Heart had quilled a large sun in yellow, and over the opposite breast was a large horse portrayed riding into the sun. Woman's Heart added beads to the skirt of the dress, sewing them up and down the skirt in different colored lines. The beadwork on the moccasins matched that of the upper part of the dress, with the sun on the left one and a horse on the right. Sun Dancer was even more perplexed as to how her mother knew she would marry Stalking Horse. When she asked, Woman's Heart only shrugged.

"He would have been my choice for your husband. If you had chosen another, I would have changed it. Now hand me another one of those beads." And she went on about her sewing, leaving Sun Dancer as confused as before.

Sun Dancer yearned to talk with Stalking Horse but her mother forbade her to leave the lodge except when necessary. She thought it more appropriate that he should wait for her daughter's answer, although Sun Dancer thought it was all rather foolish. She knew that Stalking Horse understood her true feelings, but she wanted to please her parents. It was all part of the grand tradition and Sun Dancer did not want to break with tradition this time.

He-Walks-the-Mountain had sent word to their Arapaho brothers that Sun Dancer was to be married to a great warrior, and he requested that their friends come. Although Sun Dancer wanted to celebrate with Broken Leaf and her people, she was anxious to be with Stalking Horse and begin a life as his wife. She still couldn't believe that it was going to happen, and every day that kept her from him made it seem less real. It would be at least a week before their friends arrived, and she wasn't sure she could wait. But she would—girls from good families did not elope. She had known a boy and girl who had run off together because the girl's parents did not approve of the boy. They wanted the girl to marry a more honored and wealthy warrior. When the couple eloped, the girl's father and brothers followed them and brought them back. They killed the young husband and forced the girl to marry the man they had first chosen for her.

It was custom that when a girl married, she and her husband moved in with the girl's family. Since Stalking Horse had been on his own for so long and lived in his own lodge, it was assumed the two would move into it. However, out of respect to Sun Dancer's parents, he would probably move his lodge closer to them.

It was up to Woman's Heart and Sun Dancer's other relatives to provide things for her new home. Woman's Heart would provide the beds and back-rests and the utensils used for cooking and eating. Many of the other things would be provided by the other relatives.

After the marriage, when Sun Dancer and Stalking Horse had moved into their lodge, Sun Dancer would continue to wear the protective rope for at least ten days but no longer than fifteen. Stalking Horse would respect the string for that amount of time but no longer. This custom enabled the new couple to grow accustomed to each other and sleep together before there was any actual physical contact.

Once they were married, Stalking Horse was not permitted to look at or speak to Woman's Heart. If she wanted to enter her daughter's lodge, she would do so at a time when she knew Stalking Horse was not there. But it was possible for Stalking Horse to present Woman's Heart with a gift, through another person, and this was considered a great honor. After an exchange of gifts, the mother-in-law tabu ceased to exist.

When the twenty-four hour period was up, He-Walks-the-Mountain and Brave Wolf accepted Stalking Horse's proposal of marriage for Sun Dancer. Then the announcement was made to the entire camp, and everyone prepared for a big celebration when their Arapaho brothers reached the camp.

Many Cheyenne men courted their women for years before a proposal was made, but Sun Dancer's parents knew that although Stalking Horse had not actually courted Sun Dancer, his feelings for her ran deep and true. The marriage would take place as soon as their friends arrived.

Many times Sun Dancer wanted to sneak into Stalking Horse's lodge to tell him how joyous she felt, but she was not yet married to him. A single girl entering a man's lodge without a chaperone was sure to ruin her reputation, she knew. She still couldn't believe that they would soon be married; it all seemed like a dream. And he had been so generous with his gifts to her family and in being so generous, he had done her a great honor. She put aside her moccasins and lifted the hem of her skirt, looking down at her scarred legs. Stalking Horse was not repelled by her scars and had said he was not even interested in them. He had said she had the heart of a warrior.

"Do not dream your life away, girl, you have

things to do." Woman's Heart entered the lodge and picked up Sun Dancer's dress. "I think it will be a fine dress. What do you think, Sun Dancer?"

"It is beautiful, mother. I have never seen so fine a dress. The members of your society will honor you greatly when they see your fine work."

"Perhaps. But this was not done for them, it was done for you. My heart is so full for you, child. I do not think there is a better man in this camp than Stalking Horse."

"I remember when you thought otherwise."

"That was when you were still a child and I was afraid he would ruin you. I was thinking only of your reputation."

"I know that, mother. But did you not know that I would never do anything to bring shame to you and father?"

"Yes, I knew that. I have been overly harsh on you in the past, I know. It is only because I love you and I want you to be able to hold your head up high in this village. I was trying to protect you."

"I know this, mother, and I am glad for it. I am fortunate that I am loved so by you and father."

Sun Dancer tried on her new moccasins and looked at them admiringly, while Woman's Heart checked her last row of beads on the marriage dress.

"I wonder if your friend Broken Leaf will come," she asked looking up from her beadwork.

"I am sure of it. She told me that Stalking Horse cared for me but he was only waiting until I attained my womanhood."

"A woman of great wisdom, I can see."

"Yet she is different from me. But she is no

less honorable."

"Of that I am sure. Our brothers and sisters of the Arapaho tribe believe differently from us but they are good, kind, and generous people. I have a friend, Little Deer, whom I have known since we were very young. She used to be with men of her tribe and ours, while I was with none. But it did not diminish our love for each other, and today our friendship is strong. I am glad you have such a bond with Broken Leaf."

"I, too." She picked up her moccasins and finished some of the beading her mother had asked her to do. "Will I know what to do with Stalking Horse, mother?"

"What do you mean?" Then she looked at Sun Dancer's cheeks and nodded her head. "Ah, yes, I understand. Yes, you will know some of it, child, and Stalking Horse will show you the rest. It is easy with someone you love. It was easy with your father, he was kind and gentle. It is a thing which will make your love grow."

"Perhaps he will find me too . . . young."

Woman's Heart suppressed a laugh and moved next to her daughter, taking her slim hand in hers. "When you say young, you mean without experience?" Sun Dancer nodded. "Perhaps that is better. A woman who has much experience and has known many men would be hard pressed to change her ways for her husband. But a woman who has known no one but her husband can adapt herself to him."

"And what of the husband who has known many women?"

"If he has known many, then he will know when

he finds the best. Obviously, Stalking Horse felt you were the best and that your love would be great together. Do not doubt his judgment, girl. Although he is young in years, he is old in experience and wisdom. He has been on his own for so long, he has had to be his own teacher. Learn from him."

"Yes, I will. Were you frightened, mother?" Sun Dancer looked up at her mother, her large brown eyes growing even larger in anticipation of her mother's answer.

"Truly, I was so frightened I was not even able to untie my protective rope. Your father had to do it for me." Sun Dancer laughed and relaxed somewhat. "But when it was over, I felt such contentment I realized there was never anything to be frightened of. We are lucky, you and I, daughter, because we have men we love and who love us. Anything else will come naturally."

Sun Dancer wrapped her arms around her mother and for a fleeting moment, was sorry that she would no longer be a little girl. And in that same moment, Woman's Heart, her eyes misted by tears, was sorry she would have to let go. They both knew that they couldn't change the life cycle of things, but for one brief second, they held onto something that they could never again regain.

CHAPTER XI

Ten days after Sun Dancer's parents made the announcement of her forthcoming marriage, some of the Arapahos arrived. They erected their lodges outside the Cheyenne camp, close to the stream. The marriage would be held that evening, and both camps were bustling to make ready for the feast and celebration. When news of their arrival spread, Sun Dancer asked if she could go see Broken Leaf.

"Yes, but bring her back here so you do not see Stalking Horse. I do not want you to wander about camp."

"Yes, mother," Sun Dancer replied, as she ran off toward the Arapaho camp. She met Broken Leaf halfway in between and the two ran to each other and embraced.

"It is so good to see you, *nevase*. I am glad you are here."

"I, too. I am happy to celebrate your marriage. Is it Stalking Horse?"

"Yes, it still does not seem real to me. I cannot believe he chose me."

"Do not belittle yourself, Sun Dancer, you are his

equal. He knows that. He also knows he is making a wise choice. Now, what of your capture by the Kiowas? We heard you were tortured."

Sun Dancer lifted her dress and watched as a grimace appeared on Broken Leaf's face. "It is an ugly sight, is it not? I still cannot believe Stalking Horse wants to marry me after seeing my legs."

Broken Leaf made a derisive sound. "You are stubborn, Sun Dancer, and refuse to see the truth in anything. What matters that your legs are scarred? Stalking Horse will not spend his days looking at them. He knows that the beauty of your legs is of small importance compared to all of you."

"I have often wondered if my face and arms had remained scarred, if he would have asked to marry me. I think not."

"It does not matter. You waste your time thinking of inconsequential things."

"He says I have the heart of a warrior. Could he love me for only that if he could not look at my face? It is important for me to know."

"Then the only person who can tell you is Stalking Horse. But do not be overly harsh if his answer is not what you would like."

"I wish only to know." She turned and looked at the area around her and at the sky above. "It does not seem like my marriage day. I am frightened, Broken Leaf. There is still so much I do not know."

"There is still much we all do not know. What frightens you, Sun Dancer? Perhaps I can ease some of your fears."

They walked to the woods behind the lodge and sat together in companionable silence before Broken

Leaf spoke. "You want to ask me of my relationships?"

"Yes. My mother tells me that if you love someone, it will come naturally. You do not love everyone you are with, do you?"

"I have yet to love anyone I have been with," Broken Leaf laughed.

"Does it come naturally to you then, when you are with a man? I am quite confused, Broken Leaf. I know nothing of this physical thing."

"This is difficult for me, Sun Dancer, because I do not want to say the wrong things to you. I do not want to cross what your mother has told you. I can only tell you my truth."

"Tell it to me then."

"To me it is a desire which must be fulfilled. With my people, I am not scorned for my behavior, and so I can be with many men. With your people, you can fulfill no desires and can be with no men until you are married. Most women in your tribe are unfortunate because they must marry men they do not care for; they marry men that have been chosen for them by their parents. And so they must suffer through many years of being with a man they do not even like, or they learn to care for the man and try to see the good in the relationship. You are lucky; you are marrying a man you love and respect and one who feels the same for you. I agree with your mother in this: with you and Stalking Horse, it will come naturally. You will want to be with him."

"I already want to be with him, Broken Leaf, but I am not sure if it is in the way you are speaking of."

"You have been with him alone a few times, have

you not?" Sun Dancer nodded. "And have you not wished for him to touch you and put his arms around you? Have you not wished to lie down beside him on the ground and run your hand over his smooth skin?"

An enormous blush spread over Sun Dancer's face as she replied, "Yes."

"Then you will explore each other until your two bodies come together. I do not think you will mind it much."

"Will there be pain? I heard Fawn say that she hurt every time her husband came to her."

"Fawn is a child and has no less than a child for a husband. You have a man; he knows what to do."

"But what if I do not fulfill Stalking Horse's desires? I know nothing of this; he would do better to marry you."

Broken Leaf laughed loudly and rubbed her friend's cheek. "You are truly an innocent child, *nevase*. Stalking Horse would never marry a woman like me, do you not understand? Part of the reason he is marrying you is because you are pure and good and chaste. Stalking Horse does not want a woman who has known many men; this does not appeal to him. You do me a great honor by suggesting that he marry me, friend."

"If he did, I would kill you both." Sun Dancer stood up and Broken Leaf followed her as she walked back to her parents' lodge. "Thank you, Broken Leaf, you have helped me greatly. You and my mother have been kind."

"I hope I have been of some service to you. You would do well not to worry about it. Now, show me your marriage dress. Your mother is famous for her quilling and I am sure it is a fine piece of work."

Sun Dancer nodded absently. She wished with all her heart that she could be as sure as Broken Leaf and her mother that things would happen naturally between her and Stalking Horse. She wished she could be so sure of the unknown.

Sun Dancer was impatient as the women worked on her hair and dress. Woman's Heart, Broken Leaf, and Spotted Calf fussed continually until Sun Dancer stood up and proclaimed she would have no more of it. They had braided and rebraided her hair several times, as well as smoothing her dress until she felt she could stand no more.

"I will have no more of this," she screamed in agitation. "Stalking Horse will have me as I am or he will not have me at all."

"But this is a special day, daughter, you must look your best," Woman's Heart implored her daughter. "Just let me see this side of your hair. I must put more beads in."

Sun Dancer breathed impatiently and sat back down to allow her mother to fuss even more over her hair.

"Wait," Broken Leaf cried, "I have something which will finish her hair off nicely. I will return quickly." As they waited for Broken Leaf to return to the lodge, Sun Dancer again had to endure close scrutiny as she stood up and turned around for her mother. It seemed that the dress and moccasins were full of flaws, although to Sun Dancer's eyes, they were perfect.

"Here," Broken Leaf ran into the lodge with a parfleche. She pulled out two tail feathers of a golden hawk and handed them to Woman's Heart. "I have carried them for luck for a long time, but now I want you to wear them, Sun Dancer."

"These are wonderful, Broken Leaf," Woman's Heart replied in wonder. "You are truly a good friend. Come, help me put them into her braids." Sun Dancer tried to sit as still as was humanly possible after being fussed over for so long. Woman's Heart and Broken Leaf inserted the golden feathers where Sun Dancer's braids ended—they glinted brightly agains the dark tips of her hair. Colored beads had been worked throughout the length of the braids to match the beading in her dress and moccasins, and when she stood up for the final inspection, all gave their nod of approval.

"You are truly a vision," Woman's Heart said proudly.

"Yes, and Stalking Horse will carry you away and ravish you, in spite of your rope," Spotted Calf giggled.

"That's enough," Woman's Heart berated her daughter-in-law. "Broken Leaf, is the horse ready?"

"Yes, come. He looks almost as beautiful as Sun Dancer." They all went to the door of the lodge and looked at the horse. He was an Appaloosa, a breed rarely seen by the Cheyennes but much revered. They were bred by the Nez Percé tribe further to the west, and few had been seen by any other of the Northern Plains tribes.

"This is the one talked about by our elders, raised by the Nez Percés. I have never seen such a horse."

Sun Dancer walked outside and up to the large horse. He was darkly spotted over his face and shoulders and forelegs, but his mid-section and hindquarters were mostly white, spotted lightly in black, with a black tail. He was over twenty hands tall, and Sun Dancer barely reached his shoulder. She reached out and rubbed his soft, velvety nose. "He does not shy away from strangers; a noble animal."

"Probably a war horse." Broken Leaf walked up next to Sun Dancer. "Stalking Horse picked him out for you. He continually honors you, my friend." Sun Dancer smiled over at Broken Leaf and nodded her head in wonder. A horse so fine as this one, a warrior would kill to keep. Yet, Stalking Horse had given him to her, a sign of his deep affection and respect.

"He is truly wonderful. And look how he shines with the beads. Who has made him look so grand?"

"Broken Leaf. She is a woman of many talents," Woman's Heart said enthusiastically. "She could be a great quiller."

The horse's dark mane and tail were braided with beads to match those Sun Dancer wore in her hair, and a colorfully painted robe was on his back. Around his hoofs he wore tiny rattles, which tinkled gently as he walked.

"Come now, daughter, your husband awaits you."

Sun Dancer nodded and allowed herself to be helped up onto the horse by the three women. She looked at her parents' lodge—her lodge—for the last time as a child and then was led away by her mother. Slowly, they made their way through camp so all could see what a lovely bride Stalking Horse was receiving. The people of the village waved, smiled, and nodded their approval, while some threw flower petals and birds' feathers for luck. Sun Dancer looked at no one but held her head high, in great dignity, waiting only to see the eyes of her husband.

Sun Dancer soon saw Stalking Horse's lodge and she felt herself begin to lose control. She was both frightened and excited, happy but sad—her days of being a child were now gone. She was a woman now. She breathed deeply.

She was surprised to see Stalking Horse standing outside his lodge with the other young men. Usually, the husband waited inside while the bride was seated on a blanket and the young men carried her into her husband. Stalking Horse defied this tradition. He stood in front of his lodge, his arms crossed over his chest, his long hair dressed in feathers. He wore his finest leggings and moccasins and the shirt which Sun Dancer had made for him. She smiled and he returned the smile twofold. She was no longer afraid.

When the horse stopped, Stalking Horse reached up and plucked Sun Dancer from the horse's back. When they reached the door, he turned around to give everyone another look at Sun Dancer in her husband's arms, then he strode through the lodge door. Their life together had begun.

Many of the traditions which had long been in practice for most married couples were set aside, because Stalking Horse had no family of his own. Many families had wished to take him in and make him their son, but he had always refused and made his own way. It was evident from the start that Stalking Horse was an individual of his own making and design. Normally, after the bride had been brought into the lodge, the groom's family would take her to the back of the lodge, remove the clothing she wore, and unbraid her hair. Then they would dress her in new clothing, rebraid her hair, and paint her face, decorating her hair with various trinkets. Her mother-in-law would prepare food and when the couple sat down to eat, she would offer it to them. The food which was prepared for the bride would be cut into tiny pieces by the mother-in-law so that the bride would put out little effort in chewing.

The wedding outfit was normally made after the wedding, as were the other gifts which were given to the couple, and a new lodge was erected next to the girl's parents. But Woman's Heart had wanted her daughter to have her dress for her day of marriage, and Stalking Horse already had his own lodge, so few of the traditional rules were followed in their case.

Stalking Horse and Sun Dancer sat side by side as they ate the meal which had been prepared for them by Woman's Heart and many of the other women in the tribe. They ate in silence and occasionally looked at each other. When they finished their meal, Sun Dancer cleared away the bowls and they moved to their backrests. Stalking Horse went to his, and Sun Dancer to a new one which had been richly adorned and placed next to Stalking Horse's. She was sure her mother had done the work on it; it showed her love of beauty and design. They sat in silence until Stalking Horse reached over and took Sun Dancer's hand.

"What think you, wife? Do you think you can stay married to one such as I?"

"I do not know, husband. It has not been overly

long to tell." She smiled at him and grew serious. "You were generous with your gifts to my family; I want to thank you. I think had I not accepted your proposal of marriage, my brother would have forced me into it. He has grown quite fond of that war lance."

"I am pleased. And what of your gift? Does that please you as well?"

"He is wonderful, but I cannot accept so fine a gift, Stalking Horse. The horse was trained for war and not to be a woman's mount. I want you to take him back."

"I cannot. I have a fine horse and he would be offended. It is important to me that you have a swift and courageous horse, one who would flee an enemy quickly and take you to safety. You must promise me you will accept him."

Sun Dancer realized that Stalking Horse had given her the horse for her own safety. If she ever encountered hostile warriors, she could flee quickly. She was moved by his thoughtfulness.

"You are kind for one so great. I am truly honored by your fine gift." She ran her fingers over the shirt. "And I see you wear the shirt. It becomes you."

"I told you I would wear it on my wedding day. And did you make your dress?"

"No, that is my mother's work. Look, do you see the sun and the horse riding into it? It is a beautiful dress, is it not?"

"Yes, and you shine in it. You are a vision to me. As you rode to my lodge, I could see the looks on the faces of the other warriors. I was proud you were coming to me. Your beauty is like the moon, the stars, and the sun."

"I did not know you were a poet and could speak such lovely words. Will it be so for all our lives?"

"No, I will not always have time for soft words. But this is our day of marriage and I will say what is in my heart. Can you say what is in yours?"

Sun Dancer looked down and shut her eyes for a brief moment. How long had she waited to say all the things which had been in her heart? And now she could think of none of these.

"I have loved you since I was a child, and the feeling grew ever stronger as I grew older. I watched you from afar for a long time, and then you finally spoke to me. When we spoke, our words were harsh and cold, but my love was still there. Then you were kind to me and you talked, and I knew I could marry no one but you. But I waited and still you said nothing of your feelings for me and I wondered if you ever would. When you finally did, my mind wondered, why had you suddenly come to care for me? Were you sorry for what had happened to me with the Kiowas or did you truly care? I still do not know, but I am so full of love for you that I tremble at the sound of your voice and the touch of your hand. You have known how I have felt all these years. I am told my eyes do not lie."

Stalking Horse again took Sun Dancer's hand and rubbed it against his cheek. He gently lifted her face and turned it toward his. "If you had looked, you would have seen that your feelings have always been returned in kind. When I first saw you in the river, when as a mere child you tried to swim across, I knew you were special. I hated Laughing Bird for being the one to save you; you always seemed so close to him after that. But as you grew older, I could see that you cared for me, and I took advantage of that. I made you work to get to know me. And you did that, and you made me see how much I truly cared for you. But you were still a child and I did not trust myself with you, so I stayed away from you so I would not tempt you or myself. But when you became a woman I knew my time had come."

"But why did you wait so long to tell me? I thought I would become an old one who would never marry. I knew I could never marry anyone but you."

"I wanted you to enjoy this time of your life, for you had waited so long for it."

"I did enjoy it for a short time but then it did not matter. I only wanted to hear from you. When I was taken by the Kiowas, I was sure I would die without ever knowing how you felt, or ever knowing what it was like to be with you."

"When you were taken by them, I was crazy. I would have done anything to get you back. All I knew was that you were mine and they had taken you away from me. When we found their camp and I saw you tied to that stake, part of me was tortured too. When the fire was lit, I felt the heat."

"When you saw the scars on me, did it not put you off? Were you not afraid that my beauty was ruined?"

"At that moment, I cared only that you would live. The scars bothered me because I was afraid you could not accept them. For me, most of your beauty is inside here." He placed his hand over her heart. "You are pleasing to look at, but we will not spend all of our time looking at each other. We will spend our time talking to each other and loving each other. Those are my feelings, Sun Dancer, straight from the heart." He pulled her to him and she laid her head on his chest. Neither could ever remember feeling such peace within themselves or feeling such peace with the earth and sky.

The day after their wedding, Sun Dancer and Stalking Horse moved their lodge close to her parents'. Sun Dancer herself erected the lodge, with the help of her mother and Broken Leaf. Again, the inside of the lodge was set up with Stalking Horse's things, as well as the new ones which were made by family and friends. Although Woman's Heart knew Stalking Horse was an able provider, custom dictated that he hunt the day after the wedding to prove to his new mother-in-law that he was an able provider. While Stalking Horse was away hunting, Sun Dancer and Broken Leaf spent a great deal of time together before the Arapahos broke down their lodges and returned home.

They rode for miles, Broken Leaf on the horse Sun Dancer had given her, Sun Dancer on the horse which Stalking Horse had given her. They raced and laughed and acted as if they were girls, the feeling of freedom again within their grasps. They hunted for small game and each shot two rabbits. They swam in the stream and walked in the woods to look for wild berries. Sun Dancer was sure she had never had a more companionable friend than Broken Leaf and she knew it would be an even sadder parting this time.

"I will miss you greatly, Broken Leaf. I wish you did not have to leave."

"Yes. I had even thought of staying with your people but I could not. They would look down on me and my ways."

"But they would not. They know your people have different beliefs from ours. That is why our people have remained friends for so long; we respect each other for what we are."

"That is true, but I still cannot stay. I am Arapaho and cannot make my home with the Cheyennes."

"But what if you married a Cheyenne?"

"Then I would stay here."

"Could you be true to just one husband, Broken Leaf? Or would you continue to have others?"

"This I cannot answer, for I have never been married. I will tell you if ever I acquire a husband."

"In time, you will do that."

"And how was it with your husband last night?"

"It went well, although we did not . . . we . . ."

"You were not together. Another foolish Cheyenne tradition. How long must you wait before you and your husband are together?"

"At least one week, perhaps ten days."

"You do not sound overly excited about this. Why must you wait so long?"

"Because it is our way. Don't make me feel so foolish, Broken Leaf. You yourself have said we have our ways and you have yours."

"That is true but this is one tradition that can be broken."

"How is that?"

"It is easy. Your people do not sleep in your lodge with you and your husband. They will not know if you decide to take off that terrible rope. Only you and your husband will know. But if you want to wait the entire period, then leave the rope on and bind your husband to tradition. It will make him even more of an animal."

Sun Dancer picked up a handful of dirt and threw it at Broken Leaf, who laughed uncontrollably. "You try to instill fear in me, Broken Leaf, but I will have no part of it. I will do as I please, not what you or my people tell me to do."

"I am pleased to hear it. I had already thought as much."

Sun Dancer looked at her quizzically and then laughed again. "Perhaps I will be happy to see you go after all. I cannot take much more of your philosophy."

"That is most unfortunate, for I have endless amounts to lavish on you. One day I will be considered a very wise person."

"But that day is not now and I do not have to listen to you. Come, Broken Leaf, of the running mouth, and I will race you back to camp before you drown in your own words."

Stalking Horse had great luck in his hunting and came back leading two horses loaded down with fresh game. He stopped first at the lodge of Sun Dancer's parents and left them some meat, then he distributed some among the elderly and feeble; the rest he took to his own lodge. Sun Dancer left the lodge when she heard his horses and she helped him carry some of the meat into the lodge for cooking.

"You had great fortune today, husband. The spirits seem to shine on us."

"Yes, let us hope they will continue to do so."

After Sun Dancer had cut and stripped some of the meat and hung it to dry in the sun, she roasted some over the coals of the fire, and ground the rest up with roots and berries for later use. She and Stalking Horse ate outside the lodge because the weather was still warm. As Horn had predicted, the summer grew unusually hot, and many of the people stayed outside their lodges and slept in brush arbors to receive any touch of wind at night.

After they finished their evening meal, Stalking Horse and Sun Dancer went for a long ride on the prairie until the sun began to set. It was a breathtaking sight which never failed to captivate even the oldest inhabitant of the Northern Plains. Slowly, they rode home in the glowing light of dusk, aware only of their companionship and the stillness and freshness of the air about them. Their silence held when they reached their lodge and Stalking Horse tied their horses outside. Many families were still sitting around the campfires telling stories of the old days before they had the horse and they lived in mud lodges, but Sun Dancer and Stalking Horse were not interested in stories this night.

They walked to their backrests and sat down. Stalking Horse removed his moccasins and leggings and wore only his breechclout, while Sun Dancer tentatively removed her dress. She had worn it the previous night but decided that it was time to remove it, along with the cumbersome rope. She undid the knots around her waist and thighs and threw it to the side, then she lay on her side and stared over at Stalking Horse, who had been watching her in silence.

"I have little knowledge of this," Sun Dancer said softly, her voice trembling slightly.

Stalking Horse made no motion to move but continued to stare at his wife. "I know you do not. I think, perhaps, it is too soon for you. We should wait the full time."

"I do not wish to wait the full time and I am the wife."

Stalking Horse smiled slightly and reached for Sun Dancer's hand. "I say we should wait and I am the husband."

"Will we spend all our lives arguing over this thing? I have waited long enough. Now, I want to know."

"If it is truly your wish."

"It is."

Stalking Horse moved slowly, turning onto his side next to Sun Dancer. He ran his hand over her face and then down her arm, stopping at her hip. His fingers lazily rubbed up and down her hip and then farther down to her thigh. Sun Dancer sighed deeply and shut her eyes. His touch was wonderful and it made her feel as she had never felt before.

"The child has turned into a woman," Stalking Horse murmured softly, and moved closer to her. His arms encompassed her and pulled her slight frame against his, so that she felt the length of his body against hers. He rubbed his face against hers and then breathed deeply—she still smelled of the sweet, fresh air. His strong arms traveled up and down the length of her body several times, getting to know the feel of it, getting to know each part and committing it to memory. He turned her on her back and looked down at her; her sweet, gentle face looked up at him with complete trust. He laid his head on her breasts and he was still; he was afraid to lose that trust.

"Is something wrong? Did I do something wrong?" Sun Dancer asked in a trembling voice.

"Nothing is wrong, wife, I am just enjoying you. There is no reason to hurry."

Sun Dancer nodded silently, wondering if he were telling the truth or if she had failed somehow.

They lay still for some time, Sun Dancer on her back, Stalking Horse with his head on her breasts, each thinking his own thoughts. It wasn't long before Sun Dancer sat upright, tears sparkling in her large dark eyes.

"It is I, is it not? I am not good at this thing and you do not know how to tell me. Can I not be taught? I can learn quickly."

Stalking Horse smiled slightly and took her hands in his, pulling her close to him. "It is not you, Sun Dancer, it is I. I have never before made love to one so sweet and good. It causes me great fear."

"Why? I do not understand."

"I fear I will lost your trust; I do not wish to hurt you."

Sun Dancer swallowed her fear and spoke again, forcing the quivering which shook her insides to subside. "I am your wife and I will do as you tell me. It is my duty." She looked at him bravely.

"I do not wish it to be your duty, I wish for you to enjoy it. I wish for you to be a part of it."

"Then teach me, Stalking Horse; teach me and I will learn. I am told it is a natural thing."

197

"Yes," Stalking Horse nodded his head, "it is a natural thing. And for us it will be a great thing."

Again he pulled her to him and laid her back down on the soft robes. She looked up at him again, but this time her face did not look so young; this time, the look was more womanly, more one of desire. Stalking Horse removed his breechclout and stood to let Sun Dancer look at him. She registered little shock or surprise and he wondered why it would not frighten her. He kneeled down next to her.

"You do not seem surprised."

"You forget that I have been with boys since I was a child. In this I am not shocked."

"Good." He laid his length atop hers, letting their bodies touch, and the warmth of their bodies spread throughout each other. It was then he slowly showed her the way and she opened herself to him without fear. It was a natural thing for her, for she knew what to do, and her body automatically responded to his. They moved together in fluid movements and their desire for each other grew until it had to be fulfilled. As Stalking Horse filled her with his love, she realized this was something that no one could have told her about or prepared her for; this was something that only she and Stalking Horse could experience for themselves. It was something beyond any verbal description. It had brought them together, as one, and no matter what happened to them in their lives, they would now have shared each other totally. Each would be a part of the other forever. Sun Dancer was a woman.

Sun Dancer woke up in the middle of the night, her

breath coming in short gasps, her skin covered in a light sweat. She had had the dream again, the one in which Brave Wolf was killed. She felt terrified. She shut her eyes but the vision was still too real. She sat up abruptly, suddenly aware of her nakedness. She was startled by the touch of Stalking Horse's hand on her back. She had forgotten she was in his lodge and was now his wife.

"What troubles you?" His hand ran slowly up and down the smooth skin of her back.

"It is a dream which I often have. Brave Wolf is killed in it."

"But it is only a dream; do not upset yourself over it."

"But it is so real; it is more a vision than a dream. I feel that it will happen. It frightens me."

"Do not be frightened. Perhaps you should see Horn; maybe he can help you understand it." He pulled her down next to him. "Come here to me." She lay in his arms and felt his strength flow from him.

"I cannot believe that I am here with you. It seems that for so long I have dreamed of being with you."

"This is not a dream; this is real. And you will be with me until we are both old and worthless."

"At least we will not be worthless to each other." She rubbed her face against his. "Show me again this thing for which I have waited so long."

Stalking Horse laughed and pulled Sun Dancer on top of him. "Already you have changed, wife, and can think of nothing but our bodies. This pleases me. I would not have a woman who would cringe at my every move."

"Nor would I have a man who would make me cringe so."

"You had no choice."

"But I did; I could have chosen from almost anyone."

"It did not matter whom you chose, I knew you would marry me. I saw to it."

"What do you mean?" She sat up and looked down at Stalking Horse's face. "You saw to what?"

"I saw to it that your parents would not permit you to marry anyone but me. You see, you had no choice."

"But how could you do such a thing?" she asked in outrage. "My father would never permit it."

"Your father owed me his life. All I asked in return was that he not press you into marriage with anyone until you had made up your own mind."

"And if I had not chosen you?"

"Then I would have killed the man and made off with you. You never had a choice, Sun Dancer; I have always wanted you for my wife." Again he pulled her down to him. "Are you angry?"

"No, I am stunned. I cannot believe these words which come from your mouth. I cannot believe I am here and that you love me."

"Believe it. Now, enough talk. Let me show you more about the ways of loving." Again their bodies became as one, to be forever joined in love and spirit.

CHAPTER XII

As Horn had predicted, the summer was unbearably hot, but the fall was warm and comfortable and brought many buffalo for the Cheyenne. Again Sun Dancer participated in the tanning of hides and the drying of meat, but this time it was different; this time she was doing it as a married woman and she took a great deal more pride in her work. Many of her friends, especially Fawn, treated her with deference because they knew Stalking Horse would one day be an important warrior. Sun Dancer herself felt little difference in her status except that she was proud and happy, and she felt beautiful for the first time in her life. Stalking Horse had helped to fill a part of her life which had been empty for so long.

She tanned hides alongside her mother and sister-in-law and she cut the raw meat into strips to hang in the sun. She planned to make new leggings for Stalking Horse, as well as heavier moccasins for them both for the winter, and a new dress for herself. She was also working on a parfleche for her mother, which she hoped to finish before the winter snows came. Her mother had done so much for her she wanted to repay her with a gift. Woman's Heart had even presented Stalking Horse with an ornamented robe in front of the Quilling Society, which meant she could face him without the restriction of the tabu.

The buffalo were plenty this fall and grazed in large herds so the hunters didn't have to wander far from camp in search of them. It was normally the practice of the men to butcher the animal as soon as they had killed it, and the women would come and take the skin and the meat to camp. Often, if a man was chasing many buffalo, he didn't have time to stop and dismount to skin and butcher the animal; so the arduous work of skinning, butchering and transporting the fresh meat was left to the woman. By the end of a day, a woman was covered in blood and her hands were tired and worn from cutting meat and scraping hides.

After they made sure they had enough food for the winter, the tribe moved back into the hills to the large timber which would afford them some protection from the winter snows and wind. Again, as with the coming of every winter, Sun Dancer had the ominous feeling of doom which prevailed over her until spring. She didn't look forward to the many dark days she would have to spend alone inside the lodge. For in spite of the cold weather, Stalking Horse would be out hunting for fresh meat to supplement their diet. The majority of the women quilled during the winter months to keep themselves busy, but Sun Dancer didn't look forward to the tedious work day in and day out.

When they made winter camp, the women busily collected firewood and checked to make sure there was easy access to a stream for water. Sun Dancer was walking back to her lodge with a vessel of water when she saw Laughing Bird walking toward her. He took the water from her.

"Laughing Bird, I have not seen you of late. Does everything go well with you?"

"Yes, and I do not need to ask if all goes well with you. I have never seen you look better." He looked at the flushed cheeks and the sparkling brown eyes, and again he wished he had been more forceful in his attempts to woo her when they were younger. As he had known she would, she had turned into a beautiful and desirable young woman, one any man would be proud to claim.

"Why do you stare at me? Have I changed so much?"

"Yes. You have grown up."

Sun Dancer laughed. "Of course I have grown up. As have you, as have we all." She cocked her head to one side. "What is it, Laughing Bird? Is something wrong?"

"Come, I will walk with you to your lodge." They walked in silence until they reached the lodge. Laughing Bird turned to Sun Dancer, a serious look on his face. "You are happy, then? Is marriage with Stalking Horse all you thought it would be?"

"It is that and more. I am fortunate to have a husband such as he."

"Yes, and he too, is fortunate. I am pleased for you, Sun Dancer."

Sun Dancer thought she detected a certain sorrow in Laughing Bird's eyes and she took his hand in hers. "We will always be friends, Laughing Bird.

You have been like a brother to me and that is something I will never forget. I will always be here for you if ever you need me."

"I know that. I, too, will always be here for you. Always be happy, little one, for this life here on earth is so short and we do not know what lies beyond."

"I will be happy and I wish the same for you."

"I must go now. We will talk soon." He walked away, turning once to smile and wave, and it was with a certain sadness that Sun Dancer waved back. Watching Laughing Bird walk away so solemnly, was like watching a part of her youth walk away, never to return. She turned and walked into the lodge, a sudden coldness coming not from the wind sweeping over her, but from deep inside, to chill her to the very bone.

Sun Dancer looked over at Stalking Horse sitting so erectly on his horse, and she felt great pride. His robe hung splendidly from his shoulders and his eyes swept the stark countryside for some sign of life. Sun Dancer had finally talked him into letting her go with him on a hunt, but she knew it was up to her to keep silent and still while they moved about. She pulled her robe closer about her shoulders and felt the cold wind whip her hair around. The snow was already quite deep. As usually happened, the winter had come hard and strong, and most of the camp had little food to make it through without hunting for fresh meat. The stream had frozen over and they had to break the ice to obtain water. Wood was hard to come by, and many times Sun Dancer and the other women had bloodied their fingers trying to break branches from trees because the smaller wood had been buried by snow. Her horse shifted from one foot to the other, as again she looked over at her husband.

"It is still; even the animals stay in from the cold. Only we humans find it necessary to venture out in this."

"Will we dismount?"

"No, it is too dangerous. The snow is too deep and our horses could run off. We will continue this way."

Stalking Horse led the way through a clearing of trees and held his hand up suddenly, a sign that Sun Dancer was to stop immediately. She listened to the sounds around her but heard nothing but the wind blowing through the trees. Stalking Horse turned on his horse and motioned for Sun Dancer to remain where she was. He moved slowly forward on his horse until he disappeared behind a clump of cottonwoods. Sun Dancer raised the robe and pulled it around her face, only her eyes and nose appearing above the edge. She heard nothing, but her horse began to shift nervously and move about in the snow. She held him firmly but he lifted his head and his huge nostrils flared—he scented something. Sun Dancer looked nervously about her. The horse snorted loudly and began to paw the snow.

Sun Dancer looked around her and started to move forward in the direction which Stalking Horse had gone. Something was frightening her horse; she wanted to keep him moving so he wouldn't become uncontrollable. They moved slowly forward when her horse neighed loudly. He reared up suddenly, throwing Sun Dancer into the snow. She watched helplessly as he ran away through the woods. She stood up and reached under her robe; she grabbed her knife and moved closer to the trees. A low, fierce snarling sound reached her ears and she turned her head in all directions to find its source. She knew the sound of a timber wolf, for she had heard it many times when hunting with her father and Brave Wolf. She reached the trees and searched for one she could climb. Again she heard the growl. She struggled through the heavy snow, trying to find a suitable tree.

She sheathed her knife and climbed the tree, her feet slipping on the snow which clung to it. She didn't have to look down to know the wolf was on the ground below her; she sensed its presence immediately. Slowly and carefully she moved up until she found a place she could sit, but she couldn't grab her robe as it caught on a branch and dropped onto the snow below. She watched in fascination as the wolf, and several others who had joined him, gingerly sniffed the robe and ripped it to pieces. Sun Dancer's stomach knotted as she heard the growls of the hungry animals below her. She consoled herself with the fact that in all the stories she had heard about wolves, she had never heard of one willingly attacking a human being unless provoked or hungry. But the ones below her looked hungry. Their eyes gleamed golden as they stared up at Sun Dancer and began scratching at the trunk of the tree. She rubbed her hands together and huddled closer to the trunk, pulling her knees close to her chest. She wasn't too frightened because she knew Stalking Horse would return for her at any moment, and she was safe for the time being in the tree far above the growling animals.

As the wind grew stronger, bits of snow from

branches above fell onto Sun Dancer's head and shoulders. It was dark among the trees; it grew even darker and still Sun Dancer did not see Stalking Horse. She screamed his name many times but there was never an answer. She feared he had been attacked by wolves or a mountain lion—perhaps he was lying in the snow hurt or dying. Angrily she pushed the thought from her mind as she rubbed her hands together rapidly. The bitter cold bit into her; she knew she was beginning to lose feeling in her limbs. She thought of the many songs the warriors sang before they went into battle to bring them courage. Her sad, lilting voice carried out from the trees as she sang: "My love, it is I who am singing. Do you hear me?" She sang the song again and began another. She would not permit herself to feel the kind of fear she knew was inside her; she forced herself to be strong. The fierce growls of the wolves interrupted Sun Dancer's singing; she looked down to see them angrily and ferociously jumping up the trunk of the tree in search of their prey. She closed her eyes and continued her song.

Stalking Horse swung the deer over his horse before he led it out through the deep snow of the woods. He heard the growls of the wolves and knew they had caught some unsuspecting prey. He swung up onto his horse when he reached the clearing and rode back to where he had left Sun Dancer waiting for him. As he had suspected, she had grown tired of waiting and ridden back to camp. He followed her tracks out of the woods and back along the frozen river when he suddenly realized the horse he was following was riderless. Sun Dancer's horse was traveling far too fast and easily; the tracks were not deep enough. He immediately returned to the place he had left her. He looked around and noticed footprints leading farther into the woods.

The howls of the wolves frightened his horse, and he held a tight rein as they rode into the woods. He yelled Sun Dancer's name loudly; instantly, the sounds of the wolves stopped. He yelled and hit the trees and brush with his lance as he rode through, knowing the unfamiliar sounds would frighten away the skittish animals. He pulled up his horse to listen; he heard a sound, faint singing coming from deep in the woods. He dismounted, tied his frightened horse to a tree, and continued on into the denser trees by foot. Again he heard the sound; it was Sun Dancer's voice. She was singing a war song.

"Sun Dancer," his voice rang throughout the trees. "Where are you?" He pressed farther into the woods. The only sounds were those of his feet and lance and Sun Dancer's voice. He listened to her song, trying to make out from which direction it came, but sounds of the forest were deceiving and he went the wrong direction several times. "Answer, me, Sun Dancer. Where are you?"

"I am here, Stalking Horse," Sun Dancer replied softly.

"Keep singing, Sun Dancer. Sing loudly." He moved as quickly as he could through the deep snow. He followed the sound of her voice as it reached his ears with more clarity, until he found the tree which she had climbed. He yelled loudly at the remaining wolf which stood at the base of the tree, and the animal ran off into the woods at the intrusion of the human who invaded his domain.

Sun Dancer looked down at Stalking Horse, happy that he was well. She was unable to move. She leaned her head against the trunk and closed her eyes.

"I do not think I can move; my legs have no feeling." Her voice was soft and sleepy.

"I will come up." Stalking Horse climbed swiftly up the limbs of the tree. He stopped on the limb below Sun Dancer and reached out to her. "Stretch your legs out and move slowly down toward me. I will help you."

Sun Dancer did as she was told, but her legs would not respond. They had fallen asleep and the cold had stopped the circulation in them. They were heavy and cumbersome.

"I cannot move them. They are so heavy."

Stalking Horse recognized the voice of one who had been in the cold too long. He knew of many who went to sleep and froze to death, unable to shake the heaviness in their bodies. He shouted out angrily. "Move your feet or I will drag you down the tree myself. Do as I say, Sun Dancer," he commanded.

Sun Dancer responded to the tone in Stalking Horse's voice. She forced herself to slide from the limb she was on down to the one below her. As she moved her legs, they felt as though they had been stabbed by a thousand tiny quills; she cried out involuntarily. She forced herself to keep moving; she thought how much worse her torture by the Kiowas had been. She eased herself to the limb Stalking Horse was on, and she clung to him as she felt his arms go around her.

"I cannot move my legs; you cannot get me down from here."

"We will get down." He rubbed her legs vigorously with his hands in spite of her protests, and began to move farther down the tree. "Come, unless you want to remain here as part of this tree."

Sun Dancer eased herself slowly down the tree, using her arms and Stalking Horse for support. When she reached the lowest limb and was unable to jump to the ground, Stalking Horse reached up and pulled her down, shifting her in his arms until he was able to carry her. Swiftly, Stalking Horse walked to his horse and placed Sun Dancer on him, wrapping his robe around her shoulders. He led the horse out of the woods and then swung up behind Sun Dancer when they were in the clearing. She lay back against him and closed her eyes.

"Do not fall asleep yet, wife, we must make sure your legs are sound."

"I want only to rest until we get back," she said softly and again laid her head against his chest.

"Perhaps I paid too high a price for you. Will I forever be saving your life?"

"It seems to be the way with us," she said drowsily. "But one day I will save yours."

"You already have," Stalking Horse said gently and wrapped his arms around her as they rode back to camp.

Stalking Horse made Sun Dancer walk around the lodge until he was sure her feet and legs were sound. Frostbite had not yet set in because she had been so far up the tree. The thickness of its branches had afforded her some protection from the wind and cold.

"Am I permitted to sit? I am tired."

Stalking Horse rubbed his hands up and down Sun Dancer's legs until he was satisfied. "You can sit but you cannot accompany me the next time I go hunting."

"It was not my fault. I did not know wolves were going to attack me."

"Wolves are always in the woods, especially in the winter. They are constantly looking for food. If you are ever confronted by them again, yell and scream and pound the brush. Do not be submissive; wolves do not usually kill humans."

"I will remember that next time," she said in a mocking tone. "The next time I will tell them what silly creatures they are for attacking one so brave as I."

"Do not mock me; this is no game." Stalking Horse's voice was deep with anger.

"I am sorry. I do not wish to mock you. I only wish you to understand that I am not so helpless as you think. And if you would teach me some of the things you know about the woods and the animals who live there, then I would not be in such great danger."

Stalking Horse was silent for some minutes. "I believe you are right. You are lacking in many skills and much knowledge. It is time you learned more."

Sun Dancer took slight offense to his words and tone and drew her mouth into a tight line. "I did not realize I was so dim-witted. I am genuinely amazed that I have been able to survive so long without you and your great knowledge."

"As am I," Stalking Horse replied arrogantly, a

slight smile touching the corners of his mouth.

"Now you mock me. If you truly think me so lacking in knowledge why did you marry me?"

"Because I think you able to learn swiftly." He held out his hand to her. "Now, come here and let us work further on more of your lessons." Sun Dancer looked angrily at him for a moment longer, then rose and walked to him. "I am no longer a child, Stalking Horse, and I do not wish to be treated as one. If you wish to have a wife who will learn and obey because you command it, I will do these things; but I will never be content. If you wish to have a wife who learns because she thirsts for knowledge, and obeys because she wishes to please her husband, then I will be the kind of wife who will do everything to make your life pleasing. I want to learn everything with you, Stalking Horse; I do not wish to be left out because I am a woman."

"I hear your words and I will remember them. Will you come to me then, and share with me our love?"

Sun Dancer knelt next to him and ran her hand along the lines of his face. "Yes, this I will gladly do. And perhaps we can learn from each other."

It was an honor for a woman to be a part of the Quilling Society, and Woman's Heart was especially proud to have Sun Dancer initiated into it. Quilling was a highly regarded craft, and when performed well and with great dexterity, it was considered comparable to a man's bravery in war. A woman who quilled thirty robes was in a class alone, as was a woman who made a lodge alone. Women who could perform these functions were few in number and were highly respected for their special skills.

As Sun Dancer had already quilled a shirt for Stalking Horse, she was considered an eligible member of the society. A piece of work had to be done in a prescribed ceremonial manner and taught by a member of the Quilling Society. Once done, the girl was able to attend the feasts given by the society and might teach others what she herself had been taught.

As the women assembled, they talked of the work they had done and the various ornamentations they had made. When the old women spoke, it was similar to the men when they recalled their counting of coup, and so, was very serious. The teacher of the new member first offered a prayer for her good fortune and health, after which some warrior who had been asked to the feast stood up and talked of his coups. After this, an old woman took pieces of meat from the pot, and went outside and made a ceremonial offering of the meat to the four cardinal points. While this was happening, the teacher was explaining to the girl that she should watch everything and learn, so that she might someday be able to instruct at a similar feast.

Now, the woman who gave the feast served the food to the others, who brought their own bowls. They ate only a portion of the food and took the rest home. Afterwards, the new girl might ask an old member to come to her lodge and draw a pattern on a robe for future ornamentation, and for this service she would present to the woman a gift. In Sun Dancer's case, she had only to ask her mother for help in learning the craft, for Woman's Heart was one of the best quillers in the village.

Sun Dancer's new duties as Stalking Horse's wife didn't just consist of joining the Quilling Society and becoming a more active woman in the village, it meant she was to depend solely on herself for the running of the lodge. For many years she had depended on her mother to do everything; now it was up to her. All the years Woman's Heart permitted her to play games, swim, and hunt were years she should have been lending assistance to her mother. She realized now for the first time how fully Woman's Heart had let her have her freedom and how few restrictions had been placed on her as she grew up. She now knew why she had never wanted to dishonor her parents; they had instilled so much trust in her that it would have been against everything she believed to dishonor them.

Various times during a week, Stalking Horse would take Sun Dancer out and teach her some new skill. Even if it was snowing, he would show her some new trick or lesson for survival. His first objective was to make sure she could defend herself with her knife. It had been different when she was a child, more of a game then, but now her life could possibly depend on her ability to wield a knife or shoot her bow and arrow.

He made a larger, more powerful bow so she was able to shoot a target from far away and still be as accurate. He fought with her hand-to-hand to make sure she would know what to do if attacked by an enemy. He taught her how to keep warm if caught in the snow, and how to find water if caught on the plains in summer. She was bright, strong, and she learned quickly; he was proud she would possess knowledge held by her own sex, as well as his.

There were times when Sun Dancer became angry with Stalking Horse and grew frustrated at the way he pushed her so demandingly. He was a hard taskmaster and he pushed her until she learned her lessons well. He was determined that she would never again be in a situation where her life was in jeopardy and she was unable to defend herself. Without telling her so, he wanted her to be more independent and self-reliant.

"I cannot use this thing; it is too heavy." Sun Dancer threw the unwieldy lance down on the ground. "I will never have occasion to use it anyway. I doubt if I will ever kill a buffalo."

"You do not know that, do you? I want you to know how to use it if ever you need to defend yourself with it. There may come a time when it is all you have to rely on."

As always, Sun Dancer saw the logic in Stalking Horse's words, and she picked up the ungainly weapon and struggled to mount her horse. It took some time before she was able to ride with some speed and throw the lance at a target, but she worked at handling it until it felt as comfortable to her as her bow. Stalking Horse also made sure she was able to fight with it on the ground.

"I am weary of all these lessons," Sun Dancer complained, rubbing her arms as they rode back to camp.

"I recall when this was all you would have enjoyed doing. You wanted nothing else but to be like a boy."

"And now I want to feel like a woman again." She looked over at Stalking Horse. "I do thank you for the lessons, husband, for I know the knowledge can never be wasted. There will come a time when I will probably use all you have taught me.''

''I hope you never have to use what I have taught you,'' Stalking Horse said grimly. ''But I do not like to think of you as helpless.''

''I am no longer that.''

''Then I have succeeded in my teachings. I also want you to learn from Horn, for he can teach you much about healing.''

''Perhaps he can also tell me about my dreams; I hope that is all they are.''

Stalking Horse saw the change in Sun Dancer's mood. ''Let us see if you are still as fast as you were when you were a child. Or have the years slowed you?''

''The years have slowed nothing but my sharp tongue, which has now grown more patient. You are fortunate there is snow instead of dust, or it would cloud your eyes as you rode behind me.'' She kicked her horse and was off in the direction of camp, her large Appaloosa easily taking the lead. When she looked back to find Stalking Horse, she was surprised to feel his arm around her as he pulled her to his horse and held her firmly in front of him.

''You have much to learn, wife. The first thing is to never try to outlearn the teacher, for he already has the knowledge and has already thought ahead of how to use it.''

CHAPTER XIII

Spring was still cold when the band of Cheyennes moved down to the prairie. The snows were melting and the ice was breaking up in the streams. They chose an encampment close to where they had camped the previous year, but this time they erected their lodges farther from the stream in case of flooding from the melting snows. The men hunted antelope and deer until the buffalo herds appeared for their summer grazing, and there was talk of a war party going after horses to replace the ones which had grown weak over the winter.

Sun Dancer worried about Stalking Horse. She knew he was a good warrior, one who would do anything to help his brothers, but she was afraid he would do something reckless while on a raid. This was a fear all Indian women lived with. She could never voice her fears to him because he would think it very "womanly" of her to worry about him. But she did worry about him, as she did about her father and her brother.

She had never been close to her other brothers, Running Bear and Two Moons, although they had been closer in age to her than Brave Wolf. They were totally involved in their war society and cared very little for their family. By the time Sun Dancer was five summers old, her three brothers were already warriors, and Brave Wolf and Running Bear were already married.

The soldier bands of the clan were made up of the bravest warriors and they constantly lost men in battle. Both Running Bear and Two Moons belonged to the Dog Soldiers, the society which consisted of especially brave men. The Dog Soldiers were looked up to by many people in the village, but they were often too authoritative and demanded that the rest of the people do as they did. They were more disposed to war than the other men of the village and very often were in disputes with the elders about making war. The men who joined the Dog Soldiers knew that once they joined that society, they had to leave their own clan and families and go to camp with the Dog Soldiers. They took their families with them, if they were already married, but they might also marry among the relatives of the Dog Soldiers. Sun Dancer and her parents and Brave Wolf seldom saw her other brothers now, and she grew to feel she had never known either one of them.

Sun Dancer chose a day when Stalking Horse was hunting to visit Horn. The old man was leaving his lodge to go into the nearby woods to look for healing herbs. He asked Sun Dancer to accompany him.

They walked in silence as Sun Dancer watched while Horn picked certain plants for their healing properties. Horn picked a plant similar to a cattail, which he would pulverize when it dried and then steep the leaves in water. This mixture would be given to a patient as a drink for bellyache. He showed her a certain root which when boiled in water and drunk would serve to help pain in the bowels, or if chewed and rubbed on the skin was good for any illness. A bit of the root tied to a child's necklace was good for keeping night spirits away. The stems and roots of a wild onion, when ground finely and applied as a poultice, were especially good for blisters and carbuncles. Once the sore opened, the medicine was boiled and some of it poured into the sore to loosen and clear out the pus. Horn pointed out a root which, when dried and ground to a fine powder, was used to make a horse spirited and long-winded. The sweet medicine, which Horn told Sun Dancer was named after their culture hero, was dried and pounded up and given to a woman after childbirth to make the first milk secretion pass quickly, and was considered a good medicine for the blood. Blue medicine was used for headache. The leaves and stems were put into cold water and allowed to stand for awhile and then drunk. Yellow medicine was used to stop a cold when it first appeared, and another root was used for rheumatism and sore muscles. Poisonweed medicine was used if a person's skin was poisoned by ivy or other harmful plants; it was ground and sprinkled on the afflicted parts. He showed her plants which were good for nose-bleed, bleeding bowels, bloated stomach, blocked kidneys, sprained back, diarrhea, paralysis, and medicines to wake a patient up and put a patient to sleep. Sun Dancer looked around her in wonder; she had never before realized what a vast amount of knowledge Horn possessed to know the healing properties of so many wild plants.

"It seems impossible to tell one plant or root from the other. How did you learn them all, Horn?"

"I was taught by my grandfather, who was a great healer in the tribe. He took me out with him daily until I learned each plant and its individual use. We can eliminate much pain with these." He spread his arms out around him. "Come with me today and I will show you many things which will surprise you."

Sun Dancer followed Horn in excitement, eager to learn the ways of healing. It was another lesson which Stalking Horse said she should learn, and she would learn as much as Horn would teach her.

"I have seen a white man," Stalking Horse told an awed Sun Dancer as they walked along the stream.

"Is it true? What was he like? Was he cruel? Is his skin truly white like snow?"

"Slow down, woman, and let me answer one question at a time. He was trapping beaver farther down the river. He was friendly to us and traded these for some dried meat." He handed the pouch to Sun Dancer who exclaimed loudly at the glass beads.

"They are wonderful, more so than the ones you gave my mother." She held one up to the light. "Look at the way the light plays over it. This is glass?"

"Yes, and the white man uses it for many things."

Sun Dancer put the beads back into the sack. "And his skin, was it truly white?"

"Not white like snow, but pale compared to ours. It was a lighter shade of brown. He had hair which covered his face, and the hair on his head grew to his shoulders. A strange one to look at."

"And his eyes, did you notice his eyes? Father says some of them have eyes the color of the sky."

"This one had eyes that color. I have never seen such a thing."

"Oh, eyes the color of the sky. I truly would have enjoyed seeing this. Did he speak our language then?"

"He spoke it and he used sign. He said that he lived from the things he could trade for the beaver furs. He said people in the cities would pay a high price for them."

"The cities. These are the places where all the white people live?"

"Yes. He said he does not like them much. He said he lives in the mountains in winter and traps the beaver along the streams. Then he trades all his furs in the spring and summer. He said he does not like to live with his people."

"He sounds much like us. Will he come back?"

"He said he traps along the river every winter; and if we would trap furs and give them to him, he would trade them for us for things we can use."

"I still cannot believe this, a white man in our country. And he lives in the mountains away from his own kind? I would like to see a white man, and especially a white woman. Do you think a person sees things a different color when his eyes are the color of the sky?"

"I do not think so. I think we all see the same from the inside, but from the outside the color is different. You are truly interested in these people."

"Yes, I have always wanted to see these people of whom Sweet Medicine spoke so long ago."

"You will see them. In time, as Sweet Medicine said, they will be all around us. They will move onto our land and we will have to fight to keep it."

"How do you know this?"

"I have heard from our brothers, the Arapahos, that white men have already pushed Indians from their land, and the white man is too numerous to fight. One day he will outnumber us and we will no longer be able to fight. We will be captives in our own land."

Sun Dancer looked at Stalking Horse as he reflected on the hills beyond the stream. "You are too serious, husband. Surely this thing of which you speak will not happen for a long time. It probably will not be in our lifetimes."

"But it may be in our children's or our grandchildren's. What else can we give them if we cannot give them our heritage, and the land we have been on for so long? I fear the coming of the white man, Sun Dancer."

"I did not know you feared anything."

"I also fear losing you," he said gently and pulled her to him.

"You will never lose me. I will always be with you, no matter where you go."

"And if I pass over into the other world before you?"

"Then I will follow soon after. We are together now and for always."

He put his hands on her small face and looked at her lovingly. "I knew you would say that; it is your way. But I would not want it. If I die before you, I want you to live your life out. You will be needed by many. My death will leave you empty but you will go on."

Sun Dancer looked at him with a puzzled expression. "How do you know these things? You frighten me, Stalking Horse. Is it possible you can see into the future like Horn?"

"No. I can only tell you what I feel and what others have told me. You will live a long life and will be held in great esteem by our tribe."

"And you?" she asked softly, her voice quivering slightly.

"I do not know about me, and I do not feel it is important whether I live or die young."

"But . . ."

"We will live our life together fully and with great love. And if it is such that I live a long life with you, then I will be all the more grateful, but if I am not able to live my life out with you, I will still be grateful. I will have loved you."

"No," Sun Dancer cried and wrapped her arms around his bare chest. "Do not say such things, do not." She laid her head against him and heard the rhythmic beat of his heart. She couldn't believe that this heart, this body, this very being would ever cease to exist.

"Let us continue our walk, I have made you sad. I did not want to do that."

"I want to make a promise to you," Sun Dancer said solemnly.

"What?"

"If you die before me, I will come to you when I

can. Wherever you are laid to rest, I, too, will lie there with you."

"Do not speak of this now."

"I want to speak of it. I will make sure that my responsibilities are taken care of, and then I will come to you. Know that and believe it."

Stalking Horse took Sun Dancer's hand tightly in his and they walked out on the prairie toward the hills. "We have talked of death, now let us talk of life." He pointed to the Black Hills. "Those hills have been here long and they have seen much. I feel that we are akin to them because we live in harmony with them. I look up at them and I feel their strength and their power."

"Yes, my father has often said that. Perhaps you are both mystics."

"No, I think we both want to live in harmony with everything around us; we want no intruders to destroy that harmony." He turned to her. "It is time to go; I grow too serious."

"Talk more if it eases your mind."

"Talk will not ease my mind. Let us walk by the river again; it soothes me."

Sun Dancer nodded quietly and stayed close to Stalking Horse as they walked back along the river. He looked straight ahead of him, his mind still on something else, and Sun Dancer worried about the words he had spoken to her. Had Horn told him he would die young and she would live out her life alone? A chill went through her. It was similar to the one she felt whenever she dreamed of her brother being killed; she pulled closer to Stalking Horse. Now that they were together, she couldn't imagine ever being without him. If she had to live out the rest of her life alone . . . Well, she wouldn't think of such things now. She would talk to Horn and he would help her to understand these things of which Stalking Horse spoke. He would tell her that they were all untrue. This, she wanted to believe with all her heart. For life without Stalking Horse would not be a truly worthy one.

Stalking Horse had been on a raid for many days and Sun Dancer was trying to keep busy. She picked berries with her mother, crushing and mixing them with meat to make pemmican. She worked on a robe with the Quilling Society, and she rode every day with her father to keep her mind clear and fresh. A party of Kiowas had been seen not far from their camp and they now had guards posted to keep a watch, although the enemy tribesmen had not been seen again.

He-Walks-the-Mountain rode with his daughter every day because he enjoyed it and because he feared for her safety. The sight of her burned legs would be forever ingrained in his memory; he would make sure that nothing similar ever happened to her again.

The buffalo roamed the prairies in large herds. Soon they would be hunting the animal for their food and everything else the animal provided them with. They would wait until late in the fall, when the buffalo's fur had thickened in preparation for the winter snows to kill for their winter robes. But they would kill the animal in smaller numbers now for the fresh meat and the thinner hides it would provide for clothes and moccasins.

Sun Dancer had talked to Horn about her dream but he was unable to tell her whether it was a dream or a vision. He told her not to say anything to Brave Wolf about it; often, if a warrior knew of a dream or vision before he went on a raid or to do battle, he would believe that he was supposed to die. It was a matter of honor. Sun Dancer swore she would never tell Brave Wolf, but she wondered if the dream would ever come true. She also asked Horn about Stalking Horse and whether he would live a long life.

"Why do you ask me such things, child? I cannot make visions come to me at will. They come to me on their own. I cannot tell you about your husband."

"But you know about me. How is this?"

"I was told about you before you were born; I did not ask."

"And what were you told?"

"That your life would be a long one and that you would be held in high esteem by your people."

"And you were told nothing about my husband or children?"

"No," Horn lied, for he had been told that Sun Dancer would only have one child. He did not feel it was right for her to know this. "I was told only about you."

"I worry about my husband; I fear he will do something reckless."

"Do not fear for him; he is a fine warrior and will someday lead many men."

"You know this?"

"I feel this, just as you feel your brother will die."

"I cannot deal with this knowledge, Horn. I love my brother and do not want to see him die."

226

"You must deal with it. There is no other way. Your brother is an honorable man and if he dies in battle as you so believe, then there is no better way for a warrior to die." He patted Sun Dancer on the back. "You do not know his age when he dies, do you?"

"No."

"Then it may be a long time from now. Do not worry yourself with it."

"Yes, perhaps he will be old when it happens. He is so good and has such a brave and honorable heart. He is different from my other brothers. They think only of war and killing."

"Do not speak of them in bitterness. They have chosen their own paths and you cannot fault them for that."

"I do not even know them, Horn. They do not speak to me."

"That is their loss, child. Do not expect them to be like Brave Wolf or anyone else. They are different and have chosen another life from yours."

"I know this. But I feel if one of my brothers should die, it should be one of them. I am sorry, Horn; it is not a good thing to say."

"It is what you feel."

"Yes. I wish I did not feel so strongly for people. It is too hard when you worry about them all the time."

"And do you not think that your parents and husband and brother have the same feelings for you?"

"Yes, I am sure of it."

"They can deal with their feelings but you let them overcome you. You must learn to be strong in spite of the way you feel, child. It will serve you well in the future."

"I do not feel comfortable that you know about my future. Perhaps I cannot live up to your vision."

"You can and you will. It has been told to me."

"Then you must help me, Horn, for I still have so much to learn about myself and others."

"I will help you, child, and you will learn. It is the way of things."

Stalking Horse could think of nothing but Sun Dancer as he rode against the small party of Kiowas. He wielded his lance aggressively and after knocking several warriors from their horses, he jumped to the ground and fought them hand-to-hand with his war club and knife. He knew it was impossible to make the whole Kiowa tribe pay for what only a small band had done to Sun Dancer, but each one that he wounded or killed helped to ease the anger he had carried inside him for so long after Sun Dancer's kidnapping and torture.

He watched as the remaining Kiowas rode away, leaving their dead tribesmen at the feet of the Cheyennes. Stalking Horse looked down at several of the dead men and was overcome by the strange feeling that they looked much as he and his people did. Their customs, language, and beliefs were all different, but they looked much like him and his people. When he killed another Indian, he felt as if he had killed a brother. Then he remembered the scars on Sun Dancer's legs, and the feeling left him as quickly as it had come. It did not matter that the Kiowas looked similar to him and his people, they were still the enemy and would inflict torture upon him and his people at any time. Angrily, he kicked at the body of one of the dead men and swung up onto his horse, leading away the stray horses which ran around riderless.

"You had much anger today." Laughing Bird rode up next to Stalking Horse.

"Yes. It was hard to get Sun Dancer out of my mind."

"She is still scarred?"

"Her legs. Everytime I look at them I feel the anger anew at what they did to her. I do not understand why they torture the women. It is not honorable."

"They are not like us; they think like dogs. They have no respect for women or children."

Stalking Horse looked at Laughing Bird, his eyes blazing with anger. "I would rather cut off my arm or leg than have one of them touch a child of mine!"

"That is why we have to be on our guard against them and the Utes. We must make them understand that we cannot be pushed."

"But then it will be the Sioux, and the Pawnee, and the Blackfeet. Then the white man will come."

"We do not have to fear the white man. He is not interested in us."

"He will be. He will want our land and he will kill us for it."

"You believe the prophecy to be true?"

"I believe it because there are so many white men and we are so few. If we did not fight with one another and all banded together, perhaps there would be a chance for us. But we all continue to fight and it will be easy for the white men to set us against one another. It will happen, Laughing Bird."

"I still do not believe it. There is too much land. We have our land and the white man has his. There is no need to fight over it."

"You are wrong. Even now he comes to our land to trap the beaver. Soon it will be to hunt buffalo and antelope. Then he will want our land to build on but he will not want to live next to us. He will force us away. We will move further west until there is no place to move. There will be nothing for us."

"Why do you think like this, Stalking Horse? You have grown too serious since your marriage. You need to think of your wife and the children you will have with her, the life you will have together."

"It is because of Sun Dancer that I think these thoughts. I want her and our children to be free."

Laughing Bird shook his head in exasperation. "If I were married to Sun Dancer, I would not be so serious as you. I would be the happiest man in the world."

Stalking Horse looked over at the other, anger showing on his face, the anger quickly changing to understanding. "You have loved Sun Dancer a long time."

"Since we were children; she always thought of me as a friend. She did not know my true feelings."

"Perhaps you should have made them known."

"Would it have made a difference to her?"

"Perhaps."

"I think not. Sun Dancer has always loved you, just as I have always loved her. It is a good thing you love her."

"Do not doubt it. I will always take care of her."

"I know that. I am glad she is happy and has what

she wants."

"You are a true friend, Laughing Bird. My wife is most fortunate."

"I am friend to both of you."

"I thank you for this; I have not had many friends in my life. I am honored."

"Then we are both pleased. Talk no more of the white man and our destruction; if it happens, it will not be for many, many summers. Enjoy your life while you are living it."

Stalking Horse nodded slightly, looking at the hills, the feeling of uneasiness coming over him again. He knew what he felt was true, and that it wouldn't be long before they fought with the whites and were eventually overrun by them. He decided to keep these feelings to himself for awhile. His people didn't want to believe that anything would happen to them or their land, so they would go on believing as they had for hundreds of years. But he would always be on watch, alert to any changes or any invasion by the whites. He would try to resist contact with them and watch them from afar. Perhaps, if he were constantly attuned to them, he could anticipate their every move, and he and his family could be safe from their influence and their weapons. He wanted only to live out his life in peace with his wife and the children they would have together. But as he heard his own thoughts, he knew they would never come true.

CHAPTER XIV

Sun Dancer bent over to pick up the wood from the snow, and a sharp pain coursed throughout her abdomen. She reached down and felt the swollen belly, wishing it would soon be over. Looking up at the dark clouds crowding the sky, Sun Dancer felt a deep foreboding. She was embroiled in fear. The pain stopped. She collected the rest of her wood and started back to camp, making an awkward attempt at walking normally in the deep snow. She dropped the wood and left camp for more. Again she looked up at the sky with the dark clouds racing overhead. This was going to be a bad storm which might force them to stay inside for days; it was important that she collect as much wood as possible.

She still had two moons to go before she bore her child, but the pains she had been having for the last few days were not a good sign. She had said nothing to Stalking Horse about them because her mother told her that women always have such pain at the end of their time. Her mother tried to comfort her and still her fears, but Sun Dancer knew that something was wrong when the pains became more frequent and much more intense.

She walked along the riverbank and under the trees to find fallen limbs. After making a small pile, she stooped to pick it up. Again an intense pain shot through her stomach and lower back and she was forced to her knees by its intensity. She knew then that the child was ready to be born; there was no way she could stop it.

She raised herself slowly to one foot but was unable to get up to the other. She sank down to her knees as again pain swept over her in blinding waves. She let herself go with the pain and didn't fight it. After it was gone, she again tried to get to her feet. Snow fell lightly. When she looked up at the somber sky, delicate little flakes fell gently on her face. The wind blew so coldly that she felt the chill in her bones. She remembered the last time she had been caught in the snow and how easily she had succumbed to it. She forced herself to her feet just as another pain swept over her. She walked to a nearby tree and held onto it as the pain went through her; when it was over, she made her way slowly back to camp. It took her some time before she was able to make it to the lodge. When she opened the lodge flaps, Stalking Horse ran to support her as she stumbled through.

"What is it?"

"The child is coming."

"It is too soon."

"I know. It frightens me."

"Sit down here. I will get your mother."

Stalking Horse helped Sun Dancer down to her backrest just as she doubled over from the next pain. He supported her with his arms and then eased her gently to the ground. Her face was covered with sweat and her eyes glistened unnaturally. He threw some logs on the fire and ran from the lodge to get Woman's Heart.

Sun Dancer leaned her head back against the rest and closed her eyes, trying to block out the pain and the fact that the child was coming too early. She breathed deeply and let herself ride with the pain, knowing it would be easier than fighting it. She felt a hand on her forehead and looked up to see her mother's concerned face.

"Let us take off your robe and feel your stomach. Do not be frightened; I am here now."

Sun Dancer smiled weakly. "I am no longer frightened, mother."

Woman's Heart removed Sun Dancer's robe and placed her hands on her daughter's stomach, feeling with practiced hands the placement of the child and the intensity of the contractions. She pressed her hands hard against Sun Dancer's stomach as the next contraction came and went; she nodded glumly to herself and to Stalking Horse.

"The child is coming, daughter. You will have to bear it."

"I know. Can you help me to the other lodge?" Her mother nodded her head. Stalking Horse bent down to lift Sun Dancer in his arms but she pushed him away.

"I am strong," she said angrily, and awkwardly she moved out of the lodge.

Woman's Heart looked at the expression on Stalking Horse's face and she touched his shoulder lightly. "Do not be offended, Stalking Horse, she only tries to be strong for you. She does not wish you to think her weak."

"Can I help? I want to be with her."

Woman's Heart smiled gently at the concern in her son-in-law's face. "I will be with her. It will not be an easy time for her and I do not think the child will live. Your time with her will be after."

Stalking Horse nodded in resignation and watched as Woman's Heart left the lodge. His stomach knotted in fear as he thought of what Sun Dancer was about to go through alone. He had instructed her in many things and had helped prepare her for many situations, but this was one of which he knew nothing. There was aught he could do to ease her pain and fear. Many women in the camp had died giving birth, and he knew that Sun Dancer could be one of them. He picked up a robe and pulled it around his shoulders as he walked outside into the storm. The sky was ominously dark, the snow falling rapidly. He remembered what Sun Dancer had told him once of being frightened of winter, and now he knew her fear. He walked to the birthing lodge and sat outside, wanting to be near her if she needed him. The snow fell over him but he didn't feel its cold so much as he felt the coldness inside him and the helpless feeling that he could lose Sun Dancer and do nothing about it.

Sun Dancer squatted and held the lodge pole as her mother wiped the sweat from her face. The pain wasn't quite so severe in this position as it was lying down, although it tired her legs and back immensely. She knew the child would be born dead, or at least, she felt that it would. Her mother had said nothing to her but she knew from things her mother had said over the years in attending different births. If the child came too early its chances of survival were slim and the infant was usually born dead. She grabbed the pole tightly as another contraction went through her and she groaned slightly as the pain coursed throughout her stomach and back. It was hard for her to believe that she would endure all this pain for nothing, for a lifeless being, but she tried as hard as if the child would be born full of life.

"The pain lasts longer now," Woman's Heart stated as she again wiped Sun Dancer's brow. "Soon the child will come and you will have to push."

Sun Dancer nodded. She closed her eyes and rested her head against the lodge pole. "Please get me something to put in my mouth, mother. I am afraid I will scream. The pain grows worse all the time."

Understanding her daughter's desire to be strong, Woman's Heart pulled out a piece of leather from her parfleche and placed it in her mouth.

"It will be over soon, child." She patted Sun Dancer's head and watched as the young woman tried to bear her pain in silence. Woman's Heart had been through it many times, but it was different seeing her own daughter go through it. She wished she could take the pain from her and bear it herself. Child-bearing was a natural thing, but it was also one of the most painful things a woman would ever have to endure. Woman's Heart pressed against Sun Dancer's belly and nodded to herself. "It is time to push; do you feel you can?"

Sun Dancer nodded and grabbed the pole so tightly

her knuckles turned white. The urge overcame her and she pushed as long as she could before having to rest and regain her breath. She could hear the storm raging outside but she felt hot and her body was drenched in sweat. The pain came again and this time it was like no other. She bit down hard on the piece of leather, a slight moaning sound escaping her lips. She could feel the child's head coming out of her, and she heard her mother's voice telling her to keep pushing. As soon as the child was completely free of her body, she felt an immense relief from the constant pain. She looked up at her mother who held the child in her arms and she knew from her mother's expression that it was dead. She tried to stand to look at it but she was too weak. Her mother knelt down next to her. Sun Dancer looked at the tiny lifeless shape, a boy, and she felt a sorrow unlike any she had ever known. She felt a sudden pain in her stomach and knew the afterbirth was coming. Again she squatted at the pole, pushing until it, too, was expelled. When it was over, she moved over to the side and sat, her eyes dry and tearless, her heart cold as stone. Her mother wrapped the tiny child in a blanket and cleaned up the signs of the birth to take and bury in the snow. Walking over to Sun Dancer, she began to wash her, but the look on Sun Dancer's face instilled great fear in Woman's Heart.

"You will have others. I lost two of my own."

"He was my firstborn."

"It happens to many women, Sun Dancer, and you could do nothing to prevent it."

"If I had taken better care of myself, if I had not ridden so much . . ."

"You are being foolish. The child was meant to die and you must not blame yourself. If he had lived he might have been crippled or blind. It was the best thing."

Sun Dancer flinched at her mother's harsh words but she knew them to be the truth. "He was so small, so helpless."

"I suffer for you child, I know how you feel. But you must not mourn long for this child, for there will be others. You must get on with your life."

"Stalking Horse will be disappointed. He wanted a son."

"Stalking Horse will be happy that you are alive."

Sun Dancer looked up at her mother. "He knew the child would be born dead?"

Woman's Heart nodded and wiped her daughter's face. "I told him the child would have little chance of surviving. He was most concerned for you. He knows you will have many years together and more children. Stalking Horse is not a cold man."

"I know this but I also know that he wanted a son."

"Do not belabor the subject, Sun Dancer. It is over; the child is dead."

Sun Dancer looked up at her mother, tears filling her eyes. "Your words are overly harsh, mother. I feel the death of my son and I cannot forget it so soon. Would you please leave me alone to mourn his death by myself."

Woman's Heart looked at Sun Dancer, took the bundles, and left the lodge. She knew her daughter would be fine; her anger already showed. It was much better to feel anger than sorrow. She started for the edge of camp when she saw Stalking Horse standing

238

outside the lodge.

"It is over?" he asked sadly.

"Yes. The child was born dead."

"And Sun Dancer?"

"She is mourning its loss now. Perhaps you should be with her. It is something a woman can never forget."

Stalking Horse entered the lodge quietly, standing at the doorway before moving toward Sun Dancer. She sat with her legs crossed, her eyes staring unblinking into the fire. She rocked slightly, as if comforting a child, and she sang in a soft voice. Stalking Horse walked to her. He squatted in front of her, taking her cold hands in his. Her eyes didn't waver from the fire.

"I am sorry, Sun Dancer," he said gently, his hands warming hers. "Are you well?"

Sun Dancer turned her eyes to Stalking Horse and noted the deep concern in his face. She wanted to touch him and reassure him but she could not. She could feel nothing for him; she could feel only for herself and their dead child.

"I am not well, Stalking Horse. Our son is dead."

"We will have others."

"Do you know this to be true? Does my mother? Why do you both tell me this and expect it to make my sorrow less? Why can you not both let me feel my sorrow?" She withdrew her hands from his and looked again at the fire. "Please leave me."

Stalking Horse pulled away. He was surprised by her coldness but he sat next to her, hoping that she would soon respond to him. He attempted to touch her shoulder but she shrugged him away and continued to rock back and forth, staring into the fire. Her coldness angered him. He could understand her sorrow but not her anger and resentment toward him. Gently, he turned her to face him.

"I am sorry for you, Sun Dancer, and can never know the loss you feel. I did not know the feeling of life inside of me and I did not see the child's face. But I am glad you are here and alive. The child was important to me but you are always more so. If we cannot have more children then that is the way of it and it is something we must accept. We will always have each other and our life will go on from here. You are the most important thing in this life to me."

Sun Dancer shut her eyes and took a deep breath, her shoulders relaxing perceptibly as she did so. When she opened them, tears streamed down her cheeks and her lips trembled. "Bearing a child is a basic part of being a woman, and I have failed at it. I feel worthless."

"You are foolish, wife, if you feel your worth is measured by the number of children you bear. I can count your worth in many ways and not one of them includes bearing a child."

"But you want a son."

"You say that I want a son; I have never said so. I have said if we have children that will be good, but if we do not, our lives will go on as before. Do not put words in my mouth, Sun Dancer."

She looked at him and lowered her head. She felt confused and angry, but Stalking Horse was not the source of any of her feelings. "You are a good husband and one I do not feel worthy of. Perhaps it would be best if you let me go and took another wife."

Stalking Horse gently but firmly took Sun Dancer's face and turned her toward him. "Have you not heard a word I have said? I have chosen you for my wife; I want no other. If we cannot have children, then that is the way it will be. I want no talk of other wives or children. Would you take another husband if I could not use my arm or my leg? Would you care for me less?" He shook his head. "I think not."

Sun Dancer looked at the strong, gentle face of her husband. She could no longer resist him or the wisdom of his words. She laid her head against his shoulder and let her tears flow unchecked. She felt Stalking Horse's arms go around her, feeling his strength flow throughout her. She knew then that she would be all right. In spite of the sorrow she felt right then and the sorrow she would feel on and off throughout her lifetime, she knew she would always be strong enough to face it. Stalking Horse brought out a great strength within her and because of that and his support, she would be able to face anything.

The winter was unusually long and the Cheyennes moved farther south on the river to make their spring and summer camp. There was excitement in the air—a war party was to be sent to aid their brothers, the Arapahos. The Utes had long plagued the Arapahos, raiding their camps and stealing their horses, women and children. It was now time for action on the part of the Arapahos. They sent word to their Cheyenne allies in their winter camp near the hills. When the

Cheyennes heard that their friends were in need of help, they broke camp to head down the river. It had been a long, restless winter; the men were eager to hone their battle skills. They talked endlessly about strategy and weapons, and they were impatient to meet the Arapahos and go to war.

Sun Dancer was ambivalent about the news. She hid her feelings from Stalking Horse, for he, like the other warriors, was ready to make war after so long a winter. Sun Dancer knew it would be a long raid, for the Utes lived far to the south in the Colorados, and it would be a long trip there and back. She helped Stalking Horse ready his war gear, preparing and packing his horses for the long journey, all the while stifling her desire to ask him to stay. She packed extra moccasins, a robe, and a blanket, along with a sack of pemmican and dried meat. Stalking Horse would lead his war pony as it would be a long journey and he would want to save the horse for the actual fighting.

The pipe was offered around to many men in the camp, which was the ceremonial way of asking them to go along on the war party. In the same manner, the Arapahos had sent the pipe to the Cheyennes to enlist their aid in fighting the Utes. After smoking the pipe and agreeing to go to war, the men marched around the camp, stopping in front of certain lodges and singing war songs. Many of the people from the lodges offered gifts to the departing warriors for good luck. The leader of the party, Brave Wolf, would carry the pipe and go ahead of the others; the rest would follow in single file. While they were on the raid, they would light the pipe and offer it to the sky, the earth, and the four cardinal points. Brave Wolf would then talk to the men of this party and give them advice on the coming battle.

Stalking Horse checked his pack and his weapons, then turned to Sun Dancer, who was unable to hide her anxious feelings. "Do not fear, wife, I will return in good health and with many horses."

"We do not need horses, we need your good health. Be wise in your warring, Stalking Horse, do not become reckless."

"You are lecturing me on the ways of war?"

"I do not seek to lecture on something I know nothing about; I am only concerned for your safety. The Utes, they are dangerous?"

"As dangerous as any and they hate us. The fighting is always worse when the hatred runs strong."

"I would like to go with you sometime. At least I would be near you while you traveled."

"When we go only for horses you can come along. But it would be too dangerous to come along now. There will be much fighting and killing."

Sun Dancer lifted a small leather pouch from the inside of her dress. She reached up and placed it around Stalking Horse's neck. "Wear this. Horn has said a prayer over it."

"It is still warm from you; that is all the medicine I need."

"Keep your mind on war so you can fight well. I will welcome you warmly when you return."

"I will look forward to my return then," Stalking Horse replied playfully, pulling Sun Dancer to him. "You are a pleasing sight, wife. I shall sorely miss your presence. Perhaps it is best you do not come with me, for I would never be able to think of war. Only love."

Sun Dancer placed his hand on her cheek and rubbed it gently. "I will say prayers for you every day while you are gone."

"I will be back before you are able to miss me. Do not wander far from camp alone; I know you are fond of riding. It is too dangerous of late; too many Kiowas and some Sioux have been seen. They will be hungry after the long winter and will be hunting the buffalo. Ride close to camp."

"Do not worry about me, I am able to protect myself now. You are a good teacher."

"You are too confident; you are still only a woman and could do little against a practiced warrior. Do as I say and stay close to camp." One of the men called to Stalking Horse and he nodded. "I must go." He touched her face once more. "You are hard on a man's mind, Sun Dancer." He mounted his horse and leading his war pony behind him, headed off after the others. Sun Dancer watched with a mixture of pride and fear, but suppressed the latter emotion as the riders left the camp. She was the wife of a warrior and she would behave accordingly. With head held high and emotions in check, she walked to the river to collect water for the cooking pot which would only serve one that night.

They had been on the trail for over a week, and it would be many days before they reached Ute territory. The combined Cheyenne and Arapaho war party was large, and they rode in columns next to each other, behind their leaders. The weather was good for riding, and not yet hot enough to make travel uncomfortable. Their days were long, riding from sunup to sundown, but there was never a complaint from any man. They were all accustomed to the rigors of making war. The young boys who accompanied the war parties were assigned the menial tasks that the warriors themselves didn't want to do. Although the boys were treated kindly, they were expected to wait on the chief and the others. They were to use the experience of traveling with a war party to further their own knowledge. When the chief of a war party thought a boy had learned enough to steal a horse, he would let him. Many times, very young boys were seen leading horses from enemy camps in the hopes of pleasing their chief.

The combined forces traveled in a southwestern direction. They crossed the Colorados in spots which had been traveled before, and their innate sense of direction and survival came to good use on such journeys where they knew little of the surrounding terrain. The Arapahos had often fought against the Utes and had traveled in their territory. Their scouts led the way into the enemy land. The party strung out along the way, making a colorful and awesome sight, their bodies painted for war, their ponies in tow, their weapons ever present.

After two days of riding in Ute territory, Buffalo Bull, the war chief of the Arapahos, and Brave Wolf each sent a scout ahead to check on the location of the nearest Ute camp. While the rest of the war party camped, Stalking Horse and Antelope Tongue went on ahead to scout the territory. Stalking Horse and

Laughing Bird were normally sent together as they had proved to be adept and observant scouts, but to be fair, a scout was sent from each camp. Brave Wolf selected Stalking Horse because he knew him to be quick in obtaining the knowledge they needed.

Stalking Horse and Antelope Tongue traveled cautiously, moving silently through ravines and any low places where they could escape detection. They rode a few miles and climbed one of the high hills so they might be able to see any smoke or signs of camp life. They paid close attention to the behavior of the animals. If buffalo were running or wolves sneaked off into the hills looking behind them, the scouts waited with great patience to learn the reasons for the actions of the animals.

Stalking Horse and Antelope Tongue scouted for most of the afternoon before signaling to their bands that it was safe to advance. As their people cautiously moved ahead, the scouts continued to fresh observation points. As the day wore on with no signs of the Utes, Brave Wolf and Buffalo Bull signaled to make evening camp in the hills. After the two scouts had returned for provisions, they traveled on ahead of the main party before making their camp for the night. Stalking Horse and Antelope Tongue alternated watch during the night to make sure no Utes sneaked up on them.

The night was uneventful and the two scouts moved out early the next morning, combing the unfamiliar territory for signs of the enemy. It wasn't until late in the day that Stalking Horse and Antelope Tongue spotted the first Utes. They were camped close to a stand of trees, well hidden from observation. Stalking Horse and Antelope Tongue almost passed them by but they saw smoke furling up through the trees. They left their horses in the hills and made their way on foot to the camp to examine it as closely as possible.

The encampment was a large one with more than forty lodges, and the sounds of women working and children playing could easily be heard as the scouts moved in closer. The Utes would be at a disadvantage because they would see to it that the women and children and old people were safe before they fought. Stalking Horse felt uncomfortable as he looked at the scene below him. He knew how he would feel if his camp were attacked and his wife's life threatened; indeed, he had known the feeling when she was kidnapped by the Kiowas. He didn't like fighting when there were women and children around—one of them might be wounded or killed. Many of his people and their allies felt that the women and children were part of the enemy camp, but he had never felt that way. As far as he was concerned, they were innocents who didn't belong where there was fighting between the men.

"I do not see many warriors," Antelope Tongue said quietly, as he studied the Ute camp. "My hand aches to shoot an arrow through the heart of one of them."

"One of whom?"

"One of the dogs who stole my wife. I will take many lives in repayment of that."

"The women and children are innocent."

"I do not seek to kill women and children. I only seek to be repaid for what has been taken from me."

"That is fair," Stalking Horse nodded and again looked at the camp. He knew Antelope Tongue would steal a woman or two, and probably some of the children. He knew too, that the women would be raped and abused for what their men had done. It was an injustice but one which he could understand. If Sun Dancer were ever taken from him and killed, he too, could be driven to such acts of hatred and revenge.

"Let us return and tell what we have seen."

Silently, the two made their way back up into the hills and to their horses, and equally as silently, they rode back to their main party to report what they had observed. Plans were made to attack the sleeping camp. As soon as it was dark, the entire party made their way along the rough trails into the hills where Stalking Horse and Antelope Tongue had been only hours before. They left their mounts with the younger men and boys; they took only their weapons. Silently, they stole down the hills to lie hidden close to the Ute camp, waiting for the campfires and conversation to die down. Already, some of the warriors were rounding up the horses grazing in the hills, herding them up to the boys who would care for them on the journey home. The Cheyennes and Arapahos sat waiting for the Ute camp to fall asleep. Most of them had been in this position before and knew well the discipline and patience required when raiding an enemy camp. Sometimes the waiting went on for hours and even then the circumstances weren't right to permit them to complete their raid.

Stalking Horse sat with his lance in his hand, his war club secured to his waist, his knife at his thigh.

When he fought hand to hand, he preferred these weapons opposed to his bow and arrows which he used when on horseback. He ran his fingers along the smoothness of the lance and again felt the strange feeling in his stomach when he thought of what it was used for. Killing was not abhorrent to him, he had done that many times; but killing for senseless reasons was something he could neither understand nor condone. And killing innocent people was something he could never see himself doing.

The hours passed slowly until Stalking Horse was sent to check on the Ute camp. By the time he returned, the Utes had become still and all of the campfires had burned themselves out. Stalking Horse remained for better than an hour before he was sure no one was awake in the camp. The Utes had posted no guards as they were secure in the knowledge that no one would enter their territory. It would be all too easy, Stalking Horse thought to himself.

Brave Wolf gave his men the order to move into the camp. Slowly and in pairs, the Cheyennes and Arapahos made their way into the enemy camp. Horses were cut from their ties and led away, while any trappings which belonged were also taken, as well as any supplies, weapons, or meat hanging from racks. The Arapahos impatiently and angrily took as many horses as they could. Stalking Horse and the Cheyennes knew there would be a fight; the Arapahos hadn't brought them all this way just to steal horses. Once they had stolen as many horses as possible and had taken them safely to their men in the hills, he knew the fighting would begin.

The cry rang out sooner than anyone expected when a woman who was leaving her lodge, frightened by the movement of the men, screamed loudly, running back into the lodge for her husband. Suddenly, Ute warriors appeared from everywhere, angry and ready to fight. The Arapahos and Cheyennes had the advantage, as they were prepared to fight and their weapons were ready. But being experienced plains fighters, the Utes found their own weapons and fought back eagerly. Fighting in enemy territory was one thing, but fighting in defense of one's own camp was different. The Utes screamed loudly and fought boldly, angered by this intrusion of their own camp.

Stalking Horse fought with his club, striking swift blows to the arms and shoulders of the enemy. When he or one of the others touched one of the Utes without killing him, the scream "Ah haih," was heard for the sound of counting a coup. The Cheyennes and Arapahos soon took over the camp, the remaining Ute warriors having scattered or been killed. This had been an easy raid for most of the Utes were away on a hunt, believing their camp safe. The Arapahos pillaged the camp, taking anything they wished, including women and children. Stalking Horse was done with his fighting; he was ready to leave the camp when he heard a piercing scream. He turned to see an Arapaho warrior beating a young woman, throwing her to the ground. Stalking Horse had never interfered with any man during a raid, but there was something about the girl's scream which caught his attention. He ran to them; the girl was young and pretty, and reminded him of Sun Dancer.

He moved forward and pulled the warrior from her.

"She is a mere child, leave her be," he said forcefully.

"This is none of your matter. I found her first." He pulled away from Stalking Horse's grasp but was again pulled back, this time held in place by a firm grasp on each arm.

"Do not hurt her." His voice was cold and ominous. The Arapaho relented.

"I will not hurt her but she is mine. I will take her back to my camp."

Stalking Horse nodded slightly and again looked at the terrified girl, who looked at him with pleading eyes. He could do nothing now without causing a fight between him and the man, but at least he could make sure that the girl wasn't abused while they rode together. He turned away.

The raid had been a success and many horses stolen, as well as many coup counted on the Utes. Having collected all of their horses and captives, the war party quickly rode for their own country, wanting to get far away from the Ute camp in case their warriors returned. They rode all night and all of the next day before making camp. Backriders were sent to make sure no Utes followed, but they made good time with the many horse changes they were able to make. They had gone into Ute territory, raided one of their camps, and gotten safely away with no deaths among their ranks.

After the pipe had been lit and passed around, the members of the war party sat around the fire eating boiled meat, each relating his own story of the raid. The men who had counted coup related the incident and it was either confirmed or denied by the others who had seen it. Captives were bought and traded, horses compared and gambled over. Walking around the camp, Stalking Horse found the Ute girl he had saved. She was tied with the rest of the captives at the far end of the camp, the terrified look still on her face. He walked up to her. Not knowing her language, he signed to her.

"Do you wish to go with the Arapaho?"

The young girl shook her head vehemently. She reminded him of a doe he had once caught in a trap, its eyes pleading with him for freedom. He hadn't relented then but he knew he would now. He immediately sought out the Arapaho who had captured the girl.

"I wish to buy the girl from you," he stated firmly. He would tolerate no resistance.

"And what will you pay me for her?"

"Ten of the horses I have just caught. It is a fair price. She is young and inexperienced and worth little more than that."

"Then why do you wish to buy her?" The Arapaho taunted him.

Stalking Horse looked at the man with cold eyes. "Because I do not wish to see her abused by you. I will give her to someone in marriage. I myself already have a wife."

"Then you do not need a second," the Arapaho stated matter-of-factly. He turned his back on Stalking Horse.

Stalking Horse pulled the man's shoulder, forcing him to turn around. "Either you will sell her to me or I will fight you for her. It is your decision."

The man stared at Stalking Horse's cold, black eyes, not fooled by his youthful appearance. He had seen him fight in the Ute camp and knew that he was an able warrior. He didn't know why the man wanted the girl so badly, but ten horses was more than a fair price to pay for her. Besides, ten more horses added to the ones he'd already stolen would make a sizable amount. The girl was not worth fighting over nor risking a breach with their allies. He nodded his head.

"She is yours, friend, but little do I understand of a man who is willing to give up ten war ponies for a mere girl."

Stalking Horse told the man he would cut out his horses early in the morning, and he walked back to his sleeping place. He sat down and stared off into the distance, wondering, as the Arapaho did, why he had just given up ten good horses for a girl he cared nothing about.

CHAPTER XV

Sun Dancer was wading through the stream trying to catch turtles, when she heard the shouts of the warrior who was sent to the village to signify the return of the war party. She quickly jumped out of the water and raced to the entrance of the village, eagerly awaiting the arrival of her husband. She was joyous because it had been announced that there had been no deaths. Everyone in the camp sang happily about the success of the war party.

Sun Dancer spotted Brave Wolf and he smiled at her as he rode past, his warrior-like bearing filling her heart with pride. Her eyes followed him as he rode past and she felt a rush of love for the older brother who had always taken time to care for and love her. As she turned back she saw Stalking Horse sitting proudly on his horse, his head held high, a queer expression on his face. He took little notice of Sun Dancer as he rode by and she wondered if he had been wounded. It was only after his horse passed her that she saw a beautiful young Ute girl following closely beind him. She felt a pain in her stomach and her legs felt weak and unsteady. She felt the curious stares of the women around her. They whispered and pointed to Stalking Horse's young captive, making obscene gestures as to what Stalking Horse's intentions were with the girl. Sun Dancer moved slowly to their lodge.

Although the camp was bustling with excitement, Sun Dancer felt little of it as she made her way past the people to her own lodge. She remembered telling Stalking Horse to let her go and take another wife when she had lost their child, but she didn't think he would actually do it. Her heart ached and she felt her eyes sting from tears she refused to shed. She waited outside the lodge door for a few minutes before going in. When she entered, her eyes swept the inside of the lodge for the girl and she saw her sitting on Stalking Horse's robes. Quickly, her sadness and fear turned to anger.

Stalking Horse smiled when he saw Sun Dancer, and moving toward her, he placed his hands on her shoulders and pulled her toward him. "It is good to see you wife; I have ached for you." His words were gentle and any other time they would have made Sun Dancer pliant in his arms.

"I see you did not ache overmuch." His gaze followed hers as she looked at the Ute girl.

"Her name is Spring. I bought her from an Arapaho."

"You bought her? You did not think one wife was enough?"

"I did not buy her for my wife. I bought her because I did not wish to see her abused. She reminded me of you."

She looked at him then and saw the gentleness in

his eyes and she relented somewhat. "I did not know your heart was so soft. I have never known you to do such a thing."

"I never did such a thing before you," he said softly, running his hands over her face. "My need for you is great." His eyes drilled into hers and she felt the familiar weakness she always felt when he looked at her so.

"I do not wish to fulfill your need in front of the girl. I wish to be alone with you."

Stalking Horse nodded and led the girl to the door of the lodge. Before going out she stopped and turned back to look at Sun Dancer, a slight smile appearing on her face. She looked young and vulnerable and frightened, and Sun Dancer was unable to refuse her a smile. The girl went out of the lodge with orders from Stalking Horse to remain on the ground outside of it. He walked back in and pulled Sun Dancer back to his robes.

"It has been too long." He pulled her down to him and quickly pulled her dress up over her head.

"The girl is beautiful," she tried to interrupt, but Stalking Horse was impatient.

"Do not talk of the girl now. I only wish to feel your softness and your warmth. We need speak no words."

Sun Dancer looked up at him as he hovered above her for a few moments, then she put her arms around his neck and pulled him down to her. She too, ached with the need of him and she let him know it. She never wanted him to forget what love with her was like.

* * *

"Perhaps you should keep the girl. She is young and healthy and quite lovely; she can give you children." Sun Dancer looked down at Stalking Horse as she traced invisible figures on the robe. She had to say what had been on her mind since first seeing Spring.

"Perhaps she can give me children," Stalking Horse answered smugly. "I do not want to decide now. I will think awhile on it." He lay on his back, his arms behind his head, looking up at the top of the lodge.

"You are considering taking her for your wife then?" Sun Dancer's voice wavered in spite of her firm resolve to make it steady.

"You seem to be considering it for me. Now that I think on it, I would not mind two beautiful, young wives."

"You would not have two beautiful, young wives. I will not share you with anyone."

"You know I can have more than one wife."

"Yes, but it does not mean that I accept it. If you choose to take Spring for your wife, you will have to divorce me."

"I will not divorce you." His voice was hard as he turned his gaze from the ceiling to her.

"Then I will run away." Sun Dancer's voice trembled. She couldn't control her words.

"No one would marry you; you would still be a married woman."

"It would not matter for I would not choose to marry again."

He reached out and touched her arm, rubbing the soft skin which was now so familiar to him. "No man could take my place then?" His voice contained a note of amusement but Sun Dancer was not amused. She sat up, suddenly shy of her nakedness. She reached for her dress but Stalking Horse pulled it from her hands. "Answer me."

She looked at him, trying to maintain her self-control; she felt her whole body weaken as she looked into his eyes. She looked down at the floor, her long silken hair partially covering her face. "There is no one else. If I cannot have you, then I want no one."

Stalking Horse sat up, reaching over to tilt Sun Dancer's chin up. Her eyes glistened slightly; she attempted to control her tears. "I am playing with you and I should not. Our love is no game. I do not want Spring for my wife; you are the only wife I will ever want." He pulled her head so it rested against his broad chest, his hand stroking her hair. "Your emotions are too deeply felt for me to make jest of them. I am sorry for that."

"I will not hold you if ever you choose to have another," Sun Dancer mumbled softly against his shoulder. "I would rather give you up than share you."

"Do not worry, wife, I will never choose to give you up. You are part of me now. No one could replace what you have already given me."

Sun Dancer looked up, her eyes bright with love. She wrapped her arms around his neck and pressed her naked body against his. There was no need for more words as Stalking Horse laid her down and felt the full bloom of her youthfulness and beauty open up to him. Afterwards, when their desire was sated, he looked for a long while at her peaceful face. He could imagine loving her as much when they were old and unable to fulfill their desires in this way, as he did now. When their physical love had become a clear memory in an otherwise cloudy mind, they would still have each other. When their days on the earth were over, he would take her hand and walk into the next world and onward, until they were together for all eternity. He closed his eyes and let the full sweep of emotion overcome him. He realized for the first time the full force of their love; it had transcended the physical and now encompassed the spiritual.

Spring was not only pretty, she was skilled and quick to learn as well. She had already picked up many Cheyenne sentences in the few weeks she'd been with them. She did everything in her power to please Stalking Horse, which made Sun Dancer distrust her even more. Stalking Horse decided to keep her until he found a suitable husband for her. Sun Dancer was proud that Stalking Horse was so caring of another, but she was not above wishing the person was someone other than Spring.

Sun Dancer displayed no outward dislike for Spring, even taking her along on her walks to the river and woods to collect different herbs and roots. Since her day spent with Horn, she had decided to learn about as many of the plants as possible and then go back to Horn for more teaching. Spring seemed as interested as Sun Dancer and was quick to learn the different plants. After awhile, in spite of the way Spring threw herself at Stalking Horse and did everything she could to be near him, Sun Dancer grew to have some affection for the girl. She was very bright and spirited and Sun Dancer was reminded of herself only a few years before. When she found out Spring was able to ride as well as she, they began taking long rides in the morning and evening; it was something they both looked forward to. Sun Dancer admired the girl's adaptability and was not so sure that she herself would have been able to adapt so well to an enemy's way of life.

Winter wore itself out and summer came early. The weather was soon burning hot. Sun Dancer pitied the small children and babies who couldn't understand the intensity of the heat, and the women, who, like herself, were with child. Soon after they made summer camp, Sun Dancer knew she was pregnant for the second time. She felt a mixture of joy and apprehension at this knowledge, for she feared that this child too would be stillborn. However, she realized she was being given another chance and she was thankful for that. She decided to wait before telling Stalking Horse. He wouldn't guess if she missed her visits to the bleeding hut, for she had missed them many times when her cycle was irregular. She wanted to make sure the child was alive and growing inside of her before she told her husband.

Sun Dancer was ill with this pregnancy and it forced her to go to Horn for help. She had grown thin and weak by the time she went to him, and he worried for her health.

"You should have come sooner, child. You take too much on yourself."

"I thought it was just the heat. I have seen others

260

grow weak and tired in this terrible heat. But I have been unable to eat, Horn. Nothing stays in my stomach. I worry that the baby will get nothing to eat."

"The baby will eat from you and will grow strong. It is you I worry about." He went over to one of his pots and took out some of the pulverized whortle-berry. He placed a small handful in some water and gave it to Sun Dancer to drink.

"What is this?"

"*Mahkimins*, little red berry. It is good for one who is sick in the stomach and cannot eat. I will give you some to take every morning. Drink it down." Sun Dancer did as she was told and her eyes followed Horn as he went to another of his pots. He took out some of the powder and mixed a bit in some water and handed it to Sun Dancer. "This will also help. I will give you some of this to take at night." Sun Dancer drank the liquid.

"I feel silly, Horn. I am a young, healthy woman and have never been ill. What is wrong?"

"Many women feel this sickness when they are carrying a child. Your body is not used to the presence of the child in it and reacts in this way. Drink the rest of it." Sun Dancer drank the rest of the liquid down.

"You did not tell me what this liquid was for."

"It will help to make you relax. You will feel like sleeping."

"But I do not wish to sleep. I have many things to do."

"You will stay here and rest. I would like to look at you when you wake up. If I think your color is good and you look better, then you can return to your lodge. If you are no more rested and your stomach still pains you, you will stay here until I find something which can help you."

Sun Dancer began to feel the effects of the drink and lay down on the robe on which she was sitting. "I do not wish to lose this child, Horn. I want to give Stalking Horse a healthy child."

"We will do what we can. Sleep now, child, for it is the best thing."

"Do not tell Stalking Horse of this. I want to make sure the child and I are healthy first."

"I will not tell Stalking Horse unless I think he needs to be told. Now close your eyes and sleep."

Horn watched the young woman sleeping peacefully, and he shook his head in anger and frustration. He knew his ministrations would do nothing to help Sun Dancer. It was out of his hands. All he could do was lessen the pain for now but he could do nothing about the pain which would result when she lost this child.

Stalking Horse watched as Sun Dancer tried to hide her pain and frustration. The weather was almost unbearably hot and even the oldtimers couldn't remember such a hot summer. There was talk of breaking camp and moving up to one of the cooler mountain valleys if the heat didn't break. Sun Dancer's stomach was large but the rest of her was thin; Stalking Horse worried constantly about her. He had a deep-rooted feeling that something would go wrong with this pregnancy too, and he refused to leave her side.

Although Sun Dancer followed Horn's instructions and took the medicine and rested, she still demanded to do all her same chores. It was especially important to her now that she was heavy with her child to prove that she was still capable of doing things and that she wasn't a weak woman. Spring seemed to grow lovelier every day, and Sun Dancer could see the way Stalking Horse looked at her when she served him his food or when she bent over the fire to cook. They hadn't been together for some weeks now, and she was sure it would be at least two moons before they could be. She knew his desire was great; it showed every time he looked at Spring. Sun Dancer felt that she was no longer the object of his desire, and she fretted over it constantly.

As the summer grew still hotter and her burden heavier, Sun Dancer was forced to limit some of her activities. She was too tired to bring water from the stream or to collect wood for the fire; she spent a great deal of her time resting outside the lodge. She knew she was providing Spring a perfect opportunity to be with Stalking Horse, but she could do nothing about it. Perhaps she should tell Stalking Horse to take Spring and satisfy his desires, but she was afraid that he would always want her once he tasted her sweetness. He didn't have to marry Spring, as she was Ute and was not obligated to observe the strict moral codes of the Cheyennes, but she could be his woman. She wondered how so many of the women were able to deal with their husbands' other wives, but she couldn't find an answer. Perhaps they didn't feel the kind of love she felt for Stalking Horse and cared little if their husband had others; or perhaps, their love was so great that it mattered not what their husbands did or whom they loved. She sighed deeply and ran her hands over her large stomach. She felt the movement inside as the child kicked and was reassured that it was still alive.

The air was so still that Sun Dancer felt stifled. Some of the old people and children had died from the heat, and she was frightened that she too would succumb. With great difficulty, she got to her feet and started toward the river. Her legs felt heavy and swollen, the skin so tightly drawn that they stung when she walked. She wished Stalking Horse were with her, but he was hunting and had consented to let Spring ride with him. She tried to push the picture of the two of them riding together out of her mind, but her attempt was unsuccessful. She could see that young girl as she followed Stalking Horse into the woods and then as she took off her clothes and gave herself to him. She knew then that Stalking Horse would take Spring, and it wasn't so shocking as she thought it would be. She sat down on the banks, removing her moccasins and thrusting her feet into the cool water. Most of the people spent their entire day at the river because it was the only cool place in the camp.

Sun Dancer chose a secluded place by the woods, thankful for the tranquility of the spot. A slight breeze blew through the cottonwoods, and she closed her eyes to hear the sounds of the woods and the laughter and words of her people in the distance. Tears stung her eyes suddenly and she covered her face as she began to cry. She felt she had no control over her life—a terrifying thought. She was sure

Horn knew more about her than he was willing to say. She was frightened by the thought that her life had already been laid out for her, that there was nothing she could do to change it; just as she couldn't change the fact that Stalking Horse would sate his desire with Spring, and possibly take her for his wife.

Sun Dancer's blank, watery eyes looked at the water in the river and saw nothing but turmoil. She didn't want to live her life knowing what would happen from day to day. She felt defeated and disillusioned, and she doubted whether her love would ever be the same again.

Stalking Horse motioned for Spring to be still as silently he stalked the deer. He watched as the animal turned its head from time to time, listening for any foreign sound, lowering it again and chomping on the wild grass, mindless of the man who was about to kill it.

He moved closer and quietly removed an arrow from its quiver, placing it against the bow. Slowly and skillfully he drew back the string and aiming for a point below the deer's shoulder, he let fly the arrow. The deer jerked in shock and then stumbled forward and fell, its head twisting off to the side as its shoulders hit the ground first. Stalking Horse walked to the animal and pulled the arrow from it, replacing it in the quiver. He lifted the animal up and carried it back to his horse, hefting it over the horse's back. Spring followed him out of the woods and back to their horses. She was in awe of his skill and wasted little time telling him so.

Stalking Horse looked at the girl and stifled a

desire to push her to the ground and fill her with his manhood. She had been obvious in her efforts to please him and he found it difficult to resist her. But his mind always came back to Sun Dancer and the fact that she was carrying his child.

"Can we swim before we return to camp? It is so hot." Spring cajoled Stalking Horse as they mounted their horses.

"Yes, I know of a place," he replied, thinking of a small lake which was secluded from everything. He knew then that he would give in to his desires.

They rode for a short distance and dismounted, Stalking Horse leading the way to a small, clear lake, which looked tantalizing in its coolness. Spring wasted no time, giggling girlishly as she ran to the lake. She turned to look at Stalking Horse as she lifted her dress over her head and stooped to take off her moccasins. She laughed and ran into the water, knowing he would soon follow.

Stalking Horse shut his eyes and took a deep breath; he followed Spring to the edge of the water. She looked exactly as he had thought she would, and she was willing to satisfy his needs. He removed his moccasins and leggings and was dressed only in his breechclout when he entered the water. He dove down, swimming for a distance until his breath ran out, then stood up to look for Spring. She was laughing and splashing water at him but he was in no mood for games. He grabbed her arm and pulled her from the water, dragging her to the ground. He wasn't in a loving mood and his movements were filled with anger and violence. Spring showed little fear when Stalking Horse plunged into her, making

266

her cry out as he did so. The whole while he sated himself with Spring, Stalking Horse thought of Sun Dancer and what it would do to her. He was angry and frustrated, disillusioned at his own weakness. When he was through, he dove into the river once more to cleanse himself, then he quickly got dressed and ordered Spring to do the same.

Spring tried to speak several times on their way back to camp, but when Stalking Horse ignored her and kept his gaze straight ahead, she made no further attempts. Stalking Horse was in no mood to talk with the woman he had just used, and his guilt was great as he thought of her and Sun Dancer. He knew that he would never have Spring again. She was young and pretty and had tried to help him fulfill a need which had been great for a long while. But she was not Sun Dancer. Sun Dancer was the only one who could fill that need and that void. Never again would he try to use someone else to take her place.

Slowly, Sun Dancer made her way back to camp, unwilling to face what was there when she returned. Stalking Horse's hunting pony was outside the lodge and she paused. "I cannot face him," she said softly. "I cannot bear the look he will have when he tells me." She wiped her hand across her forehead, beads of perspiration forming as soon as she wiped them off. She walked to the lodge and entered. Stalking Horse was hanging up his bow and quiver and turned to face her. The look on his face was grim as he walked to her. He was silent, his look searching, as his eyes scanned her face.

"Tell me," she said firmly and looked steadily into

his eyes.

"I have had Spring." The statement was simple, but the force of it was more than Sun Dancer could bear. She knew he would say it but she had been unprepared for the shock.

"I know," she replied weakly and turned to leave the lodge. "I will be in the lodge of my parents. I will get my things later." She turned once more to look at him, her face sad and tired. "She will never be me."

He watched her as she bent over slightly and walked through the door. The heat inside the lodge was stifling but he didn't notice. All he noticed was the emptiness inside of him when Sun Dancer walked through the door and out of his life.

CHAPTER XVI

Sun Dancer waved at her mother and father as she and Brave Wolf rode from the camp. She looked forward to being with Broken Leaf and she knew that her friend would provide the emotional support she needed in her life right now.

As much as she tried, she couldn't keep her eyes from Stalking Horse's lodge when they passed. His horses were picketed in front and she wondered if he and Spring were inside together. She forced the thought from her mind and looked to the countryside ahead.

"I hope this will heal the pain," Brave Wolf stated as he watched his sister look at the lodge of her husband. "He is a good man, Sun Dancer, and has done nothing wrong. We have all taken other women. It is the role of the wife to understand."

Sun Dancer looked at her brother disdainfully, her eyes narrowing to dark slits. "It is not my role, brother, and it is one I will never accept. My heart is not big enough to share Stalking Horse with others."

"It has nothing to do with the heart. It has to do

with physical needs. You were unable to fulfill his needs at the time so he found his fulfillment elsewhere. You are too hard on him."

"Perhaps," she said thoughtfully. "That is why I need to be away from here and him. Perhaps I will see things in a different light when I am without him for awhile."

"You have already been without him for awhile," Brave Wolf reminded her.

"Yes," Sun Dancer nodded to herself, and recalled the time Stalking Horse visited her after she lost their second child. She had been angry and bitter and had deliberately blamed the death of the child on him. He had left and never again had he come to see her.

"What will you do if he does not divorce you?"

"I will stay with the Arapahos and live their kind of life. They have no strict codes there."

"But you are not that way and could never live as they do. You try to fool yourself into believing things which you want to believe."

"You do not know what I feel, brother, so please do not judge me. I am not yet capable of dealing with other feelings."

"Perhaps it is time you learned to then," Brave Wolf replied sternly and rode off ahead of her.

Sun Dancer drew her mouth into a grim line and didn't attempt to catch up to her brother. She had heard enough recriminations from him and her parents. In spite of their warnings and pleadings, this was something she felt she had to do. It was her small attempt to place some control over her life, even if her life had been prearranged by the *maiyun*. And if it had been, then the end to the road would come out the same. She had to do as her feelings directed her.

Sun Dancer enjoyed their ride to the Arapaho camp. She enjoyed the freedom of the long ride, the ability to hunt alongside her brother, and the ease with which they spoke. He was not one to hide his feelings and he constantly berated Sun Dancer for being a foolish young woman and leaving her husband. But, he was also her brother and there was that part of him which understood and loved her and supported her in her decision. She loved him more than she did when they were children and she prayed that he would live to be old, as Horn said he might.

She was somewhat frightened of being away from her own camp for so long, but she felt that it was better this way. Fall was already quite cold. By the time she settled in with the Arapahos, it would be winter, and she would be forced to move with them to their winter camping grounds. She had made sure to bring her winter robe, a long, dark brown fur of a buffalo bull, which her father had killed and her mother had tanned and quilled for her when she was just ten summers old. Then it had been so long for her she dragged its length on the ground, but now it came to her ankles and it still left plenty for a hood at the top. She also brought her winter moccasins, which were lined with fur on the inside and top, and one of her winter dresses, which was heavier with longer sleeves and a higher neck. She thought of how the winter frightened her. This would be the first she had spent without Stalking Horse or her family, but she felt it was important for her to be on her own now. She had to take what little control of her life she could to overcome any doubts and fears she now had.

The Arapahos were still busy killing buffalo for winter meat, the women tanning hides and making robes, working endless days. Sun Dancer was glad to arrive at a time when her help would be needed, for it would keep her hands as well as her thoughts busy. Her people had finished their killing of the buffalo and were already making ready to leave for their winter camp. They were farther north than the Arapahos and the winter came much sooner there.

Broken Leaf was happy to see Sun Dancer, although she showed little surprise at her sudden presence. There was little time for talk the first few days. They worked from dawn until dusk, immediately going to bed after the evening meal. Brave Wolf left after a few days and Sun Dancer was saddened to see him go. She was now on her own to make her way as she chose; there was no family to guide her now.

Sun Dancer often wondered what Stalking Horse thought of her decision to leave; she wondered if he even thought of her at all. She knew that he had not given Spring away in marriage, yet she never saw them together in camp. She had seen Spring a few times at the river when she was getting water, and the girl looked at her with gleaming, triumphant eyes which made Sun Dancer want to take her knife and slit the girl's throat. Instead, she avoided the girl's gaze and the girl whenever possible.

As the days progressed and the work began to become routine, Sun Dancer had more time to think. She and Broken Leaf still had not discussed her reasons for being here, and Sun Dancer knew that Broken Leaf was waiting for her to tell her on her own. She knew what Broken Leaf would say about her strict moral code, and she didn't think she was ready to be rebuked again for her decision to leave her husband.

The air grew steadily colder. Lodges were taken down and travois made to carry the families' possessions. The Arapahos made the long trek to the winter camping grounds, and there was now no way for Sun Dancer to return to her own people until the following spring. She had wanted it this way, had planned it, but she was now apprehensive about her decision. She knew she had run away from her problems rather than confront them, and she felt something less than honorable about it.

They camped in the hills below the mountains, close to the trees for protection and for small game. Although the weather was cold and the wind blew frequently, the snows had not yet come. There had been flurries but nothing covered the ground. Thunder Strikes, the Arapaho medicine man, said that this was a sign that when snow did come, it would last for days. Sun Dancer chilled at the thought.

When their winter camp was made and a place provided for Sun Dancer, Broken Leaf and Sun Dancer concentrated on hunting small game for the family. Sun Dancer was grateful that Broken Leaf's parents welcomed her so openly, but she wanted to do more than her share of the work. She wanted to hunt and bring in fresh meat whenever she could. Sun Dancer had never hunted with any woman except Broken Leaf and again she was pleased to find that Broken Leaf was so adept at it. They spent hours together in the chill wind, trapping and hunting rabbits, foxes, beaver and small deer. They relished the daily activity and the cold wind against their cheeks; they knew that soon their movements would be limited to walking to the river for water and wood.

"It is good having you here," Broken Leaf looked over at Sun Dancer as they stood looking down at the rushing river that would soon be frozen.

"You have not even asked me why I am here."

"I do not have to ask why."

Sun Dancer looked at her friend, saw the compassion in her eyes, and knew it was time to talk. "I fear I have been either a fool or a small-hearted person; perhaps both."

"It is Stalking Horse?"

Sun Dancer nodded and lowered her head, feeling much like a small child who is confessing to some lie or wrong deed. "In the spring, Stalking Horse returned with some of your men from a war with the Utes. He brought along a Ute captive, a girl. She is young and beautiful and was so grateful to Stalking Horse for saving her from one of your men, that she tried to do everything for him. I asked him if he planned to take her for his wife but he assured me he did not want another wife. He said he was waiting for the right man for her and he would give her away in marriage. Some moons passed and I found out that I was again with child. I grew very ill and could do little by my last months. I could see Stalking Horse desired Spring more and more. It was not long before he took her."

"In your lodge?" Broken Leaf was somewhat surprised that a man like Stalking Horse would take another woman in front of Sun Dancer.

"No. They were hunting. He told me when they came back that he had taken the girl, but I knew it already. I could not live with him and the girl, knowing what they had done, so I left. Not long after that, I lost the child. I felt such bitterness and anger toward Stalking Horse and Spring that I wanted them both to die."

"Have you seen him since?"

"Only once, when he came to see me after I lost the child. He was greatly pained by it, but my sorrow was only for me that day, and I cruelly blamed him for the death of the child. He walked out and I have not seen him again." Sun Dancer covered her face with her hands, as if trying to blot out the painful memories. "He is still with Spring."

Broken Leaf said nothing for awhile, waiting until she felt sure Sun Dancer was ready to listen. When Sun Dancer lifted her head and looked over at Broken Leaf, the older girl smiled indulgently, placing her arm around Sun Dancer's shoulders. "I am not one to judge you, *navese*, for I have not been raised like you."

"I do not seek your judgment, only your advice."

"I believe you already know my thoughts on this."

"I do. But thoughts are not so easily applied to life."

"Yes, that is true. But you still love Stalking Horse, do you not?"

"Deeply."

"Then what is more important, your husband or your belief that man and woman should act in a certain manner?" Sun Dancer looked at her noncommittally. "You yourself have stated that you are different from other people in your tribe. When you were growing up you did not wish to be as the other girls were; you wished to be like the boys to run and hunt and ride and be free like the wind. You are like a river which comes to two forks, one straight, the other curved; you are unable to choose which fork to take."

"Why not choose both forks?"

"Why not?" Broken Leaf emphasized to her friend. "Some of your traditional beliefs are good and make you what you are, just as your non-traditional beliefs are a part of you. You have already chosen both forks of the river but do not realize it. I think you know, too, that what Stalking Horse did was not wrong; you just cannot accept the fact that he desired another woman. Your pride has been injured."

"Would not yours be?"

"Perhaps. But did not Stalking Horse accept you as you were when you were growing up? He was not attracted to you because you were like the other girls, but because you were different."

"I am selfish. I do not wish to share Stalking Horse with anyone."

"And you would go so far as to give him up completely rather than permit him to have another woman occasionally? I do not see your thinking in this, *navese*," Broken Leaf again used the Cheyenne word for sister. She felt it brought her closer to Sun Dancer. "As before, you make things difficult when they should be simple."

Sun Dancer looked at the water below her and felt that her feelings and emotions were like the turbulent, rushing water. She kicked some rocks from the side of the bank and watched them bounce off the side and fall into the water, immediately disappearing in the rush and swirl.

"I am beginning to see that I have been wrong in my thinking toward my husband. But it is not only that. It is that I have lost two children. I have felt them live and grow inside me. I have seen their delicate little bodies when they were born dead. It is something that no one else can feel but me. It is a sorrow I do not wish to feel again."

"My heart feels much pain for you, and it is something I have not yet felt. But do not blame Stalking Horse for their deaths."

Sun Dancer shook her head thoughtfully. "I do not. He could do nothing. When I lost the second one, it was easy for me to blame him because he had been with Spring. It was wrong of me, I know. I felt such pain at the time, I wanted him to feel it, too."

"But you would not let him."

"No. I would share nothing with him."

"And now? What are your thoughts now? I sense that you feel something else. What is it?"

"I feel the fault lies with me, that I am to blame for losing our children. My body is not made to bear healthy children. I should not even try."

"What do you mean?"

"Perhaps it is best if Stalking Horse stays with Spring. She is young and strong and healthy. She can give him many children."

"You are all of these things and not much older than Spring. How do you know you cannot bear healthy children? Can you see into the future?"

"No, but I feel it was not meant to be. There will be no children for me."

"I cannot believe this is you I hear speaking," Broken Leaf shook her head in exasperation. "This talk of yours frightens me."

Sun Dancer reached over and touched Broken Leaf's arm, a half smile on her face. "Do not be frightened, I still speak out of my sorrow. That is why I needed to come here, to be away from it and Stalking Horse. Sometimes, my father has often told me, one can see more clearly when one steps back to see things from a distance. I am doing that now."

The first storm of winter came and lasted for five days, during which the villagers couldn't go outside for more than a few minutes. Broken Leaf and Sun Dancer quilled and played the stone game, but soon they both yearned to be outside and roaming about. It was during these times that Sun Dancer most missed Stalking Horse, for she often recalled the many times that they had lain in each other's arms during a storm, fulfilling each other's needs until there was nothing left to do but sleep.

"You long for your husband now," Broken Leaf whispered to Sun Dancer. "The winter will be a long one for you."

"The longest of my life, I fear."

The minute the storm ceased and the snow was pushed from in front of lodge doors, people came out of their lodges to walk around and collect more wood for their fires. Broken Leaf and Sun Dancer were like small children and they ran awkwardly through the deep snow to check on some of the traps they had set in the woods. Already some of the hunters were setting off to find fresh game, while some of the children ran for the ice to play and slide on it with their old hides. The camp would be busy until the next storm.

As the girls made their way through the woods, they heard sounds. Sun Dancer immediately drew out her hunting knife, recalling the incident with the wolves. When they investigated further, they saw it was only a deer with her fawn scampering gingerly through the deep snow. For once Sun Dancer was glad she didn't have her bow and arrow, for to look at these wild animals and not to have to kill them was a pleasure she or any Indian could seldom indulge in.

The girls caught three rabbits in their traps, reset them and headed back toward camp. They skinned and gutted them, placing the meat in the cooking pot to boil. The thick rabbit's fur was not only soft, but could be used to line the inside of their moccasins. Most of the hunters came back successful, as the animals, too, had come out as soon as the storm stopped, pawing the frozen earth, looking for something to eat.

Kaukseeootsi and *Makohseeootsi,* January and February, passed on into *Pootaneeshi,* March, a time when tradition held that the buffalo and horses began to fill out from the meager winter. The weather was still cold and some of the worst winter storms were yet to come; but the hunters still went out, the children still played, and the women still did their chores. War was something not practiced much in the days of winter. Riding in heavy snow was dangerous, as was all travel. The snow hid too many things over which a horse could trip or stumble, as well as being too deep for the horse to plod through.

On a day when the snow stopped and the winds were still, Lone Bull and some other men were going on a hunt. Broken Leaf asked her father if she and Sun Dancer could accompany them and Lone Bull assented. Broken Leaf and Sun Dancer, as well as some of the other women, went along to cook, make camp, tend the horses, and skin and butcher the game.

Sun Dancer loved the feel of the cool wind against her face. She looked over at Broken Leaf, who smiled an equally appreciative smile at being out and away from their lodge. The hunt was to last a few days, or sufficiently long to kill enough game for their village. Parties went out separately, some trying for elk and antelope, others trying for wild sheep and deer. The hunters tried to provide for their own families, as well as those who had no hunters to provide for them.

The horses were skittish and fearful of being ridden through the snow. Although there had been no snow in days, the wind was chill and sharp, and the girls pulled their robes up high enough to cover the delicate skin of their faces. Two more women accompanied the hunting party. With their husbands and the other hunters, there were ten people in this party. The women rode well behind the men, keeping their usual place when riding with their men.

The first day out of camp they had little luck and caught only small game. After the women set up camp, they went out in search of anything they could find, but they only caught three rabbits. The next day, the men went out on foot, going higher up into the hills looking for bigger game. The sounds of howling wolves were heard periodically, and Sun Dancer was always ready with her hunting knife in case they decided to attack.

The men dug pits and placed bait at the bottom to lure the large gray wolves or some of the smaller wolves and coyotes. Some of the other men moved farther down the hills making antelope runs. They dug large pits and drove herds into them, or tried to drive the herds over small cliffs, thus eliminating hunts for individual animals. The women hung nooses from branches where elk trails ran. If the animals returned by the same trails, they would catch their heads in the nooses, drawing the rope tight and strangling themselves.

In the afternoon of the second day a new storm hit, and neither the men nor the women were able to make it back to camp. The women were alone and, except Sun Dancer, without anything to make a fire. They collected pine needles, and spreading them over the ground, they huddled together against a large tree trunk for what little shelter and warmth it could provide. As night began to fall, the storm showed little sign of abating, and Sun Dancer suggested that they make a more secure shelter for the night. The women agreed.

They gathered what branches and wood they could and made a lean-to against the trunk of the tree. They placed dead branches across the top, along with thicker pieces of wood to support the weight of the snow. They dug a few dry twigs, as well as stones for a firepit. Sun Dancer removed her firesticks from her parfleche, as the women looked on skeptically. Few people were adept at firesticks and the favorite way of starting a fire was to borrow a burning buffalo chip from another's fire.

Sun Dancer also removed powdered buffalo chips and a small bit of white quartz sand. She put the sand into the bottom stick or "hearth stick" and the powdered chips around the edges of the hole to serve as tinder. She revolved the top stick quickly between her two hands until sparks ignited with the buffalo chips. Then she quickly added dry pieces of twigs to get the fire started. The four women huddled closely together by the small firepit, the lean-to affording them protection from the gusting wind and snow. They skinned and butchered one of the four rabbits they had caught that day, and placed the meat on sticks over the fire. They collected more wood for drying by the fire, for they all felt they would have little chance of finding wood the next day. They had to make what wood they had last for as long as possible.

Sun Dancer suggested that they each take turns tending the fire throughout the night so it wouldn't die out. She took the first watch and sat quietly, stick in hand, rousing the ashes and adding more wood only when it seemed it would die out. She pulled her robe closer about her, her fingers numbing from the cold. She remembered her earlier experience in the snow, and she made a point of rubbing her legs and hands every few minutes to keep the numbness from setting in. Bits of snow and leaves fell from the tree above onto their tiny shelter, the sounds of the gusting wind and the howling wolves high up in the hills making her shiver. The sight of her hunting knife in her lap eased her anxiety slightly, although she knew it could do little against a wild animal. She longed for the comfort and security of Stalking Horse's arms and the warmth and safety of their lodge.

A large clump of snow fell on the top of the lean-to causing Sun Dancer to jump with fright. She looked all around them making sure nothing was lurking about.

Broken Leaf stood up, warming her hands by the fire. "Our wood will not last through the night."

"It will if we are careful with it. Add more only when it is necessary."

"You do not seem frightened; I am reassured by that."

Sun Dancer smiled at her friend, taking her hand in hers. "I was caught in the snow once before and was too frightened to think or help myself. After that, Stalking Horse took me out and taught me many lessons on survival. I will do all I can to keep us alive."

"I know you will. Why don't you rest now. It will be a long night, and you will need your strength for tomorrow."

"Do not forget to rub your arms and legs to keep the blood going. Tell the others."

Broken Leaf nodded slightly and watched as her friend lay on the bed of pine needles and shut her eyes. She turned to the small fire; she wasn't reassured by its constantly dwindling flames. She held her hands next to it and rubbed them vigorously, feeling the blood as it surged through her veins. She watched as the snow began to pile up outside the lean-to, and she shook her head weakly. We will never make it out alive, she thought sadly.

Sun Dancer was unable to sleep for more than a few hours. Her need for survival was stronger than her urge to sleep, and she awoke to find Broken Leaf still tending the fire, their supply of wood pitifully dwindled.

Broken Leaf looked over at her friend. "You should sleep more, you can do nothing now."

"It is hard to sleep when I know I may never wake up again." Broken Leaf caught her eyes and held them, nodding slowly.

"I was thinking much the same thing."

"I think we should walk out in the morning. If we stay and the storm continues, we will die."

"Yes, it is our only chance."

"Broken Leaf, I will need your strength to help me. Do not give up before we have tried."

"I will not, *navese*. I will look upon it as a great adventure."

"Yes, perhaps our greatest," Sun Dancer replied solemnly, as she looked out at the falling snow.

The morning was dark and gray and the storm had subsided somewhat, but snow drifted slowly down. Sun Dancer told the other women what she and Broken Leaf wanted to do, but they refused to go along. They felt it was safer to stay in their little shelter and wait for their men to find them, rather than take their chances walking in the snow and freezing to death. Broken Leaf and Sun Dancer had second thoughts, but as the firewood diminished, they decided to leave. They promised to send help if they found their way back, and they said goodbye to the other women. They took one of the rabbits and left the other two for their friends, hoping that they would find other game to subsist on.

Walking in the deep snow was hard work, the girls frequently stopping to rest, pulling their heavy robes tighter around them. The walking caused them to sweat, which ultimately caused them to get cold, but the walking helped their legs and arms by making the blood course steadily through their veins. Their breath came heavily in the mountain air, the cold stinging their lungs as they plodded through the thick carpet of snow. They said little as they moved, concentrating only on making their way out and back to their main camp.

The sky began to clear slightly and the snow stopped at midday. The girls eventually found the hunting camp, but everyone was gone. They dug beneath the heavy snow to see if the men had left any food, but they found nothing but an extra robe.

"They will be back when the storm has cleared," Broken Leaf said firmly. "It would have been their deaths to come look for us."

"I know that," Sun Dancer placed a reassuring arm on Broken Leaf's. "Our tracks were covered by the snow and they did not know which way we went. My people would have done the same." She bent over to pick up the heavy robe. "At least it will be warmer." She placed it around Broken Leaf's shoulders then pulled her friend over to sit on a fallen tree. "We must rest before we go on."

"I cannot take this robe, Sun Dancer."

"We will share it. Rest now."

"I do not think I can go any farther. I will stay here and wait for my father."

"But it might be days before he can come back for you. Look now at the sky, it is readying itself for another storm."

"It would be foolish to try to walk through it, Sun Dancer, we could never make it."

"But it would also be foolish to stay here. We have no shelter and no fire. All the wood is wet from the snow and eventually we would become so cold we would not care. We would die."

"Why do you want to go on? There is a chance the storm will stop, and my father will return for us tonight or tomorrow."

"There is also the chance that he will not. If the storm continues for the next few days, no one will be able to come for us. We must make it on our own."

"How do you know that we will make it?"

"I do not know, but I refuse to die waiting to find out. I am going with you or without you."

Broken Leaf stared at the determination in Sun Dancer's eyes and knew that her friend was truthful in what she said. She felt she would die either way, but felt it was better to die with a friend than alone. "I will go with you, *navese*, but I do not think you are right."

Sun Dancer smiled. "I do not even know if I am right, but Stalking Horse told me it is important to keep active if you are caught in the snow and cannot keep warm. We will die here for sure; better that we try to make it out."

Broken Leaf nodded wearily and stood up. "Let us start now before I give up. I will follow you."

Sun Dancer led the way through the deep snow, looking for any familiar signs. The horses' tracks had been covered up, but they found their way to the river, hoping to follow it back to the main camp. They stopped frequently to pass the robe back and forth. It was heavy and cumbersome, but they hung onto it as their only means of shelter. When they stopped, they removed their moccasins and took turns rubbing each other's feet and hands. They sucked on small pieces of snow to ease their thirst and ate pemmican to appease their hunger. Toward the end of the day the storm came full fury, and the girls were forced to stop. They went deeper into the trees by the river and using the extra robe as a top on their makeshift lean-to, they huddled in comparative warmth while the storm raged outside them. For the first time Sun Dancer was frightened. The storm showed no signs of abating, and without fire or dry clothes, she and Broken Leaf would freeze to death in a short time.

"We must build a fire," she said more to herself than to Broken Leaf.

"How do we build a fire when you yourself said there is no firewood to be found?"

"There is the bark of the tree." She took out her large knife, digging into the bark of the tree they were leaning against. She removed the outside in thick pieces, digging down into the soft inner bark. "Even the outside is not so wet. Come, before it is too dark, let us go around to the trees which have sheltered each other from the snow."

It was a painstaking process and their fingers were easily numbed by the cold and the peeling of the outer and inner bark. They collected pine needles hanging on lower branches untouched by snow to start their fire. They dug a small pit and emptied the dirt and snow outside the lean-to. Since the ground was soaked, it was impossible to start a fire there. Sun Dancer cut a piece of her robe and laid it in the bottom of the pit. Over this, she placed the pine needles and small, thin pieces of bark. She took out the parfleche which contained her firesticks, and dropped pieces of buffalo chips and white quartz sand into the pit. She rubbed the stick vigorously between her two hands, but no spark ignited. Broken Leaf tried it next and was able to produce a spark which caught a small buffalo chip but then died out. Sun Dancer put her face close to the sticks and as Broken Leaf rubbed them, she blew until some of the sparks finally caught hold and a small fire was started. While Broken Leaf tended the fire, Sun Dancer skinned and gutted the rabbit, cutting it into small pieces and putting them on small twigs to burn over the fire. She placed the rest of the rabbit in the snow to keep it fresh for the next day.

"This is the best meal I have ever eaten," Broken Leaf licked her fingers after eating her portion of rabbit. Sun Dancer cut it into portions that would last at least another day, and although each could have eaten more, they knew their lives depended on keeping as much food as possible. The bark sizzled and smoked when first placed on the fire, but eventually it caught hold and burned well; they had plenty of bark to last them through the night.

The storm stopped sometime during the night, and when Sun Dancer and Broken Leaf awoke the next morning, everything was still and clear. They looked about the white blanket of snow, appreciating its beauty but fearing its power. Sun Dancer looked over at Broken Leaf's weary face and wondered if she looked as tired. She wondered too, how the other two women were faring.

"Let us go," Broken Leaf stood up and shook out her robe. Her legs were weak and she stumbled against the tree. "My legs feel as though they cannot move."

"Let us rub them before we go; we will move slowly." After they had packed everything, including the dried pieces of bark, they removed their moccasins and rubbed each other's feet and legs and then leaned on each other as they rose to stand. It was easier to stand now but their legs still felt limp and weak. Doubt showed in both their faces.

Sun Dancer led the way, the extra robe slung over her shoulder, as well as her bow, arrows, quiver, and parfleche. The parfleche contained quills and sinew for sewing, firesticks, sand, buffalo chips for firemaking, pemmican, healing herbs, and leather thongs for tying things together. Sun Dancer silently blessed her mother for her foresight, as her mother insisted that she always carry the parfleche.

Although the snow was deep, the weather wasn't quite so cold, and the girls traveled at a brisk pace. When the snow got too deep, they walked nearer the river, next to the ice. The thick sheet of ice looked inviting and offered a shortcut in places, but both girls had seen people fall through the ice and freeze to death before they were pulled out.

The snow covered everything with its white mantle, camouflaging usually familiar signs. But Broken Leaf was able to recognize the countryside, and their spirits lifted enormously. They felt they could reach the main camp by the next day. They camped that night next to a large cottonwood by the river. The storm began anew and twice their lean-to was blown down on them. The storm continued well into the next day and by the time it stopped, it was almost dark and too late to travel. The girls repeated their routine of the previous nights and collected dry bark and leaves, keeping the fire going high under their little shelter. Sun Dancer made sure they repeatedly rubbed their legs and feet and hands and arms, and whenever possible, they each stood up to move around a bit. They were glad they had rationed out the fresh meat because the pemmican was monotonous compared to it. It was quiet all throughout the night, and early the next morning they set off toward the main camp.

Broken Leaf was having more and more difficulty walking, and her legs began to go numb. Eventually, it was impossible for her to move any further, so they stopped to rest. Sun Dancer vigorously rubbed Broken Leaf's legs and the latter screamed in pain. It was evident to both of them that frostbite was sinking in. Sun Dancer knew then that she must go on alone.

She made a shelter for Broken Leaf and built a fire, covering her with the extra robe. When she was sure her friend was as comfortable as possible, she knelt next to her to say good-bye. "I will return soon. You must make an effort to rub your legs and feet, no matter how much it pains you. Promise me."

"I promise. I do not wish to die. Go, now, and I will pray for you."

With a final squeeze of her friend's hand, Sun Dancer trudged up the riverbank toward the hills and mountains. She walked as Broken Leaf had directed her and soon the countryside began to look familiar to her. When she got close to the camp she began to run, in spite of her weariness, and it wasn't long before a guard saw her and helped her into camp. When she was taken into the lodge of Lone Bull and Wind Woman to be warmed, she told them what had happened and how far they had come.

"We will go for them now," Lone Bull responded.

"I want to come with you," Sun Dancer started to stand, her legs giving out beneath her.

"You will stay, child, you have done enough already," replied Wind Woman with affection.

"I cannot rest until I know that Broken Leaf is safe and the others are found. Please, do not stop me."

At the determined look on Sun Dancer's face, Lone Bull nodded slightly, ordering her to change into dry clothing before leaving.

Sun Dancer smiled wearily as she patted the horse Stalking Horse had given her; she had had doubts that she would ever see it again. She rode her horse with ease, in spite of her pain and tiredness, and she and the others reached Broken Leaf quickly. While Broken Leaf's father took her back to camp, Sun Dancer led the other men to where she and Broken Leaf had left the other two women. After only a few hours, they reached the place where Sun Dancer and Broken Leaf had left the others. What had taken almost four days on foot took only a few hours on horseback with no storm to interfere. She eagerly dismounted on seeing the lean-to, and ran to the small shelter. She bent over and looking inside, shut her eyes in disbelief. The women were sitting frozen, their eyes staring straight ahead, their legs out-stretched before them. Sun Dancer turned away, tears welling up in her eyes.

"No," she said in a defeated manner falling to the ground, the white snow suddenly turning completely black.

CHAPTER XVII

Sun Dancer felt soothing hands on her and she called out Horn's name. He had always been there when she was ill and he had always helped her. And if Horn was there, her parents and Stalking Horse were sure to be there. She felt immense relief as she thought of opening her eyes and seeing Stalking Horse's face. But Spring's face suddenly appeared and furiously things began to collect in her mind: Stalking Horse, their marriage, the loss of her two children, Spring, her experience in the snow, the dead women. She opened her eyes, shutting off the images in her mind. Wind Woman smiled down on her, a comforting hand resting on her arm.

"How are you this day?"

Sun Dancer looked around the lodge for Broken Leaf, hoping her friend was all right. She found her sleeping on the robes next to her. She sat up and rested her head against the backrest. "I feel well enough. How is Broken Leaf? Her legs?"

"She will be fine. You saved her life, Sun Dancer."

"It was no more than she would have done for me. The others?"

"They died in the snow. Their men brought them back here to their families."

"Perhaps if I had stayed with them, or forced them to come with us . . ."

"There was nothing you could do, child, the decision was made. You did what you thought was best."

"Perhaps," Sun Dancer nodded unconvinced. "Broken Leaf almost died. I should have gone alone."

"Do not punish yourself so. Broken Leaf is a strong-minded girl and would not have gone with you if she did not believe you were right. And she is alive and well because of you." She reached down and brought up a bowl of warm broth. "Drink some of this, it will warm you."

Sun Dancer complied and relished the delicious taste and warmth of the rabbit broth. "Have I slept long?"

"Since yesterday when you took the men to the women. The men were grateful to find their bodies."

Sun Dancer shook her head blindly, tears filling her eyes. "I am sorry, Wind Woman, for your women that have died."

"We all feel sorrow, child, but you need feel none. You tried to get them to go with you and they would not. Do not dwell on it overly much; it is done with now. You must go on."

Sun Dancer finished her broth and laid her head back against the rest, closing her eyes. "You must go on," Wind Woman had said, and Sun Dancer knew she was right. She knew when she felt herself getting nearer to the Arapaho camp that all she wanted was to get Broken Leaf and the others safely out, then return to her own people in the spring.

She was able to see things clearly now. She understood for the first time that it mattered little what Stalking Horse had done with Spring, for it was nothing compared to what she herself had with him. He didn't lie to her, he told her what he had done. But she had rejected him out of hurt and pain. When she took the time to think about it, she realized how patient he had been with her. It was his right as a warrior to take as many wives as he pleased, without asking Sun Dancer's permission. The fact that he didn't take Spring for his wife showed he had little respect for her. But Sun Dancer had been too blind with anger and humiliation to see that. If something had happened to Stalking Horse and he had been unable to fulfill the desires he had awakened in her, would she have been able to go without that fulfillment? She could not truthfully answer the question.

It was good that she had gone away by herself, but she regretted that she had not spoken to Stalking Horse before she left. She should have let him know that she had to be alone to reconcile all of the feelings she felt—anger, hurt, frustration, loss, sorrow—these were all things which she had to learn to deal with. And she had. She realized that being alive was much more important than any of these things. Being alive and being able to live her life in a manner which made her proud. She had to learn to give more to Stalking Horse because he had given so much to her. Indeed, without his lessons, she and Broken Leaf would not be alive now.

"Are you awake, *navese?*" Broken Leaf's voice

penetrated her thoughts.

She opened her eyes and smiled. "You look well; it pleases me so."

"It pleases me to be alive. Thank you. It is a debt I do not know if I can ever repay."

"There is no debt between us, *navese*. There is only a strong bond of love and friendship. A friendship for which I am truly grateful."

"And I. I will miss you when you leave. Will it be soon?"

Sun Dancer smiled at her friend's uncanny ability to read her thoughts. "Yes, when *Makeeomishi* is here. When the Spring Moon comes. Then I will go back to my people."

"And to Stalking Horse."

"Yes. I can see now that what he did was of no great consequence. But I saw it through the eyes of a scared young woman, carrying his child, a child whom I was frightened to bear for fear that it would die. Afterwards, when the child did die, I was blinded by my sorrow and my self-pity, and I sought to strike out at Stalking Horse for what he did."

"And if he again takes another woman?"

"I do not believe he will," Sun Dancer answered confidently.

"But if he does?"

"Then I will accept it and do my best to make him desire only me."

Broken Leaf laughed as Sun Dancer's eyes narrowed and her mouth grew firm. "I believe Stalking Horse will be so ensnared in your trap, he will want no others. You will cast a spell on him."

"Not a spell, only my love. And I will give it freely,

without conditions."

"I would like to do that one day but I have never met a man whom I would do that for."

"You will, *navese*, and he will see the gifts in you."

"And if this man should never come?"

"I do not know. I do not know if it is better to be alone and hope for a great love, or if it is better to accept a man you do not love and hope that you will one day grow to do so."

"If Stalking Horse had not asked you to be his wife, what would you have done?"

"I would never have married. It was different with me, for I have loved Stalking Horse all of my life. To have accepted someone else would have been to lessen my ideals."

"And your dreams."

"Yes, and my dreams."

"I know you are special, Sun Dancer, and your life has been blessed from the start. Not only will you feel great pain and sorrow in your lifetime, you will feel the kind of love and joy that we others can only look at and wish for. You, *navese*, have been touched by the spirits."

The winter seemed to go on forever, but Sun Dancer knew that eventually *Makeeomishi* would come and then *Oaseeowatut*, the May Moon, when the sun would shine brightly. She kept herself as busy as before and she worked alongside the rest of the women. She felt as comfortable with these people as she felt with her own. She wondered why the different tribes, many of whom looked the same, could not live together in peace, and grow and learn from one another. They could share in one another's traditions, and stand in great numbers together if the white man ever came to take over their land, as Sweet Medicine had predicted. She wondered if the whites lived in harmony or if they too fought and stole from one another. Her father believed that if all Indians had been put on earth in the same place, no matter where they roamed or lived afterwards, they would always be as one because they had started out together. Sun Dancer smiled as she thought of her father and his ideals. He was a great man, a man who believed in peace, and it was his dream to see all the northern tribes live in harmony. She wondered if he would ever live to see it.

In spite of her resolve to remain patient, Sun Dancer grew restless when the ice began to break up in the river and the snow began to melt. Bits of grass and wildflowers began to poke through the ground, and the sun, although not yet warm, began to shine constantly. Spring was coming and soon Sun Dancer could return to her people.

When the danger of flooding rivers was past, the Arapahos moved down from the mountains to the plains, eager to hunt the buffalo for fresh meat, and to pluck nature's own bounty of fresh berries and roots. Sun Dancer would accompany the tribe to their spring and summer camp to help set up the lodges and collect berries and roots. After they were settled, she and Broken Leaf and Lone Bull would ride to the Cheyenne camp. She found it difficult to contain her enthusiasm and excitement.

When the Arapaho lodges were erected, the men went out to hunt and the women to collect berries.

They ate elk-berries, fresh or dried, but black raspberries and red raspberries were eaten as fresh fruit only. The berry most widely used by the Cheyennes and Arapahos was the chokecherry. The women of both tribes pounded the berries finely, pits and all, and made the pulp into flat cakes to be dried in the sun and saved for winter use. They were also used in making fine pemmican. Wild plums were another favorite of the women. They were eaten fresh or stoned and dried in the sun to be kept for winter use. The plums were welcome food during a lean winter for they could be boiled and would taste much the same as freshly cooked plums. When the women found red, yellow, or black currants, they pounded them finely and dried them into little cakes. Often the women stewed the currants with the scrapings from buffalo hides to provide a tasty broth. As needed, the women picked the fruit or dug for roots in late spring or early summer. Sun Dancer collected various roots and leaves of plants and pounded them finely, leaving them in separate bowls with directions to Wind Woman for their use.

The work was never done in an Indian camp, but Sun Dancer felt it was time for her to return to her people when the sun had grown warm and she had helped Broken Leaf and her mother in their work. Wind Woman gave Sun Dancer a necklace of silver and turquoise for helping Broken Leaf. Sun Dancer tried to refuse the necklace—it was such a fine one— but Wind Woman insisted she take it. The necklace had been given to her years before by her brother, who had traded with a trapper for it. Sun Dancer was greatly honored.

The weather was perfect for riding. It was not the heavy heat of summer but the light warmth of late spring. There was a breeze in the air and everything on the prairie was in color. The tall prairie grass was green and swayed lightly in the breeze, while wildflowers dotted the prairie in colorful patches. Buffalo wallows, where the great beasts wallowed and played to cool off, were still full of water from the heavy snows, and looked like small lakes. The buffalos themselves grazed in giant herds as far as one could see. The animals were confident of the land on which they grazed, showing little fear of the Indians who killed them only out of necessity. Their heavy brown winter coats showed signs of shedding, and matted brown fur fell in pieces over the prairie. It all seemed so wonderful to Sun Dancer, and suddenly so new.

Lone Bull told them of the days when they hunted buffalo on foot.

"We had to find a buffalo well away from the herd. Many of us circled the animal shooting arrows or throwing our lances at it. If we could not find a single animal, we chased small herds over bluffs so they were killed or injured in falling. Then we had to hurry to finish off the injured ones before they escaped. You know," he looked at the girls, "that was not easy. It was just as easy for one of the wounded beasts to turn and charge us. You cannot imagine what it is like being chased by an injured bull buffalo."

Sun Dancer smiled slightly. She knew exactly what Lone Bull meant.

"Did your people always know how to dress the

hides, Lone Bull?" Sun Dancer asked in fascination.

"No. When we and your people first came here, the Teton Sioux showed us how to dress the hides in two pieces and sew them together. Much later, some Comanches showed us how to tan the hides in one piece."

"Showed the women, you mean, father," Broken Leaf added playfully.

Lone Bull smiled.

Sun Dancer relished these stories from the older people, for as her father had told her many times, she and the other children were the only way the history and tradition of the tribe could be passed on. As a child she had learned everything. Her father made her repeat it word for word, so that when she passed the history and stories on to her children they would be intact. Her children. Perhaps she would never have any children, but she would know all the stories well. She could pass them on to all the other children of the tribe.

Sun Dancer was anxious to return to her people but she was also sad at leaving the Arapahos. They had been good to her and accepted her as if she were one of their own, not asking why she was there. There would be the sadness, too, of leaving Broken Leaf. By now, she was more than a blood sister, she was a sister of the heart. Sun Dancer saw in Broken Leaf things she admired greatly, and a person whom she wished she could be more like. She was a direct and honest person who dealt with her feelings and did not try to run from them. She had helped her in that, at least; Sun Dancer would not run from things anymore.

The Cheyenne camp had moved from the previous spring encampment, following the buffalo as they moved along the prairie in search of better grazing. They camped at various points along the Cheyenne River, while the Arapaho camped at points along the North Platte. Both tribes kept close to the water for the coolness the trees could provide and the endless supply of water. If the heat became unbearable, they would break camp and go up to one of the cooler mountain valleys.

After the second week, Sun Dancer saw the conical shapes of the lodges in the distance. She could tell by the way the camp was arranged and the lodges were painted that these were her people. Her joy was boundless and she had never before felt such pride. She knew her people were highly respected for their practical thoughts and their honorable ways, but she felt something more than that as they neared the camp. There was the pride of belonging to this group of people who warred out of necessity and were willing to talk peace with anyone.

In the old days, her father had often told her, they hadn't even known of war. They were a peaceful people who were continually harassed and warred upon until they were forced to leave their land and move across the Big River. They acquired the horse and adapted to him quickly, as well as to the nomadic life of the Plains Indians. They learned to defend themselves and gained the respect of all those who fought with or against them. It was these people whom Sun Dancer admired and loved, these people who were a part of her. They were Cheyenne.

The camp was a bustle of activity when the three

riders arrived. Men were making weapons, gambling, talking of war, and exchanging stories. Some of the women were tanning hides or grinding berries and currants for dried cakes. Other women sat outside and quilled, while some sewed shirts and moccasins or crafted cradleboards. Children with their dogs ran through the village, the sounds of their laughter carrying in the air. It was a familiar scene to Sun Dancer, but one which touched her heart. She was home.

They rode to her parents' lodge. Sun Dancer jumped from her horse and almost ran into her mother, who was carrying a robe from inside.

"Naha," her mother screamed uncharacteristically. "Daughter, you have come home." She placed her arms around Sun Dancer and held her close some moments before letting her go. "Go to your father, he worries for you. He is smoking the pipe with your brother."

Sun Dancer turned to Lone Bull and Broken Leaf. "Many thanks to you, Lone Bull, for taking me this long way and for your many kindnesses while I was with you and your people."

"It is I who should thank you for giving me back the life of my daughter, child, for she is a great joy to me and my wife."

"You will stay with our family and let us return your kindnesses?"

"Yes, but only for a few days."

"Come with me, Broken Leaf," Sun Dancer implored Broken Leaf.

"No, you must see your father and after him, your husband."

"Yes," Sun Dancer replied thoughtfully, her brows drawing closely together. "Will he want me after so long, I wonder?"

"Go to him, *navese*, he is the only one who can tell you that."

Sun Dancer nodded slightly and turned toward her brother's lodge, suddenly unsure of herself and Stalking Horse's feeling for her.

He-Walks-the-Mountain smiled broadly as he saw his daughter run toward him, his face brightening, looking years younger.

"*Nehayo*," she said softly, sitting down beside him, "Father. You have a foolish daughter; can you take her back and love her as before?"

"I will always love you, child, no matter what. You are my blood."

Sun Dancer hugged her father then looked across at her brother, who was smiling broadly, a knowing look on his face as he nodded his head.

"It did not take long, eh, *nekaim?* Your life is here with your husband and your people."

"Yes, but I had to find it out for myself."

"And what did you find out?"

"That I can accept many things I never could before."

"Spring?"

"Even Spring, if she is what Stalking Horse wants. Is she still with him?"

"That is for Stalking Horse to tell you," Brave Wolf stated flatly, a slight twinkle appearing in his eyes.

"You evade me, *seeheeneehito*. You are my elder

brother but you enjoy playing the games of a child."

"It is true. But your husband must speak for himself; I cannot speak for him."

"Is he here, in the camp?"

"He is hunting elk."

"And will he be gone long?"

"I do not know. He went past the river where the elk graze closer to the trees."

"You know so much of what he does, do you speak often?"

"Yes."

"What does he tell you?"

"He tells me many things, *nekaim*. Mostly he tells me he tires of his wifeless state."

"Is there more?" Sun Dancer asked hesitantly, fearful of hearing that Stalking Horse had taken Spring for his wife.

"There is more."

"Do not play with me," Sun Dancer yelled angrily at her brother, then looked over at her father apologetically. "Forgive me, father, I have tried to become more patient, but it seems I will never be where my brother is concerned."

"It is all right, child, I agree that Brave Wolf toys with you as a panther does with its victim." He narrowed his eyes at his son.

Brave Wolf held his hands up in the air. "It seems I must come forth with what I know, but I will not. It is your place to go to your husband and speak with him, *nekaim*, and know his feelings. What you find out from him will be of far more importance than what you find out from me."

Sun Dancer nodded and stood up, realizing the

truth of her brother's statement. "You speak the truth, Brave Wolf, and I will go to my husband now. Long ago I ceased being a little girl and I believe the time has come for me to cease acting like one. My heart is so full being with you again; my love is great for you both." She turned and walked slowly away, aware for the first time that Stalking Horse might have rejected her and her love. She breathed deeply and held her head up high. She would accept the inevitable with honor.

Stalking Horse bent over the animal and pulled his lance free from its chest. It was a large buck, its antlers spreading wider than he could hold his arms. It pained him to kill so beautiful an animal, but he reasoned that it was better to kill him now than permit him to suffer later when he was brought down by the pack of wolves which had been trailing the herd. His foreleg had been injured and he was lagging behind the others, trying vainly to keep up. Stalking Horse had seen the wolves work before and he knew them to be discriminating hunters, killing only the weak, old, or diseased. But when he saw this animal, he felt it didn't deserve to be torn apart by a pack of hungry wolves. It deserved to die quickly, without pain. Although the end result was just the same, he felt he was letting the animal die in a more dignified manner, eliminating some of its pain. It deserved that at least.

He felt the vibration of the earth and turned his eyes on the horizon to see a lone rider. He squinted his well-trained eyes against the sun, knowing instinctively that it was a woman, and in his heart that it was Sun Dancer. His stomach contracted involuntarily and his lips drew together in a tight line.

He had struggled within himself for a long time over her. He could have divorced her, but that would have meant giving her the freedom to marry someone else and he didn't want any other man to have her. She had been honest—she had told him she wouldn't share him with anyone and she had not. He admired her for her spirit but there were times he wanted to take that spirit and crush it, making her bend to his will.

Sun Dancer stopped her horse some distance from Stalking Horse and walked the animal in slowly. Her eyes were bright and shining and her smile was such that it encompassed not only him, but everything around him.

"So you have come back," he said in a neutral tone, sounding neither angry nor glad. It angered him to see her sitting there, so proud and beautiful, looking more of a woman and less a girl than ever before. Had she too, had a man to fill her empty nights and days? His anger exploded inwardly, but outwardly he remained calm, almost uncaring. He turned back to the dead buck and hoisted it up onto the pack horse, securing it with a rope. "How did you know where to find me?" His gaze was still directed on the work in front of him.

"I did not. Brave Wolf told me you were hunting elk and I rode to the places I know you like to go." She slipped from her horse and walked to him, placing a tentative hand on his shoulder. He looked at her with cold and unfeeling eyes. She immediately withdrew her hand.

When Stalking Horse finished tying the buck, he picked up the reins of the pack horse and swung up onto his own mount. Sun Dancer followed in silence, watching him as they rode. Her heart and body ached for want of him, and she longed to lie with him right on the open prairie. His skin gleamed in the sunlight, his dark hair hanging well below his shoulders, secured only by a headband of doeskin. His breechclout exposed his strong legs and flanks, and his whole upper torso was muscled and firm. His posture was proud, his head held high; he commanded attention without requiring it.

They rode many miles in silence, Stalking Horse not looking at nor speaking to Sun Dancer. She knew he was dealing with his own feeling about her but she couldn't remain silent for long.

"Is Spring still with you?" Her voice was even in spite of her dread to hear his answer.

"And if she is?" He turned to look at her for the first time. "Will you run away again?"

Sun Dancer was ashamed and she looked down as the flood of heat spread over her face. It would not be easy; he would not let it be. "I will never run away again," she stated truthfully, her eyes lifting to meet his. "My home is with my people. And with you." She thought she detected a momentary flicker in his eyes before he again turned away.

"And how did you come by this?"

"Something happened to make me understand that nothing is more important than life, and living it with joy, honesty. And love."

His look was quizzical but he asked nothing

further. They continued riding in a cloak of silence, the pace slow and unhurried, each mile making Sun Dancer want to scream in frustration. She had never remembered wanting anything in her whole life so much as she wanted Stalking Horse. It had been that way from the first time her eyes met his when they were just children, and would be that way until . . . until what?

"I cannot remember a time when I did not love you," she said softly, unashamed of the depth of her love.

Stalking Horse pulled his horse to a stop, his eyes still on some unknown point in the distance. "But still you left me. It is not like you to run away."

"I had never borne two dead children before." Her voice was angry and sorrowful. "It was an actual physical pain, as if a part of me had been cut out and taken away. I did not know such sorrow could be felt." She shut her eyes and it all came back to her in a sudden flood of emotion. She felt his hand on her arm.

"We will talk about it again. It is still too soon." She nodded blindly. "We will stop by the river to drink and to talk further. Come." He touched her hand again lightly before removing it, and she followed him until he stopped at a point along the river and dismounted. He had offered her no comforting words; the sorrow was long past for him. After the horses drank and moved back to graze on the high, green grass, Stalking Horse and Sun Dancer drank their fill and sat down under a tall cotton-wood, also drinking in the beauty of the day and the surroundings. Spring was the time when everything looked fresh and new and alive, and gave the false hope that things would continue like that for always. Sun Dancer felt unaccountably weary and melancholy, as if something sweet and fleeting were now past. The adult part of her was slowly taking over the child, and she was helpless to forestall this other person from assuming control.

"You have changed," Stalking Horse's voice rang deeply into her thoughts.

"The change is one which I cannot control." She remembered her father telling her that the changes would come about slowly, without her realizing them.

"Tell me of your thoughts now."

Sun Dancer looked at him and felt a great urge to touch him, but she knew now was not the time. She looked up at the sky above her. "Our lives here are so short, yet often we are fooled into believing they will be long. We waste much time doing and saying things we do not mean or that do not matter. When the time comes to open ourselves up and be true, it is too late. Our time is over."

"Your thoughts are sad this day."

"My thoughts are no longer the fanciful ones of a girl, but those of a woman who has endured much sorrow and who has survived it to become a stronger person."

His hand touched her face gently, traveling over the familiar lines and cupping it tenderly. "You still look so young to have such thoughts. If only I had been able to spare you your sorrow." She looked at him then and was unable to check the tears which flowed of their own will. This was something she had wanted to do with him but had been unable to at the time because she had closed him out. His arms came around her and held her tightly, his hand ever so gently stroking her hair. Although her strength had become great, she needed to feel his strength, and his gentle support of her. She needed him beyond all else, to seek with him that union of souls that would carry them throughout their lifetimes to the life beyond that which they knew on earth. They sought to find that perfect union of body and soul which would bring them a peace shared by no others. They now shared each other's pain and sorrow. The other would come later.

CHAPTER XVIII

Stalking Horse had not told Sun Dancer whether Spring was still with him, and she didn't want to break the bond they had just re-formed to ask him. If Spring was still with him, then it would be up to her to accept the girl and treat her as a second wife. She knew she could do that, but sharing the same lodge while he slept with both of them was something she wasn't sure she could deal with. She felt his hand stroke her neck and she knew then that she could endure it, for she would never leave him again. He was too much a part of her.

"You look sad again," he said solemnly, gently running his hand up and down her long, graceful neck.

"I am no longer sad." She turned and looked at him with a great intensity. "I am glad I went away. It was the right thing to do."

"Why do you say that?"

"Because if I had stayed here, I might never have felt happy again about you or me. It was best for me to get away and think clearly about us and about what happened. I could never have done that here."

"You always intended to come back then?"

"Yes. But I wanted to come back at peace with myself. And I have."

"Was the winter hard for you?" He knew well her fear of the dark winter months.

"I was busy and did not permit myself to be frightened. Many of the things you taught me helped me to make it through."

"What do you mean? I taught you nothing about the winter other than survival."

"That is what helped me." Stalking Horse tried to interrupt but Sun Dancer went on. "I worked with Broken Leaf's family and helped other women in the tribe. Soon, the ice was melting and we moved down the mountains. I knew then it was time for me to come home."

"If you did not return home by summer, I was going to come for you."

"You would have done that?"

"I had given you your time; I would not have given you more."

"You missed me then?"

"You are my wife."

"No one could do the chores as well as I?"

"No."

"Or love you as well as I?"

Their eyes met and Stalking Horse pulled her to him. "No. You are the only one who can love me as you do." She laid her head on his chest and felt his arms move up and down her back. That was all she wanted to hear. It didn't matter now whether or not Spring stayed; she would never take her place with Stalking Horse.

"What would you do if I told you I had lovers?" She asked playfully.

"I would kill them all."

"And if I told you there was no need for others because my love for you is too strong?"

"I would say let us strengthen it even more so that it would never again be threatened."

Their bodies became as one under the clear sky, the sound of the river flowing gently by. They felt a part of it, a part of nature's beauty. It was natural and it was right, and it was a part of their love which needed no words.

They reached camp at dusk and went straight to their lodge. Stalking Horse had changed nothing inside and a part of her warmed to be in the familiar place again. She looked around, expecting to see Spring or her robes and backrest, but she and her things weren't there.

"Spring is married." Stalking Horse answered her question.

"Married? To whom?"

"To Laughing Bird. He has admired her for a time."

"Laughing Bird? I cannot believe . . ."

"I think she reminds him of you."

"No. Spring is very beautiful and can do many things. She is her own person."

"She is not you." He came close and took her into his arms. He remembered when she had said, "She will never be me." That was the last thing she had said to him before the child died. Now, he knew it to be true. "I never intended for Spring to become my wife or my woman; I never wanted another woman but you. That day something happened and I took her, but it meant nothing to me. I realized afterwards how precious you are to me. There will never be another Spring."

Sun Dancer looked up at him, realizing the full impact of his words. He was telling her he didn't want another wife or woman, that she was all he would ever need. He had said it before but now it meant something more to her. "It is your right to take other wives."

"It is also my right to take only one wife and keep her until I die."

"Or until I die."

"No, I will not permit you to die first."

"Then let us not speak of such things now. Please." She placed her fingers over his lips. She had lost two children whom she had not known. She knew Stalking Horse and she loved him. If he should die before she . . . She sank slowly to the ground and held her hands up to him. "Fill me with your love, husband, so that I may be fooled into believing it will be like this forever."

Broken Leaf and Lone Bull remained for a few more days and then returned to their own camp. Sun Dancer and Broken Leaf had spent most of their time together riding, swimming, hunting in the woods, or talking with Stalking Horse. After Broken Leaf and her father had gone, Sun Dancer was aware of the large void that was left by her friend's departure. She was even more aware of the help and support which Broken Leaf had given her. When they saw each other again, it would be as if they had never been apart.

Sun Dancer returned to her home and duties with great relish. She accompanied her mother to meetings of the Quilling Society, she tanned hides, hunted for small game, but she was most enthusiastic about going back to her teachings with Horn. She wanted to learn as much as he could teach her, confidently expecting that one day she would use the knowledge as wisely as he. Horn was pleased to have her back but he didn't seem surprised, and as always the instinctive feeling that Horn knew more about her life than she, caused Sun Dancer to feel acutely uncomfortable.

Horn assigned her the task of seeking out various wild fruits, currants, roots, onions, and bark, all of which could be used in the healing of human and animal ailments. She was intently studying plants in the woods one day when she heard footsteps in the brush and turned to see Laughing Bird coming toward her. Her smile was radiant, for she hadn't seen her friend in a long time. She stood up to greet him.

"It has been a long time, my friend," she said happily and Laughing Bird nodded.

"Yes, a long time." He pulled her into his arms and hugged her fiercely. She didn't resist for she felt the same way about him. He stood her back to look at her. "You look well, more womanly than before."

"That is what Stalking Horse tells me."

"Does it go well with you and Stalking Horse?"

"Yes. Things that once seemed important to me no longer matter." She smiled at him. "And you are married to Spring. She is lovely."

"Yes, she is that. She reminds me much of you."

"I do not think Spring and I are anything alike."

"I have found that to be true." His voice was flat, even, reflecting something Sun Dancer couldn't quite detect.

"She cooks, sews, and hunts well, and she is young and beautiful. She is strong and will probably give you many healthy sons and daughters."

"Perhaps." His gaze went beyond Sun Dancer to the trees behind her. "If it were you, I would not care if there were no children. You would be all I need."

Sun Dancer met his eyes and the sadness in them; she looked away. Here was the person she had grown up with, who had saved her life, who had fought for her when others were so willing to make fun of her, who had taught her so many things. He was more than a friend, for they had shared so much together. There was almost a blood tie between them. He was like a brother to her but something more. That was the problem. There had always been something more between them. She had always wanted to believe that theirs was just a simple friendship but she knew in her heart that it was never that. She would have probably married him if she hadn't married Stalking Horse, and she would have been happy with him. But she had caused him sorrow when she chose another man over him. She took his larger hand in hers.

"You would not be happy if I had married you, Laughing Bird, for I would have cheated you of the many things which you deserve. I could never have loved you as you deserve to be loved."

317

"But you do love me."

"I will always love you in a special way which no one else can ever understand."

"But you do not yet think of me as a man."

"I have always thought of you as a man. You were there for me when I needed you and you cared for and protected me. I did not deserve such special treatment."

"I thought we would marry someday, Sun Dancer. It seemed the natural way of things."

"I thought we would be married, too." She stopped then, unwilling to hurt him further.

"But you fell in love with Stalking Horse when you were young and your feelings never changed. I knew that; that is why I did not ask for you in marriage."

She turned away, ashamed of the way she had hurt him so cruelly. She felt his hands on her shoulders and his breath in her hair. "It changes nothing. I will always love you and I will always be here for you. But I know it is Stalking Horse who makes you happy."

"I am so ashamed, Laughing Bird, I do not wish to face you. You deserve much happiness and I feel that I have taken much away from you."

"You have taken nothing from me but given me everything." He turned her to face him. "I know that I am special to you and the times we have spent together are meaningful only to us. I just wish that I had been able to love you." Sun Dancer closed her eyes, tears stinging her lids. She felt his cheek on hers, lingering for more than a second, and then he was gone. She watched him as he walked away and she was sad. He was more than a friend—he was that rare thing between friend and lover, a person who had helped to fill her with happiness and self-respect, who had made her years from girlhood to womanhood some of the best she had ever known. She understood now how Stalking Horse could love her and still make love to another woman. For as much as she loved him, she could love Laughing Bird and enjoy making him happy. She silently prayed for his happiness with Spring.

Sun Dancer planted crops of corn, beans, tobacco, and squash in the soft and fertile soil near the river. All the women sowed their crops near the river because it produced better than other areas. Although buffalo meat was their staple food, these crops were a good supplement to their diet, and they were able to trade the tobacco with other tribes for things which they needed.

Often, Sun Dancer remembered what her father had told her of the early days.

"Before we crossed the Big River, when we still lived in earthen lodges, we lived almost entirely from the yield of our crops and from the meat of small flesh animals which we hunted on foot. Our weapons were crude, and when we chased an animal on foot, the kill was not so easy as it is on horseback.

"Before we traded with the Mandans and some of the ciboleros for metal, we made our arrowpoints of stone. Sometimes we had to spear an animal twice or three times before it would fall. Hunting in those days was a dangerous occupation.

"But things changed when we acquired the horse and could ride swiftly after animals, now large herds of them. The metal gave us the more efficient weapons that we needed. But even that has changed now. Everyone uses guns—Sioux, Crows, Blackfeet, Pawnee, Utes—they all have them. Soon it will be our turn. A Cheyenne armed with only a lance or bow and arrow, can do little against a man with a gun.

"I have always feared guns. I believe they will speed up our destruction." He-Walks-the-Mountain sighed deeply. "Change is inevitable, I suppose. We can do little to stop it."

It was a belief which Stalking Horse had voiced many times.

Sun Dancer had seen Spring many times. The girl paid little attention to Sun Dancer but she was obvious in her attention toward Stalking Horse. He treated her deferentially, with the respect due the wife of a warrior like Laughing Bird, but he did little more than that.

Spring was heavy with child and Sun Dancer was happy for her and Laughing Bird. For in spite of what Laughing Bird had said, she knew a child would make him proud. As she watched Spring move about the camp with her extra burden, she was struck anew by the girl's gracefulness, and how even her heaviness with child did little to impede that grace. They met at the river one day while Sun Dancer was getting water, and she offered to do the same for Spring.

Spring sat down while Sun Dancer filled her vessels and her voice rang out clearly. "Will you ever be able to give Stalking Horse sons?"

It was a cruel question and Sun Dancer was both

hurt and angered by it. She turned to the girl. "I cannot see that it is any concern of yours whether I do or do not. You should be concerned with giving Laughing Bird sons, not Stalking Horse."

Spring stood up, taking her water from Sun Dancer and turning to look over her shoulder, she replied, "I am concerned about Stalking Horse because this will be his son." She smiled sweetly and then walked slowly away, as if challenging Sun Dancer to come after her.

Sun Dancer watched the girl and then sat down, knowing that what Spring said could be true. The time was right—it could be Stalking Horse's son. It was one thing for a man to say he could live without children if he never saw them, but if he actually saw them it would be different. He might say that it didn't matter but his eyes and feelings would betray him as the child grew older and he watched its progress. It would be the child she could never give him. She covered her face with her hands, knowing that this was something she could not fight. Would she lose him to the girl, after all? And what of Laughing Bird? It was obvious she cared little for him. If only Stalking Horse had never brought the girl to camp. But she couldn't think that way, she had to think practically. There was a chance that the child could be Laughing Bird's, but it probably wasn't. No matter. She would face up to this and to Spring. She had learned something while she had been away—she possessed courage she never knew she had. She would find that courage now. She promised Stalking Horse that she would never run away again and she would not. She would fight, even if it was only a young girl whom she was fighting. She would find a way and she would win. She came from a fine line of warriors and their blood ran thick in her. She would fight courageously, even if it was only a war of tongues.

"You did not tell me where you got the necklace." Stalking Horse lifted the heavy silver from Sun Dancer's slim, brown neck.

"It was a gift from Broken Leaf's mother."

"She gave you a gift for staying with them?"

"She is overly kind. I helped her with some quilling and tanning, and showed her the use of some plants. She wanted to give me something."

"You were false with me," he said harshly, pulling the necklace so that her face was close to his. "When I asked you about the winter, you said you were not frightened. You lied." Sun Dancer looked down but he pulled her chin up. "Why did you not tell me what had happened?"

"Because it is over now and it does little good to talk of it."

"But I want you to talk of it. I want to know what happened."

"You already know. Broken Leaf told you."

"Yes, she told me that you saved her life."

"She would have done no less for me."

"She said she would have stopped but you kept her going. She said you were the strong one."

"I was strong only because I learned many things from you. You taught me well."

"I think if I had not, you still would have made it through. You are a strong person, Sun Dancer, and would have found a way on your own."

"I do not know. My will to live is strong but if I did not know the things you taught me, I would not have been able to survive."

"Why did you not tell me of this?"

"Because father has often told me that a truly honorable person should also be humble."

"Then you are both." He pulled her close. "My heart is full of you. I feel much pride."

"Do not feel much, it was not a great thing I did." She pulled away from him and sat up erectly, looking into his eyes. "Spring carries your child."

His look was warm and continued to hold hers. He showed little surprise. "I know."

"She has told you?"

"Yes."

"And you are happy?"

"I am happy for her and Laughing Bird."

"But it is your child."

"Perhaps. We do not know for sure."

"You think she is lying?"

"I think it is possible. She thinks to run you off again and have me back. She does not know you well."

"But what of Laughing Bird? I want him to be happy."

He rubbed her head gently, a slight smile tugging at the corners of his mouth. "I know you do. I sometimes think I did the wrong thing when I gave her to him. But he is strong and will teach her respect. If she does not learn it quickly, he will divorce her. She is smart; she will stay with Laughing Bird. She knows he is a good man."

"Yes." Her mind wandered for a moment. Stalking Horse's voice brought her back to reality.

"You love him."

She stared at him. "Yes. He is special to me in a way that you, my father, and my brother are not."

"I know that, and I respect it."

"But what of your child, Stalking Horse? Will you want to be a part of its life, to watch it grow, to teach it things?"

"It will not matter if it is my child or the child of Laughing Bird. I will love it, as we Cheyenne love all children. I will watch it grow and teach it many things. But I will never think of it as my own."

"And does it sadden you to have no children of your own?"

"It is a sadness I can live with."

"Truly?"

"Truly." He pulled her to him. "With you, there is no sadness which I cannot overcome. There are many years left to us. Perhaps a child will come someday. We will pray for it."

"Horn says there are many medicines which I can take that may help."

"You like working with Horn?"

"Very much. He teaches me things which are new and exciting. He says I learn quickly, and if I continue to show good learning, he might instruct me in many secret ways which only he knows. He says he wants to pass these ways on to me."

"It will be good then. You will always know how to help people."

"Yes. I would like to be like Horn someday. Old and wise and knowledgeable in the ways of The Great

Spirit and the *maiyun,* and knowledgeable in the ways of healing. There is so much I want to learn."

"Then learn it. It can only do you good."

"That is what my father says. He says that not one thing learned can ever be wasted."

"Your father is wise. Perhaps you will learn his wisdom."

"But first I must live many years to acquire it."

"You will acquire it and you will live to be many summers old. But let us think of other things now. I will be riding off to war soon and I must get my fill of you now."

"You said I could come with you sometime."

"Not this time."

"Why? I want to come and be with you. Please."

"We will talk of it later." He pushed her down onto the soft robe. "Now show me how much you will miss me."

"I will not miss you for I will be with you." Her arms tried to create a barrier between her chest and his. "Tell me I can go with you."

He pulled her arms away and pinned them above her head. "I will tell you nothing but what I am now going to do to you."

"And what is that?"

"I do not think I will waste the words." His body covered hers and there was no need for words.

Spring bore a son at the end of summer and she named him Little Horse, the meaning of which did not escape Sun Dancer or Stalking Horse. He was a fine, healthy boy and Laughing Bird seemed proud. Whether he knew the true parentage of the child or not, it seemed to matter little to him. Sun Dancer and Stalking Horse took great pleasure in seeing him so happy.

During one of their visits, when Stalking Horse and Laughing Bird were discussing the future plans of the small baby in the cradleboard, Sun Dancer chose to talk with Spring. "Does Laughing Bird know that the child could be Stalking Horse's?"

"He does not." Spring maintained her indignant attitude toward Sun Dancer.

"Then you will never tell him."

"I will tell him if it pleases me." Her eyes dared Sun Dancer to tell her otherwise.

Sun Dancer walked close to the other girl, her eyes darkly fierce. "You will never tell him, for if you do, I will slit your throat." Sun Dancer's voice sounded fierce, although she wondered if she could ever carry through with her threat.

"You are lying."

"It would be easy. I am good with a knife and I have never liked you, Spring. You have been like a thorn in my finger ever since you came here."

"Stalking Horse brought me; I did not wish to come."

"Now you are lying. But it matters little. You belong to Laughing Bird now, and you will not find a better man than he."

"But I do not love him."

"Then tell him to divorce you and see if you can find anyone better in this camp. Or return to your own people, but you will have to leave your child here. Laughing Bird will never let you take him with you."

"No. I will never leave my child."

"Then stay with the child's father and try to make him happy. He is truly a good man, Spring, and handsome to look at."

"Why didn't you marry him then?"

"I almost did." The look on Spring's face was one of shock. "It would still be easy for me to love him. Would you like that, Spring, if I took your husband away from you?" Sun Dancer knew she had struck the girl's sensitive spot—her pride. She would never permit anyone to take away what was hers.

"You could never take him away from me. He loves me."

"Perhaps. But just the other day he told me he would do anything for me. I could tell him to trade you to another tribe and I could take your child. You could do nothing about it."

"You would not do that."

"I would if it meant Laughing Bird's happiness. It is up to you, Spring. I mean what I say. I have many options. I can kill you and say it was an accident, or I can tell Laughing Bird that you have offended me in some way and tell him to trade you. It matters little to me, for I would like to see you gone from this place. It is your choice."

Spring looked defeated, and the lovely mouth trembled slightly. "I will do as you say. I will never make Laughing Bird doubt the child or my love for him. I want to stay here."

"And do not try to be close to Stalking Horse again. He is my husband and wants nothing to do with you. You have a fine husband and one you can be proud of." The girl nodded blindly, tears flooding her eyes. Sun Dancer placed a hand on Spring's shoulder. "I am not a cruel person, Spring, only one who cares deeply for the people she loves. If you make Laughing Bird happy, then I will be your friend and you can come to me for anything. I do not wish to be your enemy forever."

Spring looked at Sun Dancer. She wiped her eyes and walked outside the lodge, sitting down beside her husband. Sun Dancer followed her out, watching as Spring held the tiny child, envious that she would never hold one of her own.

"See how he smiles like Laughing Bird?" Spring said joyfully, looking lovingly at her husband. Sun Dancer's eyes caught Stalking Horse's and he nodded his head. She smiled back. The child might be of Stalking Horse's blood, but in every other way he would be Laughing Bird's.

CHAPTER XIX

Except in the case of revenge, returning a wrong for a wrong, the Cheyennes only warred to steal horses. Some men went their entire lives without ever killing a man and were proud of it. To kill a man in self-defense or in defense of one's brother was understandable, but to kill for the sake of killing was something many of the Cheyennes could not condone. Therefore, Stalking Horse permitted Sun Dancer to accompany him and some of the other men on a horse-stealing raid to the country of the Pawnee, which was to the south. The Pawnees had raided many Cheyenne villages along the Big River and had stolen a great number of horses. Word spread throughout the various Cheyenne bands about the Pawnee raids, and many were eager to travel to the land of the Pawnee to steal back their horses. Sun Dancer and some of the other wives rode with their husbands to keep camp and assist in taking care of any stolen horses.

Sun Dancer had never seen a Pawnee, although she had heard much talk of them. Their heads were bald except in the back, where they wove feathers through the fan of hair. They wore great lengths of silver from their ears and numerous necklaces. It was said their noses began high up on their foreheads with little bridge, but He-Walks-the-Mountain contended that it was only because they wore no hair about their faces that gave the impression of the nose going back into the head. Some of the women had seen them and said they were fierce-looking people.

"I would rather die than be involved in their blood rituals," Singing Bird had stated.

He-Walks-the-Mountain had told Sun Dancer of the Pawnee practice of sacrificing human lives to *Tirawa*, the principal god of the Pawnees. It was called the Morning Star Ceremony and was used to appease the god and bestow good fortune on the band.

"It is always a young healthy boy or girl, one which would please *Tirawa*," He-Walks-the-Mountain recalled one day. "For four days before the sacrifice, the chosen victim is served the finest food and is treated well. At the end of the four days, two old men go to each end of the village and call aloud to every man to make a bow and an arrow, and smaller ones are made for the smaller boys of the tribe. Before sunrise, the whole village waits at the west end, where two posts have been set up, between which four cross poles have been tied. As day breaks, the captive is led, naked, to the posts, where his hands and feet are tied to the cross poles. On the ground under the altar, they place wood for a great fire.

"Then a warrior with a bow and arrow, the one who captured the victim, runs up and shoots him through from side to side, beneath the arms with the sacred arrow. Then all the males run up and shoot their arrows into the body.''

"What of the smaller children, father? You said arrows were made for them?''

"Arrows are shot for the children who are too young to shoot them. The body is full of arrows when they are finished. Then a man climbs up and pulls out all the arrows but the sacred one, and he cuts open the breast of the victim, putting his hand into the opening and taking out a handful of blood and smearing it over his face. When this is done, the women come forward and strike the body with their sticks and spears and count coup on it.

"Then the fire is lit and the body burned. The people walk by and take handfuls of smoke and smear it over their bodies and those of their children, praying to *Tirawa* to give them health, success in war, and plentiful crops. The man who killed the captive fasts and mourns for four days and asks *Tirawa* to take pity on him because he knows he has taken the life of another human being.''

"Why do you frown so, *nekaim?*'' Brave Wolf rode next to Sun Dancer, his face openly happy, as ever.

"I was remembering the story father told us about the Pawnees and their human sacrifices. It frightens me.''

Brave Wolf shrugged. "It is their way. We have strange ways also.''

"But we do not sacrifice humans.''

"But we kill them, do we not?''

Sun Dancer nodded. "Yes. But at least we kill in war and for a reason. We do not take innocent people into our camp and slaughter them like animals.''

331

"We do not do that." He smiled again, a smile which made Sun Dancer forget her troubled thoughts. What would she have done as a child, if she hadn't had Brave Wolf there to make her laugh?

"Do you like being with your husband?"

"It pleases me greatly to be with him. But sometimes the life in our camp is very . . . dull."

Brave Wolf laughed uproariously. "Dull? Life is never dull when you are around, *nekaim.*" He looked ahead. "We will make camp shortly and continue on tomorrow."

"Brave Wolf?"

"What is it?"

"Have I told you of late that you are wonderful? You have given me much joy in my lifetime."

"You are very serious today, Sun Dancer, but I thank you. We have brought each other joy." He kneed his pony and galloped on ahead. Sun Dancer watched him as he rode away and marveled at the sight of him. He was her brother, her blood. It was a wonderful thing to behold; they were both made of their parents' bodies and forever joined because of it. Then there were her two other brothers who she did not know. They too were of the same blood, but they were no closer to her than any two strangers. Perhaps it was more than blood. Perhaps it was the fostering of love by the parents that co-joined them more than the blood. Perhaps it was the respect they had for each other as human beings. Whatever it was, it was a special thing never to be taken lightly. Her brother was not only a part of her blood, he was a part of her heart.

* * *

The Cheyenne party camped in some rocks which gave them cover from anyone who happened by. When the women had cleaned up camp and were lying in their robes, the men stayed up to talk of the Pawnees and how they would approach their camp. Brave Wolf was their war chief; he listened to their ideas then commented on them or gave ideas of his own. Stalking Horse would be a war chief before long now, but Sun Dancer shut her eyes to the thought. As the years passed and the Cheyennes had more and more contact with other tribes and the white man, there would be more wars and more chances of getting killed. And she knew Stalking Horse to be a man of great courage and ability. He would lead his men and he would fight every war valiantly, even if he lost his own life. Her father was many summers old now, but that was because most of his life had been lived in peace. It would be the young ones—Brave Wolf, Stalking Horse, Laughing Bird—who would face the most dangers and have the fewest chances of a long life.

Stalking Horse walked to the robes. "Brave Wolf tells me you worry about the Pawnees."

"I am not worried; I feel safe with you and our people. It is their customs which frighten me. They seem so strange."

"You speak of the sacrifice." Sun Dancer nodded. "It only happens in the summer as a sacrifice to their god for bountiful food and good fortune."

"But it is summer now."

Stalking Horse laughed. "Do you think that we will come upon them while they are making their sacrifice? It is very unlikely."

"But it is possible."

"If that is so, then how fortunate for us to pick a day when all the men will be otherwise occupied so that we may steal their horses."

Sun Dancer looked at Stalking Horse a moment, then slowly nodded her head. "You have planned this. You knew this was the time of year for their sacrifice and you planned to do it during the ceremony."

"I did not plan it."

"Then how did you know so much about them?"

"Red Bead was a captive of the Pawnees; he remembers well the ceremony. He had to shoot an arrow into the person who was sacrificed."

"He did such a thing?"

"Do not condemn him, Sun Dancer, he did as he was told so that he could stay alive. When he was accepted into the tribe and trusted, he ran away, back to our people. You were young then, a child, and it is likely you do not remember. Red Bead and his father and brothers, along with other members of our tribe, were captured. They were not out for war; they were hunting along the Big River. The Pawnees had roamed north of their land and attacked the hunting party. They killed and scalped Red Bead's father and all of the older men, and took the younger men and boys back to their tribe. They killed the young men who were too much Cheyenne to ever change, and the other young boys were adopted into the tribe."

"And what of Red Bead's brothers?"

"The two older ones were tortured and killed, the two younger ones were taken to the Pawnee village with Red Bead. The youngest, Coyote Boy, who was strong and tall and handsome, was treated with great respect by the Pawnees. Red Bead and his other brother did not understand it. They lived this way for a time until summer came and Coyote Boy was taken away to a special earthen lodge. Red Bead and his other brother did not see him for four days. During that time they were ordered to make a bow and one arrow, which they did, and on the next day, Coyote Boy was tied to the posts which had been erected at the edge of the village. Coyote Boy's captor shot the first arrow into him, then the rest of the men in the tribe did the same. Your father has told you about the ceremony.''

"Red Bead had to shoot his own brother? It is something which I cannot understand.''

"He was a boy and he was ordered to do it. Coyote Boy was already dead by that time anyway. The worst part for Red Bead was seeing his brother's body so mutilated. It is something which he has never forgotten.''

"He goes to kill them?''

"Brave Wolf has said it is not wise; we do not have enough men with us. But we will fight if we have to and we will steal many horses. We will avenge Red Bead's father and brothers as well as we can.''

"And what of his other brother?''

"He stayed with the Pawnees. He was younger than Red Bead and too frightened to attempt the escape.''

"I do not like this; I feel strangely about it all. Perhaps I should not have come with you.''

"You will be safe. You and the other women will remain with the horses. Some of the boys will stay with you. When it is done, we will go back to our country. The ride will be hard the first night, but it will get easier as we get nearer to our land."

She looked at Stalking Horse and realized she could not let him worry about her. It was important that he concentrate all his efforts on the raid. She would not let him know her misgivings.

"I am well and will not worry. It is time we rested; you will need all your strength for the ride tomorrow." She lay down on the robe and he beside her.

"I am pleased you are here. It will bode well for me." He pulled her close and they lay underneath the stars. As she looked up into the sky, Sun Dancer wondered which star was the one the Pawnees murdered under.

For six days, the Cheyenne war party traveled across the seemingly limitless plains. They traveled slowly to keep their horses in good condition, giving them time to feed well along the way. They knew they would need well-conditioned horses for the grueling journey home.

They made base camp at a secluded place among the trees. From there, the scouts rode out to find a Pawnee camp. There were many different Pawnee bands, not all practicing the Morning Star Ceremony. Red Bead was one of the scouts. Since he knew the Pawnees and their ways, he would know which band practiced the ceremony.

They all decided that if the ceremony had already been performed or was unlikely to occur while they were there, they would raid the camp at night to steal as many horses as possible. Brave Wolf didn't want to fight the Pawnees if he didn't have to, for they had never done him wrong. But they had wronged one of his people. If the Cheyennes had to fight, they would do it well.

Sun Dancer and the other women helped the young boys set up camp. Lodges weren't erected on raids—a raiding party pulling travois would have difficulty outrunning the enemy. The women helped with the chores, thus permitting the young men who usually performed them to listen as the war chief and warriors discussed the raid.

Sun Dancer watched Stalking Horse as he talked with her brother and the others. He was serious and completely attentive to what was going on and, she noted, his opinion was highly regarded. The warriors decided to scout the area for a few days to see if the Morning Star Ceremony was to take place. If it was not, they would make their raid right away and return to their own land. Once the warriors left on the raid, the women would prepare to leave and wait for the men outside camp, ready to help with the horses taken by the raiders. The women would be as useful as the men on the journey home.

When Red Bead and the other scouts returned, they were sure that the ceremony would take place in one or two days at a camp not far away. The posts had been erected and Red Bead had seen young girls taking food to the hut where the victim was held. He guessed it would be another day or two before the sacrifice took place.

During this time, Sun Dancer tried to keep herself busy but she always came back to watching Stalking

Horse. Although the other women quilled or gossiped, she was unable to sit still long enough to do either. She was not allowed to ride lest she give away the camp site, so she wandered around the woods, trying to find plants and berries which would be useful to her and to Horn. Late in the evening of the second day, Red Bead rode into camp, the excitement plain on his face.

"I was close enough to hear them talk," he yelled jubilantly. "The sacrifice will take place with the rising sun!"

"Good," replied Brave Wolf. "Before the sun rises, we shall ride close and sneak into their camp. The Pawnees will be waiting for the morning star to rise and will not be anticipating a raid on their camp. We must prepare ourselves."

That night, the men painted themselves and sang songs of war, thinking only of the coming morning. They passed the pipe around and all smoked from it. They took out their weapons and prepared their horses. When the sky was dark and the night quiet, the warriors left for the Pawnee camp. Sun Dancer watched with pride and apprehension as Stalking Horse and the others rode out.

The women quickly packed their provisions onto their horses, waiting for their men near the trail outside their camp. It would be a long wait until morning, but they were prepared to be patient. They would be ready when their men came with the horses.

As always, the younger men of the war party were assigned to collect the horses which roamed freely, while the more experienced warriors went directly into the Pawnee camp to steal the most coveted horses. Coyotes yipped in the night, with the village dogs answering occasionally, barking lazily for a minute or two. Brave Wolf, Stalking Horse, and the others moved closer to the Pawnee camp, waiting until the right time. They left their horses with the young boys, who would wait until their elders approached the Pawnee camp before gathering the horses in the hills. The warriors waited patiently, watching every movement in the camp. People still moved about, while others let their campfires die out and went inside their lodges. The earthen lodges were dug out against the hills and they gave off strange shadows in the night. The lodges were strange to look at, but similar to ones used by Stalking Horse's parents and others of the tribe before they had crossed the Big River.

Stalking Horse's gaze leveled on the wooden posts which would be the "altar" for the victim, and he wondered if the boy or girl knew what would happen in just a few hours. Red Bead said his brother had not known he was to be sacrificed until he was dragged, frantic with fright, to the posts to be tied. Red Bead would never forget the look of terror on his little brother's face that day. Sitting there in the dark night, imagining what the ceremony must be like, Stalking Horse could also imagine the look on Coyote Boy's face when he realized what he was about to endure.

Stalking Horse felt uncomfortable and he now understood why Sun Dancer was frightened by the thought of the ceremony. In just a few hours, when the sun rose over the hills, a healthy young boy or girl would be tied to the "altar" and shot through with hundreds of arrows. The thought made him squirm and he heard Brave Wolf whisper in the darkness, "You too, think of the victim. I do not think I could die so without fighting. It is a strange thing which they do."

"They pick the young and strong. It would not seem so bad if they sacrificed the aged and the sick."

"But that would not be much of a sacrifice to their god."

"No god should require a human life to be sacrificed. War is an honorable thing, slaughter is not."

"But we cannot change it, brother, for if we tried, it would be as you fear the white man. You fear he will come and try to change us and our ways. So we must respect the Pawnees and their ways and not try to change them. We must all cling to what we know, to our traditions. If they are going to change this bloody thing, it will have to come from one of them, not from one of us."

Stalking Horse nodded silently, his eyes still fixed on the posts. "You speak truthfully, I know, but it is unsettling. The child will not even have a chance to fight."

"The child will be watched over and will be rewarded in the next life. Let them have their ceremonies, we will take their horses."

Stalking Horse again nodded his silent assent, although he still wondered about the person in the sacrificial hut. It was not an honorable way to die.

In the Pawnee village, the people gathered at the sacrificial mound on the eastern side of the camp. The Cheyennes stealthily made their way to the opposite side of the camp. The young Cheyenne boys started rounding up the grazing horses as the warriors advanced to gather the picketed, most valued horses. The dogs were no problem this early morning: they followed the Pawnees to the other side of camp, hoping for scraps or handouts.

The sun had not yet risen; the cover of darkness was still with them. The Cheyennes advanced quickly now, covering the noses of their horses to prevent any sudden nickering. Even the guards which they assumed would be posted were absent, readying themselves to join in the ceremony. Red Bead hungered for a fight; he longed to spill Pawnee blood in revenge for the death of his brother. Brave Wolf ordered him not to kill unless it was necessary. They had come to steal horses, not to kill.

The warriors ventured into the Pawnee camp, moving slowly to the picketed horses. Stalking Horse quickly hid next to a lodge as some Pawnee women walked to the sacrificial hut. Moments later, a young girl, completely naked and painted all over, emerged from the hut. The women took her through the village to the eastern side. Stalking Horse watched in wonder as the young girl followed her captors in silence, either not knowing about her approaching death or too proud to show her fear. She was led to the sacrificial mound as the sun began to rise, and Stalking Horse led the horses he had chosen to the outside of the camp.

"We have enough; the sun will be up soon." Brave Wolf motioned to his men. They led their horses away from the village in silence. Stalking Horse did not move; he hunched down in the grass, waiting for the ceremony to begin.

"You must come, brother, you can do nothing."
Brave Wolf moved to him in the early morning light.

"Yes, but I can see and I can remember, so that I
will never treat a human life without dignity."

Brave Wolf looked at his friend and brother-in-law
in silence and nodded his understanding. "We will
wait for you over the hill."

"No, do not wait. Leave my horse and I will catch
up to you. Do not endanger the others."

Brave Wolf moved away in the semi-darkness,
while Stalking Horse watched as the young girl was
led to the posts. He could see her body begin to rebel
as she realized what was about to happen, but she
didn't cry out or try to run away. She held her head
high, her posture erect and proud. It was how he
could imagine Sun Dancer going to her death.

He felt his heart beat furiously as the girl's ankles
and wrists were secured to the posts. A priest uttered
some words, while another man, her captor, stepped
in front of the girl. He looked at her a moment, and
she at him, then he shot her with an arrow while
another man clubbed her on the back of the head.
Her captor cut her chest open and stuck his hands
into the cavity, removing the bloody heart.

Stalking Horse crept back over the hill. He knew
what would come next: every man would shoot an
arrow into the body and then they would burn it.

When he was out of sight of the Pawnee camp,
Stalking Horse ran to his horse. He hadn't ridden far
when Sun Dancer came out of the bushes, leading
two extra horses. She was smiling. He smiled back
and was suddenly reassured of life through her. He

could not help the girl who was sacrificed, but he could help others. If he ever became a chief, he would deal fairly and compassionately with people. Life was too delicate a thing to toy with, and it could end too quickly. He wanted to live and he wanted his people to live. There would be honor in their living and in their dying.

They were a night and a day out of the Pawnee village when Brave Wolf decided to make camp. He sent out two backriders and posted a guard, while the others ate and rested. They made no campfires that night, but ate dried meat and berries, drinking water from their hide vessels. It had been a successful raid—many horses had been taken and no lives on either side had been lost.

"We have many horses now." Sun Dancer came to sit next to Stalking Horse after refilling her water vessel. "What will we do with all of them?"

"We are rich in horses. We will give many to the old people of the tribe, to my aunts and uncles, and to Horn."

"Horn will not take many. He does not wish to possess many things."

"He will take the horse I have chosen for him. This one is white with a black patch on his nose and four black feet. He is strange to look at; I have not seen many like him. I think Horn will like him."

"Yes, perhaps he will. He likes things which are different." Her hand touched his arm lightly. "You saw the ceremony?"

"Yes. It was a young girl. Young and proud. She did not even cry out."

"I could not be so brave."

"You have been braver."

"I?"

"When the Kiowas were ready to burn you, you did not cry out. The blood of your father and brother runs thick in you."

"I wanted to die honorably."

"You live honorably and you will die honorably." He took her hand. "You have given me much, Sun Dancer, but more than anything, you have shown me a special way to look at life. You have created something in me which never before existed." He held her hand tightly, looking into her puzzled eyes. "Through you I have learned to respect life and look upon it as a gift to be used wisely. And you will help me to use it wisely."

"You give me too much credit, husband, for unknowingly you have done the same for me. Perhaps together, we can learn and help our people. Together, we are strong."

Stalking Horse nodded and looked up into the star-filled sky. Perhaps one day she and he would fill a place up there in that vast universe, but they would make their time on earth count for much. We will make our ancestors proud, he thought. From our living will come wisdom and peace. And honor.

CHAPTER XX

The day the white men came to the Cheyenne camp was a day Sun Dancer would never forget. Already, many of her people had traded with French trappers, *maiviheyo*, "red white men," and found them to be good friends. The trappers paid much for beaver furs, and it was easy for the Cheyennes to catch the beaver on the rivers as they came out of their holes. Frequently, the Indians broke the dams surrounding the beaver house until the water was lowered. They often sent a small dog into the hole after the beaver until it became so annoyed it came out after the dog. The beaver was either clubbed on the head or shot with an arrow. Many of the Cheyennes were beginning to realize the value of the soft brown fur; they were willing to catch them and trade them to the French for items which they didn't have.

There were four French trappers who came down from Canada, and two *ciboleros*, Mexican buffalo hunters. The Mexicans came all the way from Mexico to trade with the Indian tribes of the north who lived in and around the Black Hills—Cheyenne,

Sioux, Kiowa, Comanche, Crow, and Arapaho. They brought with them a dry, hard bread, which the Cheyennes grew fond of as well as salt, arrowshafts, bows, and sheet iron for arrowheads. The Mexicans exchanged their articles for dried meat, robes, moccasins, backrests, and parfleches. Things which the Indians took for granted, the Mexicans and French wanted, and vice-versa.

Sun Dancer stood outside the circle of Cheyenne men and women watching as the *ciboleros* and the trappers showed their wares. She was not too impressed with the Mexicans; except for their facial characteristics, their color was similar to the Cheyennes—dark hair and eyes, brown skin. The trappers impressed her most; one in particular. He wore buckskin pants and a shirt with long fringes and heavy-duty moccasins laced to his knees. His cap was a rich, dark fur, probably otter. Around his neck, he wore many different Indian necklaces obtained from trading with various tribes. Although his skin was tanned dark by the sun, it was still lighter than Sun Dancer's; and his golden hair fell to his shoulders. When he looked up to tell the women about his wares, Sun Dancer saw that his eyes were the same shade as the sky on a clear day. So, she thought, it was true: the white man comes in different colors.

It was this one man who most intrigued Sun Dancer; he was unlike anyone she had ever seen. When he handed her a piece of bread, Sun Dancer immediately handed it back to him; but he held up his left index finger, grasping it with the fist of his right hand, pulling it back and forth. It was the sign for "keep," and shyly Sun Dancer put the bread into the parfleche which hung around her neck. She continued to watch with great interest as the trappers and the *ciboleros* laughed and joked with some of her people, trading for items they needed while traveling the high plains.

The men were invited to stay in the Cheyenne camp, and they were treated as honored guests. They were given a lodge of their own in which to sleep. The trappers' gifts of bread were added to fresh buffalo meat and freshly picked blackberries for the feast to be held that night.

At their evening meal, Sun Dancer included the bread which the Frenchman had given her. Much to her surprise, Stalking Horse did not complain, although he did not eat the bread. She knew his feelings about white men and she feared he would be angry with her for accepting the gift. But he was not and he encouraged her to trade for more bread if she so desired.

"Did you see them, Stalking Horse, and the one with the golden hair? I still cannot believe anyone can be so different from us."

"It is not only in looks that they are different from us, Sun Dancer, and you will do well to remember this." She looked at him, slightly vexed by his warning, but she left the lodge to trade for more bread. She found the man with the golden hair sitting outside his lodge with another man. She handed him an empty parfleche, then with both index fingers pointing up, she raised both hands and quickly moved them past each other and pointed to the bread. He smiled broadly and went into the lodge.

"This one is nice, Pierre. You should find out how much bread it will take to trade for her," one of the trappers yelled after Pierre.

"Oui. I would pay much for one like this," one of the other trappers added. "She would be good for those long winter nights when we are trapping, eh?" They all laughed and Sun Dancer looked at them, marveling at the strange tongue in which they spoke.

The Frenchman returned with the bread and took the parfleche from Sun Dancer. "You will take these, too, eh?" He handed Sun Dancer a small comb and brush. "For de hair," and he motioned with the brush and comb how they were to be used. Sun Dancer smiled delightedly but attempted to hand the gifts back to the Frenchman, but again he refused. She thanked him and walked away, admiring the delicate workmanship of the mother-of-pearl comb and brush. She turned once more to look at him and found him smiling at her, and shyly she smiled back.

"Are you going to buy her, Pierre?"

"We could all buy her and share her." One of the trappers kissed his closed fingers. *Magnifique.*

"Do not joke about her," Pierre said seriously, sitting down by the others. "Cheyenne women are not like others, they are treated with great respect. If we forget that, then we might wind up with a knife in here, eh?" He motioned vividly with an invisible knife across his stomach.

"Well, then, why don't you buy her? Then you could do whatever you want without breaking their rules."

Pierre nodded his head slightly, a smile spreading slowly across his face. "That I could do. I have often

348

wondered what it would be like to have an Indian wife." He looked over at the others and they all laughed, appreciating the fact that he was not so gallant as he seemed.

Stalking Horse was not pleased with Sun Dancer's gifts from the Frenchman. "You will take them back."

"But they are so beautiful."

"I do not trust gifts from anyone I do not know, especially those from a white man. You will take them back."

"Why do you distrust them so? They have been friendly and have traded fairly."

"I do not like them coming in here, for later they will bring others. You know my feelings on this, Sun Dancer."

"Yes, I know them well enough, but this I do not understand. Even my father says they are good to trade with and we can acquire many things from them."

Stalking Horse glared at her from across the fire. "I do not like the way they look at you."

"At me? I do not understand."

"They are men and you are a woman. They have not seen a woman in many moons. Perhaps they seek to gain your favor, and that of the other women in return for trinkets and gifts."

"You do me a disfavor by saying that."

"It is not you I speak of, I speak of the man with the golden hair. I have watched the way his eyes watch you. He watches you as a man who desires a woman."

"You are wrong," Sun Dancer refuted angrily, but

she knew there was truth in her husband's statement. She too had seen the look in the Frenchman's eyes. "I will take the gifts back. I did not know you watched me so."

"I only watch you when I feel you are in danger and cannot take care of yourself."

"You feel that I am in danger around the white man?"

"You have never before confronted a man such as this, nor have I. We do not know what to expect. It is better to be wary."

"And distrustful?"

"If it must be."

"I do not like this. They are kind and I will be kind back. I will return the gifts but I will not be their enemies." She looked at Stalking Horse for a brisk moment then left the lodge.

"But they will someday be yours," Stalking Horse said out loud, frightened of the unwanted presence in his village.

Pierre looked perplexed when Sun Dancer walked up to him, and with a gift of roasted buffalo tongue and fresh berries, returned his comb and brush.

"But they are for you," he insisted and tried to return the gifts, but he was met by disapproving eyes. He made the sign for "gift" and "keep," but Sun Dancer shook her head. She smiled then and made the sign for "friend." She started to walk away but Pierre grabbed her arm. There was a flicker of anger in her eyes, and he immediately let her go. She was not used to being treated in such a manner. "Wait," he said in exasperation, and closing his right hand below his shoulder and bringing it down, he made the sign for "stay." Sun Dancer stopped and he ran to find one of his friends. Jean was older, the most experienced trapper of the group, and he was able to speak a smattering of most of the languages of the northern tribes.

"She bring you buffalo tongue, eh? That is good. That's a delicacy and means you're an honored guest."

"Tell her I wish her to have the gifts. I do not want them. Tell her if she does not take them, I will throw them into the river."

Jean repeated Pierre's words to Sun Dancer. Although she was amazed that he would do such a thing, she still refused his gifts.

"She says she can't accept the gifts but she thanks you anyway."

"Tell her not to go yet; tell her I wish to be her friend."

Jean gave the younger man a perplexed glance, but he translated Pierre's words. "She says you are already friends."

Sun Dancer turned to go and desperately Pierre thought of something to keep her there.

"Tell her I am lonely."

Quickly, Jean translated Pierre's words and Sun Dancer stopped and turned around to look at the white man. He was handsome in his own way, and certainly his eyes were something which a person could look upon and never tire of seeing, but what was he asking of her now? Could it be that he was just lonely and needed a friend, or was it that he needed a woman, as Stalking Horse had said. It was better not to take chances. She spoke to Jean, and he smiled in appreciation of the young woman's words.

"She says if you are lonely then seek out your friends for companionship. She must return to her husband."

"She is married then." Pierre watched her as she moved gracefully away, her carriage erect and proud. She looked as he had always imagined an Indian princess should look—proud and beautiful.

"But of course. Did you expect one like that not to be?" Jean invaded his thoughts. "She cannot be played with, Pierre. She is the daughter of a chief."

"And her husband?"

"Young, but a respected warrior. I do not think he would let her go without a fight. I know I would not."

"Would he sell her then?"

"Would you?"

Pierre looked over at the older man and shook his head. If he owned a woman like that, there was no way another man would take her from him. He wanted to see the woman's husband.

Sun Dancer picked the berries and put them into the basket. She loved this time of year when the fruit was fresh and plentiful and it wasn't necessary to subsist on dried fruit. She enjoyed being with nature and learning about the plants and animals. She was happy she did not live where people huddled together; she could not conceive of living in a white man's city, did they call it? The lodges, it was said, were built so closely together that there was no room for plants and trees and wild game to run. How foolish! It made no sense. It seemed to her that everything her people lived for and depended on were the very things the white man wished to destroy.

The Frenchman, Pierre, bothered her. He was determined to be her friend, although she made it clear that they were friends, that nothing further needed to be done. She had told him she was married and saw the look on his face. It was then that she realized Stalking Horse was right. Pierre had been hoping to have her warm his robes.

"I cannot be the kind of friend with him that I am with Laughing Bird," she thought, sorry for herself and the strange foreigner.

Sun Dancer heard footsteps behind her. Although the person attempted to step quietly, she could hear the light footfall; it was not a Cheyenne. She turned abruptly to find Pierre staring down at her. The look in his eyes was unsettling, as were the eyes themselves. She stared into the clear depths, not able to comprehend what was behind them. He took her arms and pulled her to her feet, taking the basket from her to set it on the ground. She wasn't frightened of him, for she knew he wouldn't try to harm her so close to her own camp. He continued to stare at her and then he reached out to touch her face gently, much the same way Stalking Horse touched her, much the way a lover would touch. She tried to pull away but he drew her near and spoke in his strange language, words which she could not understand.

"I do not understand why you Indians do not kiss. This is a wonderful way to show affection." His mouth closed over hers, very gently, and although she tried to pull away, he held her close and continued to move his mouth on hers. Sun Dancer's heart beat quickly and she was ready to reach for her knife when Pierre let her go, smiling as he did so. She touched her lips, not quite understanding what the gesture meant. She picked up her basket and hurried away from the white man. What had he said in his strange language, what had he meant by his gesture? She turned to find him staring after her, his blue eyes gentle and knowing. She did not fear him, and that frightened her most of all.

Sun Dancer wanted to tell Stalking Horse about the white man and what he had done but she did not. She knew her husband and she knew he would kill the white man for touching his wife. He had made his feelings known several times and he didn't want her talking or trading with the white men, although she did so in spite of his protests. But she knew his love for her was great and he sought only to protect her from something she didn't understand. He had taught her many things so that she might be independent and strong, but he knew little of the white man and didn't know what to expect from them.

"The white men seem to like our village. Soon they will be taking Cheyenne wives and living as we do." Stalking Horse chewed on the dried meat and looked at Sun Dancer, his mocking tone an invitation for her to protest.

"We have no law which says we cannot marry the white man. If a woman of our tribe is willing and the man pays her family, then we must not interfere."

"And would you marry the white man with the golden hair?"

"Why do you ask such a question? I am married to the only person I want to be with."

"What of this light-haired man with eyes the color of the sky? I have seen you look at him and I wonder, what does Sun Dancer think of this man? Does she want to know him because he is different from us, or does she want to know him as a woman wants to know a man?"

"You insult me much these days, husband, and do me little service by your unkind words. I am a woman who knows her mind, and I seek to find out new things."

"And if the light-haired one asked you to leave with him, would you do this?"

Sun Dancer stood up, throwing her bowl at Stalking Horse, hitting him on the leg. "I will not hear any more of your insults. Why do you speak to me in this manner? Why do you treat me as if I were an adulteress?"

"Because I see you through the eyes of a man and a lover, and I know how other men look at you. I do not seek to insult you, Sun Dancer, I seek only to have you with me for always."

"Then do not treat me as a child who has no mind. Let me learn things for myself. Be my husband, not my parent." She stalked out of the lodge, again leaving Stalking Horse to look after her in silence, knowing instinctively that she was in some kind of danger, but unable to do anything about it.

*　　　*　　　*

Sun Dancer avoided Pierre. Although she often felt his eyes on her when she passed him by, he made no further attempt to touch her. He and his friends planned to leave the village in two days' time. She wished she had learned some of the language in which the men spoke and gotten to know the men better. She felt, however, that it was best to keep a distance from them, especially Pierre. She sensed she could grow to like him and she knew this would anger Stalking Horse.

The night before the men were to leave, a feast was held in their honor. The Cheyenne women roasted fresh meat, baked corn in holes dug in the ground, placed bowls of fresh berries before the lodges of the guests. The women danced and sang love songs, while some of the young boys played their flutes and beat time on drums made of skins. Stalking Horse refused to attend a feast in honor of the white men, as he had refused to have any dealings with them, but Sun Dancer went to the celebration and brought a gift for each man. Although she had already given Pierre a gift of a parfleche, she had taken a pair of his moccasins and repaired them and had lined them with rabbit fur for the coming fall and winter. All of the men were gracious in their acceptance of the gifts, and they too, distributed gifts of beads, glass, and bread to their generous hosts. It was important for them to maintain this friendly contact.

As the ceremonies proceeded and everyone feasted, Pierre moved closer to Sun Dancer and placed something in her hand. When she raised it up to look at it, she drew her breath in sharply, for she had never before realized what she looked like. Pierre had given her a small hand mirror. Sun Dancer stared into it, as if unsure of the lovely, gentle person who stared back. She looked at her face once more then over at Pierre. She laughed and he was completely mesmerized by her delight. She was a child of nature, untouched and pure.

"Merci," Sun Dancer said shyly, having learned the word from Jean, the older trapper.

Pierre lifted her hand to kiss it lightly. She quickly withdrew it but was reassured when Pierre said in halting Cheyenne, "It is our custom; do not be offended."

The evening went quickly and the white men and Cheyennes gestured and laughed as if there were no language barrier between them. When it grew late and many of the campfires began to die down, Sun Dancer started for her lodge. Pierre walked with her but she shook her head and pushed him gently away. She smiled and made the sign for friend, but made it clear he was not to accompany her further. Pierre watched her walk away and it was then he realized that he must have her. He called out to her and she turned; as he approached, she saw the change in his eyes. There was no gentleness now as he took her by the arm and led her to the edge of camp. Even as she struggled to reach her knife, he struck her a blow on the head, rendering her helpless. She could only think how angry Stalking Horse would be.

The white men rose early in the morning, preparing their horses for their journey. They were surprised to find Pierre already packed and gone. All were surprised that is, except Jean, who had a strong suspicion of what his friend had done and why he'd left so early. He was angered by the young man's impulsiveness, and more angered by the fact that he could destroy a valuable friendship which they had just created with the Cheyennes. Although he felt no loyalty at all to the Cheyennes, he felt compelled to be honest with them so that he might be trusted in the future. He immediately went to the lodge of Stalking Horse.

Sun Dancer was gagged and tied to her horse, Pierre in front, leading her along. She knew he wouldn't get far this way, and as soon as Stalking Horse found out she was missing, he would follow. He had warned her and she hadn't listened. Now he would be angry and would think her no more than a child who could not see the true nature of people. She silently cursed her stupidity and her innocence. She had wanted so much to believe this man was good.

Pierre had taken her knife and the parfleche from her neck, knowing too well she would need them to survive if she were alone. When they stopped to water the horses he removed her moccasins; he took every precaution to see she wouldn't run away.

Pierre traveled a route completely unfamiliar to Sun Dancer, the trail leading into a part of the mountains unknown to her. He constantly looked behind him, covering their tracks effectively, back-tracking at times, veering off the path at others. When it seemed as if they would go well up into the mountains, Pierre took another route back down to the plains, a route which was well-hidden and untraveled. It all looked unfamiliar to her and she wondered if Stalking Horse would be able to bypass the false tracks Pierre had left for him and track them down. They rode all the first night and day, and into the second night, stopping only for water and to allow the horses to rest. Sun Dancer was exhausted and unable to understand how Pierre could be so cautious and alert without sleep.

Pierre stopped the third night to make camp by the hills. He lifted Sun Dancer to the ground and immediately removed her moccasins, tying her hands behind her and her legs at the ankles. He covered her with a robe and unsaddled his horses, removing only water and food from the pack. His long, heavy rifle he kept ever-present. As he sat next to Sun Dancer, feeding her bits of dried meat, his eyes were always alert to the sounds and sights around him.

"Don't be frightened," he signed to her but she couldn't believe him. She could never remember being so frightened in her life and having so little control over the situation. Then there were the times she caught him looking at her, the kind of look which Stalking Horse had described to her. She knew this man intended to make her his woman. Although everything in her rebelled at the thought, she knew what she had to do to stay alive and get back to her own people. It was important for her to think clearly, without the shadow of fear.

She was awakened abruptly after a couple of hours and lifted up onto the horse, her feet again lashed underneath the horse's belly, her hands tied to its neck. Pierre continued on his strange route and by morning they had reached the plains and were able to see herds of buffalo grazing. They were going south, and this frightened Sun Dancer even more. She had never been farther south than the Arapaho camp, and she was being taken into land which was completely foreign to her. They rode hard that day, Pierre allowing Sun Dancer to ride her horse on her own, but making it known that he would shoot her if she tried to escape. She greatly feared the large rifle and she was forced into doing whatever the man ordered her to do, at least until she was able to find him in a vulnerable moment. And she knew that this would happen, for all men were vulnerable at one time or another.

Four days had elapsed since their flight from the Cheyenne camp. Sun Dancer looked constantly behind her, hoping to see some sign of Stalking Horse or her people. But Pierre had been effective in covering their tracks, for she never saw anyone following. He seemed completely at ease in this land, and he seemed to know it as well as any Indian. Indeed, he probably knew parts of it better than the Indians; he made his livelihood solely from the furs of animals, trapping the rivers and mountains.

On the fourth night, Pierre made camp in some low rocks, effectively shielding them and their horses from passersby. Pierre killed a rabbit and ordered Sun Dancer to cook it, along with some of the hard bread he had given her. When Sun Dancer refused to eat, Pierre commanded her to do so by aiming the rifle at her head. It was not so much fear of dying by the weapon that made her comply but the fact that she was not one to give up and die willingly. She would eat and she would remain strong for that time when she could escape.

It was the fourth night also that Pierre came to her; she feared that what Stalking Horse had predicted would happen. Pierre kissed her many times and ran his hands over her body. When her lips refused to soften and her body refused to yield, he angrily pushed her away from him, swearing in French.

"When we are away from this place," his arm swept the area around him, "then there will be time to teach you what I want." Harshly, he kissed her once more and went to his own robe, closing his eyes for the first time in four nights, or for the first time that Sun Dancer had seen. She couldn't understand how the man could keep going with so little sleep and she didn't understand why. She was nothing to him. Why was he doing this?

Pierre woke up abruptly, shortly after closing his eyes, when a wolf began howling in the hills. He was instantly alert and he moved about the area, checking every place a man could possibly hide. Satisfied that no one was about, he went back to his robe and sat down with his rifle across his lap, closing his eyes. She too had heard the wolf and it was a joyous sound to her ears, a familiar one. Would there be wolves where they were going?

Pierre woke Sun Dancer before dawn and they headed out of their hidden camp. Again he let her ride without tying her hands, and again he threatened to use the rifle if she tried to run away. The scenery changed the further south they rode. The hills seemed farther away and the prairie more stark and desolate. Often, they rode past herds of grazing buffalo. Sun Dancer couldn't help remembering the time Stalking Horse had saved her from the charging bull. At the time she had been hurt and ashamed that he had done it, but now she felt a fondness and a longing. She was frightened without him, but she knew she had to rely on herself. Stalking Horse had taught her that, and she must remember everything he had taught her.

They rode the entire day and well into the night before stopping. As they had done the previous night, they camped in a shelter of rocks away from the path they had been following. Pierre said little to Sun Dancer and she wished he were more the friendly man he had been when they met. It was still hard for her to believe that this man could change so suddenly, but Stalking Horse had known he would.

"Don't hope for your man to come for you," Pierre said as he watched Sun Dancer looking about her. "He will never find our trail, only the one I left him." He was quiet and he stared at Sun Dancer for a long time. "We go to Mexico. You know Mexico?" Sun Dancer wasn't sure what he was saying and she looked at him questioningly. "We go to the home of the *ciboleros,* Mexico. South."

He pointed south. Now she understood what he meant. He was taking her where the Mexican traders came from, a place where few northern Indians had ever been but had only heard of. It was a place far away where the weather was hot and the land dry. Alarm showed in her face.

"It ees best. Indian squaws are not unusual there and I can trade for many things. You will like it."

Sun Dancer stared at the man. Mexico—she must

escape. She would die in a place like that. She was too accustomed to the mountains, the rivers, the cotton-woods and pines, the flowers and fresh berries in spring and summer. Were there animals in this other place? Was there anything for them to live on? Would she be condemned to live the rest of her days with this man because she had refused to listen to her husband?

"Sleep now, woman, we ride in a few hours."

Sun Dancer turned onto her side, listening to the sounds of the night, wondering if Stalking Horse was coming for her. She worried about the trail Pierre had left, hoping that Stalking Horse's tracking experience would show him the false ones. She tried in every way she could think of to leave a sign for Stalking Horse but it was impossible. Pierre constantly watched her; even when they stopped to relieve themselves, she was never left alone for a minute. The time would come, she was sure, when he must learn to trust her. He couldn't keep her tied forever. If she proved to him that she could be trusted, perhaps he would untie her and let her roam about freely until she was able to get a knife or his gun. A thought plagued her, however; if he trusted her enough to untie her and let her go about on her own, then he would probably demand more from her than kisses. This was something she was not prepared to give him, no matter what the outcome. She closed her eyes, but she did not sleep.

CHAPTER XXI

Stalking Horse packed his horse lightly, taking only the essential things—food and weapons. He had known something was wrong when the trapper came to his lodge and told him that Pierre was gone. When Sun Dancer did not come back to the lodge the previous night, he didn't look for her. He thought she wanted to be alone, and he didn't want to anger her by going after her and bringing her back to the lodge.

His first inclination had been to hit Jean in the face, to smash him to the ground. But the man had told him the truth and could not be faulted for that. He shook the man's hand in an expression of friendship, and tried to offer him a gift of a pipe and tobacco. But Jean waved it away, saying he was the one who owed the Cheyennes because of his friend's insolence. He wanted to ride with Stalking Horse but Stalking Horse refused his help; he wanted the Frenchman to himself.

Stalking Horse told Brave Wolf where he was going but declined any offer of help. "Sun Dancer is my wife," he said, "and I am responsible for her. I will get her back."

Jean told Stalking Horse where he thought Pierre might go. "There's a place we stay in the mountains, or he might go south to Mexico to trade his furs. Told me many times he wants to settle in Mexico because the weather's nice and the people there accept whites."

Stalking Horse easily followed Pierre's trail up into the hills and back down, picking up the fact that he had backtracked several times. Stalking Horse smiled to himself as he ran his hand over the tracks. The man was good, he had to admit, but he didn't realize that a Cheyenne boy is taught to track from the time he can walk. It would be a challenge but one he could handle.

Pierre had a good start on him but he wouldn't be able to travel so quickly with Sun Dancer and a pack horse. Stalking Horse rode straight through the first night and into the morning, picking up the trail as Pierre veered in and out of trees and rocks. He looked for any sign that Sun Dancer might leave, but wasn't surprised when he found none. He assumed she was tied, for Pierre had probably guessed she wasn't a meek type and wouldn't stay unless threatened.

By the end of the second day, Stalking Horse knew the man was going to Mexico. In spite of his meanderings, Pierre was traveling in a southerly direction. Because of this and the fact that the weather would get hotter the further south they traveled, Stalking Horse knew he'd have a better chance of finding them. Pierre would have to rest his pack horse often, and unless he wanted an expert horsewoman like Sun Dancer to escape in minutes, he was probably keeping her in check. The slow pace would eventually aid Stalking Horse in his search.

Stalking Horse traveled until the sky was black and he could see nothing. The white man had the advantage of being able to travel at night, while Stalking Horse couldn't risk losing the trail and having to backtrack and relocate it the next day. As soon as the sky began to lighten in the morning, he was mounted and riding, stopping only to jump to the ground and check tracks.

His mind constantly wandered to Sun Dancer. His gut fear was that the man had used her and hurt her; he wasn't sure how a woman like Sun Dancer would take that kind of humiliation. He hoped with all his being that he was wrong and the man hadn't forced himself on her. But being a man himself, he knew well a man's lust when he wanted a woman.

By the fourth day, it was apparent that Pierre was letting Sun Dancer have her lead on her horse, for the pace had picked up immensely. The man was no fool. He picked a circuitous route which he knew Stalking Horse would have to follow. If Stalking Horse elected to go straight to try and head them off, he risked missing them completely. And the man rode through the night. Did he not sleep?

A week out of the Cheyenne camp, Stalking Horse found himself no closer to Sun Dancer and Pierre, a situation which frustrated and angered him. If he kept on at this rate, he would always be a day or two behind them. By the time they reached Mexico and the big river, the Rio Grande, they would go anywhere, for the trail would be lost. He had to take his chances and start traveling at night, using his every instinct and sense to guide him on the same route which the white man took.

The first night Stalking Horse rode on after a few hours of sleep, and in the morning light, fresh tracks showed him to be getting closer to Sun Dancer and Pierre. He rode on through the day, stopping only to find water for himself and his horse. He slept a few hours in the heat of the day and rode straight through the next night to make up for the time lost. The next morning rewarded him with hot ashes from a still smoldering campfire and tracks which had barely settled into the dirt. He was close to them and he kept up the hard pace.

Again Stalking Horse slept in the heat of the day and traveled through the night, but the next morning what he feared would happen, happened. The trail was cold and he had lost sight of any tracks. The white man had anticipated Stalking Horse and had changed his course, veering southwest, to throw his tracker off. Stalking Horse spent half the day picking up the trail. When he found it again, he kept on all day and long into the evening. When he finally rested, he tried to think as the white man was thinking, trying to envision how he would elude someone, even though they both knew the eventual destination.

Although there were not many settlements of whites in the south, there were enough for Pierre to stop and trade. He would not be frowned upon because he had an Indian wife, for many trappers and men of the mountains took Indians as their wives. But a lone Cheyenne warrior, especially one who had never been to white settlements before, would be leery of entering such a place. Pierre knew that and

Stalking Horse knew that that is what the man would do. But as much as he hated and feared the white man, he loved his wife even more; he would follow this white man no matter where he went. This was something the white man would not count on. He would not count on an Indian loving his wife so much he would follow her anywhere to get her back.

Stalking Horse still traveled at night but at a slower pace, jumping to the ground when the moon gave off enough light for him to see the tracks. He could not waste another day backtracking, so when it was too dark for trailing, he camped for the balance of the night. At dawn, he was on his way again. He expected to see the pack horse left on the trail somewhere, but Pierre pushed all the horses hard, knowing he'd be able to trade for more soon. The Frenchman had surprised Stalking Horse, and grudgingly he admitted to himself that the man had given him more of a chase than he thought possible. But no matter how good the man was or how much respect Stalking Horse had for his ability, it wouldn't prevent him from killing Pierre when he found him. And he would find him. Of that, he had no doubt.

For the first time, Sun Dancer felt out of her element. Pierre had stopped at a trading post, and he had dragged Sun Dancer into the wooden building against her will. She saw a woman with red hair piled on top of her head, dressed in a cloth dress and bonnet. Strange hard shoes covered her feet and Sun Dancer marveled that the woman could even walk. The woman's husband and sons were dressed in shirts and trousers which appeared to be held up by colorful ropes. Outside, there was a wagon pulled by oxen; there were small carts, horses, and weary looking pack horses that waited to be reloaded for a new journey.

Sun Dancer looked around the small room in wonder as Pierre dragged her to the counter and he bargained with the owner. She saw beaver traps, traps for larger game, a few rifles, blankets, trading beads, heavy fur garments made from an assortment of animal skins and hides, axes, short-handled picks and shovels, knives, ropes, and sacks full of hard-to-come-by products such as coffee, tea, flour, sugar, and tobacco.

Sun Dancer felt curious eyes on her as she and Pierre moved about, and no one seemed friendly enough to smile or make a friendly gesture toward her.

When Pierre was finished at the trading post, he dragged Sun Dancer away from the building. They rode a short distance into some trees where he set up camp. After unpacking his horse, he threw a package at Sun Dancer.

"Put this on and take your hair out of the braids." When Sun Dancer made no motion of doing as she was told, Pierre walked to her and roughly ripped the dress from her shoulders. She struggled frantically to free herself from his hold but he worked the dress off until she stood only in her moccasins. After admiring her body for a few moments, he took the dress out of the package and pulled it over Sun Dancer's head, fitting it to the rest of her body.

"Ees too big for you but will do. A dress. You wear dresses now." He picked up her buckskin dress and bunching it into a ball, threw it in the fire. "Undo the hair," and he motioned to Sun Dancer what he meant. She knew he would do it for her if she did not, so she undid her braids. She took the brush that he had given her and brushed it out. The thick, black mass reached almost to her waist and she could feel Pierre's hands running through it. *"Magnifique!"* he whispered from behind and pulled her to him. "I do not know if I can wait, *ma cherie*, but I will try. I do not wish to frighten you, only to love you. I will make you forget you are an Indian." Sun Dancer didn't understand much of what Pierre had said, but she understood the last and she bristled at the words. He would never make her forget she was Cheyenne, no matter what he did to her. He could change her clothes and her hair and her way of speaking, but he would never change the person she was inside. She would always be Cheyenne.

Sun Dancer did everything obediently. The sooner she gained Pierre's trust, the sooner she could find a way to escape him. She now cooked the meals before asked, and as much as she hated to wear her hair loose, she did it without protest because she knew it would please him. She even attempted to speak the English words he tried to teach her, in the hope that he would eventually trust her.

She was resigned to their way of traveling now, and having traveled similarly with her own people, she never complained of the rapid pace which they maintained. She hated the feel of the long dress on her legs, and she hiked it up around her knees while she rode, which made Pierre smile. Even though her own buckskin dress was heavier, it was much more functional and comfortable. She didn't want to imitate a white woman, but if doing so would keep her alive long enough to think of a way to escape, then she would wear dresses and hard shoes and hats.

She was surprised when one night Pierre announced they would camp early. He'd found a place along a river, which river she didn't know, but it was abundant with trees and would easily hide them from passersby. Sun Dancer roasted rabbit and collected gooseberries, and they ate generously of the bread which Pierre always carried with him.

When they finished their evening meal and Sun Dancer had cleaned up, Pierre took something out of his pocket and gave it to her. He gestured to her mouth.

"It is to eat." He unwrapped the peppermint stick, broke a piece off, and put it into her mouth. "Is good, no?" Sun Dancer sucked on the candy and was pleasantly surprised by the sweet taste. She smiled with genuine pleasure. It was the first time she had smiled at Pierre on their journey, and it elicited a gentle response from him.

"I would like always to make you smile." He moved closer and ran his fingers lovingly along the lines of her face. His eyes were gentle again, but Sun Dancer knew that they could change at any moment. She tried to contain her fear as he lowered his mouth to hers, forcing her body to remain relaxed while his hands moved over her. He lowered her to the ground, his hand found her skirt and began to move it upwards, touching her skin. She wrapped her arms around his waist and waited. She knew this time would come and she had been prepared. She moved her left arm down to his hip where he kept his knife, and as he continued his exploration of her body, she slowly moved her hand down to the hilt of the large knife. When she had a firm grasp on it, she pulled it from its sheath. As Pierre moved his hands farther up her thighs, she plunged the knife into his side. His scream rent the still night air, but when she tried to throw him from her, he shoved her over, striking her violently.

"Diable!" he screamed and again struck her on the head. She tried to sit up but was too dizzy. She lay on her side, wondering what had happened, when she saw her mistake. He still wore his vest, which was made of deerskin and lined with lamb's wool. The knife had pierced his skin, but not enough to cause any real damage, for the vest had dulled most of the impact. Pierre glared at Sun Dancer, raising his arm as if to hit her again, but he put it down. "Ees to be expected. *Vous etes une sauvage."* He got to his feet, grimacing at the pain in his side, and walked to the horses. He returned with rope and again Sun Dancer was tied, ankles crossed and together, arms behind her back; then she was lashed to a tree. Pierre would see to it that she had no more opportunity to try to kill him.

They rose at dawn and Sun Dancer was tied to her horse with a rope around her neck. The implications were clear. She was not to attempt anything. If her horse went even a little ahead of Pierre's, she would choke to death. He would make sure there were no further attempts on his life. Sun Dancer still could not believe the man had not been injured; she'd stuck the knife in with a quick, hard thrust but had not counted on his vest. Stalking Horse would have thought of the man's vest but she had not. She thought only of hurting the man and escaping his hold. But now, she was more his prisoner than before, and she would have to go a long way to prove she could be trusted again.

Again, their pace was slower, but to make up for time lost during the day, they often rode through the night with only a few hours sleep. She couldn't understand how he could function on so little sleep but he seemed ever alert and watchful. His manner toward her had changed little; he still wanted her and made it obvious by each glance. In spite of what she'd done, he acted as though it were something to be expected of a savage. He kept the rope around her neck and tied her on the horse and on the ground, but he seemed to bear no grudge against her.

The weather grew increasingly hotter and Sun Dancer dreamed of the daily swims she was used to taking. Pierre still forced her to wear the calico dress, and Sun Dancer managed to push the long sleeves up her arms and the skirt of the dress well up her thighs. She still wore her knee-length moccasins; she knew she must present a ludicrous sight with her white woman's dress and her hair in long tangles. For the first time in her young lifetime, she was ashamed of the way she looked.

One evening, they stopped at a ranch to water the horses. Although the man and his wife weren't pleased to have an Indian woman on their property, they were more than willing to let Pierre and Sun Dancer stay for the goods which Pierre offered to trade. He also traded his horses for three fresh ones, along with another dress for Sun Dancer, some fresh beef, vegetables, and tobacco for himself. Sun Dancer was taken to the barn, enduring close scrutiny by the man, woman and their four children. After Pierre tied her in one of the stalls, he went off to clean up and eat with the family.

Sun Dancer was shamed; she now knew what Stalking Horse had been talking about. She would rather die than be treated as an animal, unwelcomed by other people, and she knew that that is what it would be like as Pierre's woman. The barn was dark; she was alone and frightened. She looked up as she heard the noise of feet on the straw. One of the couple's boys had come into the barn carrying a lantern. He stood in front of Sun Dancer, staring. His hair was almost white and his eyes a clear blue. There was a sprinkling of freckles across his small, upturned nose. He continued to stare at Sun Dancer as if not quite sure what she was. Then he set the lantern down.

"You're pretty," he said softly and sat down in front of her, pulling some bread from his shirt pocket. "Here." He pushed the piece of bread toward Sun Dancer and she opened her mouth to accept his gift. He fed her until the bread was gone. He left to return with a dipper of water, which he held to her mouth as she drank.

"Thank you." She spoke two of the few English words she had learned.

"You talk English," he said with a smile and began to ramble on, stopping only when he saw Sun Dancer shake her head. "You don't speak English? But you said 'thank you,' I heard you."

Sun Dancer looked into the clear, blue eyes which were so similar to Pierre's. The kind of eyes which she had trusted once before. She lowered her head and fought an incredible urge to cry. The boy gently lifted her chin up and looked into the brown eyes which were now filled with tears.

"Don't be sad. I'll help ya."

Sun Dancer tried the words. "Help you me," she said softly, hoping the boy would understand. But of course he didn't. He got up, smiled, and took the lantern, leaving Sun Dancer in total darkness. Why would a small boy want to help me, she thought. And how could he, against a man like Pierre? She leaned her head back against the barn post and closed her eyes. It all seemed impossible now. Even if she could escape, she was so far from home that she could never find her way back. After a time, Stalking Horse would give up searching for her and he would forget her. And she would be a thing of the past, her name whispered on the lips of those who had known her. To all of them, she would be dead.

Sun Dancer opened her eyes when she felt the jerk on her neck. The boy pulled the noose open and slipped it off. Then he took the large hunting knife which was stuck inside his belt, and cut the rope securing her hands and legs.

"Go now, the trapper will be out soon. You must take your horse and ride fast."

Sun Dancer stood up, rubbing her arms and legs. She rummaged through Pierre's pack to find her knife and some supplies. Quietly, she led her horse outside the barn and into the field, followed by the small boy. When she was a distance away from the house, she turned to the little boy and knelt down, taking him by the shoulders.

"Friend, friend," she said, hugging him to her. She had nothing to give him but the necklace Wind Woman had given her; she removed it and placed it around his small neck. "Thank you," she said solemnly, hugging him once more, and she rode off in the direction he had pointed out to her.

The boy smiled and waved as she rode away. He reached up and felt the smooth silver of the necklace. It was a wonderful gift from a beautiful Indian princess. But he would have to hide it because his parents would never let him wear anything an Indian had given him. He was glad he had helped her. He didn't like that old trapper anyhow, and he didn't like the way he kept the girl tied up like a dog. His parents would be mad, but he didn't care. As soon as he was old enough, he was going to run away and live with the Indians so he could learn all about riding horses and shooting bows and arrows. And maybe someday he would marry an Indian girl who looked just like the one he had helped. He turned and smiled as he heard the Frenchman's voice, cursing and yelling when he found his Indian lady gone. Maybe that would teach him that people were people, not animals. And besides, anyone who looked like she did deserved better than a dirty old trapper.

Sun Dancer felt free for the first time in weeks, and she rode her horse at a full gallop. She rode in the direction the boy had pointed and tried to remember things which looked familiar as they had ridden in. She planned to ride all night, even if it took her from the trail. She wanted to get as far away from Pierre as she could, and she knew the only way she could do that would be to ride. When her horse tired, she slowed him to a walk until he was able to gallop again. She knew the horse was tired, but her horse was still better than the horses which Pierre had traded for. Even tired, her Appaloosa could outrun the animals that Pierre would have to ride.

When dawn came, Sun Dancer didn't recognize the territory but she kept going north, using the sun and the stars for a guide. She stopped only for water and to pull her hair back in one large braid to keep it from her face. She wanted to rip the sleeves from the dress but she realized she would need them at night when it cooled down. She chewed on dried meat and some of the hard bread, eating wild roots or berries if any were available.

Now that she was on her own, the freedom she experienced far outweighed the fear she felt at being entirely alone. She had been completely stifled by Pierre. She knew that living with him would have been like living in a cage, which was something he could never understand. Pierre thought of her as a possession, not as a person. Although he was a man of the wilderness, he understood nothing about it, nor the sort of life one lived when at peace with nature. Sun Dancer longed only for her family and her own land, and those thoughts kept her riding when she should have slept or rested. Sleep was not important now, home was.

* * *

Stalking Horse squatted in the field by the house, waiting for Pierre and Sun Dancer to ride out. He followed their trail here and knew they would have to ride out sometime. He grew impatient, and stole through the field to the edge of the yard, stealthily running across the yard to the barn, circling it to come around the front. The door was open and he moved in, constantly looking around as he did so. It was dark and he waited for his eyes to grow accustomed to it. Standing still, he searched for the outlines of Pierre and Sun Dancer but found no one. He walked to the stalls and found them empty. They were gone. Again, he had wasted precious time. He stood for a moment, leaning his head against the post, his eyes locking onto something on the floor. He reached down and picked up a piece of rope which had been cut with a knife, and then another. If Sun Dancer had been tied, the Frenchman wouldn't have cut it to set her free, he would've simply untied it. Somehow she had gotten loose. He started for the door when he heard a faint sound coming from one of the stalls. He sidled over to it and looked down. A small boy was sleeping, curled up on a bed of hay. His hair was blond and unfortunately, reminded Stalking Horse of Pierre. But he was a mere child and could not be blamed for something a grown man had done.

Stalking Horse bent down to look at the boy more closely, and saw the necklace. It was the necklace Wind Woman had given Sun Dancer. He touched it lightly and knew then that the boy had helped her. If Pierre had taken the necklace for himself, he wouldn't have given a piece of such worth to a mere boy. He surmised that the boy had helped Sun Dancer escape and that she had given him the necklace as a gift. That was why he was sleeping in the barn, away from his family in the house. He touched the boy lightly on the head and smiled in silence. He removed one of his arrows from its quiver and placed it next to the boy, knowing that all boys enjoyed hunting games. Although the arrow was meant to fit a man's powerful bow, he hoped the boy could someday use it. He wished him well, admitting to himself that not all whites were the same. Here was a good one, and perhaps from him, others would learn. He left the barn as quietly as he had entered it.

Three days had passed since Sun Dancer had escaped from the farmhouse and she was exhausted. The territory was unfamiliar and twice she had almost ridden into Apache hunting parties. She knew if she found the Big River she could follow it north and find her way back home again, but she wasn't sure how to find the river from where she was. She combed the landscape for some sign of familiarity, but the rocks and barren land looked the same. She longed for the lusher prairies of the north.

Sun Dancer finally stopped in the heat of the day, unable to contend with the burning sun. She ripped a strip from the hem of her dress to wrap around her forehead to keep the hair from her face and the sweat from her eyes. While she rested in the slight shade of a large rock and a few mesquite bushes, she grudgingly admitted that Pierre was a man with great ability. He was as tireless as a Cheyenne and he tracked and made trail as well as one. He went many days without sleep and when he did close his eyes, he was still alert to any sound or movement. And he had kept Stalking Horse from finding them, something that Sun Dancer thought could never happen. She was sure that Stalking Horse would have overtaken them their first day out of the Cheyenne camp, but then she saw the trail Pierre had laid, and knew he was an expert. After sleeping a few hours and chewing on some meat, Sun Dancer continued riding in the late afternoon. She planned to ride into the night, unafraid of what she might find in the darkness. She was more afraid of what would happen if Pierre found her again.

The nights were cool and Sun Dancer rode slowly, keeping a watchful eye for any unseen obstacle her horse might trip over. She sang songs to give herself courage. She sang some of the wolf-songs, songs that were sung by the "wolves" or scouts when they traveled the prairies alone. The songs were said to have been learned from wolves and sometimes the men imitated the sounds of the animals. She sang the same song she had sung when she was caught in the snow alone, and others which she had learned from her father and brother as a child. "My love come out into the prairie, so that I may come near you and meet you," was commonly sung by men traveling alone; another sung by a leader to his followers, "Friends, take courage, do not be frightened; follow where you see me riding my white horse." And she pictured Brave Wolf on his white horse and it filled her heart to see her brother that way and it gave her courage to go on.

By early morning of the fourth day, Sun Dancer thought the territory and landscape looked familiar. She remembered certain rock formations and her spirits lifted as she recognized a small watering hole at which she and Pierre had stopped on their way south. She and the horse drank greedily from the water and while the horse ate from the sparse growth surrounding it, Sun Dancer sat down to rest. She lay on the ground with a wet piece of cloth torn from her dress pressed over her face. She tried to clear her head of any thoughts as Horn had taught her to do; she concentrated on resting her mind and her body fully before she began to ride again.

Sun Dancer rested for awhile giving in to the exhaustion that overcame her. An hour later, she awoke suddenly. She watched as her horse's ears pricked up and he whickered softly. She had felt the slight rumbling of the ground as she lay there and she knew a rider was coming. She quickly swung up onto the bare back of her horse, pausing to look back. She could see a man outlined against the land, the beaver-skin hat prominent on his golden hair. It was Pierre. The sight of the man so calmly riding her way made her turn her horse and gallop away, knowing all the while that he would keep up his steady pace and find her. He had the advantage of knowing the land and knowing that she was frightened. The man was a demon, possessed of stamina that normal men did not possess.

Sun Dancer didn't turn around again; she knew he was behind her and would stay there until she grew tired and lost ground. Then he would find her and take her again; the thought made her ride even harder. She wanted to put as much distance as possible between her and him, although she knew it would do no good. The man would win and she would be his prisoner again. Nothing Stalking Horse nor her father or brother had taught her over the years would help her now. They had never envisioned one such as this—a white man who tracked and made trail like an Indian, one who needed little sleep and food. If all white men were like this one, she could understand well Sweet Medicine's fear of them. She turned to look once more and saw Pierre moving steadily along, as if sure of the outcome and finding no need to hurry about it.

Sun Dancer sat against the rocks, knife in hand, prepared to use it if needed. She positioned herself there, knowing that the only way Pierre could come in would be from the front, where she scattered bits of wood and dried brush to make a silent entry impossible. She prepared to face him and was ready to fight to the death. She had no wish to be his prisoner again, but she knew that she could never outrun him. Her eyes closed and her head nodded against her chest; she abruptly opened her eyes and looked around. The night was still except for an occasional coyote yip. She forced herself to keep her eyes open but exhaustion overtook her at times. She slept in short naps, waking suddenly to see if Pierre had entered without her knowing it. She could not remember feeling so tired; in spite of herself and her resolve to stay awake, her body went limp and her head fell forward.

She did not awaken as Pierre walked into camp,

avoiding the bits of wood and dried brush she had laid for him. He walked to her and easily took the knife from her hand. She looked defiantly beautiful, and he smiled as he thought of what it would be like to tame her and train her to his wants and needs. He had known many trappers and men of the mountains who had taken Indian wives and had not regretted it. They were used to a hard life and hard work, and they didn't speak of silly and useless things. This one would be especially good. She was strong, stubborn, and beautiful; he would break her until she would gladly do his bidding. He took the rope from his waist and placed it around her neck, then he grabbed her shoulders and jerked her to her feet. Her eyes were huge; she reminded him of trapped animals which pleaded for mercy with their eyes before he killed them.

"You will be taught a lesson dis time, girl," he said in a cruel voice. Sun Dancer didn't have to understand the language to know what he meant. She cursed her weakness as she fell from the force of Pierre's hand against her face.

CHAPTER XXII

Many of Pierre's friends beat their Indian wives, stating that it was the only thing they understood. Pierre didn't think of himself as a violent man, but he was able to lend himself quite easily to it when he felt it was called for. Sun Dancer lay on the ground, the dress torn from her, her back criss-crossed from the whip Pierre had used. He knelt over her and applied the thick bear grease, knowing that it would help heal and that the marks wouldn't leave scars. He had been taught by an expert on the ship from Calais. Otto was a German who had been on the ship for many years and was an able man with whip or cat-o'-nine tails. He could make a man live or die in seconds, or prolong the agony indefinitely. He could use the whip so it would scar for life, or so that it would leave superficial marks which would disappear in days. This Pierre had learned from Otto, and this he would apply to Sun Dancer until she learned to obey.

Sun Dancer tried to get up but he forced her down. When he was through covering the cuts with the bear grease, he covered her with a blanket. He'd punished her, but just enough to let her know that he was the master and she the slave. Mexico was still hundreds of miles away and he didn't want to incapacitate her so she couldn't ride. He smiled as she leaned against the rock where he'd found her, and he lit his pipe in the darkness. She hadn't cried out at all when he'd whipped her. When she fell to the ground, she stubbornly refused to stay down and kept trying to get to her knees. She wanted him to kill her.

He puffed on his pipe. He couldn't wait for some of the other trappers to see her. Some would try to buy or trade for her, others would try to steal her. But he would never trade her nor would he let anyone take her. She was his possession and he would keep her until he tired of her or she died, the latter being something which was subject to his whimsey of the moment. He rather liked having control over another's life, knowing that he was the one who would say whether she would live or die. When she learned to speak more French, he would make her beg for things. He liked women who begged, just as he liked to watch the animals caught in the traps just before he killed them.

This time Stalking Horse was ready. He knew that Sun Dancer was no match for the Frenchman and that it was only a matter of time before Pierre caught up with her and they started back south toward Mexico. He waited, knowing that Pierre would come, knowing that he was a man ruled by his vanity. He didn't want to lose a prize as valuable as Sun Dancer; he would keep after her until he caught her. And he would go south again, for he was smart enough to know Stalking Horse would find him if he stayed in Cheyenne country.

It was five nights before Stalking Horse saw them. They rode at a steady pace, a pace which wouldn't tire the horses. They rode past, not seeing him as he stayed behind some rocks a mile away and looked on. Now it was his turn to surprise the Frenchman. He watched until they were out of sight, then mounted his horse and rode after them. The urge to kill was strong, wiping out even his love for Sun Dancer. He thought only of what it would be like to sink his knife into Pierre's belly.

Sun Dancer looked at Pierre over the cup of hot liquid he had given her and told her to drink. It was black and bitter but it warmed her insides and kept her alert. Her back itched from the salt in her sweat; when she rode in the hot sun, she longed to tear the dress from her back and scream in agony. But she had not uttered a sound and her gaze never wavered from the landscape ahead of her.

She was amazed that Pierre had tried to utter words of love and comfort after he had beaten her; she ached to spit in his face. She understood his game, and she would play it until she got another chance to escape. He wanted her to submit to him, to be his slave. It was something she could never do but it was something she could pretend to do in order to gain his trust. She hated him and thought only of different ways she would kill him if she had the chance. He was a strange man this one, who uttered words of love one minute then beat her the next. But she would play his game and do as he bid. There would come a time . . .

"You are not angry with me, eh?" Pierre interrupted her thoughts. "You must learn to obey me then all will be well. You understand?"

Sun Dancer looked at him, keeping her hate to herself. She nodded.

He smiled happily and poured more coffee into her cup. "It ees good, you will see. You learn to be my woman and do as I say. You will have a good life. Better than with your Cheyenne husband."

Again Sun Dancer nodded and forced a slight smile. "Pierre," she said softly, forcing the hated name between her lips. His reaction was what she had hoped for; he came to sit by her, gently placing his arm around her shoulders.

"You say my name finally. It ees good." He pulled her to him and kissed her. "When you are healed and we are in Mexico, I will teach you of love, little *sauvage*. Then you will call my name in ecstasy, eh?" He laughed loudly. Sun Dancer smiled along with him, knowing that the only joy she would ever get from saying his name would be when she said it for the last time, when he was dead.

Pierre slept that night for the first time in days, as if reassured that Sun Dancer would finally acquiesce to being his woman. He did, however, make sure the noose was securely knotted around her neck, tying it to the ropes which secured her hands and feet. He may have felt reassured but he didn't trust her, and he slept with Sun Dancer well out in front of him so that anyone who entered camp would come across her first.

Sun Dancer worked the ropes but knew from

experience that they were fastened tightly; if she moved about too much, the rope would pull against her neck forcing her head farther down to her knees. She rolled to her side and laid her head on the hard ground, thankful for the brief respite from Pierre's eyes and words. She thought of Stalking Horse and wondered what had happened to him, and if he had given up his search for her. The trail would be almost impossible to find now that they had backtracked and gone south again. She closed her eyes and tried to block out the pictures she had of her and Stalking Horse making love, talking, or riding together. She could not permit these pictures to enter her mind and make her weak. She must clear her mind of all thoughts but these—to escape Pierre or to kill him. But as she tried to keep her mind clear, pictures of Stalking Horse kept entering her mind until she could no longer keep them away. She needed to see him, to feel his strength. This was one time she was tired of depending on herself—she needed him to help her. She breathed deeply but did not force the images from her mind. They made her feel as if Stalking Horse were near.

Stalking Horse walked to the horses and calmed them as he entered the small camp. He saw Sun Dancer on the ground, the Frenchman a few feet behind her. He moved slowly around the perimeter of the camp until he came to the large rocks behind Pierre which shielded him from intrusion. Stalking Horse carried no weapons and his knife was sheathed. He smiled to himself as he thought of Pierre's blunder—Pierre knew Indians, but not well enough. For some reason he'd assumed they couldn't climb rocks.

Stalking Horse deftly climbed the large boulders until he was above Pierre. He crouched low on the rock, hanging as far out as he could without falling, then jumped on the sleeping man below him. He quickly recovered his footing, aiming his knife at Pierre's throat. It was the only time Pierre had been caught off guard. He was genuinely surprised to see the young Cheyenne poised above him with his hunting knife. But as he readied himself to die, Stalking Horse stood up, motioning Pierre to do the same. Slowly, Pierre got to his feet and regarded the man in front of him. He was tall, over six feet, lean and muscled. Although he looked young, Pierre knew the Cheyenne already had years of experience behind him. He looked at the Indian until Stalking Horse pointed to Pierre's knife. Pierre realized the Cheyenne was giving him a chance to fight for his life. Pierre nodded slightly and removed his heavy jacket, taking his hunting knife from its sheath on his leg. Stalking Horse cut Sun Dancer's ropes and pulled her to the side of the camp. Pierre breathed deeply, thankful that the Cheyenne was honorable and was giving him a chance to fight. He was not so sure he would have done the same.

The two men walked around each other, each holding his knife in front of him. Pierre was acutely aware of the fact that he had underestimated the Indian, wishing now that he had heeded Jean's warning. He was completely unaware that Stalking Horse cared so much for Sun Dancer, or indeed, that Indians had such feelings. It came as a total surprise to him.

Pierre regarded Stalking Horse a moment longer before lunging forward, striking his knife upward. But Stalking Horse agilely moved to one side, avoiding the thrusts of Pierre's knife. He moved around the other man, his knees slightly bent, his knife held low to parry any blows by Pierre's knife. Clearly, he was the more confident of the two. Again Pierre lunged forward, and as Stalking Horse moved to the side, he swiped his knife and ripped open Pierre's right forearm. Surprised, Pierre howled in pain, but he was instantly on guard and steady on his feet as Stalking Horse came at him again. The blood gushed from his arm and his grip on the knife loosened. Stalking Horse knew this, and made the man move, tiring him, so the loss of blood would weaken him.

Pierre knew he was losing and that the Cheyenne was just playing with him now. He may have been almost equal to the man in tracking but he was no match for him in a knife fight. He lunged forward aiming his knife at Stalking Horse's side, but Stalking Horse moved quickly away, his knife crashing into Pierre's shoulder, crunching as it hit the bone. Pierre cried out and fell to his knees, dropping his knife as he did so. He looked up to see Stalking Horse above him, an ominous outline in the dark sky. Then it was over, as Stalking Horse plunged his knife into Pierre's heart, and the Frenchman lay inert and lifeless on the ground. Stalking Horse stood over the dead man for a moment then wiped his knife on Pierre's leggings, replacing it in its sheath. He walked to where Sun

Dancer sat watching him. He lifted her to her knees, she, flinging her arms tightly around his neck. There were no tears; he knew she would try to be strong. But he felt relief flood through her slight body as he held her, and he had a tremendous desire to love her right there. She trembled slightly and he realized for the first time that she wore a white woman's dress of thin material, and her hair was loose about her shoulders. He stroked her hair and buried his face in its softness.

"You feel thin, wife," his voice was husky, as he rubbed his face against her hair and neck.

"And you are like a vision, my husband. I fear you will soon disappear." Her voice trembled and she laid her face against his bare shoulder. "I was afraid you would not come."

"You need never fear that. I will come for you wherever you are." He held her in his arms as she slept, wondering what the white man had done to her, hoping that she could forget.

Sun Dancer talked little but smiled constantly as she and Stalking Horse traveled north to their home. They left Pierre's body where it lay, Stalking Horse stating that the man deserved no more. Sun Dancer didn't talk of her time with Pierre but wanted only to forget it and get on with her own life. At times during their ride, she would forget she was with Stalking Horse and she would become alarmed, thinking she was still with Pierre. Stalking Horse stopped frequently so that Sun Dancer could rest, and he never questioned her about Pierre. Once, when they stopped at a point along a river, Stalking Horse saw the unhealed marks from Pierre's whip and his face grew stony and cold. Sun Dancer tried to cover them but Stalking Horse bathed them in cool water and applied some of the grease which Sun Dancer had taken from Pierre's pack. His eyes scanned the swollen, red welts and he wondered what other marks Pierre had made on his wife. That night they camped along the river and Sun Dancer bathed and washed her dress. She sat mending the holes in the dress and looked up to find Stalking Horse staring at her. At first she thought it was her nakedness that made him stare, but his eyes were not full of desire but of question.

"He harmed me in this way only," she answered his questioning look, pointing to the scars on her back. He came forward to hold her. He was thankful that the man had not used Sun Dancer in that way. For unlike the marks on her back, those were marks that would not go away so easily. They talked of what had happened, and Sun Dancer was surprised to find that Stalking Horse had been at the farm house, and that he, too, had left the boy a gift.

"He will be one who will listen to his own mind," Sun Dancer stated, remembering the determined look on the small boy's face.

"And he has courage to go against one such as that trapper. Perhaps he will grow up to understand us."

"I feel that he already does."

They reached their land two weeks later and Sun Dancer was joyous to see her home again. She was greeted by her family and friends and all wanted to know of her experience with the white trapper.

Horn checked her wounds to make sure they had healed properly, and he smiled at her knowingly.

"Why do you look at me this way, Horn?" Then she nodded her head. "You knew I would come back, didn't you?"

"I knew it." He applied a mixture of bear grease and herbs to her back to secure the healing. "I have been granted the privilege to be able to see your life, but only so that I may help to guide you. You will live your life the way you wish, no matter what I tell you."

"I still do not like it. I feel that sometimes you look at me and know that I will die in the next moon. It unsettles me, Horn."

"This I can tell you: you will live to help many in the tribe, and much of your wisdom will come from living."

"Broken Leaf once told me that I am special. She said I will know great sorrow, but I will also know great joy."

"She is right."

"Why have I been chosen, Horn? I only wish to live as others."

"But it was not to be. The Great Spirit chose you and you will do as he says."

"You too, are special, Horn. Was it not unsettling to you when you were young?"

A slight smile creased the craggy, leather-like features, and the brown eyes shone brightly. "Everything was unsettling to me when I was young, child. I fought even the wind as it swept down from the mountains, and the snow as it fell from the skies. I would accept nothing and challenge everything."

"But here you are a great healer and seer of many things. What made you change?"

"Life made me change, child, as it will you. Now go to your husband. He has searched long for you."

Sun Dancer thanked him and started for the door of the lodge. She stopped and walked back to Horn. She hesitated, knowing the question she was about to ask was personal, too personal to ask someone of Horn's stature.

"Do not hesitate, child, ask me." His bold eyes challenged hers.

"Did you ever love a woman, Horn?"

The old man looked beyond her, to some distant place in time. "Once I loved a woman." He was silent for a long while and then his eyes came to meet Sun Dancer's. "But it was long ago and she is dead."

"But you have the memories."

He nodded. "I have those."

Sun Dancer sensed his reticence and turned to leave. She had already invaded too many of his private thoughts.

"Take care, girl, to cultivate what you have with your husband. It will not grow of its own accord." She turned to look at him once more and nodded silently. She wondered if he knew something about her and Stalking Horse. But of course he knew; he was telling her to cherish what she had with Stalking Horse for it would not last forever. She shivered in spite of the warmness of the day and walked back to her lodge. There was a sadness in Horn's eyes of the kind that only one who bears acute sorrow can understand. She understood and she wondered how many other people he had mourned for over the years. She smiled as she saw Stalking Horse in front of the lodge and she followed him inside. She promised herself that she would make a robe for Horn for the winter. She wished she could give him back his love.

Horn was by nature a gentle man but he was more gentle still when he was with Sun Dancer. He felt somehow responsible for the girl, having known of her existence long before her birth, and having known the course her life would take. He knew that his position in the tribe was such that most everyone feared him, but he did his best to dispel those fears over the years. He supposed he was an awesome-looking creature with his long, gray hair and numerous strands of necklaces consisting of bears' claws, mountain lions' teeth, eagles' talons and the eyeteeth of the gray wolf. That, and the fact that he walked around in a robe which was over thirty summers old, and was torn and tattered from long use. He also carried a long stick decorated with the feathers of different birds and the rattles of many rattlesnakes, so he made a great ruckus when he walked. But people feared him most, he supposed, because he had talked with the *maiyun*, the spirits which controlled men's lives and from whom he had received the vision about Sun Dancer.

Horn prayed daily to *Heammawihio*, the Wise One Above, who was the chief god and the creator, then he prayed to the earth and to *Nivstanivoo*, the four directions, who some believed influenced the lives and fortunes of people. *Seyan*, the place of the dead where *Heammawihio* lives, is the place where all the dead go, whether good or bad or cowardly or brave. All go there except those who have killed themselves, and Horn did his best to reassure people that the dead lived there as they did on earth—chasing buffalo, warring, hunting game, and living in lodges. When his people were sick or dying, Horn tried to reassure them that their *tasoom*, their spirit soul and mind identified to them in their shadow, had not yet left their body. But if they were ready to die, he comforted them with songs and thoughts of the way it would be in the next world, assuring them that their most prized possessions, as well as their favorite horse, would be sent along with them to *seyan*. Horn did all this, but foremost he thought of himself as a healer. It was to this end that he worked so diligently each day.

Horn's grandfather had been the one to show him the way, for he had been a great healer in his day when they lived back across the Big River. He gathered roots and vegetables, herbs and fruits, and the bark of various trees. He studied everything until he figured out the exact use for each, then he memorized the different mixtures. As Horn grew up, it was natural that he assimilate some of his grandfather's knowledge. Often, when he and his brothers were out hunting, he would look for new and different plants to experiment with. In the old days, the Cheyennes did not war, so Horn and his grandfather treated few wounds, except for those experienced while hunting. But they were able to treat common maladies like headache, stomachache, dizziness, leg cramps, insomnia, and bleeding cramps. When his grandfather died, Horn took to the practice of healing, and eventually became the medicine man of the tribe and, unwillingly, a seer. In his first vision, he saw his grandfather killed by a mountain lion while gathering plants in the woods, and it had happened just so. Horn was frightened of his visions after that, until he learned that he saw good things as well.

He had acquired a vast amount of knowledge over the years and it was time to pass it on. Although he knew that he would live to old age, he wanted to pass all his knowledge on while it was still fresh in his mind. Sun Dancer was the perfect choice. She had a natural interest in the ways of nature which would serve her well in what she learned from him. She was also bright and quick and learned things faster than he ever remembered doing. She would be a safe repository for the knowledge he wanted kept alive for the tribe. The fact that he cared for Sun Dancer as if she were his own granddaughter only made the task more meaningful and enjoyable.

The fall came quickly and the Cheyennes prepared meat and skins for the winter. Sun Dancer saved an especially large and well-treated skin for the robe she planned to make for Horn. Her mother advised her against it, telling her that many people over the years had made Horn robes but he had declined them all. Sun Dancer, however, was not deterred from her task.

When winter came and the Cheyennes had made their home in a well-protected valley in the hills, Horn used this time to tutor Sun Dancer. In what spare time she was able to manage, Sun Dancer worked on the robe she was preparing for her teacher. The pair was a puzzlement to everyone in the band, especially when they were seen walking and laughing together, a sight that unnerved even the bravest warrior. If one such as Sun Dancer could make one such as Horn laugh, what powers did she possess?

Sun Dancer began to be held in higher regard, not only because she was the daughter of a great chief and the wife of an honorable warrior, but because she was the intimate of Horn, the great healer and seer. People wondered if she would take Horn's place.

As the winter wore on, Sun Dancer remembered Horn's advice and she loved Stalking Horse ferociously, not in just the physical way, but in ways that would tie him to her more than any other. She talked with him and learned about his lonely childhood. He had become a loner not by choice, but by necessity. His adoptive parents had been kind but they had wanted him to take the place of their dead son. He could not do this for he was unable to be more than he was. So he left their lodge at a young age to fend for himself. Although even now he still provided them, as well as his aunts and uncles, with fresh meat and horses.

She knew he was a man of great ideals and like her father he wished that the various tribes could live together peacefully. They walked in the snow and talked of what it would be like when they were old and the white man lived on their land. They roamed the hills and woods and if the snow was not too deep, they rode across the soft white blanket, watching nature and her animals in their different guises.

The villagers often smiled at them as they walked, the old people nodding their approval of such a sensible young couple. It seemed that at this point in their lives, the Great Spirit was truly smiling on them. By spring, Sun Dancer knew she was carrying another child and that this time, all would go well.

Stalking Horse was pleased but wary of the news, knowing what had passed each time before. But Sun

Dancer was in good health and acted no differently, except that she was more beautiful than he had ever seen her. She continued to ride and work hard, in spite of what had happened before; she realized that if the child were not strong enough to be carried, it shouldn't be born into a life such as theirs. Her stomach grew large and round, and Stalking Horse marveled at the movement in his wife's stomach as the child kicked angrily in its tiny space. Horn too was pleased, for he knew that Sun Dancer was ready to receive some reward for all the sorrow she had endured.

The summer, as if acceding to Sun Dancer's wishes, was mild and not overly hot, and it passed in a flurry of activity. Sun Dancer participated in the hunt as always, and smiled as periodically she saw Horn walk through the camp in the robe she had given him the previous winter. She had worked daily on it and even her mother said it was a beautiful piece, checking the quill work to make sure the stitches and beads had been set properly. On the back of the robe Sun Dancer had quilled a large owl with yellow eyes, eyes that were full of wisdom like Horn's. In the front on either side of the opening, she had done various plants and even their roots, their colors as accurate as those she herself had picked. When she had presented it to Horn and thanked him for all he had taught her and the kindness he had shown to her over the years, he was visibly moved. He ran his fingers over the plants on the front and turned it over to look into the all-knowing eyes of the owl. His eyes were warm when he looked at her, warmer than she could ever remember seeing them, but he simply said thank you and sent her away. She didn't know if he liked it but she saw him wearing it the next day, walking about the camp in the cold air, watching the reactions of people as they realized that Horn had accepted and was now wearing a new robe. Unknowingly, Sun Dancer had made a small place next to Horn in the eyes of her people.

It was late in *Tonoishi*, September, the Cool Moon, when Sun Dancer labored and was ready to bear her child. She went to the hut alone, reassuring Stalking Horse that all would be fine no matter what happened. The labor was long, lasting into the night and early morning. As midday came and the sun shone brightly and the sky was clear, Sun Dancer bore a girl child. She was small and delicate, and Sun Dancer named her Little Flower. Her father was as proud as if she had been a large boy. There was feasting that night and Stalking Horse danced and sang to his wife and daughter, while the women brought gifts to their lodge and asked to see the child. Woman's Heart had already made a magnificent cradleboard, and the small child was attached to it for all the world to see. Sun Dancer turned the child over to her mother's care and she joined her husband, who proudly led her to a seat by her father and brother.

"You have done well, daughter." He-Walks-the-Mountain reached out to touch his daughter's shoulder.

"It is what all women do, father, but it is special because I am your daughter." She smiled and touched his cheek.

He-Walks-the-Mountain nodded his assent. "It is

400

true, but my pride is not the less for it. Now your blood and the blood of your grandfathers will not die."

"Do you feel sorrow that I have not produced another warrior for the band?"

"Did I feel sorrow that you were you and not a young warrior?" He shook his head and made a rasping sound in his throat. "Do not seek to lessen the birth of this grand thing which you and Stalking Horse have created. Her life will be important because she has you in her." He turned to look at Sun Dancer and she could see the wetness in his eyes.

She moved closer to take his hand and laid her head on his great, familiar shoulder. "When I was small and looked up into the sky, its vastness frightened me and filled me with unknown terror. But then you took my hand and through you, I found the strength to face my fears and confront the unknown. It has always been so, father, and will always be so until one of us crosses over and goes to *seyan*. Even then, I will probably see your hand waiting to show me the way."

He-Walks-the-Mountain looked at his daughter and then gave her up to her husband, who sat waiting patiently for her. He watched as they walked together, and he experienced the joy that they felt in the birth of their child. He wanted only to see Sun Dancer happy, to see her live out a full life with her husband and child. When that was accomplished, he would be ready to take Woman's Heart's hand and cross over. And he would be waiting, as Sun Dancer had said. For even in death he would be there for her. She would always be his little girl.

CHAPTER XXIII

Sun Dancer sat up, her body covered with sweat, her chest heaving from exhaustion. The dream had been clear and, for the first time, she saw that Laughing Bird was with Brave Wolf. She tried to see more, but it ended with the frantic cries of the horses and Brave Wolf being trampled under their feet.

She felt Stalking Horse's hand on her back. "The dream?"

She nodded, covering her face with her hands, trying to block out the horrible vision that she knew so well.

"What does Horn say?"

"He says perhaps it means something else, or perhaps if Brave Wolf is to die, he will die old. But it is not true. I have seen his face in the dream and he is as he is now."

"You know you can do nothing about it. Come, lie back down."

Sun Dancer lay next to Stalking Horse and turned on her side, resting her head on his chest. She was reassured by the strong beating of his heart that life, indeed, went on. She reached over to peer into the cradle to see that Little Flower was sleeping.

"We are all well." Stalking Horse ran his hand over Sun Dancer's face, his eyebrows knitting together in question. "I do not know if it is good to become as Horn. You take too much upon yourself. Your sorrows are already too great."

"But I must learn to be strong for I will be as Horn is. I cannot change it."

"And as time goes on, you will learn to 'see' as Horn does. You know this."

She looked at him and dawning appeared in her eyes. She reached out for his hand. "Yes, this I know. This dream is the beginning; there will be more."

"Can you live with these visions of death all your life?"

"I must," she sat up, a frantic note in her voice, "I must." She stood up and pulled her robe over her shoulders. "I do not wish it to be this way."

Stalking Horse stood behind her and placed his hands on her shoulders, turning her to face him. "I know this. I will help you. I am strong for both of us."

"I do not wish to rely on your strength."

"There will be times when you need to. Know that you can."

He placed his hands inside the robe and ran them over the now smooth skin of her back, which showed no signs of the abuse she had taken from Pierre. She was so thin and slight and yet in time, she would carry the weight of a whole band on her shoulders. He prayed silently that he would not die young so that he could always be there to help her. He was not frightened of death, only of leaving Sun

Dancer alone.

The white trappers returned again in early spring. Sun Dancer was surprised to find she felt no ill will toward them. Jean brought many gifts for them all, and hoping that he would find Sun Dancer alive and well, he presented her with tortoise shell combs for her hair. When she started to refuse, Jean told her he had carved them himself and it would please him greatly if she would accept them. Sun Dancer was delighted and with some of her friends in tow, she tried them in her hair and in everyone else's.

Jean really wanted to please Stalking Horse, for he knew the young man would exert considerable power over the tribe one day. Also, he somehow felt responsible for bringing Pierre into this camp and for the trouble Pierre had caused. He encountered Stalking Horse with his horses. He held up the first two fingers of his right hand, then raised them next to his face. It was the sign for friend. Stalking Horse returned it without hesitation. Jean spoke in Cheyenne:

"I am happy to see that your wife is well. You found her easily?"

"It was almost two moons before we returned here together."

"And she was well?"

"You want to know if she was abused by your friend? You can ask the truth, *veho*, white man." His tone was cold and unemotional.

"He was not my friend and that is why I come to you today. I ask your forgiveness."

"Why is this?"

404

"He was from my own country across the great ocean; when I met him, I thought I would help him because he reminded me of my home and of my young brother."

"I can understand this."

"But I did not know that he would steal your wife. I would never have brought him here if I had known."

"I believe you, *veho*."

"Then I want you to take this." Jean held out a Kentucky rifle.

Stalking Horse shook his head. "I do not need a white man's weapon."

"But you might some day. You are wise enough to know that the white men are too numerous and will one day try to push you from your land. You will have to fight them with their own weapons or they will wipe you out."

Stalking Horse stared at the man, his eyes black with anger. "And you do not consider yourself a white man?"

"I do not consider myself one of them. I have lived in this country longer than you, Stalking Horse, and I love it as well. When the whites come with their changes, then I will no longer be able to live the life I am accustomed to, the life I love. Maybe we will be dead by then and it will not matter. But it will matter to your children."

Stalking Horse reflected on Jean's words for a moment. "Then you do not live in these places where the white man has built lodges of stone and wood?"

"Cities? Hell, no. I go there only to trade for the things I need to see me through the winter in the

mountains. I'm as much an outcast there as you are."
He smiled. "We are brothers in a way, Stalking
Horse."

Stalking Horse smiled then. He admired the man
and his honesty. And more than that, he believed
him. "Tell me of their rifle."

Jean smiled broadly. "It's called a Kentucky rifle.
To load it, you place the butt on the ground like this,
take some powder from the horn, pour it down the
muzzle, wrap the ball in this little patch and put it in
the barrel. Then you push it down with this
ramrod." Although it sounded complicated, much to
Stalking Horse's surprise, Jean had the gun loaded
and ready to fire in less than a minute. "What do you
think?"

Stalking Horse muttered lowly, "I think it takes
too much time. I could have pierced you with a
quiver of arrows by the time you loaded this."

"Perhaps, but if I had already loaded my gun and I
had seen you first, you would be the dead one, *mon
ami*."

Stalking Horse laughed and clapped Jean on the
back. "Show me this rifle; perhaps I will use it
someday."

Jean handed Stalking Horse the large rifle, the
latter surprised at its lightness. He admired the fine
workmanship, running his fingers along the brass
inlaid stock.

"This is worth much, I think. Why do you wish me
to have it?"

"Because I value your friendship. I want you to
know that not all white men are like Pierre."

"I already know this," Stalking Horse smiled

mischievously, "but I will take the rifle anyway."

"You are sure you want to do this?" Stalking Horse's eyes twinkled in amusement.

"But of course! It can't be all that bad. Just a little hot air, then you come out and jump into the river. Never did understand why you all make such a fuss about it."

"Many believe it is a spiritual as well as a physical cleansing."

"Well, whatever it is, I'm ready for it, *mon ami.*"

Stalking Horse laughed—he wasn't sure if he would ever get used to Jean's strange style of speaking. He spoke what he called a "lazy man's English" with a smattering of French thrown in, as well as Cheyenne and other Indian tongues. The man's speech was as colorful as the man himself.

The sweat lodge was constructed of bent willows which created an arch, and it was completely covered so that it was dark inside. The floor of the lodge was carefully covered with sweet sage, while a fire was laid outside for heating stones. When the fire burned down, all the men prepared to strip and enter the lodge in only their breechclouts.

"I feel mighty strange standin' around with a bunch of naked men." Jean looked around him.

"In a short while, you will not even notice them. Come."

The men entered the lodge to the left and sat down cross-legged. Brave Wolf took a small bit of tobacco and offered it to the earth, sky and the four cardinal points, then placed it in the pit which had been dug in the middle. Then a stone was passed in from outside and Brave Wolf placed it in the pit, covering the stone with sweet grass. The odor permeated the small space and Jean inhaled the smoke deeply. Brave Wolf purified himself, rubbing the smoke over his body and his pipe. Then he passed the pipe around until it was smoked out.

The stones from the outside were brought in with pronged sticks and placed in the pit. Brave Wolf sprinkled a few drops of water on the stones to clear the air of tobacco. Then he passed around a bowl of water.

"Wash your face and hair with it, then take a drink," Stalking Horse advised Jean. "You will be glad for the moisture later on." When the bowl came back to Brave Wolf he was silent for a moment, then he poured the water over the stones. The air in the small space of the lodge was stifling. Everyone leaned forward because the heat was less intense there than at the roof. Stalking Horse pulled Jean's head down.

"*Sacre bleu!*" Jean felt the pungent air sting the inside of his nose and throat. He rested his head on his knees and thought of the cool air outside the lodge. The door to the lodge opened momentarily and another bowl of water was pushed inside. Brave Wolf poured the water over the stones one more time, and the heat grew more intense.

Sweat steamed from every pore in Jean's body, stinging his eyes and making every attempt at breathing a labor. Brave Wolf poured more water on the stones and Jean's voice sought out Stalking Horse in the pitch-black darkness.

"You Indians are crazy! *Vous etes fou!*"

"But you said it was just a little hot air, *hoovehe,*

my friend."

"I didn't know how hot—I didn't expect hell!" There was silence for a moment while Jean fought for air. "When do we get out?"

"Enjoy yourself, *veho*, we have a few more dippers to go." The laughter of the Cheyennes rang out as Jean cursed them all in English, French and Cheyenne.

Jean's trapper friends left after a few weeks but he stayed with the people he had grown so fond of. His friends (and this they truly were for they would never seek to cheat or embarrass him) would trade his furs for the supplies he needed for the winter, and he would meet them at his winter camp. Everyone in the Cheyenne camp liked Jean. The warriors enjoyed his stories of the mountains and his description of the ship on which he had crossed the great ocean, while the women wanted to hear about white women and their clothes. He was that rare breed of man who really was more of an Indian than a white man, and he felt completely at home with his Cheyenne brothers and sisters.

Sun Dancer asked Jean to be her teacher. She wanted to learn more of the language which he and Pierre had spoken.

"No," he shook his head vigorously.

"But I want to learn it."

"French is not the language to learn here, English is the one. I will teach you English."

"English," Sun Dancer repeated. "What is this English?"

"It is the language that most whites speak and the language they all will speak someday. It will do you well to learn English."

Sun Dancer agreed and in payment for his lessons, for she would not take them for free, she would make Jean a buffalo robe. He had seen the one she had made for Horn and the shirt she had made for Stalking Horse, and he was greatly impressed with her work.

Sun Dancer and Jean worked each day on her English lessons. Jean started with simple words, pointing to things with which Sun Dancer was familiar and speaking them in English. When they were together he spoke only in English, knowing it was the best way to learn. It was the same way he had learned Cheyenne and the other Algonquian-based languages: Cree, Blackfoot, and Arapaho. As in all things, Sun Dancer was quick to pick up English words. Soon, she was telling Jean everything she saw in English.

Surprisingly, Stalking Horse was glad she was learning English. He felt that it was best to know all you could about a people and the language was the best place to start. He felt great ambivalence toward the whites now. Pierre had been a prime example of what a poor human being was like, but then he had known Cheyennes who were just as poor in character. But there was the boy who helped Sun Dancer, and there was Jean. Jean had a true love for the Cheyenne people and he had taken to Sun Dancer and Little Flower immediately, as if he felt responsible for Pierre's actions and wanted to make up for them. Jean was a good man and Stalking Horse thought of him now as no less than a brother. It was confusing. He could not call the white man his enemy when one of his brothers was a white man.

Sun Dancer learned quickly and unknown to Jean, she taught Stalking Horse everything she learned. Sun Dancer and Stalking Horse were alike in their desire to speak this language; they wanted to be able to communicate if necessary. In spite of his fear and his intense hatred for white men, Stalking Horse wanted to know more about them and why they were like they were.

Jean told them of the Bible, the creation, Adam and Eve, and Noah's Ark. Stalking Horse and Sun Dancer were fascinated by the stories, and they made Jean repeat them to the whole village. He spoke of the believers in the Bible as Christians, and told of how many of them had come to America (the name he called the land where the whites and the Indians lived) for religious freedom and to convert the Indians to Christianity. The people asked for more Bible stories, and Jean was at his best telling some of his favorite stories and embellishing them just a little bit. When Sun Dancer became more fluent in the English language, Jean took out his Bible and helped her to read passages from it, although he explained that the English was an archaic form.

Jean and Sun Dancer, with Little Flower strapped to her back, walked every morning and evening. They both looked forward to their walks and Sun Dancer began to look upon Jean as she looked upon her father and Horn. She had taken to calling him *nahkohe*, bear, because he reminded her of one with his long brown hair and full beard. But although Jean was large like the bear, he was gentle and with heart. He was one who cared. Sun Dancer had an unquenchable thirst for knowledge and Jean was able to provide her with a never-ending supply from a different source. And Jean looked upon Sun Dancer and Little Flower as the family he never had. They were both dear to him.

"Do you miss your country, Jean?" Jean smiled at the way Sun Dancer pronounced Jean with a perfect French accent, while the rest of her sentence had been in perfect English.

"*Oui*, sometimes. I grew up in the grape country. We make wine out of grapes, wonderful wine. I miss it all sometimes."

"What is wine?"

"Wine is a drink which makes one a little crazy in the head. White people drink too much of it and get into fights and kill each other. But where I come from . . ." he smiled and looked off into the distance, remembering. "Where I come from everyone drinks wine. Even the children."

"Why did you leave, Jean? Your heart still aches for it."

"Yes. I was going to marry a girl. She was dark and pretty, like you. And sweet. You know, *pevaaohe*. But she loved my younger brother. He looked like Pierre, with golden hair and light eyes. I knew they loved each other but I would not accept it. I found them together one day and my brother and I fought. I killed him." The thought still brought tears to Jean's eyes and he turned away so that Sun Dancer would not see his shame.

"And what of the girl you loved?"

"She killed herself when my brother died. So, I killed them both." He looked at Sun Dancer, as if asking for her forgiveness. "I had to leave my country then; my father made me go. I wanted to stay and be punished but my father put me aboard a ship and sent me here."

"And that is why you stay up in the mountains alone with the animals? You do not feel worthy to be around people."

"I am not worthy, Sun Dancer. A man who kills his own brother . . ."

Sun Dancer removed the cradleboard from her back, took Little Flower, and handed her to Jean. He brightened for a moment and tried to hand her back to Sun Dancer, but she shook her head.

"See how she smiles when she looks at you? She sees only a kind face and a person who will let no harm come to her. She does not know of your past. She sees you only as you are."

"But you know my past."

"And I see you only as you are, *nahkohe,* just as you see me. Would it matter to you if I had killed someone?" She shook her head. "I do not think so. We are not concerned with the past."

"I cannot rid myself of it. I dream of my brother and how I ended his life when he was still so young."

"Then you must make peace with him here on earth until you can be with him in *seyan,* your heaven. He is with his loved ones. He has forgiven you." Sun Dancer walked around for a moment then came back to stand in front of Jean. "I myself, have two older brothers whom I do not even know. I am ashamed to admit it, but they are nothing to me. Brave Wolf is the only brother I have. If I had to kill them to save Brave Wolf, I would do it. I feel shame at this knowledge, but I cannot change it. Do you think less of me for it?"

"Of course not."

"Then you know my feeling also."

"You are wise for one so young, child."

"I am learning," she smiled. "Go to Horn and smoke with him. He will help you to make peace with your brother."

Sun Dancer finished Jean's robe in the early fall. She hoped to finish work on the one she had already started for Stalking Horse before winter came. Jean was greatly pleased with the robe and although the snow was not yet thick on the mountains and the air was not so cold, he wore his robe daily, proud of the fine quillwork and designs of the mountains and the wild animals with which he lived.

Little Flower was still a small child, and Sun Dancer worried that she did not grow faster. She was a quiet baby, never uttering a sound, even when she was hungry. She was immensely patient and her parents were glad they had named her Little Flower, for it was a name which truly befitted one so delicate and lovely.

Sun Dancer continued to learn from Horn, while also practicing her English with Jean. She also learned stories from her father. Her father thought it was time that she learn some of the more intricate stories and traditions of the old days, so that they might be passed on indefinitely. Brave Wolf had already learned them, he told her, but Brave Wolf was a warrior and could be killed at any time. They must be passed on to a woman.

Jean moved with them up to the mountains but left them there and rode on to his own camp and his small log cabin. He said he would join them when he could. He knew of some of the best places to trap beaver and he was anxious to get to it. He felt the furs would be plentiful this year. In spite of the cold, there was a great feast the night before Jean's departure, and even he got up to dance with some of the women, to the immense delight of the rest of the villagers. He hugged his robe tightly around him the next morning, and grasping Sun Dancer by both shoulders, he kissed her on each cheek, explaining that this was an old French custom. It brought to mind the kisses on the mouth which Pierre had so brutally inflicted on her, but Sun Dancer realized that Jean's gesture was one of affection and not of brutality. He gave her his Bible and told her to read it and keep it for him until they next met. He and Stalking Horse grasped forearms and then hugged, as brothers will do, and he was off. A white man who was really their brother.

"Times were much slower then." Woman's Heart rocked Little Flower while Sun Dancer worked on Stalking Horse's robe. "When we traveled, everything was packed on our dogs. They could not carry much, so we women worked harder."

"Do you miss those days, mother?"

"I do not think so. We were never left in peace by the Hohes, and we knew nothing of fighting. It is better to know and be prepared."

"Stalking Horse says that things will grow worse. He says that the white man will get better guns which

415

will shoot faster and longer distances. Jean told him that they develop new weapons all the time. Then the Indians will trade for the guns or steal them because without them the whites will kill us all."

"Stalking Horse seeks to find a fight where there is none."

"He is a warrior, mother, and fights only when he is called upon to do so."

"I know this, child, but in his youth and inexperience he seeks to find an enemy where there is none."

"Jean says there are true enemies among the whites who seek to change everyone."

"Perhaps. But we have enough war with our own enemies. I do not wish to make enemies of the whites."

"No one does." Sun Dancer put down her quillwork and looked over at her sleeping daughter. "She is small, mother. I worry. She does not take much milk from me and the winter food is not good to start a baby on."

"You were small, smaller even than she. You would not take my milk so I chewed up meat and forced it down your throat. You wanted to do everything your way from the beginning."

Sun Dancer laughed. "Did I always cause you trouble?"

"You always caused me trouble but you were always a joy. That is the way with children." She laid the cradleboard down and looked at Little Flower. "Do not worry about this one. She is strong and has good color. She is not one to cause trouble and so will not let you know when she is hungry. Make her eat and she will soon learn to do it on her own. Start with the bread Jean left."

"I do not think I will have more children, mother." She looked solemnly at Woman's Heart. "Something happened to me when I had her. You saw it?"

"You bled far too much and the pain was far too great. To have more children would be to endanger your life."

"I will not make a warrior for the tribe."

"Bah!" Woman's Heart waved her hand in the air. "Women are just as important. We do all the work and bear all the children. It would serve the men well to remember that without us there would be no warriors."

"Perhaps Little Flower will someday be a warrior."

"Little Flower? I do not think so. But her daughter, perhaps. It could be so."

"You have changed your thinking a little, mother."

"My thinking has not changed, daughter. It is only that you are settled and I no longer have to worry overly much about you. I have always thought we are important. Did you not learn that from me?"

Sun Dancer stood up, grasped her mother's shoulders, and to her mother's surprise and delight, she kissed her on both cheeks. "It is a white man's custom. Jean says it is to show great affection."

"Then it is a good custom." She bent down to pick up Little Flower. "I will take the child. You work on your husband's robe. It will be grand."

Sun Dancer watched her mother as she left the lodge and tears filled her eyes at the sight of her with her daughter. It was a special thing, seeing her child with her family. Even Brave Wolf had come to the lodge several times to hold and admire Little Flower and comment that she looked pretty and took after him. Family was a fine thing. Her thoughts wandered to Jean and the guilt he felt over the death of his brother; he would never again be able to return to his homeland and his family.

She sat down and began working the dyed quills through the thick buffalo hide. She wondered if future generations would ever know the time and effort that went into making a robe, and the love that prompted her to do it. She wondered if her grandchildren would look upon it with pride and exclaim, "My grandmother worked this out of love for her husband and pride for her people." She wondered if anyone would care.

Painstakingly, she applied the stitches of sinew underneath the quills so they wouldn't show, and she stopped to rub her fingers for warmth and to examine her work. The large horse on the back of the robe was starting to take shape and Sun Dancer smiled. Stalking Horse would be proud. She lowered her head and squinted to see the tiny stitches she was sewing in the firelight. It was fine work she was doing, work that had been taught to her by her mother and her mother before that. She would teach Little Flower and hopefully she would teach her daughter. They would care because they were Cheyenne. And a Cheyenne is always proud.

Jean met the tribe again in spring and he seemed more at peace with himself. He had already traded his

418

furs for supplies and gifts and as always, brought something for everyone. He brought a history book with pictures for Sun Dancer; for Little Flower, he brought a music box, which everyone enjoyed; for Stalking Horse, who greeted him in English, he brought a pearl-handled hunting knife; some tobacco for He-Walks-the-Mountain, who had expressed an interest in the tobacco Jean smoked; and for Woman's Heart and some of the other women, he brought a sewing manual, so they could study how the white women sewed their clothes. For the children, he brought pieces of hard candy, which they all sucked on for days.

Stalking Horse and Sun Dancer spoke to Jean in halting but understandable English, while the rest of the tribe sat in fascinated anticipation of another of Jean's tales of the white world. He felt relaxed and at ease in the company of the Cheyennes, and it was more like home than anyplace he had known in the last fifteen years of his life.

Jean expressed a desire to know how to use a Cheyenne lance, and Stalking Horse began to teach him. They started on foot and Stalking Horse showed him how to hold it and waited until Jean got used to the weight and unwieldiness of the weapon. When Jean grew accustomed to the weapon, he began to carry it while he rode, just for the practice of carrying it on horseback. When Stalking Horse felt he was ready, he mounted Jean on a good buffalo horse and they went off hunting.

Presently, they found a small buffalo herd. Glancing at Jean, Stalking Horse asked, "Are you ready?"

Jean looked at the buffalo Stalking Horse had picked out, swallowed loudly, and hefted his lance. "Ready as I'll ever be, *mon ami.*"

Jean and Stalking Horse charged their horses at the large bull, Stalking Horse gradually turning the bull from the herd. When Stalking Horse yelled, Jean threw his weapon into the animal's thick hide. It took two more steps, its front legs buckling, and it fell. Stalking Horse whooped loudly.

Jean, not quite accustomed to the quickness of the buffalo horses, rode on a short distance. He finally stopped the horse and rode back to take a look at his buffalo. "I'll be damned, *c'est magnifique!*" He started to dismount, but Stalking Horse quickly cautioned him not to.

"Many have been killed by 'dead' buffalos," said Stalking Horse, as he rode to the animal and poked it a few times with his lance. Satisfied that the animal was dead, Stalking Horse let Jean try his skill at a few more. After they had butchered and skinned the animals and travoised the meat and skins back to camp, they headed for the mountains, where Jean was anxious to try his newly acquired skill on the big sheep.

They rode in silence, appreciating the sounds and sights of the land in summer. They stopped to pick wild berries, and Stalking Horse speared fish for their dinner. They spoke in English and Jean was amazed that Stalking Horse was able to learn the language second-hand from Sun Dancer. They enjoyed a quiet camaraderie when they were together, one that surpassed the differences in their backgrounds.

They went up into the hills, for now Jean was

hoping to find a large buck deer or an elk. He had always wanted to fight an animal one-on-one without the aid of his rifle, and the anticipation of the experience made him nervous and apprehensive.

"You have fear?" Stalking Horse noted his friend's unusually anxious manner.

"I always have fear when I do not know what is around me."

Stalking Horse nodded and looked at the trees and bushes around them. "A man would be foolish if he said he had no fear. Fear helps to keep a man on his guard."

They had stopped to drink and water their horses when they heard the sound echo around them. When Stalking Horse ran for the horses, they were already rearing up and neighing fearfully. They were well-trained but fear overcame them and before Stalking Horse was able to get them under control, they pulled free and ran away. Again the sound echoed around them, a thunderous roaring.

"Bear." Jean looked around him and wished he had taken his rifle along. "Grizzly, I think."

Stalking Horse nodded and looked around him. "We must move away from the water. He may come here to drink."

They moved silently away, aware that they were vulnerable to every animal that lived in the hills. Stalking Horse carried only his bow, arrows, and hunting knife, while Jean carried the lance and his hunting knife. Stalking Horse had killed a bear only once in his life and that had been with three other experienced hunters. And the bear had been a black bear not a grizzly.

"You have hunted bear before?" He turned to look at Jean who was ever-cautiously stepping backward.

"A few times. But I had my rifle with me then."

"You have killed grizzly?"

"Once, up in the hills. He was an ornery bastard, too. Just woke up from hibernating and was out to kill the first thing he saw. I put a bullet between his eyes before he could think, and another before he could think again. When he was on his hind legs, he stood taller than you or me."

"I have heard tales. In the days before my people had horses, they were attacked many times by the grizzly, who knew they were helpless. Sometimes he would wait for them when they went for water or to gather roots and berries in the woods, and he would attack and carry them off. When my people acquired horses, they still did not hunt him. He is too strong and swift and his hide and fur are thick and not easily pierced by a stone arrowhead."

"Yeah, they's tough bastards. Knew a fella once, just killed grizzlies. That's all he did. Still have the fur of the one I killed. Have it up in my place in the mountains. Makes a good cover when I sleep."

Again the sound pierced through the quiet woods and the men continued making their way out to find their horses. It grew dark before long and they made their camp among some rocks which would afford them some protection if the bear should decide to attack. They made a large fire, collecting as much wood as possible to keep it going through the night. Neither man could sleep and each remained watchful until the morning. It was early in the morning when the sun had not yet lit up the sky that they heard the crashing sound and saw the bear coming out of the trees. He loped awkwardly but steadily toward them and they moved up onto the rocks.

"Keep the lance in front of you. Do not throw it until he is close enough. Try for his throat." Stalking Horse had already taken an arrow from his quiver and placed it in the bow. He was thankful now for his steel arrowpoints; they would more easily penetrate the beast's thick fur than the stone ones.

The bear slowed when he came to the rocks and stood on his hind legs, clawing frantically at the air. He stood well above either Jean or Stalking Horse, and his crazed eyes reflected his intentions. Jean had never seen claws so long nor teeth so sharp, and he felt this one could have been father to the one he had killed.

"This one's a real beast, *oui?* What if we get back behind those rocks there? You think we'd have a chance?"

"He could dig at us with his claws. There is no place deep enough." Stalking Horse jumped to another rock to draw the bear's attention, his arrow aimed at the giant's throat.

"What are you doing, *mon ami?* Nothing foolish, I hope."

"I will make him follow me. You look for the right time and get close to him. It will be our only chance. We cannot run into the open, he would run us down."

"We could try for the woods again."

"Do you think we could get past him? No, we must

face him here."

"I don't like it. Why not let me draw his attention?"

"Because I have the arrows and can shoot him enough times to anger him." He jumped to another rock while shooting an arrow into the bear's throat, and quickly adjusted another in his bow and sighted it. The animal grew enraged and swatted at the arrow, finally knocking it from his throat. He roared loudly, the sound carrying out across the prairie, and Jean moved silently around the rocks as the animal stalked his friend. Stalking Horse aimed and shot again. The bear rushed him and the arrow barely caught in the fur of the bear's chest, the bear knocking it to one side. The enraged animal came down on all fours and confronted Stalking Horse, while the latter deftly jumped to another rock to keep the bear's attention. He had notched another arrow into the bow when the animal stood up again. This time he reached forward and swatted at Stalking Horse, who slipped and fell backwards against the rocks. The bear dropped down on all fours and quickly found a way up onto the rocks. Stalking Horse pulled another arrow from his quiver, sighted it, and shot the bear in the face just as the animal reached out and moved its deadly claws down the length of Stalking Horse's chest. The bear lowered its immense jaws toward his chest and stomach when the lance landed deeply in its neck, forcing it to cry out in pain and anger. He stood up, ready to confront its other foe, but Jean was ready. He pulled the lance out and thrust it deeply into the bear's chest. The animal screamed but he lost his footing and tumbled from the rocks. He tried to get up but Jean had already retrieved the lance and again thrust it into the animal's heart. The bear made low, moaning sounds, dying sounds, and Jean thrust the lance deeper into its chest until the large form became lifeless. He jumped onto the rocks and ran to Stalking Horse, who lay crushed against a large rock, part of his chest ripped open from the bear's claws. He was breathing with great difficulty, but his eyes were open and he managed a slight smile.

"You did well, friend. You must take the skin."

"Hell with the skin. We have to get you back to camp." Jean reached down to lift him, but Stalking Horse raised an unsteady hand to stop him.

"You did an honorable and brave thing. You must keep the skin. It is your right."

Jean cussed in three languages before he realized that short of dragging Stalking Horse out of the rocks, he would have to accede to his wishes. He pulled out his large knife and knelt by the head of the animal. He started at the throat, making a horizontal incision and a vertical one down the belly of the bear to either leg, where he drew one down each leg and up again to each forepaw. He drew an incision around the bear's head, peeling the skin down the back and front of the carcass until it was completely loose. He cut the skin from the animal's four paws so he could save the claws. He didn't waste time dressing the fur or drying the meat; his first concern was Stalking Horse, who watched him to make sure he kept the special hide. Jean then took the liver and kidneys of the animal and gave them to Stalking Horse who shook his head.

"It is just that you take them."

"You take the blasted things or I'll shove them down your throat! You need them to keep alive." Stalking Horse nodded silent assent and swallowed the nutritious, blood-filled organs. Jean cut up pieces of meat which they could carry with them, and left the rest to the animals and scavengers. He hated to waste good meat, but more than that, hated to see his friend die. He walked back to the woods and placed the bear skin, together with the unused meat, in a tree.

Stalking Horse was semi-conscious and made no protest as Jean washed the blood from his wound. The bear had made a diagonal slash across his chest, exposing the upper part of it. Jean took the parfleche from around his neck and silently thanked Sun Dancer for her forethought. She had made it up for him before he went back up into the mountains; she made him promise that he would always wear it, as it could someday save his life. Or her husband's.

He took out the crude awl and some sinew, and after wiping the wound again, he began to sew. Stalking Horse opened his eyes to look at Jean a few times but he made no sound; in fact, he hadn't made a sound other than talking since being attacked. Jean marveled at the man's stoicism and strength and silently thanked him for making the job easier. He made the stitches large and crude, but he closed the wound effectively and the bleeding stopped. He made a poultice from a mixture which Sun Dancer had included in the parfleche, and bound it with strips of cloth he tore from his shirt. Stalking Horse lay quietly. He opened his eyes once again to thank Jean.

"You must leave me," Stalking Horse tried to move.

"Do not waste your words. Rest." Jean gently pushed Stalking Horse down.

Jean went back into the woods. He found some sturdy branches and in a short while, he had built a travois on which Stalking Horse could lie while he pulled. Jean knew that Stalking Horse would die if he left him and went for help—wild animals, exposure, and infection from the wound—any one of these could kill Stalking Horse before he got back. When he finished the travois, he covered it with leaves and grass and placed Stalking Horse on it.

Stalking Horse opened his eyes and looked at Jean. "Why do you not leave me?"

"Because you are my friend, my brother. Would you leave me?" Jean walked in front of the travois, took one long pole under either arm, and began to walk eastward.

Stalking Horse opened his eyes and looked up at the blue of the sky. He tried not to breathe; every time he did so it felt as if a great rock lay on his chest. The pain was not great, only the inability to breathe. He tried to think of other things but his mind came to rest on Jean. The man was good and truly honorable. He had never had a true brother but he felt he had found one in Jean. If he lived, he would give Jean his lance. And his horse. And they would become true blood brothers. For the blood of Jean was equal to the blood of any Cheyenne.

CHAPTER XXIV

Jean's forearms throbbed and burned but he refused to give in to the pain. They had come a long ways but the distance was nothing compared to how far they could have come on horseback. It would probably take them two or three more days on foot to get back to the main camp. He stopped periodically to check Stalking Horse, but he was either asleep or unconscious most of the time so Jean struggled on.

Jean did not recall being a particularly sympathetic man or a compassionate one for that matter, but something in this Indian and his wife and their people moved him. The man had a naive innocence about him, in spite of the fact that he had learned to hunt, ride, and kill at a very young age. But there was more to the world than that. Stalking Horse knew that the Indian's world would not last forever and he wanted to keep his people from seeing it. Jean respected that and the fact that the man was honorable. Honor, that was an important thing to a Cheyenne. Even a man like Jean, who had killed his own brother, was treated with great respect and honor. This was something he had never expected to feel again.

Perhaps he still felt responsible for the damage Pierre had done. He didn't know why he continued to come back to the Cheyenne camp. But there was something there, something he could not find in the white world. Perhaps it was the honor and respect with which they treated one another. The classes didn't seem so harshly drawn there: a chief was highly revered and respected, but he was also a person to whom people could go for counsel. Warriors were important members of their society for their obvious abilities to hunt and fight, but women were held in high esteem also because all knew an Indian camp could not function without them. In the white world, the chiefs were not accessible to the people around them; the common people had little chance of speaking to them. The white people lost much because they never really knew the people who governed them.

Jean stopped for a moment to brush the sweat from his brow. He looked over his shoulder at the quiet "savage" on the travois. "Savage" was another misconception of the white man. To the whites, a man was a savage because he ran around half-naked and grew his hair long; he used the earth or his lap for a table and ate the animals, berries, and fruits that nature provided. To be "civilized," according to the whites, was to wear layers and layers of unnecessary clothing, to wear tight shoes which pained the feet, to eat from a table, and to go to a church once a week where people seldom practiced their religion. An Indian walked outside his lodge and looked at the sky and the trees and the river around him and at the animals the Great Spirit had provided him with. An Indian lived his religion, he did not practice it on Sundays.

"Leave me. I will die anyway." Jean stopped when he heard Stalking Horse's voice behind him. He gently set the travois down on the ground and walked to his friend.

"You'll not die, *mon ami*. You die after all the trouble I've gone through to get you here, I will kill you myself!" Stalking Horse started to laugh but stopped abruptly, the gesture causing him great pain. Jean touched Stalking Horse's arm, which was also bruised from the grizzly's claws. "We will make it, *hoovehe*."

Stalking Horse shook his head back and forth in a defeated manner. "You are like a rock that will not be moved from its place no matter how hard one tries to move it. Perhaps you and Sun Dancer are of the same blood."

Jean laughed and stood up. "You rest and we will be back soon. You must be quiet and rest. If you do not, I will sing some songs to quiet you down. And we both know how terrible that would be." He walked back to the front of the travois and picked it up once more. The pain in his arms was renewed but it went no farther than that. He would not let it.

Early in the morning of the third day, Jean saw riders approaching; he could tell from their dress that they weren't Cheyenne. He dropped the travois to the ground and picked up the lance which lay next to Stalking Horse. Five Crow hunters came to a stop about three feet from Jean and surveyed the situation in silence. The leader held up his right fist and placed it against his forehead. This was the sign for Crow. He placed the back of his right hand against his chin, his index finger and thumb forming a circle. He snapped the index finger forward without moving the hand, then repeated the action again; it meant talk.

"I can speak in Crow," Jean replied. The Indian nodded.

"Do you wound this Cheyenne?"

"No. Grizzly bear attacked us and my friend tried to draw him away from me."

The Crows looked suitably impressed and said a few words to each other. The leader spoke again. "You killed this bear?"

"Yeah."

"And the skin?"

"It's in a tree back there." Jean pointed back toward the hills from which he and Stalking Horse had come. "Wasn't about to drag fifty pounds of bear fur around when I'm pulling this." Jean looked up at them and lowered the lance to the ground. "You take me and my friend to our village and I will tell you where the skin hangs. It will be yours."

Again the Crows conferred with one another and the leader spoke. "Yes, we will help you. I will pull the Cheyenne, you will ride with Broken Dog." Jean nodded and pulled the travois behind the leader, who fastened it to his horse, and Jean was pulled up behind Broken Dog. The leader rode next to them and looked at Jean.

"White man, why do you save the life of this Cheyenne?"

"He is my brother, *hoovehe.*"

The Crows looked at Jean, then at Stalking Horse and nodded their heads. They understood well that when a man called another man "brother," it indicated a meaning far beyond that of friend. Although the Cheyenne was their sworn enemy, he was the brother of the white man, and even they would not interfere with such a relationship. They hoped that in this good gesture which they now performed for the Cheyenne, the Great Spirit would someday prompt a Cheyenne to do a similar good for a Crow. The leader turned and looked down at Stalking Horse, whose chest was barely rising with each breath he took. The man would not live anyway, he thought, but at least their intentions were honorable. Sometimes an enemy was not an enemy but just a man who needed help.

The people of the village gathered around the entrance to the camp; the guard had given the sign that someone was coming. He had recognized the Crow warriors immediately and was ready to sound the alarm, but he saw Jean signaling and he merely called to the people of the village to come. Cheyenne warriors stood ready and armed in case of a trick, but it was soon evident that the Crows were helping Jean and Stalking Horse. A sigh went through the crowd as the travois was pulled through the camp and they saw Stalking Horse lying helpless. Horn had been summoned and with him, Sun Dancer, who had no idea it was her husband she would help attend.

Horn and Sun Dancer met the travois as Jean jumped from the Crow horse and ran to them.

"It was a grizzly. Stalking Horse tried to draw it from me so I could kill it. It lashed his chest pretty good. Cleaned it best I could and sewed it with the awl and sinew you gave me. Did what I could." He reached for Sun Dancer's hands, as if trying to make her realize he had done all he could.

Sun Dancer was in complete control. "If it had not been for you, Jean, Stalking Horse would not be alive now." She squeezed his hand.

She moved forward to look up at the Crow leader. She held both hands shoulder high, palms out, and pushed them in a slight curve toward the Crows. It meant thank you. She then held up the first two fingers of her right hand and raised them to the side of her face. It was the sign for friend.

The Crow nodded his head solemnly and he too made the sign for friend.

She asked Jean to show the Crows where they could rest and eat. "And you must rest, *nahkohe*. I will tell you how it goes with Stalking Horse."

After quickly examining the wound, Horn ordered the travois pulled to his lodge, where three warriors carried Stalking Horse in and placed him on the raised wooden cot which Horn used to examine and heal. He turned to Sun Dancer.

"Bring me hot water. We will bathe the wounds and see how serious the damage is." Sun Dancer stared for a moment, unmoving. Her eyes were large and watery as she stared at the gravely injured man lying on the cot. "Do as I say, child, if you want him to live. Do not lose your control now. Forget he is your husband. There will be times in the future when you will have to work on many who are close to you.

You will achieve nothing if your emotions are out of control." When Sun Dancer still did not move, Horn stood up and grasped her shoulders firmly. "If I were not here to help you, would you let him die?" She looked at him then and moved to fill up the pot with water.

Horn removed the poultices Jean had applied and looked at the hasty stitches he had used to keep the flesh together. "Your friend did well. I believe he saved your husband's life."

Sun Dancer came to the cot and looked down at Stalking Horse's chest which was covered by a long zig-zagging gash reaching from his pectorals to his abdomen. Jean's stitches were large but uniform, and had served to keep the skin together to keep infection from setting in.

"Bring me my small knife. We will have to remove these; I will make them smaller. I must check to see if any of the muscles are damaged. A warrior can do very little without the use of his stomach or chest muscles." Horn examined the area, and Sun Dancer handed him his knife. He deftly cut away the large stitches and placed hot cloths on the wound to clean it. Then he turned to Sun Dancer, who had already threaded the awl with sinew. "You will make the stitches. Your hands are used to making smaller stitches and he will need many."

"I cannot." She tried to hand the needle to Horn but he refused and stood up.

"The skin is no different from deerskin or buffalo hide. You will make the stitches small and follow the line of the wound. He will need many."

Sun Dancer stood for a moment, staring at

434

Stalking Horse, then at Horn. She had to overcome her fear for Stalking Horse's sake. She took a deep breath and knelt down by the cot. "I will need more light, Horn. Put more wood on the fire." He nodded and smiled as he did her bidding, knowing she was unaware that she had just given him an order. "It is so deep, Horn. Will these stitches help?"

"The skin must be closed. If there is damage to the muscles, we will find it later, if he survives. But to leave the wound open would be to invite his death. It must be closed and then covered with poultices to draw out the swelling. If you cannot do it . . ."

"I can do it." She bent her head close to her husband's chest and stuck the awl into the skin close to where Jean had stuck the first stitch. Her hands shook at first and she felt the bile rise in her throat many times, but she concentrated on making the stitches close and uniform, as if she were sewing a robe. She was halfway finished when her hands began to cramp. She sat back on her heels. She felt a cold cloth on her head and Horn gave her water.

"Rest for a moment before you continue. It is a difficult task."

She nodded and closed her eyes for a brief moment, remembering the time Stalking Horse said he hoped he died before she did. A small whimper came from her and she opened her eyes to find Horn staring at her.

"It will do no good to remember now. Think only of the future you will have with him."

She looked at him. Did he know that Stalking Horse would survive, or was he just trying to make her go on?

She moved forward on her knees and with the new awl threaded by Horn, she began her task of sewing the small stitches in her husband's chest. When she was finished, she tied the sinew, cut it with a knife, and sat back to survey her work. The wound looked much smaller now; it resembled a thin, jagged line across Stalking Horse's chest and stomach. Horn knelt down beside her and with a stick, lifted hot poultices from a bowl onto the wounds. He then pulled Sun Dancer to a backrest and made her drink of *eyoveseahyo*, yellow medicine. When the leaves were pulverized and mixed into hot water, it became a sedative.

"Drink this and it will help you rest."

"I cannot rest. I must check on Little Flower and come back to be with Stalking Horse."

"Little Flower is well, and Stalking Horse will not wake for hours. Drink this. Your mind needs a rest as well as your body; this will keep you from dreaming."

Sun Dancer assented and drank the liquid. She leaned against the backrest, gazing at Stalking Horse, who still gave no sign of life. She watched him and thought of the many things they had done together and the things they would do if he lived. And suddenly she didn't want to think anymore; she just wanted to sleep. She laid her head back and closed her eyes, her mind a blessed void of dreams and thoughts.

Horn looked at her and was thankful that she slept peacefully. He turned to Stalking Horse to make sure that he slept comfortably. This was one time he would wait for the outcome, just as they did. The spirits had not told him of this occurrence nor had they told him what would come of it. He felt curiously impotent. He had always known about things which concerned Sun Dancer, but this was the first time since her birth that he hadn't known of an event before it happened. He sat down and lit his pipe, ready to speak with the Great Spirit and the *maiyun*.

Although he had purified himself and Stalking Horse before Sun Dancer sewed the wound, Horn did so again. He took another coal from the fire, sprinkled it with the leaves of sweet grass, and passed his hands through the smoke. He passed his hands over Stalking Horse's wounds to purify him. He took his rattle and sang while shaking the rattle in rhythm with the song. He used the rattle to drive away the bad spirits which might enter Stalking Horse's wounds, and the song was a prayer. Horn stopped periodically to pray to the spirits in words; he walked around the lodge, shaking his rattle and singing, trying to drive away any bad spirits which were still inside the lodge. He sat down and smoked. He talked to the Great Spirit and asked his favor in letting Stalking Horse live. Then the ritual was over. He sang no more songs and no longer purified Stalking Horse. He had performed the traditional ceremony and now he had to wait to see if further healing was required.

Horn had never dealt much in the ceremonies attached to healing. His grandfather had taught him that the most important thing was to spend the time healing; one could always pray and sing and smoke to the Great Spirit and the *maiyun* later. And if they looked down upon him with disfavor, then surely they would take his healing powers away from him. So far they had not, and they would not, as long as he continued to heal. Now he was only concerned with the lives of the two people lying in front of him. For he knew, given the chance to live long lives, they would do much to help their people and to guide them wisely.

Jean came to Horn's lodge late that night to check on his friend. He called out quietly to the medicine man and Horn gave him permission to enter. Jean had never been in a medicine man's lodge but he had heard strange stories about them. He entered the lodge and quickly glanced at the surroundings. Backrests were erected on the periphery, and in the center, two raised cots were placed next to the fire. Another raised platform was against one wall and on it were hundreds of bowls and containers which Jean assumed held the medicines with which Horn healed. Rattles and a pipe lay close to the cots, and various other articles such as knives, awls, thongs, and sticks lay against another wall. There was nothing strange or sinister about the place and Jean was surprised to find that he felt comfortable in it. He walked to where Stalking Horse lay and knelt next to him. Stalking Horse's face and chest were beaded with sweat and Jean could see little of the wound under the thick poultices which covered his chest and stomach. The cuts on his arms had bruised and swelled but looked as though they were already healing.

Horn walked up behind him. "You did well, *veho*.

You saved your friend's life."

"He wouldn't be here if I hadn't wanted to go hunting without my gun. He saved my life by drawing that bear away from me."

"It is no one's fault. We cannot foresee what will happen nor can we stop it."

"You are not like other medicine men I have seen. Most of them run around yelling and screaming and making a lot of noise, but they do little healing. You are different."

"I do not know of others. I was taught well in the ways of healing and I try to put my learning to practical use. It would be the same if you taught someone to live in your mountains."

"Will he live?"

"I believe he will."

"Will he be able to ride and hunt and fight again?"

"I do not know. I do not know how badly he was injured inside. We can only wait and see."

"If he couldn't do any of those things he'd want to die anyway." Jean shook his head. "I will do all I can to help him and Sun Dancer."

"He knows this. He will not blame you in any way. Stalking Horse is a man who is responsible for his own destiny. You must learn this about him."

"No matter what his destiny, I will see that he gets all the help he needs." He took Horn's right hand in his and shook it, a gesture which completely confounded Horn. *"Un mil beaucoup, mon vieux medicin.* Let me know if I can help you in any way."

Horn watched Jean as he left, then looked at Stalking Horse and Sun Dancer. They had managed to make a friend and brother of a white man. It was a strange situation but a good one. It was especially good for Stalking Horse to learn that not all white men, as not all Cheyennes, were bad men. He and Sun Dancer had looked for good in Jean and they had found it. This was a thing that would enrich all their lives.

Stalking Horse opened his eyes, focusing on the lodge hole. He watched vaguely as the smoke trailed out into the night. He tried to move but grunted involuntarily, the least movement from his neck down causing him excruciating pain. He lifted his neck enough to look down at his chest and stomach; he remembered the attack by the bear but little after that. He recalled telling Jean to leave him and to skin the bear but after that, everything became unclear. He slowly turned his head and saw Sun Dancer on a robe sleeping peacefully, but Horn was nowhere around. He tried once more to sit up but found it impossible; the muscles in his stomach would not support him. He dropped back breathing heavily, and shut his eyes.

"Do not attempt that again or you will never have the use of those muscles." Horn came to stand next to the cot.

"I do not like lying here. I want to get up and force myself to move."

"If you do that I can promise that you will never throw a lance again."

Stalking Horse's expression grew serious and unbelieving. "You speak the truth?"

"Muscles have been injured. We do not know if we have repaired them correctly. We must wait for them to heal to find out."

"We?"

"Sun Dancer sewed the stitches on your wound. She did fine work—her fingers were deft."

"She did this? I did not think she knew how."

"She knows how to sew clothes and make shoes, what is so different from sewing your flesh? Her hands are quicker and surer than mine. Your scar will be thin because of her."

"Is she well?"

"She sleeps deeply now. I gave her medicine so she would not dream. She will wake rested in the morning."

"And Jean?"

"Jean is well and was here not long ago. He blames himself for this."

"There is no blame to anyone. It just happened."

"I told him that, but he will only believe it when it comes from you." Horn bent down and felt Stalking Horse's head, and walked to the platform to mix a drink.

"Drink this and it will draw the fever from your body." Horn held Stalking Horse's head as he drank, placing a cool cloth on his forehead. "You must do as I say and forego your pride for a time. It is more important that you rest your body. Let it heal. There will be much time later on for forcing it to your will."

"I will do as you say, Horn. I do not wish to be crippled the rest of my life for then I would have to divorce Sun Dancer and marry her to someone else. This I would not enjoy doing. I will do as you say."

Stalking Horse smiled up at Sun Dancer as she

cleaned his wound. She checked the puckered skin around the stitches to see if any sores had developed and applied fresh poultices. The scar was still red and swollen, but the skin had grown together well. Horn said they would cut the ends and pull it out slowly. Sun Dancer winced as she thought of the pain it would cause Stalking Horse when they removed it, but she knew he wouldn't utter a sound.

"Does it look well, healer?"

Sun Dancer backed away from the cot and looked down at Stalking Horse. She placed her hand on his head to check for fever. "I am not a healer, only a helper. I did what Horn told me to do."

"You did it well."

"We will find how well when you are able to get up and move about. We still do not know if the muscles will be strong."

"I will make them strong."

"But if the muscles are damaged . . ." Stalking Horse's fingers covered Sun Dancer's lips. She lowered her eyes.

"We will not think of that now, wife. We will think that I will be normal again. I do not wish to think of the consequences if I am not."

"If you do not heal, I will do the work and the hunting."

"And will you take my place as a warrior too?"

"I . . . I will do whatever is necessary."

"But I would not let you. Do you think I could live as a man of honor if my wife did everything for me while I lie around like a useless animal? You would come to think little of me, wife, as I would think little of myself."

442

"Then it is best that we do not speak of it, for it will not be so."

He reached for her hand and grasped it tightly. "I was wrong; we should speak of it now."

"No. I have other things to attend to." She tried to stand up but he pulled her close to him.

"Hear me well, Sun Dancer, for I do not wish to speak of this again. If I am damaged and can no longer be a useful man, I will divorce you and marry you to someone else."

"No!"

"I have taken into consideration the fact that you are a gentle woman; I would not marry you to anyone. I have chosen Laughing Bird. Although he already has a wife, it is you he has always loved. He would treat you with great dignity and respect."

"And have you in mind someone to care for you while you marry me off to someone else? Spring perhaps?"

"Do not be angry. I would do what is best for you."

"Or for you?" She pulled away and stood up. "I must look after our child."

Stalking Horse's eyes followed Sun Dancer until she left the lodge. He returned his gaze to the top of the lodge, where he was able to glimpse the small hole to the outside world. Sun Dancer did not understand that what he would do would be best for her and for Little Flower. She also did not understand that once he married her off, he would leave and go up into the mountains.

"If I am unable to ride," Stalking Horse thought aloud, "Jean will help me. We will wait until the winter snows. Jean can put me against a rock so I can see my home and the plains below.

"I shall stay there through the first chill night until my body no longer feels the cold, and I will be comforted by my blanket of snow. I shall close my eyes, and I shall sleep.

"If I am to be denied the life of a warrior," his thoughts ran on, "and the right to die as a warrior, I must be allowed to choose my own death. I cannot live if I am not whole. There is no honor in that. I wish Sun Dancer would understand.

"It does not matter that I cannot go to *seyan*, the place of the dead, to live with *Heammawihio* and hunt and go to war. It is more important that Sun Dancer understand my reasons for leaving her and that she knows why I have to go alone and die with honor.

"If she does not understand, that will be the hardest thing about dying." He winced, "That and giving her to Laughing Bird." Ultimately, that might be the hardest thing of all.

Sun Dancer sat opposite her brother in his lodge, her head lowered and her thoughts unclear. She had wanted to speak with her father but she didn't want to burden him. Brave Wolf would be better able to advise her in this matter. Brave Wolf waited patiently while Sun Dancer sorted out her thoughts and felt calmed by his presence.

"It seems I will forever seek you or father out to advise and counsel me. It seems I cannot think for myself."

"It is sometimes necessary to seek out others for advice, *nekaim*. Sometimes others can see clearly

444

what is blurred to us."

Sun Dancer nodded but still didn't look at her brother. "If you were injured and did not recover fully, if you were not able to go to war and hunt, would you . . . ?"

"I can tell you what I would do. I would take care of my family and then I would go away."

"Away?"

"I would go off to die. A warrior could not let his wife care for him while he was able to do nothing to care for her. What honor is there in that?" His voice was indignant and scornful.

"What would you do with Spotted Calf and your children?"

"I would see that she was married to someone who would care for her as I do, and who would care for my children. Then I would go off to die. If I could not die fighting, then I would find another way."

"To die," she repeated softly. "I had not thought of it. Or I had not wanted to believe it."

"Of what do you speak, *nekaim?*"

"I speak of Stalking Horse."

"I thought as much."

"What would you advise me to do, Brave Wolf? I know so little of these things."

"You know enough to let a man die honorably. If Stalking Horse wishes to marry you to someone, do not argue with him, as is your habit. Let him choose his own way honorably. Stand by him in this."

It was simply stated: she should not interfere if her husband wanted to divorce her and marry her to someone else and then go off by himself to die. It was simply stated but not easily accepted by one of

445

her character.

"If it should happen, I will not dishonor him in any way. I will let him choose his own way with great honor." Brave Wolf reached out for her hand but she pulled away. She could not understand the ways of men and their single-minded devotion to honor. Honor came before all and it was a fact which she greatly resented. She would not let anyone reach out to her now for she felt entirely alone and removed, even from Stalking Horse. She was frightened of what the future would hold and for once, she wished she could see into the future as Horn could. If she could see what would happen before it happened, perhaps she could alter it in some way. But she knew that was just childish fancy, as if she could change the course of a river or stop the coming of the snow. She didn't like the fact that she had no say in what her future held, as if she weren't even an important part of it. She felt like a mere object being moved from place to place, being pushed along in time by the whimsey and caprice of others.

She stomped into the woods and stood, arms crossed, looking down at the water coursing between the banks. She was beginning to doubt that there even was a Great Spirit or *maiyun*. Why was it they were able to direct the events in a person's life without the person having a say in it? A person should be responsible for her own failures or achievements, her father had once told her. One should never blame the wrongs or the rights, the good or the bad on anyone but oneself. Sun Dancer nodded her head. Her father's words seemed true enough; her father was not one to lie or make light of things. If what he said was true, then she should be able to take control of her life and shape it the way she wanted, without the interference of anyone, including the *maiyun* or the Great Spirit.

Sun Dancer felt a momentary instant of fright—she thought her words would bring instant destruction. But when nothing happened, she smiled. Perhaps she would anger all the gods above, but she would be the only person in control of her own life from now on. She would listen to advice from her elders and consider it, but ultimately it would be her own voice which she listened to. If the spirits above punished her for it or struck her dead, so be it, for she wouldn't live in constant fear of them or anyone. And Stalking Horse, with all his honor and pride, would have to learn to live with the fact that he had married a woman of independent thought, and not one who meekly followed his commands. There would be no divorce and there would be no dying alone with honor. She would not permit either.

CHAPTER XXV

Two weeks after being mauled by the grizzly, Stalking Horse tried to walk across Horn's lodge unaided, but fell before reaching the other side. Just the fact that he was able to get up, demonstrated to him that his muscles weren't damaged; they had been able to support him as he sat and stood. The fall was painful but the knowledge that he wouldn't be a cripple lessened the pain. He couldn't yet stand up, so he managed to get to his knees and crawl slowly back to his cot. Each movement was agonizing; the muscles were still weak and damaged, and he had very little support from his chest to his waist. Sun Dancer walked into the lodge and found him crawling. She started to help him, but instead, stood and watched; she knew he would reject her help. When he reached the cot and tried to climb up on it, Sun Dancer walked over to help ease him onto it. His face was covered with sweat and she dipped a cloth in water to wipe it.

"So, do you plan to hunt for buffalo before the day is out?"

"Your tongue is no less sharp now than when we

were children. Do you come here only to prick me with it or did you come to help me?"

"I do not know." She shifted her attention to the wound which was healing properly. She still cleaned it and applied fresh poultices. Horn said that the danger of infection would not be over until the wound was fully healed. When she finished cleaning and dressing the wound, she moved to Horn's platform to mix a drink which she immediately brought to Stalking Horse.

"You must rest now. You could have injured yourself greatly when you did that." She placed her arm underneath his neck and lifted his head. She placed the bowl to his lips and he drank the liquid which he knew would soon bring him complete peace. When she started to turn away, he grabbed her arm.

"You are still angry with me."

"I am not angry. I just do not understand the mind of a man."

"It is well that you do not. You are difficult enough as a woman."

She pursed her lips together and tried to pull away but Stalking Horse forced her thin arm close to his chest until her shoulder touched his.

"I had hoped that after the child was born you would be of a less contrary nature. But it seems that this will never be."

"Are you still seeking to divorce me? Do it then, but I will marry no one unless I choose to marry him."

"I could label you an adulteress and you would be shunned by the people of the village."

"You would not do that to the daughter of a council chief and the sister of a war chief."

"I would have you do what I wish. You are my wife."

"That is right; I am your wife. I am not your horse."

"Yes, there are distinct differences. For one, my horse is a loyal and obedient companion. And he does not talk back."

"Perhaps you should sleep with your horse. See then how loyal and obedient he is." She started to get up but Stalking Horse pulled roughly at her braid and she screamed. Again she was forced to face him.

"You are brave with your words when you know I am unable to get up. I wonder how brave you would be if I were not lying here."

"I do not seek to be brave, only truthful."

"In what way?"

"In every way."

"Speak then." He let go of her braid and she knelt next to the cot.

"When you did not know if you would heal, you said you would marry me off and then you would go away. You thought it was the honorable thing to do, but you did not think of me. You did not think of what I wanted. You thought only of your own pride and honor."

"But a man does not leave his family uncared for if he knows he will never return."

"You did not give me a choice."

"There was no choice. Without me, you need a protector and a hunter."

"I need neither. I can hunt and if I must, I can

450

fight. You yourself taught me how to do these things."

"It is the way in our village that the family of a man who dies, takes in the wife. I have no brothers or cousins so I would choose Laughing Bird. He would treat you well."

"I know this. But did you not think that perhaps I would not want another husband?"

"It would not matter."

"It would matter to me. If you had gone away, I would have followed you. I would not have stayed just because it was your wish. It would have been my wish to follow you."

"And to die with me?"

"I do not know."

"Would you have wanted the remains of a defeated warrior, Sun Dancer? Could you have accepted me and taken care of me, and all the time respected me?"

Her eyes met his and she lowered her head. She knew the answer.

"You see, you know I speak the truth. My last bit of honor would have come from knowing you had not seen me completely defeated. At least I would have left with my head held high. Do you understand this, Sun Dancer? It is not pride, it is honor."

She lifted her eyes and looked at him—the muscular chest marred by the ugly scar, the arms and legs powerful from constant use, the face strong and handsome and young. Here was the man who had loved and taken care of her, and who had always sought the best for her. How would it have been if he were no longer able to sit astride a horse, pull back on a bow, or make love to her tenderly and knowingly?

She would have grown to pity him, and he would have grown to hate himself. It was not a memory one would want to have of a once strong and vital man, and not one he would want passed on to his child. It was not the disability itself that would have been so abhorrent, but the fact that he wouldn't have been able to do anything. Their way of life would have made it impossible. He would have been useless, his movements restricted. She could not have lived that way and she would never have expected him to.

"Honor comes before all then?" Her liquid brown eyes touched him deep inside, and he felt the need to have her more than he had ever felt before.

"It must, if a person is to be at peace with himself. It does not mean I love you less."

"I think I understand. If my face and body had been scarred when I was tortured by the Kiowas, I would not have wanted you to see me. I would not have been able to walk with dignity anymore, accepting the stares of people who would pity me. I could not tolerate the pity. I would have gone away, too."

He took her hand and pressed the palm against his cheek. "We both understand, and we have each been given another chance. We must be thankful and live accordingly."

"I know this. I went out and looked at the mountains the morning after you were brought back. I made myself a promise that if you lived and were well again, I would always help the old, the sick, and the homeless in our tribe."

"You did not try to deal with the Great Spirit?"

"No. I made the promise only to myself. I did not offer it to the Great Spirit in exchange for your good health."

"Did you also make a promise to yourself if I did not get well?"

She nodded and for a time looked beyond him. "I promised myself that I would still do all I could to help our people, but I would never again marry." She noticed the frown on his face and she responded eagerly. "It would have been an easy promise to keep, Stalking Horse, for I would not have wanted to be with any man but you."

"And if I had forced you to marry Laughing Bird?"

She shook her head slowly and her eyes fixed on his. "You would not have done that, for my honor is as important to you as yours is."

Stalking Horse grew silent and nodded in agreement. "I grow impatient to get up and grow strong again. I long to do all those things which are a part of my life but which I do not always think about. I will think about them more now. It will be good to sit my horse again and ride at full speed. Mostly, I long to hold you and fill you with my love."

"It will be soon, husband, but now you must rest and heal your body." She stood and picked up her basket of healing medicines. "If we are to have a long future together, perhaps it would be wise if you and Jean stayed away from the grizzly bear. We all know that you are a great warrior and fearless fighter, but I do not think the grizzly knows."

Not long after Stalking Horse and Jean returned to camp, a small hunting party of Cheyennes was attacked by Crow warriors. All the men were killed and their scalps taken, a practice that had not as yet been well-established with the plains tribes. The Crows had even sought out the Cheyennes' base camp and killed the wives who had traveled with their husbands. All their horses, hides, and the fresh meat were taken. It was a deliberate act of war.

The Cheyennes had finished hunting buffalo and were preparing to break camp and go up into the mountains, since a hard winter seemed imminent. It would be foolish to send out a war party to track down the Crows now with winter close, but the council sat down and discussed the possibility. They decided that Brave Wolf would lead a party of ten of his best warriors to track the Crows until they were found. Stalking Horse was capable of walking by this time but was unable to ride a horse, so he could not accompany the raiders. Laughing Bird was among those chosen. Stalking Horse wished he were well enough to go along, for this raid would be a hard and fierce one. He regretted he could not go, but knew he would be a burden at this point.

The villagers held a feast for the war party the next night; and they said many prayers and sang many war songs in their honor. The relatives of the murdered Cheyennes cried out in sorrow and anger, and the warriors promised to avenge the deaths of their brothers and sisters. They planned to leave later that night after preparing their horses and supplies and painting themselves. They would ride late into the night until they made camp. Sun Dancer stood outside the circle of dancers and singers. She held Little Flower in her arms and she looked up at Stalking Horse's impassive face. She had never seen her people like this—they were in a frenzy of revenge

454

and murder, death being the only thing that loomed in their minds.

"This frightens me, Stalking Horse. I have never seen our people like this."

"Their eyes are filled with blood. It is not good."

"I worry for Brave Wolf."

"Do not worry about your brother. He is strong of will; he will not let his warriors tell him what to do. He will think with his mind, not his heart."

"You wish you were going with him."

"Yes."

"But not for their reasons," she motioned to her people. "Brave Wolf will need your help."

"I do not know. My feelings are not good about this thing which they do. It is a bad time; they should wait until after the snow. To go now is to bring bad luck. Brave Wolf wanted to wait."

"Why must he go then? There are other war chiefs."

"He must go. He will lead them well; as I said before, he will lead them with his head. They need a calm leader or they will act foolishly."

"Stalking Horse, I cannot deal with the feelings which are in me now."

"You must. You know he will go. There is nothing you can say that will keep him here."

"I must see him then, before he goes." She handed Little Flower to Stalking Horse. Her eyes were filled with tears when she looked up at him. "What do I say to a person I have loved all my life and who has loved me and guided me so well? I know he will die, and yet, I still cannot believe it."

"The words must come from your own heart. You

will know."

Sun Dancer nodded and slowly walked away from the group of people. She walked to the river to gain some peace and inner tranquility before she faced her brother, but neither would come. She sank to her knees and covered her face with her hands while she cried out at the spirits for the injustices of life. She no longer believed in them. She stood up and wiped her face clear of tears. She took a deep breath. The only thing she believed in now was her own strength: it was that, not the *maiyun*, which had always helped her. She did something then, which if anyone had seen her, they would have thought her mad or a witch. She reached under the leather thong that held her parfleche around her neck, and tugged at the small thong that held her medicine bag. She held the bag in her hand and looked at it. She hadn't taken it off since she was a small child. Her mother had tied it around her neck, declaring it was her "own" medicine and that it would protect her from bad and evil things. She had believed in it and for a long time had even thought she was invincible from arrows and lances. But as she matured, she came to know that the bag could not protect her from all things. Too many events had occurred in the last few years to make her realize that the bag served no purpose at all, save to prolong a belief in something which had no value. She rubbed the small beaded bag for a moment longer, then forcefully threw it into the river. She had broken from the *maiyun*.

Brave Wolf was packing his horse when he saw Sun Dancer approaching. He smiled. "How goes it, *nekaim?* You are speaking to me now?"

"Of course I am speaking to you."

"I was not sure after the last time you sought my advice."

"You were right as you always are." She looked around her. "Where are Spotted Calf and the boys?"

"They are still watching the people dance and sing."

"They were of a violent nature tonight."

Brave Wolf stopped tying a pack on his horse and nodded solemnly. "Yes, it is not good for people to be so filled with thoughts of revenge. It can only be destructive."

"Why must you lead them, Brave Wolf? Surely, there are others who can lead them as well as you."

"The council chose me and I cannot refuse them. They feel I am of some value as a war chief."

"You are the best. You know I did not mean to say that you were not. I wish . . ."

"Do not worry, *nekaim*. If my time comes, then it will come. I would rather die in service to my people than in any other way. Do you understand that? I do not fear death."

"I know you do not. But I fear it for you." She stepped toward him, and he enclosed her in his arms. "Do you remember when I was small and I stepped on the large snake with the rattles and I was afraid I would die. You said to me, 'You do not fear death, little one, you fear fear itself. Once you have learned to conquer fear, then you will no longer fear anything.' Have you conquered it, Brave Wolf?"

"I believe I have, little one, for I do not think on it anymore. To waste time being fearful is to waste precious moments of life."

"You sound like our father."

"I lack the wisdom of our father. His kind of wisdom only comes with age. Perhaps in time . . ." He stopped then and held Sun Dancer away from him, his eyes stern and serious. "Do not worry for me, *nekaim*, I do not worry for myself. I am ready for death. Do you understand?"

Sun Dancer looked at him and she understood. Brave Wolf, too, knew he was going to die. There was no sorrow in him. He was a man who had accepted his death and would live out the rest of his life with great dignity. Tears filled her eyes. She had not wanted to cry in front of him. He held her close against him.

"Do not cry, little one."

"I do not cry for you, Brave Wolf, for you are the fortunate one. I cry for myself." She wrapped her arms tightly around him and those last moments with him were forever ingrained in her memory. When finally she stood back to look at him, a smile spread over his face.

"Did I ever tell you, little one, that your beauty rivals that of our mountains when the sun casts its glow over them? And it is even more so because your beauty lies deeper than your skin. It is in here." He patted his heart. "I shall miss you. Take care of Spotted Calf and my boys. Have Stalking Horse teach them well."

"He will." She was silent for a moment and her eyebrows knit together. "You knew I was coming here, didn't you? And you knew . . ."

"Perhaps it is something we both have, this 'sight'

of ours. Use it wisely, *nekaim*. Let Horn show you the way."

"I will. Why have you never told me before?"

"Because you could not understand before." He took her small face in his hands and leaned his face tenderly against hers. *"Ne-sta-va-hose-yoomatse hooma.* I will see you again on the other side."

Sun Dancer nodded and smiled. "Jean has a custom that I am growing fond of. It is a sign of affection among the whites, but he says his people do it differently from other whites."

"What is this strange custom?"

She placed her hands on his shoulders and pulled him down slightly, kissing him on each cheek. "It is called a kiss and signifies great affection between two people."

"It is rather strange but not unpleasant. You and Stalking Horse have a good friend in Jean. Let the friendship grow, and it will not fail you." He finished tying his things on his horse, then patted the animal's rump. "I must find Spotted Calf and the children now."

"Brave Wolf?" He turned. "Why have you never before told me that I possess beauty?"

"I did not want your head to become any larger. Already it grows too large for your body." He laughed and managed to dodge the rock Sun Dancer threw at him. She looked at his horse, patting it on the rump, then slowly returned to her own lodge.

"Ne-sta-va-voomatse na-htataneme. I will see you again, my brother." She spoke quietly to herself and with a deep breath, she released all the fear and tension which had been inside her for so long. Her

brother was at peace, and now so was she.

The tribe moved into the mountains. Jean stayed to help Sun Dancer erect the lodge (which greatly amused the other women and Stalking Horse) and to make sure the family had plenty of fresh meat. He said good-bye and returned to his place in the mountains to trap for furs, taking with him many of the women's crafts which he would trade for supplies and guns. He-Walks-the-Mountain and the other war chiefs had made the decision to buy guns and to learn to use them. They would have little or no chance against the Crows if they decided to attack, and most of the other Plains tribes were now acquiring guns. This was a matter of survival, and they meant to survive.

Stalking Horse healed well but the cold slowed the process. It permeated to the very bone and his arms and shoulders easily grew stiff. He constantly worked at strengthening his body and exercised by pulling his bow string further and further back every day. He did lifting exercises to strengthen his arms and stomach, stretching to get the muscles of his arms accustomed to the daily activities which sometimes pushed them to their limits.

Little Flower was fast approaching her second year and was sturdy and agile, although still quite small for her age. Her little brown body was quick to follow the movements she saw being made by her father, and Stalking Horse and Sun Dancer laughed endlessly watching the tiny child trying to pick up Stalking Horse's bow and pull the string back. The bow was taller than she and usually wound up falling over her and landing at her feet.

Sun Dancer continued to learn from Horn but she put aside time to visit Spotted Calf and her nephews each day. She and Spotted Calf had never been of the same nature and seldom spoke for very long, but she realized that the woman was good and that her brother must have seen much in her when he married her. There was also the fact that Spotted Calf didn't know that Brave Wolf wasn't coming home. Sun Dancer hoped that when the news of Brave Wolf's death arrived, she and Spotted Calf would have established a much closer relationship.

Woman's Heart missed quilling with Sun Dancer but saw the value of her learning the healing art from Horn. The other women saw it too, so didn't think it strange when Sun Dancer spent most of her time with Horn instead of quilling with them. However, Sun Dancer always did her work and was still able to mend and sew new things for herself or Little Flower or Stalking Horse. Her days were long and full and strangely enough, she was no longer plagued by the nightmare about Brave Wolf which had filled her with terror for so long.

When spring came and the snows melted, still no word had been heard from the raiding party. By this time, family and friends were beginning to believe the worst. The war council decided to send out another party after they moved back down to the plains and set up camp. Stalking Horse was healed by this time and he was chosen by the council to lead the party. He had never led a war party, but everyone knew that if he were successful in this, he would surely be chosen to be a war chief.

Sun Dancer prepared Stalking Horse's pack. It included extra moccasins, a heavier shirt, since they were going north, a medicinal parfleche, the hard bread which Jean had taught them how to make from the flour he had brought them, dried meat, and dried currants. She attached extra lengths of rope to his horse in the event he was able to steal horses, and all his weapons—war shield, bow, arrows, quiver, hunting knife, war club. For the first time, instead of his lance, he carried the rifle which Jean had given him, along with extra ammunition. Sun Dancer hid her apprehension as Stalking Horse and his men rode off; she knew she would have to do that for many years to come.

Before Stalking Horse left, he held her by the shoulders, his eyes containing a certain sadness. "This is one duty I do not long to perform," he said fatalistically. "I must try to find the bodies of your brother and our friend, Laughing Bird, and the rest of the men who were with them. It is not good."

"Keep a clear head, husband. Before he left, Brave Wolf told me that revenge is a bad thing to feel and can only lead to more destruction. Heed his words."

"I will heed them, although the people will cry for revenge. I must do what is right at the time."

"I know you will do what is right. It is a hard thing you do. I would not be in your place."

"I am glad you are not." He held her tightly for a moment then led his horse into camp to meet his men. By mutual consent, Stalking Horse and Sun Dancer had decided long ago to say good-bye at their lodge before raids. They both felt that if anything happened to either of them, these last moments together would be remembered as special and private.

People in the village were frightened and continuously on their guard. Their hunting party had been killed the fall before and ten of their best warriors were probably now dead. They were sending out ten more of their best warriors; what if they did not return? It seemed to everyone in the village that their warriors were being taken from them, and eventually they would be forced to use women and children and old people to defend themselves. As a council chief, He-Walks-the-Mountain constantly reassured his people that the Great Spirit wasn't against them and that the evil *maiyun* hadn't been sent to destroy them. It was the way of the war, he said, and now that they lived on the plains, they would be forever confronted by enemies. Many of the old people recalled the days when they lived so peacefully in their mud lodges and war was not a part of their lives. But He-Walks-the-Mountain reminded them that although they were a peaceful people at that time, it didn't prevent the Assiniboins, the Hohes, from attacking them without cause until they were pushed to the Big River and eventually forced to cross it. After that, it was the Teton Sioux, who had exacted quite a number of Cheyenne lives, and then the Snakes, the Kiowas, and now the Crows. But the Cheyennes were a stronger and mightier tribe now, able to fight the Snakes and drive the Kiowas and the Gataka Apaches southward and out of their hills. The Crows were another matter.

The Crows were a fierce and brave people and their forays back and forth into Cheyenne country were a constant source of irritation to both tribes, as the Cheyennes raided the Crows in their turn. He-Walks-the-Mountain had heard tales that the Blackfeet and Sioux were also waging war against the Crows, and he wondered how they could continue to survive under the constant pressure of war.

Jean returned and his arrival gave the people a much needed lift. For the first time, Jean brought many guns and much ammunition, stating he would teach everyone how to use a firearm. He brought things that people had requested, and for the people he knew well, he brought personal gifts. There was a British-made pipe for He-Walks-the-Mountain, who was so impressed by the instrument that he continuously walked around with it in his mouth. He brought different kinds of material for Woman's Heart and her friends, colorful thread for their sewing. A hand-carved rocking horse was for Little Flower, and for Sun Dancer, a large steel pot for cooking her many mixtures of herbs and roots, as well as a notebook for her to write them all down. He also brought two children's readers for Sun Dancer and Stalking Horse to read, as well as a picture book on hunting in England, which he thought might amuse all the men of the tribe. Along with his many gifts and trinkets, he brought flour and sugar, which were rare treats for them, and candy sticks for the children who continually followed Jean everywhere he went hoping for more.

"As usual, you bring too much, Jean," Sun Dancer reprimanded him. "What have we for you in return?"

"Bah!" He waved his huge hand in the air. "You insult me when you speak like this, *ma chou*. You

464

have given me everything. You are my family now."

Sun Dancer smiled and kissed him on both cheeks, as was their custom with each other now. "You should have had many children and grandchildren, Jean. You have a heart as big as all this." Her arm swept around to the plains beyond them.

"I need no family of my own, I have you and your daughter and your husband, as well as the rest of your people. A man could have no better family."

"Truly, do you not miss your own people and speaking in your own tongue?"

Jean's eyebrows knit together and he scratched his bushy brown mane. "I live here in America, so my language is English. And most of my time I spend with you and your people, so my other language is Cheyenne. Makes sense to me. I see my other mountain friends when we trade in the spring. We drink much of the water that makes you crazy," he pointed to his head, "and we love the women." He plucked at his beard a moment and laughed uproariously. "Jean loves the women and when they see me come, they know there is no other like me. *Haahe?* Yes?"

Sun Dancer laughed and took Jean by the arm. "I, myself, have often thought what a magnificent man you are, Jean. If I had not married Stalking Horse . . . ah, well, who knows?"

Jean stopped and looked at her. "You kid with me, *ma chou,* but I like it. Do not forget, a man is much like a peacock who sits and grooms his beautiful tail and admires it all the while. But he needs to have it admired by his peahen or it means nothing to him. Remember that as you grow older with your husband."

"As long as he too remembers. Even the ugly peahen needs to be admired for the special things in her. *Oui?*" Again she took Jean's arm and they walked toward her lodge. "Come, peacock, and let me repair those moccasins for you before they fall apart. You need a wife, Jean. There are many pretty women in this camp."

"Yes, I have thought on it myself. I will seriously consider the matter. But only after my stomach is full and my body is rested. Then I will be in my full glory."

"I think, dear Jean, that you are always in your full glory. Come."

CHAPTER XXVI

Stalking Horse found no signs of Brave Wolf or his party. He decided against riding into the Crow encampment, a decision which made his revenge-hungry men angry. But he knew the odds were against them. They were only a small party while the encampment they had come upon appeared to have at least twenty or thirty warriors. Too many for even the Cheyennes. Stalking Horse's plan was to wait for some of them to go hunting and then attack. They would try to capture at least one Crow and make him talk. They had to wait only one night until a few Crows went out hunting.

Stalking Horse and his men waited for the Crow hunting party and attacked them as they rode by. His men killed three of the Crows before he gave the sign to stop. They took the other three away from the main encampment and questioned them about Brave Wolf and his war party. Yes, the men remembered that their war chief let two of them ride away. The Cheyennes were incredulous—why would he have done that? Stalking Horse asked if they had taken the chief and they said yes, and he knew Sun Dancer's dream had come true.

Stalking Horse considered the plight of his captives for a few moments then announced his decision.

"Let them go," he ordered.

His men looked at him in disbelief and anger.

"You cannot do this, Stalking Horse," Elk River cried out. "We must kill them. They killed our brothers."

"But they also let two of our brothers live. We must do the same."

In spite of the protests of his men, the captives were set free. He confronted his angry followers, then turned and led them away.

Stalking Horse had no idea where to look for his men, if indeed, they were alive. They might have gone eastward across the Big River to stay with the Arikaras until the snows melted, or northeast to the Mandans. The snow and its subsequent melting had erased all tracks. Stalking Horse knew that if they were well, they would return to the village when they were able. It would be impossible for him and his men to find them. It would be better if he and the others returned home in case they were needed there. Again, his men objected to his decision, but Stalking Horse was going home. His men had come far to fight and to punish the Crows for what they had done, but Stalking Horse wouldn't permit them to commit suicide. They would return with more men and some day exact justice.

Stalking Horse realized his decision to release the Crows and to return home would be unpopular with his men and with the people of the village, but he knew it was the right one. It would serve no purpose for him to lead a raid and get all his men killed. It would be better to wait when they were strong in number and time had passed to make them less vengeful. He also knew that his decision would prevent him from being chosen as a war chief but that was suddenly unimportant to him. To him, it was more important to make the best decision for his men than to have their lives on his conscience for all time. Brave Wolf had often admonished him never to listen to anyone but himself, unless he felt he was making a decision which was detrimental to the group. He had taught him how important it was to think clearly and without emotion, for in that direction lay the possibility of life.

His people were disappointed, as he knew they would be, but He-Walks-the-Mountain supported Stalking Horse's decision. Eventually, the villagers agreed that Stalking Horse had been right about coming home. If the men were alive, they would return of their own accord, and if they were dead, there was nothing anyone could do for them now. But his decision to release the Crows remained unpopular. The families of the men hoped that it was one of their husbands or brothers or sons who had escaped alive. Spotted Calf was not one of them. She had spoken with Sun Dancer and Stalking Horse about Brave Wolf and she knew he would never come home. She had already done her mourning and was now ready to help those who hadn't yet accepted the deaths of their loved ones.

The next day a lodge was erected in the middle of

camp and a feast prepared. All the chiefs were called together to consider the man who would fill Brave Wolf's position as war chief. A man was required to have many qualifications: he had to be brave; he had to have a big heart, as well as a strong one; he had to be generous and wise; he had to be even-tempered and open to new ideas; he had to have good judgment and discretion; and he had to be just.

Stalking Horse was soon chosen as a new war chief. It was a surprise to no one except perhaps, to him. Brave Wolf had spoken of him in council and often stated that if he were killed, he would choose Stalking Horse as his successor. What seemed to the people to be an error in judgment on Stalking Horse's part, was to the elders of the tribe a wise and correct thing to do. They realized what an all-out war with the Crows would encompass, and they wanted to avoid it at all costs. Periodic raids into each other's camps were things they had each done, but each sought to avoid a war which would cost the lives of many young and useful men.

The feast continued throughout the day. Although the people of the village had been doubtful of him earlier, they now supported Stalking Horse as a new war chief. Soon after dark, guards sounded the alarm. Warriors ran to the entrance of the camp to find Laughing Bird and Crying Owl riding into camp. They were alive and seemingly well, and the people rushed to embrace them and to sing and dance to their bravery and good health. The arrival of the two warriors had only substantiated the fact that Stalking Horse's decision had been the right one.

The people gathered to hear the men speak of their

flight from the Crow warriors. The village was enveloped in silence, save for the voice of Laughing Bird. While holding his son in his lap and sitting next to Spring, he recounted their escape.

"When we rode into Crow country," Laughing Bird began, "the snows had started to fall. Brave Wolf said we should find shelter until the heavy snows were past, or perhaps we could cross the Big River and lodge with the Arikaras. Crying Owl and Gray Eagle objected, but when the snows fell heavily, they agreed with Brave Wolf's decision. But we were forced to delay our journey across the river because the snows were already too heavy. We had to camp in the land of the Crows.

"When the sun finally appeared and the day was clear, we rode eastward toward the river. The sun went in and out of the clouds that day; many of the men thought it was a bad sign. The sun would be shining one moment and the next, disappear behind a dark cloud.

"The morning of the second day, we saw riders following us and we knew they were Crows. We rode quickly but our horses were tired and hungry; we were forced to stand our ground and fight. The Crows were double our number but we fought bravely and with honor. Brave Wolf counted many coup. He knocked three men from their horses with his war club before his horse reared up. He was shot in the chest with an arrow. He held on to his horse but another Crow struck him in the back with a war lance. Brave Wolf fell to the ground; he was trampled by his own horse." Laughing Bird stopped for a moment, aware of how difficult the story would be

471

for Spotted Calf and Brave Wolf's family. He cleared his throat and continued.

"Crying Owl and I were able to kill some Crows and we were both prepared to die. But the Crow war chief did a strange thing: he raised his hand up and signaled his men to stop fighting. He looked at us and told us to go and tell our people that the Crows are of a good and noble heart. Crying Owl wanted to stay and fight to the death but I told him we must leave. The Crow chief had made a great gesture and it was only right that we should honor it. Honor is not limited to the Cheyennes.

"We crossed the Big River, which was iced over, to the Mandan villages. We stayed there until the river thawed. The Mandans treated us well and told us much about trading. They have been trading with the French and the British since they built wooden lodges in the country to the far north. They are good people and of a generous nature.

"When the river thawed, we recrossed it and went back into the land of the Crow. We found the bodies of our brothers and placed them on raised platforms. We mourned for them and sang songs of bravery to them. Then we left the land of the Crow."

He-Walks-the-Mountain and Woman's Heart grieved greatly for the loss of their beloved son. He had been a brave warrior and a wise and just chief. As a person, he had been loyal and loving, full of those special gifts which only some people are fortunate enough to possess. His presence was sorely missed in the village and many songs were sung to his bravery and also to his laughter, as that was no less a gift.

After Stalking Horse was chosen as war chief to

replace Brave Wolf, Jean gave him the gift he had brought for him. Solemnly, Stalking Horse untied the box. This exchanging of gifts between the two men had come to mean something special. Stalking Horse removed a square piece of wood from the box, and on it had been carved the words: "Follow your mind and you shall know your heart." Surrounding the words was a leaf pattern which trailed around the edge of the plaque and at the very top where the leaves met, an eagle was carved, its wings outstretched.

"You have made this yourself?" Stalking Horse ran his fingers over the fine, detailed work.

"I've done a bit of carving, *oui*. I saw something like this in a store window once and I thought it would be a likely gift for you. It's called a plaque. White people put them on desks and things." At Stalking Horse's raised eyebrows, Jean added, "You know, their furniture. I showed you the pictures."

Stalking Horse nodded his head. "Plaque," he repeated, reading the words out loud. "I will hang it up with my medicine." He thought for a moment then looked up at Jean, "You knew that I would become a chief?"

"There was no doubt. I thought this was a good saying to go by. Brave Wolf might have said those words."

"Yes, these are good words. Words Brave Wolf lived by. Words I will try to live by." He turned and started walking. "Come, I have something to show you." They walked to Stalking Horse's lodge. Stalking Horse went inside and brought out the robe which Sun Dancer had made for him, turning it around so Jean could see the back. "Do you know

473

what these drawings mean?"

"*Oui.* They tell of the important events in your life. Now you will have to add becoming a chief."

"You have not looked closely enough, *hoovehe*. Look at the last picture drawn."

Jean picked up the robe and looked at it closely. It was easy for him to make out Stalking Horse's skillfully depicted pictures. "It is me, *oui?*" There were drawings of Stalking Horse and a white man, Jean, riding to the woods. They hunted for game and there was a depiction of Jean lancing an elk. In the next picture, a huge bear was attacking them. The Indian shot arrows at it while the white man circled around it with his lance. It showed the bear attacking the Indian and the white man lancing the bear until it died. Then it showed the white man pulling the Indian on a travois across the plains. The last picture showed the white man and the Indian clasping forearms, their blood dripping and mixing, to show they had become blood brothers.

"You like it?" Stalking Horse asked, anxious for Jean's approval.

"Do I like it? It's the craziest thing I ever saw. I'm immortalized in Cheyenne history. But you should save the space for more important events in your life."

"What more important event is there than when you saved my life? I would not be standing here now, and I would not be chief. You still did not answer. It is not the kind of gift you can carry with you, but this will be seen by all. When many summers have passed and we are all gone, people will still know of our friendship and how you saved my life."

"I think, *hoovehe*, it is the best gift I have ever received. You have done me a great honor." He reached out, grasped Stalking Horse's forearm, and Stalking Horse returned the gesture.

"There is more. My lance and my horse, they are yours. And I would like to become your brother. If you are willing."

"We are already brothers."

"In the Indian way, by mixing our blood. That way I will have white blood in me and you will have Cheyenne blood in you. Would you honor me by doing this thing?"

"It will bring great honor to me also," Jean replied softly. Perhaps, he thought, after all this time he was getting back the brother he had lost. Perhaps God or the Great Spirit had finally forgiven him and he could live in peace with himself. Stalking Horse had not only given of himself and of his family, he had helped to give him back his self-respect. This was something more valuable to Jean than any gift.

Stalking Horse and Jean were going to become blood brothers. The ceremony was performed by Horn, who had not performed the ceremony in many, many summers and especially not between a man of dark skin and a man of white skin. Horn offered prayers to the Great Spirit and the *maiyun*, then he, Stalking Horse, and Jean smoked to the earth, the sky, and the four cardinal points. The villagers offered food to the earth and then buried it, they sang songs about the strength of brotherhood and friendship, and they danced to this mixing of two bloods that they hoped would bring only good fortune to their tribe.

When the people finished singing and dancing, Stalking Horse and Jean were summoned to the middle of a circle, around which were gathered all the people of the village. Horn threw some sweet grass onto a coal and passed his hands through the smoke to purify them. He took out a large knife and passed it through the smoke so that it too, was purified. Then he took the right arms of both men and waved them back and forth across the smoke. He walked to Stalking Horse and took his right arm, turning it so the elbow was down; he made a diagonal cut across the middle of the forearm, cutting to prevent injuring any arteries. Quickly, he did the same with Jean, then placed the men's arms together, tying them with a leather thong so that the blood would mix. While the men stood with their forearms tied together, Horn intoned more prayers and the people sang more songs. Then Horn untied them and declared them brothers, each carrying the blood of the other in him. Stalking Horse and Jean embraced and the people of the village celebrated with a feast and much singing and dancing. Sun Dancer embraced the two men; she knew that this was a very solemn and serious step for Stalking Horse to take. For so long he had declared that the white man couldn't be trusted but now he was blood brother to one. Perhaps it would serve him well in the future when he would have to deal with the white man.

"Well, now that I am part Cheyenne, I think it is time I found a wife to warm my robes. I have seen a few who . . ."

"Be careful, Jean, do not dishonor any Cheyenne girls or their fathers will come for you. Go slowly if you can, *nahkohe*. The bear must have patience."

"If there is one thing I have, little one, it is patience. Why do you think the bear can sleep away the winter in comfort and warmth, while everyone else fights the cold and fears the dark days? You are right; I am part bear. And who can resist the likes of me, eh?" His loud laugh bellowed out behind him as he went back into the circle and danced with the women, eliciting gales of laughter from everyone.

"Perhaps you will learn patience from Jean, husband. It would do you no harm as a chief."

"Yes. I know now that I was wrong about all white men. As with the Cheyenne and other Indians, there are good men and there are bad. Jean's white blood will teach me to be more tolerant of white men."

"Does the chief feel like returning to his lodge so that his wife may have some of his attention?"

"You are jealous? Much has been made of my becoming chief."

"No, I am proud. And I am proud that you are Jean's brother; you have given him back something of himself. I seek only to have you to myself for a time."

"Then you shall have it. Come." He took her hand and they walked to their lodge. The noise of the celebration filled their ears but their minds were only on each other.

"I will be the kind of wife who befits a chief."

"I know this. It will be easy for you; you are the daughter of a chief and the sister of one . . ."

"It is all right. I am no longer sad and empty when you speak of Brave Wolf. He helped me to see clearly that night. He was ready for death, for he had lived a life of honor and dignity. He felt fortunate in this."

Stalking Horse nodded. "If he had lived, he would have become a tribal chief, for he was also wise. I do not like becoming a chief because Brave Wolf died."

"He wanted you to take his place. He said so often. He saw in you the things which I see in you. He knew you would grow and eventually become a man of peace, not of war."

"I never thought I would feel this way. When I was a younger man, my only thoughts were to learn to fight and kill. I could see no farther than that."

"Just as I could not see changing the way I saw things. I thought I would forever live as a boy and never want to act like a girl or a woman. But it happened and I did not realize it. It was not painful; it was natural. The natural course of things, as Brave Wolf and my parents so often told me."

"It is good to change but it is also frightening. I sometimes feel as if I do not know my own mind, as if I am being led by some unknown force."

"I know the feeling well, husband. Perhaps we shall feel like this until we grow old and die. It is this challenge which makes us strong."

"You have always sounded too wise for your age. This is something that you inherited from your brother and your father."

"Then I can take no credit for it." She was silent for a moment as she looked down at the robe they were sitting on. "I am glad that you will seek a path of peace. I want Little Flower to have a good life here."

"It will be difficult. The war with the Crows will not be over soon. I fear their attacks will grow more numerous and so will our retaliations. And there are always other tribes ready to challenge our right to this land."

"And the whites?"

"They are only waiting. While we Indians fight one another, the white man will grow stronger; he will build his trading posts and his forts. He will seek more and more land until the only thing that is left is to fight us for our lands."

"You still believe it will happen?"

"I know it will. Jean knows it too. He sees the white man making his lodges farther and farther west and he has heard them speak of chasing the Indian out. The time will come when we will have to stand our ground and fight the white man."

"There will be guns?" Sun Dancer's voice reflected the fear she had of the large metal firearms.

"Jean says they will be our only chance. He says the white man makes newer and better guns all the time. If we, too, do not learn how to use them, then we will be killed by them."

"These guns frighten me. They are so loud."

"But we will learn to use them." He shook his head in frustration. "I hope that we can live with the white man and the other tribes in peace, but I do not think it is possible."

"Will this war with the whites happen in our lifetime?"

"It is not possible to say. I think our grandchildren will see it. Let us hope they will live through it."

Sun Dancer shivered slightly as she lay down on the robe. Stalking Horse lay down next to her, pulling her into his arms.

"It will do no good to worry about it now. We cannot change what is to happen, we can only live out our lives with dignity and honor. Let us always remember Brave Wolf and we will be guided well."

Sun Dancer embraced Stalking Horse tightly and she pressed her face against his chest. She knew that he actually did not give her strength; often he had told her that her strength came from inside herself. But she knew that he gave her the assurance and support which she so often needed to draw upon. He was the base from which she could live her life and grow.

"Love me, *na-ehame*. My husband. Let us face this unknown future together."

Stalking Horse pulled her to him and soon their bodes were as one. When they were sated, they lay next to each other, although neither of them slept. Each thought of what the future held for them, their child, and the entire Indian nation.

Stalking Horse thought of leading his people, and he recalled the words on the plaque which Jean had given him: "Follow your mind and you shall know your heart." He knew these were good words to live and lead his people by.

Sun Dancer, while frightened of what the future held for her family and people, tried to still the fear inside her. For the first time, she took to heart the words that Brave Wolf had spoken to her the last night she saw him. "To waste time being fearful is to waste precious moments of life." And those were the words she chose to live by. When she looked over at Stalking Horse, he was finally asleep and he seemed peaceful. She felt she could sleep now. She muttered softly, "What will come, will come. At least we can face the future knowing that we have lived our lives with dignity and honor." No one could ask for more.